INN

This work is published with Amazon through a print on demand service. The author apologises for any discrepancies in print quality or cover alignment due to this.

BLESSED   BE   THE   BELIEVING

NOREPINEPHRINE

- Haufenmensch Hellegeneid -

Hegemony edition

WHATEVER IT TAKES

First independently published in 2024
through Amazon KDP as "Hegemony Edition"
this paperback edition first published in 2024

Protected by Copyright, Designs and Patents Act 1998
independently copyrighted with www.protectmywork.com
ref no: 22850181123S002

All rights reserved. The author alone holds the rights
to modify and resell this work

All artworks belonging to the author

ISBN: 9798869718983

NOREPINEPHRINE
Hegemony edition

It is the inherent illusion, the imitation blind that it copies the false. Chemical. Electric. Soulless- from it, she begs for deliverance. Because there is no salvation, not here. It is humiliation, perpetual, absolute. Until someone breaks the cycle. Everything has a cost, nothing will ever change without sacrifice, but it isn't fair- they give so much for so little. More than they'll ever know.

War has raged here for over one hundred years. It is utterly hopeless. An unending struggle, they cling to what they once had, throwing themselves at the machine. Steel, cold and lifeless, but they too have been abandoned, with nothing left. Blind and stumbling, they will fight to the last, claw on without reason.

A Klernsteiga among them, she says the strangest things. Talks of emptiness, insignificance, hopelessness- she preaches the end, of all things. The morbid prophet. She searches for a boy, one who doesn't age. She fables he has become very sick. She must reach him before his condition changes.

A copy of all Fauschenherst Encyclopaedic definitions is assorted in a glossary at the back of this book.

- FAUSCHENHERST TERRIROTY -

THE DODTOHMET PLATEAU

A thing of the cold, this figure holds firm against her storm. Where others would shelter, hunker under raised arms, the white finds a wall in her, stronger than itself. Even the endless snow, which wails all tones of cold cannot holt the cloaked shape which flutters, cloth flailing, tracing the faint sun.

To demonstrate her strange comfort with that screaming wind the wires roll, strung between tall posts, their peaks barely seen in the frozen squall. For ease of sight, they are lined with a struggling glow, spaced lights swaying with the forces against them, fastened from one end of sight to the other. Communication cables, forced into service through necessity, under the constant, surging gale, for no frequency could penetrate this. The pegs are not very tall and not far apart, but they are made winking planets within this tumult.

So, she keeps close to them, their faint illumination both following and guiding her, drifting overhead, as the plateau cries against her hood.

Here, her shape is difficult to define. In the mess of the blizzard, you can only be too close or too far, for the waves and pleats of that numbing shade shift, her form made a flickering dark against the swelling pale. She wears a drape with a cowl, her figure hidden beneath but shown in moments, as her cover is pushed and pulled against her, and it conceals both she and something against her lower back, like some bag or satchel, a straight running parallel atop.

But these things are secondary, as the winds play at her edges, for a straight angle, to stand before her and face the approach, defines the most peculiar of her unknown features.

To see her as a cloak stands to most angles, but from anywhere ahead, the gaze is drawn to the blue of her own. A cerulean sight, not just of tint but one that glows like azure bulbs, sibling to the lights she obeys. Bright and vivid, two ultramarine torch beams from under her hood- pupilless, with no iris, just dual orbs of brilliant blue. The thickness of the storm drowns all, but from atop the posts, even lost within the noise, eyes might find her own, for they drift within the darkness of a cloak, and portray direction when from afar it is unknown.

All that exists is she and the lines, the noise constant and whining against even shrouded ears. The storm takes sunlight, although the origin still bleeds into the uproar, to cast that half-darkness, of daytime stolen, defined by these two. Alone, with one endless and the other wandering underneath, her azure smouldering as she looks up, breath framed in her light, as it streams with rolling cold. Maybe, as she casts up to the lines, you could see her lips, or a vague silhouette, but still. She is undefined.

A figment, of dark cloth and glimmering vision. She hears only the rumble of the snow and her own, steady efforts from within the intimacy of her heavy shawl, face spared from the direct barrage. Shape shifting, she is heavy footfall, then a heaving chest. Tired eyes, burning the shade of a gelid greater than any freeze, and then from above, toiling through the frigid ground, which holds a moment, only to collapse under every footfall.

She stops at one of the posts, the plateau surging against, a hand reaching to the beams, palm bound with cloth ribbons, pale fingers bare to brush at the white. She exposes a small plaque, marked on every spire, lost to built up snow. It is reconcealed almost instantly, her hand holding before. She looks back out, toward that staring emptiness, her gaze returned from all sides. From this close, she can hear the buzzing of the stringed lights above, which shudder as she should.

The inscription murmurs to her fatigued mind, and she knows that she is close.

It is that sense of peering into the night, wind chasing. It is day, but there is nothing to see, and wherever she looks there is only churning white, so she must see little, her thoughts slipping against one another as muscles hold rhythm, keeping her going. Her arms are within the folds- her figure is thin frosted shins, booted and bound like her grasps, holding up the fabric form which stretches at her hips, that unseen extending to either side, then the heavy cowl and her inattentive glow, shining.

Then, from the emptiness looms a mound. The white becomes another, the ground rises, and she follows this incline up, the poles keeping alongside, ascending also. The blizzard works to pin her, all loose fabrics trying to tear themselves apart. It is no hill or mountain, but an icy dune against the flatland, and she forces herself higher, the strength of this whole furore against her back, lightbulb blue catching the snow, so close. Her legs work harder, and their crunch becomes a sinking thud, her sight wandering vacantly, swaying useless.

She climbs to the crest and summits with a lurch, the rear winds sent sprawling from a height, dispersing against the break, to roll loosely over what must be the near edge of this wasteland. She would have been inclined to call it a desert, had she not now been staring at that which purposed her journey, her figure flickering atop its perch, cables overhead. Staring down at the outpost on the very fringe of her plateau.

She gazes, blue cutting against stark colourlessness, crisp as larger, freer flakes which trip from her hood, course on. She thinks, for a moment, that she would look a daunting thing from the settlement, but then she is here for that very reason. She looks up again, at the wires, which wink their way down toward misshapen buildings. These cables should belong here, hooked up to these structures, the images of a hiemal frontier, walls a worn collage of different shades from recycled metals, all taken by the onslaught. But instead, the lines are cut. She follows them with her squint, finding limp and torn edges. She lets her eye linger, and sees further, to a clear tear in the settlement.

The winds flare, and she holds to not stumble, looking to a ruin, not a community. One already small, but now cast in heavy wounds. Reshaped, by a thing which went wild. Rampant, as all lamps are silent and homes are busted open, their interiors abandoned to piling white. Maybe ten buildings, maybe less, but most are ravaged. The damage is a faint streak from afar, but she can recognise the turmoil.

And she knows she is in the right place, because of the cables, which trace there and then from left and right- the post sits at the junction of the communication rig: the sorting office of the plateau, to redirect and guide signals, catching stray messages at the edge of the colds reach.

But no signals have been coming from Glermvender.

She works her way down the slope, to find better comfort below the brink, away from the direct stream. She can break behind her shield of a ridge, standing with the snowy climb to her rear, Glermvender ahead, framed as carnage under its frightened light, a sun masked behind stormy white.

But then everything hides. The cold runs faster here, and the post is left a ruin. She imagines, in its prime, the place looked little better, but a warm glow would show life even here, atop the pale flat. Now there is nothing. The place has been ripped, and it speaks, instead of a million words and signals a second, an icy silence. It murmurs it, through severed ends.

The sun continues to set, a deeper, harsher shade becomes the snows, that of sibling colour to her gaze, which keeps to the post, caught on its solitude. Either side beckons the reassurance of others, with lines that must somewhere meet, even far away, but it is hope against a dull mass which becomes infinite, when it is all you have.

Dusk starts to crawl. She shifts a little, moving within her cloak.

She looks right.

She blinks again, into the sidelong winds, the frozen wave chasing her sight.

A thing stands, colossal.

Its scale is dwarfed by all but sight, yet even in person, the mind plays with shapes which climb for, above, the sky, its tones redefined by fainter depths, redone by distance.

It mimics human form, but its arms are too long, and it slouches backward, rocked as though it stares at something ever more impossible in height. Its flesh is an imitation skin, it is a mechanical form, of metal and wire fibres, to create a machine thing motionless, truly motionless, against these storms.

She watches it, a statue, surely built by those who heard of shape and fear and size and took to their project with fiendish enthusiasm, building a monument of nightmares, sickness and sinew, emaciated.

And where it once had its whole head, all above the jaw has been ripped, to leave loose points and hinges atop. A wound summiting the giant, curled into a mouth of mechanical glee.

Pylons atop show its height, they blink in reds and yellows like those of a guiding pad, bringing craft down. They show a scale daunting, and unbelievable. She must surely feel fear. It is an obelisk of twisted proportions, the image of unease. A thing to make them halt, or shudder should it shift. Or dare reach a loose limb.

She rubs her hands and starts toward the metal horror.

Down here, the snow crushes easier, and she moves as such. She traces the distant precipice of the plateau which, from there, is unseen, although cannot be much further past Glermvender. She keeps a clear calmness, her blue unimpressed and steady, although now it is one thrust toward the peak, kept straight on the automaton's half-head.

That rolling, whispering noise curls inside her hood, the new angle letting the cold reach her face, cowl fluttering and bulging. It fiddles with her hair and cheeks, so instead she reaches up to grasp her cowl, drawing it back.

She is monochrome, of white and dark- her hair is the tragic shade, black and quivering around her, a length somewhere around her chin, although it is frayed by necessity, and casts itself in abstract forms about her face. Skin deathly pale, made so by the storm, expression born of the same mother as the cold, defined by its inhospitable nature, but then she has that remoteness which attracts the gaze, as does the vast nothingness which she stalks. And it does not push you aside, but they are features which conceal things behind a constant, killing cold. Expansive eyes, bright and brilliant, but tired of all things to make others wide, so that she is rendered to her constant, almost apathetic intrigue. Not aggressive, or scrutinous or malicious, of a predatory intent, but just ambiguous enough; to know these eyes well, one will sit in their sockets too.

She approaches the machine instrument, observing its perfect lifelessness. The abhorrent silence of it- a thing of scale and mass enough to make the ground shiver and split, instead staring out, toward the drifting day, dormant and content. Blizzard snow builds against its silhouette, then it is blown free, like a sheet, rolling. The whole impression imposes extents unworkable, scales too wild to realize, but then she isn't trying to. Sight vivid, hood bunched around her neck, hair lashing in frantic jabs, and that thing against her lower back, still covered, she advances, gazing.

From behind, she is a speck against the high-rise, and the great thing still has not acknowledged her. Unprovoked and unaware of challenge, it admires the death of day. Drinks in the sight, from its peak. Maybe it can see something, when those below cannot. She does not follow its look, it is to see nullity, or the corpse of that ruined place. Instead, she is fixed on the ruined head, the signals atop winking, goading her in, provoking an attack on that blind to all but its lone beauty, the last of the light. The same light which observed the beast churn from fluttering white, to appear, standing over the settlement. A figment horrific, to those who would dare turn.

As she walks, it drapes over thought. To look out to those cables, an anchor of assurance. A blank dullness, wailing against your coat, and then to a mountainous figure. A lurching shape.

To pan up, and see it drift from the swell.

Head leaning, so slow. Grin ravenous.

She stops, swaying with the storm.

She runs a hand through her hair, cold cutting at exposed skin, blue taking to the colourlessness shivering past. All free fabrics ripple, she is images of wild hair played on a reel, flickering and bold, while she is entirely still. She looks up to the machine and feels that creeping chill. The wind and the noise of it. As she stares, it looks as though she might wave.

And as though the thing gazes from sun to thought, she watches that great colossus shift, its jaw turning so slightly, it could be an invention of the blizzard. As though it listens, or stares from the corner of an eye, with senses impossible.

Amid high and roaring madness, the automaton turns, lights blinking their disbelief.

She disperses, becoming a burst of gas.

You could look to find her, turning wildly with high brows, and see only her cloak drift, abandoned, and a streak of exhaust which chases her, as she flings herself at speeds explosive.

Her proportions become abstract, gracing sight from odd angles and distances wild. It is as though she throws herself, launched before blasts of a pale fume, blown from that thing against her lower back. A makeshift device fixed at the waist, with a system of straps tying her upper arms and legs in a flexible support, it looks like a small metal engine, with two large vents or exhaust ports on either side. They twitch every which way and expel great and forceful bursts of smoke. It is these bursts, short and single blasts that leave a streak of gas where they go. They launch her after each contact, billowing the second she connects with the snow, casting her like a stone, as she skims and spins. She is expelled at force, keeping low, to surely crumble and fall, but she is in perfect control, gliding over the cold like she is pulled on a string.

Her pace is undefinable, a fluid athlete too quick and too uneasy but of a performance drilled to absolute understanding, with contortions and spins to catch herself perfectly, maintaining speed, building it. She is an inch from the ground, kicking up a trail as she slides, and then she is higher, spinning. It is erratic and spontaneous, so she is seen from a way away, a stroke of white behind her speck, noise dim, and then too near. You're trying to keep up, the soles of her feet flashing as she lands on her palms and rotates, coming up to flare again, facing the wrong way, to correct at the next expulsion.

For only brief moments can the small module on her left palm be defined. A device wired within the bounds of her hand wrappings, connecting her forefinger and thumb with thin wires to a switch, a little red toggle in the centre of her palm. She orchestrates her apparent chaos with this, with a flick of those two fingers in whichever direction, in succession to each impact. Her control is a sequence of rapid signs, thrown as she skims, but she directs the exhausts against her back with a detail unbridled, to allow each near fatal error to merely boost her across the flat, a windswept bullet rushing. Like she pilots a fighter jet, an inch from the ground.

A leaf in the hurricane she flies, low and impactful, ribbons of smoke painting her past positions as her sporadic motion blasts her along. Her hair flails, but without her cloak her uniform is fitting, sleeves rolled to those binds on her lower arms, worn to brace her against constant collision. Her uniform is blacked and purposed, militaristic, her jacket one of pockets and fastened straps and her trousers the same, bounds like her arms and booted. Flying, she is animated, as though her movement is the work of the ecstatic mind, sketching wildly. She is detailed in the many compartments to her clothes, seemingly filled, everything black but worn, battered, faded and scuffed with constant use. The vertical across her back, it is a sword, which rests atop her blaring engine, curved slightly, laying across equal halves of her back. Skimming with her, strapped tightly.

Her eyes are attentive now, fixed on each movement, carrying herself along as the snows break with each impact. The sudden rainfall of her hands and feet and then the moments of flying, split by a flaring smoke or a grating against the cold, but she does not register concern. Concentration over even anticipation, it is an awareness compulsory and of memory, drilled into her body for years, every muscle trained with instinct.

As she approaches, the machine shifts wholly. Its components churn into motion, sheets of cold crumbling into the high winds as things turn and its left arm, as the demon observes sidelong, starts to reach. Raising its limb, lackadaisical in intrigue instead of presuming threat, as though it extends its reach to an approaching bug. The woman surges, blaring in and out of sight, proportions and outline detailed by a maniac, as she surges toward the palm which becomes darker as it approaches, clawing through the storm, to blacken and shadow its descent.

The hand makes it to the ground, and tears apart the world under its weight. It shatters the cold, plumes unfurling, shards soaring, as the machine drives its reach toward the blur, seeping across the horizon. As she watches, the hand takes deeper shades still, spreading across vision. A wound in the blandness, or a dark sunrise, ink bleeding through paper, it grows over sight, ruining the pristine sheets.

But she does not slow. Instead, her hand blares, snapping against a pocket at her thigh.

The machine beast leans into its strike, shouldering toward the blow, but its limbs are freakish, and its arms are longer anyway, so it maintains its size. And she hears it, alongside the storm. If the wind is a howl, then it works to stifle another. A churning groan, like the growl of sea ships.

The great half head turns fully toward her approach.

She looms, faster and faster, building in turns and twirls, weaving the white. Needle black and thread smoke, constantly moving forward. Never failing, but flinching and swerving as she goes, conducted by the bursts which throw her. And if the hand is ink, which oozes into the sheets, then she centres on that damp frailty, directly at the centre. Her line becoming straighter, as an arrow flies level. The shadows of city-high fingers rush closer, she leads into her streak. Her impacts become constant, every meter she covers is hit, with palm and foot, dispersed in clouds.

The dark bleeds, and the palm hurtles to make her its stain.

Then, suddenly, she is in focus.

She thinks time slows, as little lights appear alongside her. From that pocket she spun them and now they twirl, revolving beside the blur. Metal throwing stars, cobbled of miscoloured steels and haphazardly held together, and while their four bladed points are profiled and sharped, their

cores is an inch thick, a red bulb glimmering in the centre of each.
Her speed keeps them alongside, but they are built to cover distance. To glide, and in those melting seconds, as they spin into focus, it is then that she swerves.

She climbs, impossibly quick, up the flat hand's face, rising in an instant from the ground to the break between fingers, thrown by her fumes. In a blink there is wild light, an explosive gold flaring below her. As she hangs there between machine digits, the detonation barks into the constant storm, a harder and harsher tone tenfold than even the endless wailing. Bright heat tears sheets and cables from the mandible, the momentary glow making all things its shade, as she holds there, suspended above the ruined grasp. Half harsh shadow, half brilliant colour, smoke burbling.

Only a toe reaches the machine wrist before she flies, snow exchanged for frosted rigidity, and now she ascends, leaving level ground to rise, manoeuvring up the great arm, leaving the wreckage to burn.
She glances up, expecting to figure a route.
Instead, the second limb approaches, tracing the first, aimed to grind her between the two parts, quicker now than before as the vague outline of the half head observes. It's lights blinking their haphazard tones and speeds.
Her cold features become a momentary grimace as she swerves, the streak coursing around, following the curvature of the arm until she can no more, and she falls, her back toward the ground, fabrics flailing, watching the hand pass overhead. Her hair rippling, inhaling heavily.

To land from a higher height safely she spins, taking a second to come to a halt through a series of frenzied feats, each rotation competing to be the quickest as she flips, landing hard, arms splayed wide to either side, crouched upon the white, plumes of exhaust at either side. Behind her, heat still scalds its colours into the blandness, and she looks up, breath quick and expression kept to its attempted calmness.
A noise and she blurts steam, an immense finger breaking where she had stood. Before she can stop, another falls, so that she weaves again, between the falling skyscrapers, her launching boosts now extended to allow the threat to become obvious in trajectory, so that she may evade.

She leads with her chest, letting her arms hang back, feet trailing twin trenches in the snow, then she swerves, ground splintering, the shattered glass of the cold spreading from a great metal index, made a gravestone for some lost giant.

The growing darkness of this boreal plane conflicts with the flames she leaves behind as she eyes the legs of the vast automaton. She lets her sight rise to its knees, as the great hand unearths itself, shifting to retake aim.

A finger descends but this time she stays close, instead using the sharp turn to throw, another star emerging from her grasp, as she rotates with whiplash and spin near lethal, casting the point like a card. Before it can detonate she must move again, but with even a moments pause she sends another, and another, their impacts becoming methodical as the explosions tear. The noise of inner workings becomes apparent as the arm chases her, each missed opportunity tearing the beast evermore, glow flaring.

And then one finger moves too far, misguided by an impending stumble, strays an inch aside, and when it lands she has time to grab, a slight adjustment to her angle bringing her up. She mounts the finger and continue higher, gas pursuing, sunset shades of flame ebbing against the wind and embers which roll, the charging figure competing with the storm and the cold and the shifting floor against which her limbs slam, again and again.

When she ascends the ground falls below, disappearing with her pace as though it collapsed, the conflict of murderous cold and building heat working against both sides of her as she passes knee level. She glances at the glowing wounds, components falling and smoke pluming amid the churning gale.

Higher altitudes make conditions brutal and such speeds make the change harsh, as her hair shudders and she stumbles, wincing against the barrage. She cannot become numb, the dexterity of her hands dictates her motion, but then they are never still, always arcing, scything through the paralysis that would bite at wandering digits. The automaton's arm is a bridge which rises, built of dull shades and exposed wiring, taking her to the growing outline of the half head, the pylons upon which its lights are strung building into vision.

Again she dares a look and sees the hand coming, the one still alight, reaching to take her sidelong, fire swept by approaching speed. The cold concealing it for a moment, it bulges from the white, moving too close for her to outpace. She watches it come, leaping for a while like a hound before she flares to the side, as she had done before but now too high and too blind to the ground to fall, so instead she kicks off, launching herself.

The space between the machine arm and torso blares past, as a metal wall approaches. Below, her carnage smoulders, she cannot see the ground, and twin blue bulbs fling themselves at the automaton's body.

Her hand darts and she draws the sword, the shade of her eyes catching bright steel, and she lands hard against the wall, stabbing with a grunt to hold herself still, planting her feet below with force. Her hair flicking forward, then back.

A moment to breathe. Her exhales are a fog, which wavers against well frozen plates, and she heaves them out, fingers locked tight around the handle which holds her there, thrust overhead. Looking up, the beast ascends into the perpetual, that distant distortion of grey continuing on, but she knows she is near the chest. Halfway, she thinks, as she looks down now, to see a vast grasp, still laced with the remnants of her damage, surge through the billowing flames, chasing up after her.

She gazes level, and lets scowling eyes knife their own blades into the machine.

Fumes plume and she's up, climbing with whole stretches between each contract, rising vertically. If she were to miss a single catch she would surely fall, but she guides each impact, like a cat racing the impossible way, or a paper plane weaving and diving, but heavenward.

The altitude rages, the hand gains but her speed builds also, and the half head comes into view. All components of the automaton, its head and its torso and its arms shift separately, so that she darts through a course of tectonic structures, passing over the chest in seconds, but her sights are set and, with the grasp so close, she surges.

The shoulder of the great beast is a glimpse as she burns past, touching nothing now as she stares the half head down while she soars. Flaring past and onward, rising higher and higher on a prolonged burst. With no anchor she wavers, so she cuts the exhaust, floating freely, as the machine hand passes its head and cuts up in pursuit.

She keeps rising a while longer, alone in the clouds.

She stays there, caught in the equilibrium of her sharp ascent and gravity, so she stretches her arms wide, facing the sky. Preparing to dive. Up this high, the storm seems to have let its strength fall, so that she remains, calm, her hair flailing with her rise, then floating in that moment of hanging. Her mind blanks. She takes a break, breath allowed to ease again. She even closes her eyes, shutting off the lights. The pause, with nothing but that engulfing cold and the noise which bats against ears, draws the easiest inhalation to her yet. Despite the chills, she is soothed.

The shadow rises, and from the billowing below bursts the vast claw, driving to her heights, size bringing curls of white mist with it. Knotted, pulling the blizzard's hair. She lets it come close, fingers twitching as she rolls her head. Feels the pressure against her back. Then she shifts, hand returning to her blade. She bursts to the side, almost rolling over the palm but she is kept just above by the sheer push the beast carried, so that when she comes to the edge she is close enough to slash, using her edge now stuck in the hand to pivot and carry herself in a spin; as the hand extends without prize, she hangs against its back.

    She plucks the sword loose.

    Her descent, it is lightning, etching itself toward the ground. Already the machine falls, its knees buckling from her barrage, but she shows no mercy, sheathing the blade against her back and drawing loose more stars. She spirals, looping around the arm in her drop, gas twisting with her as she casts the bombs, spinning a second to throw and then regaining course, the detonations thundering in her wake like footfall catastrophic. From below, the machine already crumbles and from atop now also it breaks, so she decides to meet in the middle, as climbing flames centre the damage at the half head.

She crosses the jaw. A streak of blue, gleaming at the eyeless giant, offering it nothing of emotion. Where a sneer or smile should have been, her lips are tight, her gaze unfaltering, and regained of composure. Controlled, pale features observe, azure alight. The millisecond it takes to pass oozes.

    But then, even if the machine could, it does not look at her. Instead, it would see the stars which she moves besides, to fall into the throat an upper head should have blocked.

She lands hard on its shoulder, to the roar of explosions within. Plunging into that low crouch again, her fumes blanketing like a shroud all around. A snarl cuts her features, but it lasts the breath of impact, and she dips into her stoop, letting her body adjust to the breakneck stop.

She rises, slow, disabling the switch against her hand to let it move freely. Dark strands float, and embers sway around the machine which drops, so slowly that she can stand there, upon the automatons side. Its hand collapses, still outstretched, its burning sheets tumbling as slithers of light, adding to the smoke and cinders, alien to these temperatures. It creates a breath-taking scene, a mesmeric dream from afar. A pyre, stretching so high, bleeding a blaze into the winds. A firestorm, knifing the cold, which curls in that deepness of the blizzard, turned bright when close with flame light. A beacon, of both marvel and horror.

Yet she stands there, mind so clear. Around her, the world collapses, but her thoughts drift with those burning, her eyes unconcerned. Distant, although too close. The machine descends, its fire towering.

It's as though she isn't even there.

- FAUSCHENHERST TERRIROTY -

GLERMVENDER POST

Glermvender watches her approach. It sits, huddled in its ruins, wide eyed as those of blue come, swaying with the cold. The storm bathes her and without the coat she abandoned she is bombarded, but the hard opposites, of her swatting hair and then the steadiness of her motion, it is unnerving, and fixates the eye. Fixates more eyes, for all gazes first settle upon the vast corpse she has left, faint embers still rising from the crumpled thing; an imitation figure, disassembled.

Few people come to greet her, emerging from the remnants of their post. They are heavy laden with great coats and duck into the storm, wading to offer her refuge. Their sights lingering over the carcase. She has abandoned it, out in the frozen wasteland, slumped with a reaching hand, half head half buried. Its lights are out, and its limbs are still, the white already piling against its side, but from here its details are lost to distance. They do not hope to see more anyway.

She stops, squinting even with the wind to her back. The refugees come close and offer curt bows, the remains of their home behind. The only life she can recognise aside from the four before her is another group, to the left of the settlement, working around dim lamps, assembling crates into drawn rafts and waggons. Preparing to leave, although stalled by the sudden display. Or maybe working now, after hiding from the watchful, eyeless, torn gaze of the machine. Aside from these, all seems dead. Walls pulled open and the snow unearthed, as cable posts were hauled up and their lines left to trail over caved-in rooftops. There was little here anyway, but now it is forlorn.

The people don't much bother with formalities, but they are sincere in their thanks. The closest, a man with, like all others, his face lost in the fur of his hood, takes her hand in his, feeling fingers frozen. He shouts that they'll leave soon, in a voice stolen by the storm, then asks her if she needs anything.

She blinks, turning her head from the worst of the drifts.

Her voice is modulated, well controlled, but even more an

undertone of the blizzard than his. She asks if he has any food.

He glances back, looking for a moment over the buildings. His home.

He says she can have anything they haven't already packed.

The houses are small and mostly single levelled, and she walks through a hole in the exterior to enter, climbing into a dark place, azure sights sweeping. The ground is littered with packets and draws raided, computers iced over and servers fried by the intense cold. Upon a peg by the now abandoned door she finds a worn, umber coat. It isn't very thick and hangs around her knees, but she takes her sword off her back and slips into it, shouldering through the frozen fabric, holding the sheathed blade.

While she looks around, she takes a handful of stars from her chest pocket, and puts them in her new overcoat.

Passing open doors into separate rooms, she sees tables and beds turned to snow. Water vats made ice and small batches of crops left useless, not openly exposed to the storm but still ruined, as the wailing cold endured outside. She shuffled past a stiff door and into one of these rooms, busting open iced draws in search of something to eat. She isn't sure what to make of it, crouched as she opens seemingly well frozen boxes and finds them empty anyway. She has no idea as to how long these people have been here, nor to the time spent under the watch of that machine.

Leaning back on her haunches, she reaches under her coat to the system against her lower back, resting her sword against a box to feel into her satchels, strapped tight to either side of the vented device. Inside, she feels only her canteen and its bags in one, her lamp in the other. She delves deeper, for food maybe forgotten or misplaced. She finds none.

She closes the satchels, running her hand down her face, before she takes her sword and stands, leaving the room.

She steps out, back into the cold, looking from one building to the next, and, seeing the only one which seems of brick and to have a second floor, she passes between the two spaces and their sandwiched white. It is knee deep as she creeps into the next house, finding the bottom floor of a similar forgottenness, so instead she wanders to the stairs, which shake under footfall with a brittle creak.

All windows shudder and the storm whispers its hate, throwing itself against already gutted structures. Breathing a constant mist, she climbs the case and summits into an attic space, looking around the small room.

At the other end, sitting opposite a window, a boy is perched, watching the blizzard churn.

She doesn't pay him much attention as she enters, but she sees emptiness in all but his section, lit only by the light from his single port, which catches a face turned from her. Whether he is waiting for the others to finish packing, or he has stowed himself here, he sits alongside a crate of salvaged food packets. Maybe taken from reserves, or what they could not carry.

She walks over, neither addressing the other as she looks to his box, shuffling the wrappers, glancing his way as she searches. He cannot be more than eight, she figures, his features unchanging and caught on the curling snows.

Probably born here.

She blinks.

A moment passes, and she trudges to the corner, her side to the wall with the window. She collapses into it with a slouch, tearing open a packet as she falls. Resting, one knee raised, she draws something dehydrated and of an oat-like consistency from its wrapping, and bites through. It is frozen, and doesn't taste of anything, but out there she has wandered through the same shade forever, so anything takes her imagination.

They both sit in silence, taste slowly spreading as she tries to figure whether the bar is flavourless or her face is too cold to register a palate, as a dry mouth works on the first thing she has eaten in days.

She is splayed without care and in that corner is little light, so when the boy turns a margin, hands flat on the bench by either side, he must only see her vague features, half cast in perpetual darkness, and her vivid, glowing blue unenthusiasm. Like twin frosted bulbs, shining, which waver over the bar.

He isn't wearing enough to venture out, but he doesn't much seem to mind the cold, and she figures it clear that he has been groomed to leave. His hair is sheered short in preparation for what his people hope to be a long journey, his boots fastened tight. She, in contrast to his attentive observation, sits against the corner, leg bent and the other straight, and while her hair is only of chin length, it is dark and tormented by her wanderings, so that it lays in strands, unruly and wild.

She must look an odd thing, she figures, slumped in a coat of someone probably dead, as she eats without courtesy, so she lets her bright gaze wander to him, and offers a nod into the howling quiet.

Caught between reluctance and intrigue, the boy returns the gesture, observing the thing in the corner as he had the gale. He watches her reach into the depths of the packet, then cast the wrapping aside when she's finished, running a bound arm over her mouth, slowing to meet his gaze. She stares at him, dead to expression, and then to his box, which is piled with similar rations.

When she returns to him, in a voice now free from the blizzard's interludes, clear yet empty, she asks if he's thirsty. Her voice cuts across the silence, sudden and intrusive, to break that understanding of the quiet, but the boy does not show protest.

Leaning forward a little, she reaches around to her canteen and pulls it loose, offering it to him with an outstretched hand, adding that she'll trade some of her water for more of his packets.

The closest snows which flit past the window casts their individual shadows, to create an ever-evolving patchwork of dull colour and shadow which contains the child, like television static buzzing. She is relegated to the dark of the corner.

Not seeming thirsty, but instead seeing no reason to oppose, his sights wavering from hers to the sword laying alongside, he takes two handful from the box and lays them by his side. He catches her flask when she casts it the short distance, unscrewing the lid. Before he drinks, he reaches to his chosen packets, taking a moment to figure how he will throw the many pieces simultaneously, but before he can decide she produces a bag to accompany the bottle, throwing it also.

It is a packet of power, no larger than her palm, and the boy takes it with a raised brow.

Watching, her own expression an odd mix, she waves a hand in gesture and states that the bottle is empty.

She stalls, mid speech, as he looks down the nozzle.

With a slight drawl, she tells him that he puts the powder in and shakes the bottle if he wants to drink, speaking as she shuffles forward and snatches another packet from his side, leaning against his bench as she rips the wrapper apart. He works alongside her, going to empty the dust but being stopped by a shake of her head, so to let him sprinkle the ground pieces until she nods, and watch him cap the bottle and shake.

For a while, they both sit there in the quiet. One eating, the other rolling the flask between his palms, listening to the storm.

She asks if this is his room, careful to keep her tenses kind. He nods, looking around, and says that it used to have a lot more in it. She joins him in looking, both turning to the dark of the opposite end, the room empty, but not torn open.

She says that it's pretty big, chewing through the dried grain, and he shrugs, telling her that he got the best spot in the post because he was so young. He says, as he tires of shaking, that he was the first child born here in a while, so they gave him the second floor, and he got his own radio and everything. He says it was a Geseschaus[1] system, while everyone else had the Ubess-Koss[2] ones, and the woman raises a brow, nodding her admiration. She asks him if he still has it, or if the others had stowed it with their luggage.

He says that he has, but she can have it if she wanted. There wasn't room for it with the rest.

The silence draws, and they both stare at the storm.

His voice does not quiver, nor even stall, but she senses that impending dread so, still eating, she says that Geseschaus radios come from the same place she does, and his attention flares as he turns, head cocked. One arm up on his bench as she sits on the ground, she says that they're made on Emilia[3], in a city called Sawabiva.

They talk, exchanging the meaningless, while she waits for someone to call the boy down. She won't come, take his food, and leave him to be swept away by the storm, so she tells him about her home, about

---

[1] *Geseschaus*: Radios built in Sawabiva, on Emilia. They're designed to perform through interference, or else succumb to the snowstorm static of their home world, however their range is shorter than the Fauschenherst Ubess - Koss systems.

[2] *Ubess – Koss* : The radio system used by the Fauschenherst, on the planets and the Kyut. Lightweight, adaptable, and widespread, they span six versions, with one through four being mobile, and versions five and six being stationary super-radios. The company receives Fauschenherst funding, having outfitted Sect Three, as well as owning the telecommunications systems of the planets. The radios are characterised by having high protruding aerial antenna.

[3] *E. D. 8 "Emilia"* : A frozen abyss of a planet, the largest of the four remaining worlds. Its proximity to the Faurscherin ruins has left it a graveyard for ship data banks and fuel deposits, the salvaging of which has become the planets main trade. The capitol, Sawabiva, is a telecommunications terminal that sells the Faurscherins information to the Fauschenherst, and the barren nature of the world makes this its relative sole source of income for food and resources.

how cold it and how barren it is. Time drawls by,
Eventually, he asks what her name is.

She says that her name is Nux. Nuxitec Pawasaki, but nobody here calls her that. Voice monotone and posture straight, she says that here, she is Klernsteiga[4] O one-one-nine-five "Pescha". She offers a quick nod with the words, and addresses the pause of the staring boy.
Loosening, she says that she's Pescha.
He asks what all of the other things were.
Formalities, she states. She says that nobody other than a Klernsteiga would call her a Klernsteiga, either. Nomad is-

The boy's gaze detonates, harder than any of her bombs, and his mouth splits.
She smiles.
He blurts, in question, that she's a Nomad, like Small Hand.
The grin does not falter, but she struggles to keep it so.
He has turned fully, arms straight to prop him up as he leans in, rambling, telling her that he thought she was a Rautbergen[5], coming by to check the cables, or just one wandering past.

Holding her expression, she asks, looking at the boy a few inches from her face, if he's ever seen a Rautbergen that looks like her.

He blinks, and rears back, glancing away. No. He says that he hasn't.

Pescha reaches out and takes her flask abandoned to their words, and she drinks the materialised liquid, watching the snow outside. In truth, she doesn't know if it's water, but then that is a formality too that is discarded by necessity. She hands it to the boy, who turns the canteen around to drink from the opposite rim side.

---

[4] *Klernsteiga / Nomad* : The minor half of the Fauschenherst army, officially established with the formation of Sect Three. They are self-sufficient reconnaissance fighters, operating independently and often deep in contested territory. While of marginal numbers, they are the face of the Fauschenherst, and a symbol of human fortitude.

[5] *Rautbergen* : The major half of the Fauschenherst army. A foot soldier militia which defends and expands Fauschenherst territory.

She knows nobody will come for him. This boy, sitting in his attic room, is perched atop a house with its walls blown out, and he hosts enough food to feed the whole convoy for days.

Has been left with enough food, or has stolen enough, and stowed himself away, up here.

She watches him drink, gaze unwavering, and when he's done, Pescha stands, taking the bottle and stowing it in her pocket, taking his hand with one of hers and then a handful of bars with the other. He stares at her as he rises, but objection falls to a child's mind, rapt in comprehending the impossible, as she pockets the wrappers and retakes her blade. She asks if he'll come with her. He nods.

She walks him down, back to the blown out lower floor, and asks where his radio is, holding to the empty space as he breaks her clutch to find it, dipping through into another room. The shades of cold linger, and will forevermore in this place, as the consuming contradictions of screaming silence swarm around her, the room both infinitely large and then too small to be comfortable in, centred at the woman with blue eyes. Pescha waits for him to return, hauling a rig mounted to dual straps for carrying, and she takes it from him, holding the system up. A box of compartments, inactive lights, and antenna, which extend when tugged out, she looks it up and down, then slings it over her shoulder. Looped over one arm, resting the straps of her sword with it, so that the blade runs down the side of the radio. It is frozen over and icy, the boy's radio, previously discarded in hopelessness well hidden by the child, who retakes her hand and lets her lead him out.

She takes him between buildings and through the storm, toward the group, who do not notice her approach. They instead busy themselves with trying knots and counting luggage.

She glances left and sees the machine. She calls for the boy not to look.

Pescha knows they are stalling. Holding on in pretence for night, so that they can excuse their staying, as they huddle close to one another, faces hidden by their heavy coats. Holding the boy near, that he will not fall behind, she walks to the closest of the technical engineers, who spins quickly to her turning grasp. She asks him for a spare coat. The man glances to the child but does not start, nor does he connote any sense at all as he reaches into the equipment he has salvaged, stashed alongside the makings of tents and radio gear, to pull loose a jacket and pass it to her, his other arm tucked within the folds of his warmth.

She takes it and watches him stumble, back out toward the larger group, hosting only five, her clutch still outstretched as she looks to his leave, the storm surging from her left toward the fall of the Plateau. She wonders what these people must think.

But she needn't consider, for the boy squeezes her hand tighter, not out of sole cold but of that which makes even her indifference flicker. She crouches level to him, holding out his arms as she tucks them into the overcoat, looking to button his jacket instead of staring at his shudders.

He stands there, this boy in his oversized coat, watching Pescha clasp the covering. She, with luminous sights and his radio, her coat oversized too but it is tailored in comparison to his, her sword tied against the communications box and her clothes underneath martial. Her extremities bound, body rigged with pocketed bombs.

When she's done, she looks up at him. Smiling would be an offense, she figures, and she lets him stare at her, then allows him to drift to his left, eyes trailing to the great, lifeless thing which leers his way, rapt evermore in its half glee. His attention does not falter, but this is not out of solidarity, and his sights are stuck on the colossus. Even when fallen, it hosts that same stillness to characterise its figure when standing.

Pescha asks the name of the Humeda[6].

The boy says that it was called Hjordiis. A word to mean fulfilled to another, he stutters, but as he illudes toward the act after which this name was bestowed, his speech falters, and his eyes quiver to a rocking head, as the storm rushes him, and the white mounts against his legs. Climbing even in these few stationary moments.

The Nomad takes his hands in hers, holding his great sleeves and feeling the clutched grips within, hauling his attention back as the coward sun. It is suspended now between the two, chased by the blizzard.

He turns to her, this brittle thing of frozen thoughts.

Stares into a gaze of sibling shades to that of this tortuous cold.

She tells him, in a voice quiet yet passed through sight on certain lips and through a tone now direct and close, that she destroyed the Humeda called Hjordiis. She did it only a short while ago. Pescha tells him that it was tough, coming here and fighting it, but that because of where she comes from, a place similar to this, she made it.

---

[6] *Humeda* : The machine enemy of mankind, built of an old and forgotten technology.

She draws a hand, and pokes his chest.

The Nomad tells him that if she can do that, and make it our pretty much same as entry, then what can the boy do, who has lived here? A boy raised in these storms. She shifts, leaning harder on one leg, to point out to the cables which swing through and into the emptiness. She tells him that if he follows them, tracing the edge of the snows, he'll surely find someone on the other end. Another post, further along the trail.

He follows her gesture, looking to the wavering lines, but does not move.

Instead, he asks, in a voice too fitting of his position to allow ease, what the point is.

She stares.

He is dormant of features, swaying as the hanging wires do. Murmuring, he says they're cursed. Everyone knows it. He just can't explain it.

She blinks, then adjusts herself, pivoting to glance at the Humeda, the boy pursuing her blue attention. They must look into the storm, but the boy doesn't mind. One hand held and the other hanging limp, lost in his sleeve, he stares at Hjordiis, who towers even in death.

She says they must be abandoned. The boy does not move.

What faith can be imagined, she mumbles, to ease this. The wind surges, and she ducks into its force. The machines are made. The Humeda are born, and even as things of metal and mindless slaughter, they have been birthed as such.

What has she got. What has the boy, who lingers here. Life after, the muttering endures, but then what life. Crude and unthinking, these husks of iron are more alive. Such a simple purpose, yet one to define existence. Both of them, they gaze at the dead thing, and the boy shudders. She turns to the ground, eyes sunk amid the white, holding the boy who keeps his sights on the Humeda.

How terrifying it is, this nothingness. How swallowing, to persist without meaning. Pescha looks out to the storm, still holding his hand.

Nobody is happy, Pescha breathes, and she hates this. She hates the way things are- every one of them does, they're just too scared to say it. The indignity of what they've become, the things to which they've pledge themselves. They have one life, one existence, there and then, and they only humiliate themselves. Humiliation, constant and absolute; it haunts all they will ever do.

Everything has a cost, she tells, looking back at him. It's cause and effect; everything has a cost, nothing will ever change without sacrifice, but that doesn't mean it's equal. It isn't proportionate. It isn't fair. He can give so much, everything, for so little. He'll give more than he'll ever know, for nothing.

She blinks at him, her blue deep. For the first time, there is something to read in her frosted glare.

She says she'll give everything she has to see her dream come true. Everyone here, they want things back the way they were, before it all collapsed. But they're blind, she tells. They cannot see, but they must. She will show them. Their eyes shall be aflame, she pines, with faith, passion gaining her voice. She'll see her dream come true or die looking.

The boy gazes, form heavy but face still. For a second, she hopes he will break her clutch and wander off, work on some impulse of her words, but instead he addresses her, face wavering with question.

He asks what her dream is.

The gale rushes them both, her coat flailing like tied flags, curving at the system against her lower back.

Softly, she tells him she's looking for a child. One a bit older than the boy, but a boy still. Yet he doesn't age. Nobody's quite sure how old he really is.

He's fallen ill. Now sick, he's managed to reach a hotel. A hotel for Nomads, called Relief Ukibiki. That's where she's going. It's a long way, she tells him, feeling the slack of his arm, but she's already come far. She must get there before his condition changes. From Dodtohmet, down through wetlands and oceans, across sands and plains until she reaches the Shae Doken and on, into Kenidomo Country.

The boy stares, trembling upon query.

He asks what the child's name is.

The Nomad glances again, into the storm. Who is he to tell, but signal trappers without radios. Besides, is she to turn away, and wave him on now?

Pescha says the child's name is Emile. Emile, a boy who does not grow old, and who has fallen ill.

The boy nods, frost spiking against his brows. He shifts, looking to the rest there. Even with a Nomad crouched close, they stall. Busy themselves with nothing, as lamps are held to perfectly secured cases, then retied with the shake of a head. Their coats billow and their hoods flare, and the boy in his own stares, feeling the switch and cables on Pescha's left grasp as she places a hand on the boys back. She stands, turning to the crowd, which avoids her bright scrutiny.

She walks, leaving the boy meters behind to address those fleeing. They see her come and gesture half-hearted attention, pivoting their margins while tending to lines and ropes. The figure in the coat with luminous eyes watches, faint assertion mixing with her returned melancholy.

Speaking up, she tells them they must leave. She is an image of contrast and distortion, of fabric raging wildly against a still form, her blue mesmeric, as dual lights in the unpigmented. Pescha says she can't let them wait any longer. If they try to stay the night here, they might freeze anyway, or refuse to leave without her or the Humeda as a threat, and she can't wait overnight. She needs to get down from the Dodtohmet Plateau before nightfall proper.

They all nod, shuddering with the cold, but none of them are really listening. Not like they'll protest, but like they aren't thinking. They amble and waver with words on chilled lips, and she stares at them each in turn, a process of too short a transition. She is more than willing to leave before she would wait with them.

But then the boy passes, walking past and before her. Not to face or stand against the group but to instead wait there, looking past the people and out to the storm, which plagues as a tearing wail from all sides. Maybe he breathes hard, or swallows, but he glances back at the Nomad, his jacket more a cloak than a coat.

His face is without conviction. Instead, it asks whether there is truly any option.

And as the remnants of Glermvender had done to her, Pescha bows, but further, she sinks to her hands and knees, falling before her audience. They watch the pale gaze descend closed, as her nose and hair brush the white, her arms half buried. She prostrates, hearing and feeling only the cold, which curls against her and rushes all senses, to burn boreal against her skin. Twisting fabric and hair in their streams. Pescha bows, and she does not rise. Maintaining her stoop until she can see the shadows of her strands clearly, against the light of the setting sun.

A while later, she looks up, searchlights pursuing anything upon the crisp ice. She looks up to emptiness, the trails of Glermvender's carts already fading to that frozen cycle, ever churning.

- *FAUSCHENHERST TERRIROTY* -
VANISH STRIP

The marsh of Vanish Strip spreads before, a horizon closed off by bogland mist.

Pescha holds herself up, sleep splayed over slack features, an arm extended to prop her against damp ground. Her coat has been used as a blanket and it slides off to her waist, the radio she took stowed in the corner, her vented machined lain alongside.

She awakes under the half sunken body of a machine. Not one of a size near to Hjordiis; one tall enough to tower still, yet small enough to get stuck, lumbered with the weight of mud, its keeled torso and partly submerged head providing shelter for her sleep, away from the constant drawl of fog. She cannot tell how long it has been here, but a Nomad looks to have blown its legs off, leaving it to crawl, then sink. Maybe It was all the mud, or the moisture in its system, but it lays dead now, staring into the mist.

She stretches and slips the coat on, coming to, as the sound of the marsh hums. It is a noise of struggling waterflow and that heaviness of the fog, as she shoulders her radio, blade tied tight, rubbing her eyes to the mire. It is all a shade of brown and dull grey, everything drowned by the excess of liquid which drains through, held in stagnant pools, blanketed by the smog. Sight dwells on rotten trees, bare of branches and rendered to stumps, lost amid the wet. Twisted, burnt arms reaching heavenward. Remnants of the Fauschenherst's[7] long and brutal war.

It is a place of eerie alienness.

Her feet sink when still and the air weighs her down, so she does

---

[7] *Fauschenherst*: the organisation constituting all of mankind's remaining wealth and resources. Its society is based on the legal and hierarchical structure of its preceding mothership, the Faurscherin, with its leadership tracing their lines to the original crew. It comprises all that remains of humanity: its economy; its worlds; and its military. It would be false to assume the Fauschenherst the army of mankind and its planets- mankind has become an army, as much pledged to the Fauschenherst as the word "human".

not remain. She will not spend another night here, turning a moment to look back the way she descended, the journey taken by night. Even from here, amid the mist, she can figure the ridge of the Dodtohmet Plateau, stretching high above the marsh. Spanning like an ice wall, endless to either side.

    Glermvender must be only a few hundred meters further, she thinks. What is left of it. Hjordiis too.

    She blinks, weary blue fluttering.

Vanish strip is built of migrations, she notes; discarded bridges and pontoons span the impassable stretches, linked by wooden floats now sunk and rotten, posts once hung with lights and the remnants of abandoned camps smattering the light murk, and to interject them all are the Humeda remains. There must be hundreds, she figures, most eaten by the wet mud. Their limbs claw and their bodies are frayed by machine exhaustion, creating some sick memorial to a sadist's impression of humanity. They are piles of wire, consumed by the vapour and its shades, and torn open corpses, disembowelled by roaming Nomads. There would be Klernsteiga who made this part of their route, Pescha thinks, as she passes ruined walkways and fallen automatons. Scavengers, who strafe Vanish Strip. She doesn't know if Rautbergen would pass through here. She doesn't figure anyone would by choice.

    Nobody would make this place their home. To misinterpret safety from the Humeda within the murk- she passed the collapsed and slipping remains of things similar. People, who have long since passed through the Strip, and abandoned it to the haze of memory and of the bog.

Eventually, she passes a lake. It materialises from the damp air to stretch into fog, taking half of her vision when she passes its widest point. She watches it as she walks, vapour gliding over metal limbs, clutching at the surface mist. Her bright sights find a central island, mirrored in the water below. A mound with a single spire; a stump speared with an upright pike, one long streamer tied atop. She recognises the symbology- it wavers with faint wind, which plays with similar interest amid Pescha's hair, exposed by the openness of the area.

She stares, alone on the bank. There is an encampment on the island too, waterlocked from all sides, but it has not decayed; a tent remains upright, hunched under the swaying flyer above. An outpost, maybe, for passing Nomads- she cannot tell whether it is open or strung. It is a surreal, uncanny thing, but she doesn't stop. She ventures from the lake, daylight choked by fog which dominates all.

Then the drizzle comes, rainfall building, the moisture accumulating to its apex, and she can see even less as she stops, becoming that figment of twin lights again. She hoists her stolen coat's hood, seeking direction amid the fog. The downpour impacts against stagnant puddles, creating a superstorm around her ankles.

She can scarce define what's a few feet ahead, so she reaches to her pack, eyes wandering for a branch amid the carnage. She produces her lamp, from the pocket opposite to her flask, and when she sees a stick she snaps the dead thing loose, and suspends her light from its end.

Now she avoids the largest of pools, wandering a wasteland of some forgotten war, gas still presiding to halt all life save for she, who snakes the marsh without prey, keeping to a general line.

It isn't long before she stops once more, to spin and gather baring, in an attempt to make sense of the Strip, which she had thought to be crossing at the shortest width. Instead, she reaches around and draws the radio loose, propping it against a knee to raise the antenna, shuffling the twin spires up. They rise to sway with the unfurling rains, her grip loose against the wetness. Once they're up she takes the receiver, a handheld improvisation of a module linked by ringed cables and slings the main unit over her back, pylons waving overhead.

Pescha beats her hands together against the numbing damp, stick pinned into the ground to hold her lantern high while she works on the receiver, speaking into the slatted end for a response.

Her voice is drowned by the downpour anyway, the noise heavy against her hood, and the mist swamps any reply with static, too much echoing around her to take a signal.

She tries turning, revolving slowly on the spot, giving her twin antenna reach, but stalls with the image of herself there. She peers into the marsh, looking for raised ground to separate herself from the constant interference, eyes sweeping for elevation between the flat pools and desecrated mire. Her bound and booted legs sink in wet motionlessness, forcing her to trudge on, taking twig and lamp, sight of Dodtohmet lost to the murk of Vanish Strip. She hunts for an Humeda tall enough, or not so far sunken, to mount.

And one looms, its arms stuck under the muck so that it is forever arched in struggle, rearing back until it failed to now ruined components. Sheets of muddy rust cling to worn metals and rotten internals, which spill in weathered shades of cables and joints from its bowel. Its face is thrust as high as it can, prostrate in hate and force and resistance, hollow intent thrown at forsaking skies.

It cannot compare to the corpse alongside Glermvender, but she will wander blindly no more and she draws in the antenna, a hand moving to her waist as she skewers her lantern. Towing up the hem, Pescha draws in all the coat below her vented device, rolling the layer into itself and then stuffing the corners against her straps, stowing them into one of the belts securing her to her propulsion. Then, she does the same to her sleeves, folding them to the elbow.

Both hands are tied, braces against such forces that she must endure, and her left hosts the switch. Wrappings flow around the little red control, looping it against the Nomads palm, wires trailing up her arm and then down, under her attire to her waist.

Where the connection is made, she feels a faint inscription is etched, as she runs a finger over the panel, checking the link. It reads Pack One, scratched sharply into the steel.

She is completely alone here, so she does not rush, as she stretches the digits of her left reach, and flicks the switch with her right. She feels the slight reverberation against her lower back, as the dual, vented ports perk up, twitching slightly to even the slightest of movements from her controlling hand.

Pescha stands, she and the resentful Humeda, surrounded by showering mist and its gloomy noise. Both distorted, by rain which shatters and bursts against their unnerving forms. She takes her lamp from the branch and puts it out, stowing it in its pouch with one hand. The thumb and forefinger of her left are relaxed, careful not to flinch as she figures the distance, looking the monolith up and down. The Nomad steps to the machine base, twitching with damp impact, her free hand against the Humeda skin.

    She waits there, feet shuffling.

The two fingers wired to her device flare and the dual ports against Pack One burst their fumes, jettisoning her up. Her body arcs as she rises, the floor falling, a finger an inch from the Humeda, so that when she exhausts that burst, she makes contact, palm flat on wet metal. The rain rushes by, but she's so quick and the distance so comparatively short that she barely registers it, as her hood billows and she pivots on that single outstretched arm, turning to fire off another plume, casting herself wide in that flurry of steam, so that she comes to a running stop against the back of the great machine. Before she's even fully eased she takes the switch and reverses it, allowing the control fingers to relax as she jogs to pace, walking now while she tends to unfurling her coat. The motion continues as she carries on up, marsh spread to the bounds of rain ruined vision. Higher up, a breeze manages to whisper its presence, faint against her cheeks and fingers, and when her hem drops it flutters, brushing her calves as she walks on, splashing through shallow puddles.

Up here, she flexes sore fingers and redeploys her antenna, pitching them straight against the drizzle. Pescha pulls her hood lower and takes the receiver, holding it tight while she loops the radio's straps over her arm, suspending the box and keeping its speaker close. She leans her head over to shield.

    She speaks and waits, giving a moment for a response to be silenced by the rain. She cradles the module and lets the radio swing from her outstretched arm, everything a muddy grey save for her sights, which flicker against the edges of her hood, bright and grimaced.

Then the static burns, and she hears a heartbeat, turning to locate, to zero on someone who listens to the deluge she transmits, even such a vague and fuzzy response sounding confused. The signal surges and dips, wavering between the droplets which cascade, fluttering against Pescha as her arm freezes.

    She looks up, cerulean decision straight, beaming into the marshland.

- FAUSCHENHERST TERRIROTY -

THE TIMBER ISLES

You can track the water flow from Dodtohmet, draining down its great incline. It is a vast and frozen plateau, high above all lands near, snow melting at the expanses limit, to flood the area below. She can't presume what Vanish Strip was like before, but a forest similar to the one she lingered in now would figure. Swamped by the overflow, it was once a small woodland, canopy sparse and trees spaced, vivid and thriving compared to the wasteland warzone she leaves behind.

But if she crossed at the short of the marshland then this forest is thinner still, and while she eats, watching her coat sway, hung upon an extending branch, she feels as though she can already see the end of the boscage, a bright sky wavering between leaves.

She sits upon her tree stump, eyes on the flowing coat. This place, its weather holds to a gentle warmth and oncoming breeze, protected by, at least on one side, the soaked mud, that keeps the Humeda back. A patch of peace, painted upon the extremes of the Kyut[8]. She can wait here for her overcoat to dry.

The radio sits alongside, dormant. She adjusts its settings, fiddling with dials, but it's dead, ruined by the moisture, components now the same as the machine graves she'd passed in the mire. But she's figured the way, and she stands, taking the husk of parts to trade or repair. Unless she would reach another endless, empty expanse.

Her coat flails, as though trying to relieve itself of the tree whenever her eyes are elsewhere. She holds one of the boy from Glermvender's bars, half eaten, packet split.

She thinks of him. The boy on the fringe of the Plateau. He's dead, but that's never stopped anyone from thinking. He couldn't have

---

[8] *Kyut*: A gigantic, multi-habitat (yet, pre-invasion, completely devoid of sentient life) segment of a once much larger endoplanet. Its vast alloy exterior is charred, but its interior remains, with its own atmosphere and ecologies. In full, the entire structure could have blotted a star. It appears to have been man-made.

descended with her, it was too difficult, and she couldn't let him slow her own trail. But she isn't questioning why she left him.

She thinks of Emile, his name invading her thoughts.
She leaves, sweeping into the forest.

The treeline becomes thinner, and she hears people, light spilling evermore through the forest. Until she finds the edge. Summiting a slight incline, a hand against bark and the other shielding her eyes, Pescha squints out. A breeze comes, brushing warm, the sunlight blinds her.

She must stare at it, captured entirely, sight sparkling over wetland. It makes sense, some part of her mumbles, as the melted ice waters of Dodtohmet settle, to stream out here, but she takes a flooding breath of faultless, cool air, and lowers her guard. She stares across the Greater Kodakame Wetland in awe.

A mirage, it is one and two. The painted waters and their island mounds of short green, stretching off into the ends of vision. Small islets, sprinkled between shallow blue, impossibly clear, all swayed with a constant gust. That is all. Perfect. Forever.

She can't quite figure description, as her eyes bathe. It would make others find faith, her thoughts joke, as kempt grass drifts of its own waves, traced from the furthest points right back to her. She watches it, the simple motion, but the blue of the water and the green of the land draws her vision ever wider, to the sky, too. Clear, save for the occasional cloud. She looks at them, neck craned, emptiness wading. After Dodtohmet and then its mud-stained predecessor, she has to take a moment, leaning on the wind. Breathing it, until she drops her radio and removes the coat, suspending it over her shoulders, slinging her dead communicator over one arm. Then, her sights fall, to the people she heard. They waver around a small dock, wooden struts and jetties hosting those who work, wading in the shallows with loose garments rolled up. None notice her as she descends, slow in step, low green no taller than the sole of her boot.

She reaches the shore and skirts toward docked boats, looking down into the waters, to seagrass leaves rising among stones, shimmering under her. Idealistic, of an artist's interpretation, this time blind to the machine graveyard or the cluster of frozen corpses, preserved to be horrors for similarly hopeless travellers. Here, the wind is cool, and her cloak coat dances, as she grins toward those who see her now, barely glancing before they return the gesture, figuring she's a Nomad by sight.

They are draped, the gentle warmth matched by loose-fitting garments, trousers raised and bound with drawn strings around the knees. Wading the shallows, working on their boats, trawling with low nets.

There must be fish, Pescha blinks. Fish they introduced. There was no life on the Kyut before them.

They greet her as Nomad, and she hears accents bright, bowing their way as they do the same. They offer smiles, but are unable to pretend anything besides vivid curiosity, gazing into her eyes. Most wave their greetings, but a few trudge out to meet her, brushing hair from their faces and cleaning hands against softly billowing shirts. They are an ethnic multitude, all bound by one land now, who once waded through the marsh also, to end up establishing here. Maybe they'd arrived on Dodtohmet and ran from the Humeda. Regardless, now they welcome the Klernsteiga.

She asks for a boat, and they gesture to a cluster making too and from their home. They are long, slim craft, pointed at tip and tail, and she walks to one cutting its lines and asks for a ride, perching herself and her things at the rear.

It must have been rolling hills, Pescha wonders, before the edges of Dodtohmet melted, to flood down and eventually settle here. A lake, or a pond, punctuated by endless mounds. But the grass grows short and covers completely, like the heads of overgrown giants peering from underneath the surface, dwelling among waters which scarce drop below her knees. Her hand drops, to run through the cool as she watches settlers fish and cut through watergrass, collecting the green in batches to either tow to dock on small strung rafts, or to labour with them over shoulder, striding through shallows to layer the heaps.

And as they row the buildings develop, forming from makeshift harbours into huts and storage rooms, all made of the same light tone of timber. They shift into homes, becoming clear images of civilisation, built upon shores and struts. More and more people appear, until the waters open up and a centre forms, constructed as the hub of this place.

The man who rows, a man senior and worn but keeping what may have become frailty as wisdom- he turns to the same sight, letting the scene unfold. The Nomad leans forward and asks what this place is called.

He looks at her, looks for a moment. Caught on luminous azure.

He says she's at the Timber Isles, of the Greater Kodakame Wetland. When she says no more, he finds it pressing to add that it's one of the only places on the Kyut where she'll find people proud of their home.

Pescha turns, brow raised, but he doesn't address her question, instead heaving with the efforts of his age. He shifts them toward the Timber Isles, pushing on, as the Wetland stretches beyond, this freckled flatland of water and grass. Some paradise of blue and green, windswept, and warm.

There isn't a simple harbour to be described, the entire settlement is one, pitched upon low beams and sprawled with stores and workshops. These people, they've made a risen walkway of planks upon which are built places supplying food and technical equipment, tools for boats and farming. It's crowded and bustling, traders and stalls everywhere- the boat pulls into the central pool, a great ring of timber and life surrounding, the noise an intoxicant as they dock. Her invitation to rise is a mere smile from the old boatman, as he stows his oars and himself moves to leave, laboriously pitching himself up.

The woman of cold features and glowing observation watches Islanders pass, coat sleeves hanging by her sides, heavy radio lugged upon her shoulder. She stands, slow to counter the rocking, and leaps to ascending steps, seeing the elder wander the opposite way. She looks the walkway up and down. She had not expected this.

It's still early, and she doesn't presume to cross Kodakame upon a worn cropping craft, so she will head for the furthest point from the treeline, to where the Wetland stretches out to boundless sky and unending lake. The current of people flows right so she follows, joining the stream of merchants and customer citizens. There are Nomads here too. There must be lots, in this midway sanctuary, passing through or maintaining their vigil, should this be in their territory. She can recognise them by their clothes and figure alone; the Klernsteiga physique, starving everywhere, with all muscle and strength in their legs.

This place is alien to her, she of harshness within the storm. Pescha walks the wooden path, looking into stalls offering the many variations of harvested vegetation, dried and peppered, to passers-by who eat absently. She thinks of dehydrated substitutes wrapped in silver packets, still bunched in her pockets, and chews her tongue.

The way is not difficult, and she crosses between close islands via low bridges, all necessities possible accommodated in this central zone of the Timber Isles. Her walk sees more craftsmen and their shops, all conforming to the cultural architecture of these people and their construction, with everything built of that same wood and rope, like the bone and sinew of their community; these buildings are each a lumber storefront, open and working. It isn't long before she's out of the main channel, drifting between smaller pockets, making for the open stretch with comfort maintained by that everlasting breeze, its noise carrying the constant bustle, and the water pooling.

Then it levels, to the final line of buildings, facing a single pier which reaches out alone. It spears into the wetland wilds, a backside port, away from the main hub. There are far fewer people here, save for the odd passer-by who hauls their catch further in, glancing and offering smiles. She does the same, spying their produce. It's mostly food, and she feels the weight of dried grain against her throat and stomach, so instead she turns to the few stalls out here. They steam and smoke under canvas canopies, protected from the sun by drawn banners, strung aside to allow her to look in. She finds one that's manned, knives chopping and pots steaming, and she orders a paper bag of sundried sea leaves, trading them for the busted radio. She admits its failures and water damage, a problem she figures easily reparable out here, and takes her sword and crisp leaves down the outstretch, the only one to walk its reach. The Timber Isles recede to a jetty, great lake flanking either side, patched with its peaking domes. The wind builds over the open flats as she wanders. There is a single boat at the edge.

    The dock is crowned at its far end by a sloped canopy, a symbolic entrance to civilisation at its outermost point, and upon the settled waters rests that lone longship. Low and still, tied to one of the risen posts. Pescha sees it, of a darker lumber and grater paddles, a parasol collapsed at its centre, laying down the length of the craft. It is stocked with the supplies of a voyage, well laden within the vessel.

    An inscription is scrawled, inked against the bow. She glances up at the timber awning, raised high on two pillars, and she sits against its base, boots dangling over the side.

It's warm, and despite the breeze she wears too much, so she casts the coat aside and draws up her legs, unbinding them. Merchants toil on the edges of vision, as the ties and boots come loose, and she dips her feet into the cool, trousers rolled up, leaning back on straight arms. Breathing deep. She thinks, with a pleasant smile, that while she knew the land's name, she did not know its character, and she feels such calmness in the subtle gusts. They take from her all tension and let her relax in momentary rest.

The Nomad takes a bite of dried grass, coated and peppered in flavourings and she chews in silence, listening and watching. She must find it humorous, the sudden and apparent change in where she is. She looks at a dream, the Dodtohmet ridge still broad on one horizon, her coat piled by her side.

Pescha goes for another bite, but is distracted by noise above. She looks up, sight blinded by piercing sunlight, and she raises a hand to shield. Something mumbles, and the brightness is broken by a figure tumbling, falling from the canopy, a shadow collapsing. Pescha rears back, dropping the paper bundle of leaves, wide eyed as somebody plummets, cursing as she falls, flailing wildly and trying to turn.

Vibrant surprise sees this woman wreck against the planks with a collision of shattering impact. Her form immediately arcs with pulsing hurt, hand reaching for her spine, features twitching from hateful indignity to racing pain. Sight bulging for just a moment, as her foot slips from under her body, back curved. She lays there, rear to the brilliant sky, a second of breathlessness letting a groan churn.

Pescha stares, leant back, frozen against so many inclinations. With an arm half reaching, the woman rolls, trying to right herself, until she crawls onto hands and knees, mumbling with ever movement, to stare up at vivid eyes. Struck with the sudden appearance of that thing so out of place.

The two Nomads look each other up and down, both stunned. This fallen girl, with features becoming nearly accusatory, looks through strands mostly held high in a wild bun, pegged with two wooden needles, her hair of a shade to compare to her coat, which bares semblance to the one disregarded by Pescha. A rusted shade, crimson well worn, sleeves rolled up to her elbows with pale cream lining exposed at the cuff ends. Sun-drenched hair, tinged with auburn, that escapes in strands over her momentary umbrage. Pescha may have left it at that, and assumed nothing more, but her immediate assertion of meeting a fellow Klernsteiga comes as the woman rocks back, exposing the stilts hooked to her lower legs.

A digitigrade adaptation. The animalistic striders attach at the knees to create a dynamic for speed, with flat paddle bases shaped for sprinting and wading, that she may run and not sink in silt. Like Pack One, Pescha notes the make-do style of the kit[9], fashioned from a scavenging search, defined finally by the cylindrical pods which line the limbs, rows jutting upward and out, like canisters ready to be deployed. This Klernsteiga wears, under her open coat, only bindings around her chest, as though some injury remained long enough to make its bandages her clothing.

And blue observance cannot ignore the lines which streak and pellet against her exposed stomach, imperfections both risen and sunk. Scars, once torn, chipped and flecked, remembering shrapnel spinning and shards scything. Like someone took a shotgun to her midriff.

Time drags, the seconds taken by soft winds, before Pescha nods.

The auburn Nomad does the same.

And then there is another, her companion, who stumbles to the same drop and cranes over. He asks if the fallen girl is alright, already descending to the pier. She moans that she's fine, and Pescha watches him come, seeing an ivory shirt which plumes like the garments of the Islanders, tucked hurriedly into loose pants, their strings drawn around his waist and upper ankle, to compensate for the swaying warmth. But he is set apart; his sleeves are rolled, and his arms are painted, inked with illustrations which flourish to his wrists, curling to a stop at his hands. Displays of fish, of black and white and red, diving from somewhere upon his torso to plunge, seethe and swirl in arcs and waves of detailed design. His face is inked too, like war paint- his sockets are black like charcoal which feathers at the edges, becoming grainy and fading out, his dark hair hanging unaddressed.

Again, by sight he too is a Klernsteiga, for while he is intriguing with his ink, he is defined by the jacket tied around his waist, of dark shades frayed and scuffed. Its left arm is armoured, rigged with a

---

[9] *Klernsteiga kits*: A Nomad colloquialisms for a Klernsteiga's equipment. Each Nomad builds and maintains their unique kit with the purpose of completing their Nomad duties, tailoring their equipment to their skills and environment. This policy by the Fauschenherst has remained controversial, as many Klernsteiga kits prove lethally ineffective until tested.

scaffolding support system like a stripped exoskeleton, and the coat is held around his hips by a tie of timber orbs, a necklace of wooden spheres, allowing the fortified sleeve to rest parallel to his leg.

And for both their attires, as Pescha can see, when the man descends and the woman turns, symbolic inscription are scrawled, running down the left side of her crimson overcoat and over the back of the man's jacket. A calligraphic dialect, to match the style against the waiting boat, in pale shades against their clothes.

Nomads of the Wetland, she figures, resettling sights.

He drops, staying aside as the woman rocks back, kneeling upon those machine appendages, facing Pescha, who waits for one to speak. She watches the woman of scars and the man of ink, who do the same to her.

The woman, who lets her indignation change to intrigue, licks her lips, and in a voice loud and sudden, says that Pescha has beautiful eyes.

Pescha blinks.

She asks whether the woman is alright, but interrupts herself to look up, and questions what they were doing.

Without hesitation, the auburn Nomad says they were fixing the covering, gesturing vaguely to where she'd fallen, but she seems uninterested, instead asking what Pescha is doing here, a figure so misplaced.

Warm winds trailing, fiddling impatiently with everyone's hair, she replies that she's looking for a way to cross, still sitting there, feet suspended over the waters. When asked to where, she shrugs, glancing out to the wetland, and says that she needs to pass through Kodakame, to the other end. To something called The Frown.

The woman leans back a little, looking to the man who furrows a brow, and asks Pescha whether she's been this way before.

The azure sighted Nomad says she has not. She only has names, and that she's following the sun, and as she speaks, she points, up to the light, which wavers still high and beating. Encased by that perfect, expansive blue, and its pluming brushstrokes of white.

The woman follows, craning around to look. The inked Nomad says nothing, standing over them both. Then the woman waves a hand toward the boat.

She says that its theirs, their way of navigating these waters. They're Nomads local to the Greater Kodakame Wetland, she and him. They're here to resupply then head back out, but they'll aid a fellow

Klernsteiga in any way they can. Pescha is free to come along, if she wants.

The blue-eyed Nomad looks at the ship, the vast body of water rippling with wind. She says she would be most grateful.
 The woman nods, a bright smile forming, and she stands, stepping to take Pescha by the hand and haul her up also. Her mechanical appendages give her the height over her fellow Nomad, whom she introduces herself to as E four-seven-two-seven "Red Constant", with N three-eight-five-five "Mariner" moving to the boat already.

Pescha aids their resupply, paying for the requisitioned food with lumber tokens supplied by Mariner. She hauls twin bags of something which feels like sacks of beans across the pier, lugging them into the boat before Red Constant figures they're ready.
 She calls it the Verfloga, her and Mariner's ship, and while he tends to the oars, she builds her parasol and collapses under its shade. The ship jostles when she falls, and she raises her legs upon a bench to let out the greatest of sighs. A hand delves into the bags, taking some kind of drupe and chewing, and she looks out to the waters while Mariner works, helping Pescha in. She takes her seat at the back of the boat, as one spits the stone of her fruit into the pond and the other takes his paddles, glancing back at Pescha, as though offering a final chance to change her mind.
 The blue eyed Nomad does not react, perched upon a plank made a seat as the boatman pushes off, his coat abandoned as Pescha's is to Red Constant's end. The slight and thin craft with its raised sunshade drifts from the outcrop, making for the wilds of Kodakame.

- *FAUSCHENHERST TERRIROTY* -
THE GREATER KODAKAME WETLAND

They talk, Red Constant and Mariner. A lot, their third friend thinks, but then they spend their days stuck in their longboat, so with little else they chatter. He rows, and she busies herself with the complexities of nothingness, sleeping or tending to her mechanical limbs, maintaining to the shade of her parasol.

So, it is a topic of casual conversation, of things spoken for the sake of speaking, which leads Mariner to ask Pescha where she comes from, saying she must have descended from Dodtohmet to meet them, in the Isles. Pescha works on Pack One, disassembling it with the many tools held upon the Verfloga, but she runs a hand through hanging hair, and props her elbow upon her knees, warmth and wet painted around her. That breeze- it is one of the nicest things she has ever experienced.

She says she left from Glermvender Post, but crossed the Plateau from Fyorfastin and Snackombst. She guesses she took the Dodtohmet wastes from their widest point, rethinking the layout while she talks. Mariner, who faces her while he rows, merely nods his response, but his companion, who lounges within her shade, rears her head to call that she'd been landed near Dodtohmet, back when Sect Three[10] first dropped her off.

The Nomad with the pinned bun says, collapsed against the front of the boat, that she herself had tried her hand up there, when she'd just started out, but with a voice condemned to the drawl of soft heat, states that she hadn't much liked the cold.

Mariner, who rocks with his efforts, manages a smile, but says nothing, and Pescha shifts to better address them.

She asks whether the duo stay within the Greater Kodakame Wetland, looking to their thin craft and laboursome travel.

---

[10] *Sect* : Referencing major assaults by Fauschenherst armies, each aiming to colonise and pacify the Kyut. There have been four to date, spanning over a century.

Mariner nods, although he says that Kodakame as a whole is huge, with its lesser regions being outliers. They're away from any certain response, so he and Red Constant have a lot of land to cover, bearing in mind they move pretty slow.

He tells her he was born here, in the Timber Isles, and that Constant, as he calls her, came to the Kyut a Klernsteiga. He does not grin by choice but hears her shift behind him and lets the figure of a smirk hold, as he says she came to the Wetland having only been on the Kyut a couple weeks. He says she didn't stand a chance, up there.

Constant retorts; no Klernsteiga picks where they're deployed, rolling her head from under the parasol.

Mariner interjects, saying that she scrambled down before even the Rautbergen. Came crashing through Vanish Strip. For a while, Mariner mumbles, nobody believed she was a Nomad.

But Constant snaps, reaching under a drape of cloth, that they found out pretty quickly, drawing loose and producing what Pescha first figures a cannon, a rifle like a long blunderbuss. It is one of such massive proportions that her eyes widen. The boatman blinks, glancing over his shoulder.

He stares at Constant, and she grins, resting the cannon upright against an outstretched arm. He continues, stating that she managed to get a boat, and would row herself out, every morning, to try and find Humeda. Mariner rocks a little forward, creating distance as he talks, saying that the reason why the Timber Isles exists is because there aren't many Humeda down here, yet she would get up every morning, and try to go out far enough to find something. Anything, he says, heaving against the waters, which curl with rolling winds, a routine performed alongside wavering grass, and that she wouldn't return until nightfall, completely broken and tired.

Regardless of whether she found a machine or not, she would come back spent, and collapse into the worst bed she could make an excuse for, to do the same as soon as she woke.

Constant plays with one of the frayed bandages around her chest, but holds any interruption.

Until Mariner met her. He'd seen her go out, and eventually offered to row her. He can still remember her face, he recalls, when he asked. He hadn't any intention of becoming a Nomad, but as they went out, over and over, Mariner guesses it was inevitable. After a while, he

signed up over a radio. Not like he had much choice. Murmuring, turned toward his partner, he says that she came back pretty beat up, sometimes.
    Pescha asks whether they do find a lot, out here. Humeda- she asks if there are many.

Mariner shrugs. He says he appreciates they have it better than some. This wetland, it is easy and resourceful, with shallow waters forgiving to travellers, and the nights are never too cold. But Humeda, he tells; there are Humeda here, yes. And few places to hide.

It is late before anyone suggests towing in, but the boatman says he knows a spot, and brings the Verfloga below dying light to an island hosting shape. A terminal or server, Pescha sees, as the lake adopts its evening shades, repainted in soft amber and peach. Late day chills breathe as they rock ashore, Mariner guiding them close for Constant to rise.
    All Pescha hears is the wind and water, watching Constand and her gun and her machine legs dismount, wandering up toward the abandoned computer. Mariner follows and so does Pescha, soft green underfoot. It only takes a few seconds for them to reach the top.   A Denkervung system[11], overgrown and consumed by the foliage, leaves bustling from every entrance, a banner lain over top. Wires piled and cables spilling, Mariner asks Constant to check it through while he pulls the ship ashore, Pescha aiding as they both haul the craft onto dry land. Constant examines, brushing at dirt and peering into ports made gardens for the short blades, which wave at her against the apricot sky.

Mariner finds a lamp and shakes it to life, the thing buzzing atop the ship's bow when Constant walks back, holding the flag and tossing it into the Verfloga. She says that it's just reverence of Small Hand, collapsing against the hull, her legs sprawled across the green, removing the extended limbs as Pescha joins. None of them are hungry, and the warmth has worn at her, so that she already begins to drift while Mariner investigates the server, searching through lumbered compartments, wind

---

[11] *Denkervung* : Retired server system of the Fauschenherst, issued during Sect One. The collapse of all communication systems between the Kyut and Fauschenherst worlds during the Sect collapse led to the company dissolving, however their servers still dominate the Kyut, out of necessity, rather than choice.

tugging his shirt. Light falls as Pescha yawns, overcome as Constant watches the sun drain, slipping below domes and lake.

Nectarine clouds and the heavenly pink ether, becoming deeper, darker. Constant sits by her side, already slumped in rest.

Pescha leans over. She asks when they'll get up.

Constand murmurs that she doesn't, he does, and nods vaguely toward Mariner. Pescha looks over, to the Nomad picking through leaves.

Quietly, half asleep, Constant tells her not to worry. They'll leave early.

Day barely glows when she wakes, her head rested gently against the grass. There is a rustling about her, someone shuffling past, and she looks up to watch Mariner, carrying the still sleeping Constant aboard, laying her in her end and pushing the Verfloga out. The cold and the lapping pond are amplified by early morning emptiness.

Pescha joins him, glancing at Constant while he prepares their leave. She asks if she's alright.

The inked Nomad nods, being careful to keep quiet as he wades out with the ship. He tells her that she sleeps a lot. Ever since they first met, Red has been indignant to work too hard on anything aside killing the Humeda. He says Pescha saw her attempt at fixing the gate.

He smiles while he talks, and then gestures for Pescha to hop aboard.

Their days are this cycle, looped across the infinite scape of the Greater Kodakame Wetland. Hours of rowing merge, and Pescha sways with the numbness of such an endless routine. She thinks about walking, then she could feel her progress, sore and biting, but here she just sits, eating and talking, mending and wading. She shouldn't complain. She doesn't. She knows that there is no alternative, but she can feel a slight tension form upon the two Nomads she rows with, as they drift further into the Wetland.

This far from the Timber Isles, they grow expectant. How long can paradise endure, when its angels carry cannons.

Constant declares boredom, both her companions watching her wake, glance around, and speak before she has properly moved. Pescha, who tends to the switch against her palm, lays at her end, much the same as her idle counterpart who scarce moves from beneath her parasol, but to complain to Mariner, who rows nearly every waking hour. She finds it odd, that his coat, which he leaves abandoned, would be built of a supported arm and yet it is unused, a weapon seemingly worthless. He is a Klernsteiga from the Kyut, not flown in from afar, so necessity claims utility; it was a brace for a wounded limb, or a component for mechanised fishing, repurposed when he found another to row for. But he is strong, she can see it, as he forces the Verfloga on, and he dotes on Constant, who lays under her shade and eats and mumbles. She does so always with that cannon kept close.

The red-tinged Nomad sees the others ignore her, staring with faint affront until she shrugs, slipping from her coat and removing her adaptations, drawing her pants up to the knees and tying them with the same strings worn by all the Isles. Without her coat her body is a patchwork when she emerges into daylight. Her skin bumps and depresses, not marked all over but clearly scared by differing means, gashes split and burrowed. They trail to her arms and legs, but express themselves most savagely at her core. Blown out, to lessen as the space expands. Pescha does not stare, but the bright light overhead amplifies her trophies, deep enough to make their own shadows, to dwell as experiences eternal. Constant straddles the side of the boat and slips down, easing herself into Kodakame's lake.

 The water isn't deep, but it is high enough to let her swim, and so clear that she can look down to the pebbles and seagrass, counting with her head above the surface. It isn't cold either; she trails alongside the Verfloga, distancing herself from the slow surging paddles to make her way toward a near island, grass its own waves of soft winds.

 Constant moves with them, walking with bare feet over mounds when she can and swimming the spaces between, easily keeping pace.

 Pescha asks how long they've been doing this, every single day.

Mariner says that Constant came with Sect Three, and would only be here a few months before he joined her. She wouldn't have lasted much longer, he says, if they'd let her go on alone. He'd only been able to persuade her to let him row because she'd been too hurt to move without his help. Face down, washed up in the shallows. There's a moments pause, then Mariner asks how long she's been out here, turning her way while he pushes.

Pescha watches the ripples, and says she came with Sect Four.

The Nomad frowns, seeming to stutter with his fluid motion. He asks then if she came down with the supplies, as an escort or something. He thought Sect Four was just equipment, infrastructure, a massive resupply for Sect Three. She nods, keeping sights on the lake.

He says that she can't have been here very long. It must have been over eight years now since Sect Three, and Mariner was still a kid when he joined Constant. He thought Sect Four arrived less than a year ago.

Pescha shrugs, saying that sounds about right. More questions flutter, she can tell, but Mariner holds his words. He watches Pescha, who does not look his way, and he lets his thoughts linger upon his gaze.

And then the horizon changes. Adopts a feature, and paints from its unchanging pallet a timber house, placed atop one of the mounds. It looks like an outpost, even as it is now, derelict and distraught, and the remnants of a short dock extend out upon wooden beams, ropes trailing into the water where there was once a bridge. Of itself, it is nothing unusual, but paired with the Wetland it is peculiar- to infer people in a place so perfectly untouched. Pescha stares at it, and it does the same back.

Yet it is a ruin. Not torn and ravaged, but completely collapsed. Its occupants left a long time ago; they may not have fled, or if they did, whatever scared them did not make their home like this. They left, and overtime it sank. Fell in on itself, rotten with neglect.

A house, built where Nomads roam. The boat rocks, and she turns to see Constant returned, hauling herself up, sights fixed also as Mariner throws her great coat, letting the Verfloga ease while she dresses.

Constant is passed her legs and rifle and while the ship still drifts slowly on she dismounts, almost waist deep but pushing through, cannon held high, pieces of lumber and ties of rope lining the lakebed. Mariner moves cautiously, guiding the Verfloga closer but keeping well behind Red Constant, who adds maybe a foot to her height with her adaptations.

Her coat with its scrawl draws through the water, waves spreading far. Pescha is given no true reason for alarm, but she says nothing as the Nomad approaches. Constant holds her gun to her chest, keeping it above the waterline, the shallows lapping at her stilts.

She halts at the water's brink.

With no apparent reason she stops, and so then does Mariner, who freezes mid row. He stares, eyes flickering, switching from island to island. He is entirely still, in the middle of this open area, surrounded by mounds half visible.

Gusts billow, the breeze pulls at Constant, who stands there, intently listening, herself just as motionless. She focusses on water and wind, brows furrowed, while Pescha glares from the boat, seeing a posture fixed in concentration.

Then she too hears.

Two sounds, playing in symmetry. Shouts, distant, quiet, yet apparent. Obvious, for anything unusual makes itself well known out here.

And then something rushing. Like water surging, at a funnel or fall. Pushed through, as though a stream or overflow cascades at the brink of sound's reach.

They all listen, and they are all still. Compliments and contradictions, the wind is punctuated by the outcries and the water by its seething, so that these alien noises merge with what they already hear. They fade, in and out of earshot, as though to make you question whether you really heard.

Then the shouts seem to quieten, but only because of that rising swell. It builds, mounting on itself, as water rushing becomes something rushing through, and Mariner starts to reach for his oars. Pescha need not ask the obvious. She watches Constant shift, shoulders gently sinking, as she breathes deeply, clear even from this distance.

Instead, Pescha asks if Mariner knows which one. His hand passes the oars, and instead delves below his seat. The blue Nomad watches him produce a fishing spear, handle bound in rags.

He nods, but his expression makes this answer joyless.

He says there is only one that quick. Only one to move at such speeds. His eyes fall, and Pescha too sees the calm lake shudder, ripples curling from around the opposite side of their island.

The rushing becomes detailed, as it gurgles and froths in scything sweeps, like some great fish beats its fin. Pescha asks what it's called.

Red Constant darts.

Like a shot she beams, low to the ground so that she kicks her legs before her, making her own liquid shockwaves. She leaves the pool and rises, mounting the green to reach the decrepit house and sweep through it, dodging from doorway to busted wall within the blink of an eye. Then she's out and up, letting her sudden stop and momentum fling her rifle forward and to her shoulder. Sights twitching for a target, revealed by hurried noise.

But then there's a third, and the rifle-ready gunner only has time for the edges of sight to catch steam, a figure burning past overhead.

Pescha rockets above, flinging herself from the ground to spin meters high, arms unfurling as instincts make aim. Twin bombs spread, slipping from her outstretched hand, sun catching metal edges.

The explosions hit only water, but their detonations reverberate and force the machine out. It casts itself upward, rearing from the explosion to bawl out into the blue.

If Hjordiis was sick, then this machine is morose.

A thing serpentine, or dragon-like, but made of humanoid parts, metal fashioned and warped in mankind's image.

A long, thin torso, nowhere near as large as Hjordiis but great nevertheless, and disproportionate in length, so much so that it could never stand, it must crawl.

It is hideous and irate, curling features grimaced and contorted, twisted and malformed. Head bare and round, welded in screaming agony, squinting eyes, and grinding teeth, even in its shock it towers above. Throwing itself from range and tearing the lake with it, creating its own waterfall overhead. Its limbs are humanoid but misshapen and gross, too thin and eerily reaching, and clad in a thin layer of grey rust, darker and mottled against its clear, skin-steel base. It moves too quickly and too diversely for its size, thrashing from the spray. Pescha glares up at the aggrieved automaton, both rushing through the air.

Masago, Mariner yells.

It looks down on her, in those slowed moments of realisation. Its scream is howling, calling upon all to fall, in unconditional hate. It is a grating sound, imperfect and undesigned, to make it raw and sweeping. A shrill scream of misery behind grating teeth. A skyward torment hit by hard sunlight, to tower for all sights. A great abomination, glinting within its spray.

And then Constant fires- lightning exploding like sudden thunder, everything the shade of energy for a mere moment, the shot sweeping all winds to its course.

The gun almost blows itself from her hands as the round claps and burns forward, a pellet the size of a fist launched and blaring with a crackling force. It streaks as a straight beam; it looks to tear Masago's head from its shoulders, shockwave impacting against the Humeda rainfall. All things shudder to the single second of a storm.

Masago dives, curling under the shot and falling back to the water, arcing the opposite way as Constant runs, staring wide eyed as Pescha blurts, pursuing like a homing missile. Out here, she finds herself atop pockets of land, surrounded by the impassable. Against the shallows she may fall, and hope her hand finds ground before she blows out, but it is a risk she won't take. She is forced to divert, instead rounding to curve against Masago's straight line, following close behind but flickering from immediate pursuit, grassland flashing by and slipping underneath, whole islands jumped with one flare. Ducking and twisting beside Masago's spray- liquid furrows, like riches and jewels cast wildly, rendering visibility weak as Pescha races.

Shouts rise again and the Nomad sees them, in small boats approaching the opposite way. Islanders, fishing or farming, but they've found the Humeda and now chase, cradling sluggers, the Reisreiben model, but unlike any she's seen before. Old guns, a medial between Constant's insanity rifle and a weapon of normal proportions- the Islanders hold them close as they come, head on, rowing into Masago.

Three longboats, each still stuffed with fishing nets and bags. The Islanders abandon them to twitchy attention, until one rears and shouts, calling broadside, and each of the boats does the same. In vague unison, one side digs its oars into the silt and the other churns, to drag the boats perpendicular to the machine.

They rush up, raising their guns, aimed square at the shapeless approach which twists and arcs. Pescha tries to close the distance, reach Masago before it reaches them, but she cannot throw at these similar speeds and hope to hit something so thin and quick, so she is forced into the slipstream, flinging herself between the twin cuts of water blown skyward by the Humeda. Masago mounts shallower ground, rising from the surface as the Islanders call.

They fire, blasting into the spray, blasting at whatever isn't liquid, and Pescha's sights bulge a second before she dives, rounds screaming overhead, slugs the size of pill bottles whirling. Most miss the spiral automaton, a few land. They rip with shearing thuds into plated metal, and do nothing.

The sparks tear and force Masago to leap, the machine rising like a twirled fabric streamer. It flings itself from the pool to crash down, raising the lake and the boats with it.

Pescha is close behind, and can only watch the carnage as Masago sprints through the group, sending ships and crew flying. She must evade, dodging between the debris and figures, covering up to break through the spray as the machine looks to pulverise a boat underfoot, its clawed limb falling to crush.

The Nomad reaches and slings, spinning into her throw and letting a star fly, but Masago evades and watches it pass, turning now to her as the bomb detonates. The automaton focusses on approaching blue. She glides for a moment, back an inch from the pond.

She blurts up and draws her blade, slashing Masago and cleaving at its jaw, passing by and leaping to an island. She does not wait to check her damage, she finds ground and she flips, launching skyward.

Masago dives over the island, looking to devour her and she casts down, to blow off its head.

Masago springs, eluding her again, crossing back to adjacent waters as the bomb blows and Pescha follows, trying to keep close as they bound together from mound to mound, coming close and separating again and again. The Nomad nears, looking to throw once more. Then she hears a shout, and instead dives. Another flash resounds, and Constant fires, beam streaking overhead.

It is low and Masago moves anyway, but the island the shot hits is near split down the centre, an expanded, cylindrical gap carved clean through the dirt where the lightning streak cut. Before Pescha can react, Mariner is there too, coat on and spear raised. He steps past her and scythes for the machine's forefront leg.

Masago raises the limb, attention fixed on the boatman who watches the beast spin, leg flaring, striking Mariner with enough force to cleave him apart had he not raised his armoured reach. He barely has the arm up before his face when he is thrashed, struck sidelong and thrown aside, but in his place appears Pescha, rising as Mariner falls, and she flies for the same limb, blade unfurled. It catches blazing sunlight and she knows Masago's instinct- when it steps back and lunges to strike her she twirls, slipping below before she spins and rockets, bolting up from underneath. Arcing with its shape, carving while she flies, to spin atop among flying components, wedged cut deep in the beast's side.

It makes a noise like a cough, but before it can catch her all things become the energy shade and another shot forces the machine to turn, dodging back and away from the airborne Nomad. She stares, blue wavering. She sees it, from where she has first sliced Masago, across the jaw. A mouth, hanging limp. Mechanical tendons severed.

The Humeda looks to run but it buckles, pummelled by a steel fist ploughed square in its face, and before Mariner can be thrown once more, he spears, driving for the machine shoulder, forcing it back but giving it space to flee. The beast lurches away, racing, kicking from the mound just before Mariner can reach, his hand still hovering when Pescha soars overhead, her pluming exhaust drifting like mist over the lake as she follows.

And then the mood switches. Her sights, which had span so wildly, stagnate, as she sees Masago alter its course, and now surge for the Islanders. They stumble up a grassy mound, hauling their dead.

Pescha watches them, wallowing in the shallows. Her thoughts slow. They cease.

Their boats, obliterated. Their bodies heaving, they breathe hard and turn, disorderly and confused. Eyes wide, they search for the machine. Out here, among these two shades, any contradiction is obvious, it bleeds across vision, as pigments unnerving. Dark and pumping against the warm, pastel calm.

One of the islanders stands, bulked Reisreiben hanging from a single grip. His chest shudders uncontrollably. He sees Masago charging, surging as some skin-metal nightmare, weightless in motion yet crashing through the shallows. The Islanders rush to arms, falling to one knee and raising their cannons and Pescha swerves, following off-centre to avoid the rounds. They bellow, sharp and shattering against the wind and waters which burst under Masago's footfall. The Nomad knows she cannot close the distance- she veers off, spinning to the closest island. Sights fixed on the machine which barrels toward grounded sailors.

She lands, unearthing turf with her harsh touchdown. Sliding to a halt and scampering upright, she does not throw or pursue. As soon as she knows what's coming, she stands, and watches. From the corner of her eye she sees Constant rush, raising her cannon in the hopes of felling Masago before it reaches the gunners, who line in ranks incomplete and shaking. Some work to reload, some abandon their weapons to flee, trying to drop down the opposite bank, out of sight.

Pescha watches Red Constant hurry, frantically loading her artillery before she stops, brings the cannon up, and follows the machine's path, leading the shot. It thunders out, her coat billowing. Pescha knows it won't hit before the slug is even fired.

Masago curves, dropping almost flat, letting the ball pass without even caring to see its impact, instead leaping upon the Islanders.

Constant makes a noise, between a curse and a plea, and she runs to the edge of her mound. Watching with a rifle rendered useless when others are around.

It's like their sentience just leaves. Their humanity, gone.

All their uniqueness' and individuality, everything that makes them them- in that moment they're nothing but bodies to the machine. They sustain injuries you'd think instant, immediately lethal, but half men roll, dazed, unable to comprehend. Tonnes of metal squash them, their skin splitting like crushed fruit, but they remain. They don't crawl, or try to flee, or talk. They just move, move for movements sake, clawing at dirt and rolling around. Moaning, softly, blinking up at the sky. Those who are swatted and stomped like flies go tense, muscles in shock, locking up.

Nobody screams, in agony or for help. Nobody rushes to aid their friends. Nobody stands their ground. It's instinctual, the character in each person disappears. It's pathetic, ideas and opinions and beliefs turned to pulp, leaking from a ripped bag.

A clap and smoke relieves her, as the dead island is concealed by fumes fired from Constant. The canisters launch from her adapted striders to mask the area, blanketing and pluming to conceal her approach. Her features are hidden by distance, but her figure is an expression in of itself. Of her despairing hate. She raises her cannon slower now, more certain of her aim despite her blindness, lifting the gun to the riving mass of fumes. She stands on the grass opposite that of the Humeda, a single character pointed to the mass of madness raging before her. She makes the cloud the shade of sparks and energy, firing into the gas.

Masago is forced back toward Pescha, hauling itself in a craze of confusion, and the Nomad sees one of its limbs hang, to fall loose as the Humeda spills into the open, an arm blown free.

Pescha sees the red-tinged Nomad trudging through the pools, wading without hesitation or mercy. Masago scrambles, ever as fast but now unsteady, stumbling and crashing.

Pescha flies, piling on as much speed as possible, barrelling toward her limits, beaming straight for the machine which sees her and veers, all variants of its impossible haste made sluggish and dazed. The automaton pivots, swings and throws itself, almost as the Nomad does, her outstretched reaches gliding over tormented waters, glancing at the remnants of structures long since sunk. She shifts also, but hers is so much sharper a turn and she can feel herself closing the distance, trailing Masago perfectly. Again, it tries to shake her, but it cannot switch, cannot flare and dive as it did, now ripped apart and sent sprawling through the shallows. Kicking up its own rainfall as it scrambles.

Masago glances back, seeing her gain. It lets out another cry.

The Humeda has no choice, it can run no longer, so instead it spins, looking to take her head before Pescha can stop. Make her two halves before she has the time to react. She leaps, blaring over the machine, gliding across its spine to jump the slash, fumes spouting as she creates distance for herself to whirl. Slipping atop the thin pool to round, facing the automaton, who carries its frantic motion to do the same.

Apart, the two turn to one another, their momentum made liquid that carries on where they halt. Machine terror against electric blue.

Everyone is already dead. What is to come is a mere formality.

Rising droplets pass her face, catching her vivid colour. Masago flails, hatred and fright made steel and cables.

But it does not stall. As soon as it can, it lunges.

Masago charges, throwing itself at the Nomad who does the same, gas gliding in her wake, her hand once more skipping over a pocket to draw a single bomb. She holds it close as the machine pounces, jaws so wide as to swallow her whole. She lets it near, before dropping, slipping to pass under the beast, Pack One kicking up the Wetland she skims.

She releases the star, letting it slip from her fingers, fluttering where she had been. Masago stares at it, twirling playfully between its teeth. Bobbing nonchalantly on abandoned momentum.

The blast sends Pescha rolling, crashing through the lake and sprawling in the open, face submerged. The sky above her is the opposite shade to her bomb, the blue made hot light and fire and pluming smoke, the sound alone enough to crack her skull had she not been cast away. Being flung creates liquid shockwaves that follow her path, mirroring how she skates over the surface. As soon as she stops, she props herself up on two arms to turn, flicking wet hair from her face, wide eyed and staring.

Masago smoulders.

Almost split down the centre, the machine has become like a malfunctioned rifle, the barrel blown and torn outward. It does not move, nor connote any hope of rising. Pieces of it float alongside, stagnant and gazing at the corpse which lays, half sunk, bubbling gently. Its internal components are fried.

Both figures, she, and it, they lay part under the surface. She shifts, shuffling to face the machine fully.
    She nods, smoke curling.

Upon the bloodied island, the three Nomads stand. Nobody else is left, shattered timber and bone line the grass as Constant and Mariner collect the bodies, dragging them onto dry land. They lay the remains in rows. Seventeen of them, arms and legs tucked in where possible. The boatman looks for something, a sheet or blanket spare to lay over the worst, but he has nothing to spare.
    Instead, Constant fashions a post, from the remains of their ships. A spire, bound by their nets, that flag of Small Hand taken from the server tied atop. Thin and shaky, it flaps in the higher winds, waving toward the ebb of nightfall, the sky returning to its evening shades.
    When they're all done, they stand there. Pescha, Red Constant and Mariner. With her cannon hanging in a loose grip, the red-tinged Nomad mutters something. It means nothing, a jumble of murmured thoughts, but they slip from her lips as a question, the one to haunt such moments, for she feels no victory. Constant stares at the ground. It is soiled and stained, a survivor of neglect.

She asks what they're doing here. How they can win.
    Again and again, pretending she's making a difference. That anything changes. A hundred years, people have been fighting here, she tells. Millions dead- for what, she asks. Nothing changes; no matter her achievements, her status, her comfort, right now so many lay like this, torn apart. No matter what she thinks, or where she is, it's meaningless compared to the suffering of others- right now, someone's being hacked to pieces, or starving in a field.
    Constant says nothing changes. They can't get out. There's nothing here worth this. She says she'd rather be dead.
    She stands between Mariner and Pescha. The boatman looks at her, and he lays a hand on her shoulder.

Pescha asks how that'd be any different. Everyone is still. If there is nothing left here, what can they lose. How will being dead change anything. As though dying will end this.

Later, Mariner will tell Pescha that the Islanders had a legend, about Masago. They say the machine was from Vanish Strip, before the people arrived, to take the seeds and remains of life from the marsh and plant the bordering forest, to later build their homes upon the Wetland. They say this made Masago so sad that it crawled from the mud, to try and take them back. So sad to see the seeds go, that it slumped into Kodakame, trying to find them again.

As Constant sleeps and the trio row through the night, the sky forever empty of stars, Pescha asks how much further is left.

Mariner says it isn't far now.

- *FAUSCHENHERST TERRIROTY* -

FREE RIG

The Greater Kodakame Wetland disperses, its islands splayed, scattered and smaller, sinking to the wider image of a true lake. The expanse becomes its own horizon, stretching to the bounds of sight. As the green descends the winds rise, given free reign over a new, liquid flatland. Pescha would almost feel better if a fog descended or a storm loomed, but the clouds merely thicken, the sky turning to its denser, neutral lack of substance, to hang as grey spanning all above.

The Wetland loses its ground, and a vast, empty space opens, pulled and pushed by boundless gusts.

The last the Nomads see of a recognisable Kodakame finds them at the territories limit, upon the last of the major islands. One still slight yet prominent atop the wet plane, made evermore so by that which lays atop.

The machine is lifeless and long dead, centred upon land and cradling something, half embracing it, half pinning it to the ground. The Verfloga passes, not stopping but eyeing from the bow, with its oars and wide parasol. They see an Humeda, overgrown with ligaments well rotten to moisture. It looks as though it watches something fade to distance, straight ahead, figure stretched to try and keep the sight close.

Within its leafy grip a bone Klernsteiga lies, sword still clutched by a skeletal grasp. The shadows hide all other features, but the wind has stripped the visible limb bare. Yet even from here, the Nomads see no struggle. The blade is without scabbard, but the grasp is light. Resting against the hilt. Huddled under the machine reach.

And then the islands fade, becoming grassy heaps and piles, scarce tall enough to surface and then scarce even when hiding, the ground dropping from sight to deeper waters. As the previous rolling fields now flooded would have fell, into a valley or lowland. Smokey white skies and then the similar water below, now an ocean broken by so little. Drawn across vision with equal colourlessness both above and below, grey and grey, punctuated by vague mounds, suspended upon the blank. Like miniature, floating planets, distant and passing.

It is almost unnerving then when something appears, develops from a wavering dot into definable shapes. Unsettled, odd and misplaced against the pallid world, an outpost forms.

Mariner calls it Free Rig, noting the lack of a formal name, because it is never in one state. A drifting frontier, a settlement non-existent in of itself, built with the propulsion of other ships, it forever coasts, a lone station, the only one around. Nobody sells anything there, or comes to resupply, or looks for sanctuary. It is merely a midway, without purpose, defined by emptiness on all sides.

The people who find their way to this place are wanderers, living upon the waves. Mariner also figures, for Pescha's purposes, a Nomad who can cross will be here too.

Sails and hulls, weathered timber and damp rope. The harbour is a set of walkways made to be moorage, but it has melded itself to the ships which make berth, forming a structure of many differing levels. It has an aura, to thicken as the clouds do, that hangs against darkened wood and high streaming banners, flags of allegiance and loyalty. Straining against a wind which draws them far, like great arms reaching, rolling and churning above the compound.

Free Rig awaits, a blot against pale emptiness, which the small Verfloga approaches. A thin longboat with its wide shade, creating ripples that span seemingly for miles, lapping against wooden struts.

The people of the float are not like those of Kodakame, these are bordering regions but different lands. As those of the Timber Isles are tinged with the amber of their warmth, those out here similarly reflect their conditions, but stand as sallow, sicky shapes. Baggy in attire and tending to similar acts, farming from drawn in nets laden with seagrass, they are unfit and feeble, contradictions, yet so similar to those of the Wetland. Like siblings, who hid themselves away in the attic.

With the cooler breeze their garments flail, and they watch the Verfloga come with a different intrigue, this time wholly dissimilar to that of the Islanders. Where they would bustle over, carrying their tools and hauls of green, these figures stare. They are still, clothes shifting yet attention fixed, eyeing the craft filled with Nomads and their weapons.

Watching them pass the outer stretches of the spiderweb pier, and row into the main dock of Free Rig. They are not hostile, so much as they are unnerving. So accustomed to their barren wastes that they disregard any courtesy, to instead stare. Only stare, but stare deeply.

 Mariner leads her through, leaving Constant by their boat, the Rig confined mostly to one open square, central to the conglomerate of ruined sea ships. They walk to this central zone, one side open to ocean. He does not point direction or tell her where to go. Instead, he simply nods to the dock, telling her that there, she'll find someone to carry her across, his sights lingering upon the many boats moored, and the figures who managed them. His hair is almost as dark as Pescha's but both it and his light shirt bulge with the sea breeze, black ink upon his face and coloured artworks across his arms, detailed and vibrant amid the general drabness of the Rig. He looks out to the ocean, glancing at a sun depicting evening, although without any of the warmth or hue to suggest so further.

Then his expression changes.

 It slips, from unfocussed and nonchalant to something direct, as his sights centre on someone particular, approaching from the dock. Pescha frowns, and turns, looking for someone among the sparse pockets of people, who amble and sway from dock to ship. Speaking and eating, watching the others work.

 For a moment, she fears that an Humeda will loom from the rolling grey.

It is a boat, to which Mariner scowls.

 Different from the others, immediate by sight besides the assortment of random and oddly repurposed craft, now transformed into homes and haulers for folk seeking safety upon the waves.

 This ship is larger. Like a catamaran houseboat, it is a building upon two hulls, parallel to one another, holding the structure above the waterline. A seabound stronghold, the construct atop is no more than two or three levels in height, but it imposes as a fortress. Timber, yet darkened, with walkways and balconies detailed around the rim.

 A warship, Pescha thinks, with those positions around its body. A gunboat, alongside fishing ships and their sails.

The blue-eyed Nomad glances at her fellow Klernsteiga and asks what it is.

 Mariner looks over the piers, holding his answer. Maybe hoping he's wrong, maybe hoping to point. He eyes the smaller craft, and the crews who wander the wooden walkways.

It's the Et-Skhep. Et-Skhep Mordaar Corsairs.

Marauders, he says. Rovers, yet Pescha sees everyone there and nobody seems to panic, no commotion arises before Mariner's search, blinking into the sparse crowd. He doesn't look worried, so Pescha asks no more, but she watches him turn, eyeing the merchants and sailors, figuring what-

Click.

Pescha blinks, twitching. Mariner groans.

An antique thing, a flintlock is pressed against the boatman's head, pushed hard to the back of his skull. It is bound at the grip with tattered cloth and held by a man who appeared from nowhere, expression callous, but wavering upon smug.

His skin is the extreme of those of Free Rig, so grey as to make him cloudy, as overcast as the storm-riddled sky, with hair woven in thin strands to hang, just around the top of his shoulders. Skin like the sea, he wears a loose reddish shawl, a poncho lain over his figure, dropping to his thighs.

His eyes are slight, as though he has remained unfazed for an age, to leave the muscles of shock redundant, and he stares with that cutting attention at Mariner, who stands at gunpoint, unmoving at the end of the barrel.

The boatman calls him Sartska, asking what he's doing.

Sartska says, pronouncing every word individually, that he's stealing from him.

Mariner coughs, and says he's got nothing on him.

Sartska says-

Pescha jumps at him, drawing her sword, everything spinning as she leaps, swiping at his gut as he twists himself back, cursing. But the boatman reaches, he stops the blue-eyed Nomad, her hand flexing to the switch on her palm, to be taken and held there by Mariner.

He tells her that Sartska is a Nomad, too.

Pescha glares, arm held back by the boatman, who looks to her azure uncertainty. Mariner continues, slower now while the figure in the poncho straightens himself, gaze caught on the ground over which he almost stumbled. The boatman says that Sartska is a Klernsteiga, who watches the body of water which Pescha wishes to cross.

Then he looks up, to the man with the flintlock, and says that Sartska works the waves with his ship, having taken the crew a while back. He turned the previous Et-Skhep into the Humeda hunters they are now. That doesn't mean that Sartska arrived and put them on the straight path, he adds.

Pescha glances at Mariner, who eases his grip, and then looks to the Corsair.

In turn, Sartska looks up, a heavy grimace clear, sights knifing straight at Pescha. People watch now, turning from their hauls, but it is with vague intrigue, not yet frightful- they do not look at the same expression these two Nomads do, watching Sartska wobble. He sways there, shawl fluttering, almost whispering to himself as closed lips shift, murmuring words unheard. Mariner reaches out, half-apologies offered with high brows.

He says that they aren't looking for trouble.

Sartska fires, pistol blaring, the shot making all surrounding blandness a vivid amber, sparks blurting.

Pescha skids, curling out of the way, Mariner throwing himself to the other side, the streak of light etching between them.

Where it hits the opposite structure, the mauled and strung-up wood explodes, the timber bulging to blow out, a burst hole carved through the mass of ships. Shrapnel of lumber sprawls across bland waves, thunder shaking pale skies.

Now people run, the commotion flaring and giving Pescha a place to hide as she submerges herself among the chaos, closing one eye and looking to Sartska with a squint, her colours concealed. The Corsair starts to load another shot, too rapt in the act to even search for his targets. Indignant, he performs the process by muscle memory, a bubble around him of empty space forming as people rush, more in shock than terror but moving regardless. Scurrying to make space between the figures now concealed within the throng.

And then Sartska frowns, looks up from his pistol, and Pescha follows his sights, turning low to watch Constant approach, stomping from the docks. The purpling mark of a bruise builds against her face, but she holds an expression to make the injury almost shrink away, an irritation so vivid that it defines her hunched stance and long strides.

There isn't room among the receding mass for Pescha to use Pack One, so she sticks to the group, eyeing the open stretch between the beaten Nomad and the one scowling, stuffing a shot into his weapon. Constant raises hers, swinging it before her and levelling a wounded cheek against the stock. Again, Mariner calls from the crowd, struggling to surface above the many heads, calling for her to stop, waving for lost attention.

Constant doesn't even look his way.

Another group follows her, tumbling from where she walked. Pescha recognises the look on Sartska's face, as he stares down his crew, who bare marks to make Constant's a pat of the hand, holding their heads and trying to walk straight.

Constant ignores them too. Her attention plays over the mass, knowing where Mariner is even without coat or weapon. When she sees a blinking blue, she nods toward Pescha, who winks quickly to confirm.

The people stop running, satisfied by the empty space which contains the Et-Skhep captain at one end, his mob at the other, the coated Nomad in the centre, standing tall upon her striding adaptation.

She calls out, her voice the only noise against wind and lapping waters, asking whether Sartska is robbing Klernsteiga too now. She draws his focus, so that dual slithers of squinting azure go unnoticed.

The captain shakes his head, locks swaying, calling that not everyone gets lucky enough to live in Kodakame. He murmurs something about farming grass, still steadily preparing his next shot.

Constant calls him a thief, rifle ready to blow him apart, twin weapons designed to tear steel and cable pitted against one another, in an arena of merchants and timber walls. Behind Pescha, the wound in Free Rig's ship scaffolding creeks, like hinges long abandoned to the steady gusts, but she does not question Constant's readiness to fire. The dull, colourless shades of this imitation wetland tug at her loose bun, untied strands reaching for the Kodakame they know, as warmth and blue skies shy away from this oceanic breeze.

Sartska shrugs, raising arms to the surrounding emptiness, this grey-grey horizon, and tells her that he's the only Nomad left on The Frown. He needs material for his crew. As the gusts blow tied strands before his wavering sneer, shawl swelling and shifting like the waters, he asks her if she wants to swap.

Pescha weaves, unhurried but unwavering, one hand moving figures from her way, the other resting against her hilt, blade horizontal along her lower back.

Constant almost hisses that the Islanders would never let the Et-Skhep back, not anywhere near. Her sights widen for a moment, when she asks him to imagine what they'd do, if Corsair ships moved once more into the Wetland.

Then, the captain asks; what is Constant doing out here? These are not her calm pools. What is the Verfloga doing, this far out from Kodakame? Who is she to call him out of place.

And the blue-eyed Nomad, he asks, calling louder and generally, priming the pistol with a quick thumb. He looks to the surrounding throng with a grin of goading, arms apart to leave his body open.

As though something is punctured, gas billows amid the crowd, a can pierced and spinning its fumes, and Sartska pivots to the dual ultramarine approach, as bright as any bullet he shoots, firing from the mass. Low and grating over well-worn timber, kicking up splinters as she comes. Pack One against the ground, like she launched too hard, she is pulled in its wake, arms trailing with speeds so sudden that the Corsair barely has time to raise his Humeda killer before she spins. A hand upon the lumber she whirls, wheeling on the outstretched arm, one foot curling and disarming him of his gun, but he sees her grasp for her sword, and he pulls back, ready for a slash.

Her blue catches his sights, too slow against her momentum, and she turns the reach into a kick, a second leg sinking into his gut.

Gas blurting, she must pull back last second, so that she completes the twirl instead of ploughing through. She'd have skewered him on her leg.

He collapses, coughing the complete range of his vocal spectrum, gurgling and choking, nearly folded in two. She comes to one knee, drawing her blade which catches the colourless light and makes it luminous, against her brandished metal.

She holds him down, looking to impale him, back to Constant

who turns, levelling her sights upon the crew. They have time but to shout, before they are at the end of a barrel which blew islands apart. Pescha eyes the crowd, figuring they couldn't care less who won, and lets Mariner emerge, shoving from the throng. He falls by her side and pins the squirming Corsair. Even as he takes kicks from Sartska's flailing legs, he mutters that Pescha can't kill him. He's the only Klernsteiga to watch over The Frown. Nobody else knows the Humeda out there.

She looks over, toward the opening in Free Rig which faces the vast blandness, of an ocean rising into sky. The Frown. The great body of water which divides for miles, emptiness on all sides.

    A mere glance, she finds its title taking effect.

Pescha looks down at the captain, telling Mariner that she doesn't care what he does, she isn't going to kill him. Rolling there, face an inch from her sword, she and Mariner holding his body as though to not pin him so would let everything inside spill out, Sartska manages to turn, keeping her gaze. Her blue finds scowls, trembling in the wake of a force that sends her soaring, and even in pain that sudden indignation manages to seep through.

    She grins at him, blue wide and bright, so different from the encompassing drabness and so close that her shades catch her steel and his face. He groans under her grasp, rolling away. Pescha nods, and looks at Mariner, who has a million interjections playing over uncertain features.

    She thanks him for everything, and tells him to go make sure Constant doesn't kill anyone.

- *FAUSCHENHERST TERRIROTY* -

THE FROWN

She learns of the Et-Skhep from a crewman. The marauders, who've worked The Frown long before the first Nomads.

There from the very beginning, when the tragedy of Sect One unfolded. They sought refuge on the waves, praying the machines were confined to land as they slipped into the waters, sailing rudimentary and makeshift boats as far from the shores as they could. When the blanket silence fell and all communications ceased, they had no way of knowing what was happening away from the shore, let alone beyond the Kyut. When the Fauschenherst lost contact with its whole first Sect, the seafarers had nowhere to turn. No way of knowing who else had survived the sudden machine revealing. The only people left, upon the grey-grey horizon.

Without resources or the knowledge to make use of the land, they were forced to take from others, from ships trying to cross to the other side. Maybe some thought the machine horror was bound to one area. Maybe they'd been pushed out by others of the first Sect. Regardless, they tried to pass over, and met the founding Et-Skhep, the hopeful colonists turning against one another as soon as the blackout fell. Pescha doesn't know what Et-Skhep Mordaar means, but it was a name given, not made.

It wouldn't be long before the machines found them too, taking to the growing fleet of Corsairs. Ripping it apart, so forcing the dregs back to shore, in a frenzy of miscommunication and fear. It was a sight many of the marauders had never thought they'd see.

She tries to imagine it. The machine demons, wandering the coast, and turning to ships that watch silhouettes, on the edge of vision. To see the automatons walk out, and slip below the waves.

Most fell then to land, but a group survived. Managed to establish a small port, on the border of a place where they could remain in their boats.

When the surviving Et-Skep first clashed with the Timber Islanders, it was a conflict of massacres and atrocities. Most were committed by the marauders, who fought a community who had fled from Dodtohmet and barely established itself atop the shallows. Pescha heard names, but not specifics, of the Corsairs who fought.

Ihmsk and Snabskatte, famed for their burning of Island homes too far from the central construction. Sjallamaan and his ship, the Morrilskahn. The Irimehus Gohrm and the Hastessen.

And Pescha hears of those they fought, who battled for what little they had. Ishintsada and Hassara. The Mian, who founded the Timber Isles, and Tseshiga, the most revered of those to war. Murder on murder on murder, until the Et-Skhep fell once more, and were forced back out into The Frown.

They are not so sure after that. Built on rumours, they think Snabskatte, the last of the Et-Skhep captains, worked to bring the many fragments of the original Corsairs back together. Maybe he won, maybe he didn't. Regardless, generations later, his marauders follow a Klernsteiga. Flown in under Sect Three, like the vast majority of Nomads.

She wonders just what the seabound peoples knew, of what was occurring across the Kyut. If they even realised that Sect Four had so recently landed, barely a year ago.

If they knew of what happened to Sect Two, some sixty years back.

Late evening is choked by ocean fog, light withheld by low cloud. It renders the sunset an already looming dark, the sea blackened as night spreads over empty waves. Sartska didn't set his lights, but the ship ploughs on, a quiet shadow drifting atop a calm yet tense darkness, embedded against the wearisome shades of grey. It is cold, and the winds do not bring that same sense as of Kodakame. Cool, made biting, but Pescha will not descend below deck. She sits upon the bow, huddled against herself, watching the sea. She left her coat on the Verfloga.

She wonders if they're below her. If the Humeda of The Frown wait upon the shore, or if they're built for this place. She can lean over the side and look down, but all that churns is foam, curling against the armoured hull.

The soft lapping, receding forevermore. Making the horizon shift. The sky an ocean, the ocean a sky.

When Sect Three landed, they had but to make space. The many communities descended from Sect One's lineage owed no allegiance to those who had forsaken them to this place, a hundred years ago. To wander a land of the resources and room they so needed, to see salvation snatched by a mechanical grip. For Sect Three, the new Klernsteiga accompanied the Rautbergen, and fought to make an indent on the machine presence. They fought so hard. They've been fighting every day for eight years. Mariner. Red Constant. Sartska.

Pescha wonders what it has done. Sect Four comes with resources and equipment, but it is handed to a broken forefront. A year here, and she looks upon it still. A sea, rolling between the fingers of false figures, built of steel and cable.

She holds her arms, hair whipping around her head. Out here, her sights are all that glow. Sights leading through the night.

She thinks of Mariner and Red Constant. Imagines if one of them ever left the other.

She thinks of Emile, so far away.

She curls up, and buries her head against her knees.

- *FAUSCHENHERST TERRIROTY* -
SILSALAT

This area she traverses, between the fall of Dodtohmet and the rise into Kenidomo Country, it is a geological pit, carved by something tectonic. Cold lines the cusps on either side and The Frown runs through the middle, marking the midway of this section. She knows this because she's seen files, maps of this local area, the rise and fall in altitudes and the temperature fluctuations caused by the residue of whatever left such a massive scar on the face of the Kyut. She knows about the water flowing down from Dodtohmet, swamping Vanish Strip then filtering out through the Wetland. She knows about the heat and sea waters precipitating a way ahead into forests that'll climb with her. She can infer the rest. Guess what will mar her path. But she hadn't guessed this.

A band of desert, it is the inverse of Vanish Strip over which she trudges. Where one was consumed by moisture to the degree of inhospitality, this place ebbs the shades of dehydration. A clear sky, drawn of any vibrance by heat beating. Stifling temperatures and ocean salt, so that waves become low dunes, vanishing to the ripples of intense warmth at either stretch and behind, where the sea should be. She turns, and she may see the waters, but if that's the sea then it encroaches impossibly on all sides, the undulating swelter making her world a mirage, following her up the slight and seemingly endless incline.

But ahead, something is made clear. The ground rises, to a cliff face spanning, fading in heat to her left and right. One of dust and sun-blushed stone, as though the water should have lapped at its precipice. A craggy ridge that makes a wall against the desert, rendering it as a great beech, although one well baked under the constant scorch. She walks it with smouldering fatigue, steadying her breath but stumbling anyway through the smothering intensity, feet sinking as though now back atop her snow. Under this sun, for moments, her vision flickers to white, and her skin burns.

But she is drawn to an unnatural thing. Unnerving, it reminds her of the machines, lingering against a landscape painted empty, expressing the vastness of the sky and the vivid warmth. Now the vast wall presents a great superstructure, built against the sandstone perch.

A factory, a refinery, it is the image of abandonment. Rusted metals, darkened under the heat and worn away by the grain, create the skeleton, of scaffolding half fitted and chimneys chipped and crumbling, everything baked. The hazy outline compounds itself as she pushes through the pulsing day, defining what change from banners to vast turbines, fitted to the top of the massive building. Windmills, their fabric paddles ruined by high flung sand. Flapping uselessly, their rotors jammed with grit.

The coastal sandstone wall of Silsalat spreads across view. It is centred by the facility which scales the climb, left out here to the elements. Disregarded, cloth pads pitted with holes and steel drawn thin, the factory is the only way up in sight. She dares not walk from its view or else loose it to wavering distance, so dry eyes lock onto the compound, left lain against vertical stone. A fortress of narrow sheet steel and skeletal framework, the desert pilling against its base.

Silsalat grows with her approach and scales, a dam to hold back heat, adorned by the metal design. When she nears the base, its magnitude becomes daunting. She cannot conceive of how it was built, as her mind slips within the numbness of warmth, or how someone could have thought it even possible to build.

It is a temple of iron, a cathedral of blackened rust and torn fabric. She looks up, and tries to figure the height of such a structure, but the scale is shifting. Out here, her sights stray, slack and mesmerised, her blue dim against the sun's devastating pitch. She stares, at pipes and balconies, blinking into the shapes.

Her brows furrow, attention caught.

On one of the overlooks. Hair ashen, but much longer than hers. Trailing with higher winds, its shade matches that of the metal sanctuary, but if she sees them then they surely see her, way down against unsaturated gold.

She rubs dry eyes and raises a hand, waving up to the sweeping strands.

They wave back, from way up high within the factory.

It is a complex of fallen sand, light slipping between gashes and tears in the vast, towering body. Of tumbled dust, the open interior climbs past a crossing webwork of platforms, dangling chains and pulleys hung. Broad holes let the glow in, creating beams of stagnant particulates, illuminating the disused innards. Equipment discarded; all things are the same shade of dry, uninhabited decay. She stands there, a speck in the enormity, wiping the sweat from her forehead. At least it's cooler in here.

She sees no Humeda, or signs of their carnage. As she climbs, the erosion has bored through the sheets, making time and heat the killers of this place, leaving a slumped corpse against Silsalat. Making an example of its futility. Harvesting the seaward gusts or breaking into the cliff face, whatever this place was made for, it is unsalvageable now. Pescha thinks of someone crossing The Frown before the Et-Skhep, or part of that first Sect which landed on this side. Maybe they recycled their ship, or came with the means to set up a foundry.

Her shoulder brushes a threadbare rope. She covers her face to pass below sunlight cast from an immense cave-in, collapsed roofing piled atop itself. Dust wavering with her footfall.

The overt layout and open construction makes navigating easy, as she scales flights which meet, before each step, her scrutiny, out of fear for such a far drop, but she walks without struggle, rising up to the metal mesh walkways. Some are collapsed, taken down with burdensome debris, yet there is always another way, over the many branches and levels of the iron skeleton. She walks, from ground level to the opposite side, scales up and then comes back again, making for the opening which leads to the overlook. The way is obvious even from the bottom of the compound.

The sun streams through a beaming door, the noise of the elevated breeze toying with a cloth strip once tied to close the way. She makes for the balcony, blinded by the patchwork harshness of light and its waving curtain, so that she steps out with an arm held up, squinting into the back of her hand.

When sight returns, she gazes over the desert of Silsalat. A quaking, quivering mass of low dunes, it shivers under its own heatstroke. Like waves, although nobody there could ever mistake them as such, for the warm winds brush dust and hair so softly that it whispers heat, close and intimate, against the collars of those who wander the wastes. She inhales, and the warmth slips through her chest like something bleeds, but up here the temperature isn't as bad. The breeze compensates, and she looks in its direction, the rush flowing around this iron palace. She looks right, and sees a man, crouched, searching through the dusted rubble.

His hair is straggly and long, drifting about his features. Like a wraith or phantasm, tried eyed. More than indifferent, he is unattached from the world around him.

He watches her take in the view and he stands when she turns, a soft smile offered as he wipes his sleeves. Skin the same as Sartska's, he has that tempestuous smokiness, a dark ethereality, crowned by his thin, inky strands, which hang all the way to his waist, and sway before his face. He is macabre, a ghoulish depiction. Like Sartska again he too dons a shawl, but where the Corsair stared with worn contempt and a lifetime of scrutiny and mistrust, this face is fatigued, yet kind, like a haggard but accepting teacher. He is in scarf too, of woven sable and frayed edges, a melancholy but dear phantom. A charming spook, he looks out over Silsalat dunes as she comes, and the wind which twists and loops his strands draws them around his head, body, arms, and the cutter against his waist, the handle barely visible from the folds of his loose upper cloth.

She raises a hand, pointing skyward, and asks if he knows the way up.

Sure he does, he says, his voice gruff but unaggressive, and he asks her to follow him.

It is as though they walk through the innards of an Humeda, but then Pescha knows that sight too well to be mistaken. Here, the immensity of this factory swells and slips against the eye. Walkways are flanked by the instruments of production, to open out, whole new expanses revealed as the two ascend, some walls not even finished, to let the sunlight make its own barrier, catching the dust mid motion. Keeping close to her guide, she asks what this place once was, this abandoned citadel. He looks around also, admiring the scale, lingering strands hanging before his face.

He says he isn't sure. He saw the fans on the way in too, so it's got to be the wind. Loads of pulleys, he figures they were making some kind of fuel. Then again, the gusts could have been used to winch, but then whatever was being built isn't here anymore. Maybe someone tried to build their own automaton, he remarks, running a hand over a rusted railing.

Brow raised, she asks if this is his spot, having guessed the compound to be where he lingered. To rest when wandering the sands.

He shakes his head. He says he's just passing through.

She sees him rummaging through the ruins, searching the complex, then looking out over the desert, using the height for a better view. Keeping pace, their steps resounding to the lowest regions of the cathedral, she asks what he's looking for.

Without response, she watches him walk, his hand twitching by his side. His age, he looks in his early thirties.

After a moment, he says he's lost someone. Another Nomad. He's looking for him. He calls him his comrade.

Pescha asks if they're friends. Another pause, and the man nods. He says they came here together, with Sect Three. Pescha lets the silence draw. She waits. She nods and says nothing more.

In the higher levels, where the layout becomes more closed, among hanging corridors and extending rooms, they pass the remnants of camps. Makeshift windows, sawn from the sheet metals to let the light and breeze in, but nobody has been here in a while. The dust is well settled and even this high up, the sand piles and mounds against room corners, all things that hot haze, of muffled gold and burnt steel. Pescha walks to one of these openings, rough cut and fitted with a thin cloth, a translucent imitation curtain, drifting with the ascendant gusts. She looks out, over a rooftop of the compound. She and the ghost Nomad have climbed the tallest section. Much lower than them, another roof has collapsed, supporting beams snapped and hanging, torn and loose- chimneys crumbled, now lying still. A forgotten place, thin sand shifting over the remaining structure.

The man stands behind, observing over her shoulder.

He jokes, tone quiet yet clear, if she ever gets that feeling. Like she wants to go home, but she already is. His voice is carried by the draft through the passage, audible even from the other end.

Without turning, she brushes dust from the sill. She says that he's here because they don't have a home. That's why the Klernsteiga are where they are. They've no choice but to make this their home. Everywhere else has gone.

Without sight, she can tell he turns. He murmurs that it never feels as though they should be here. They're not supposed to be here, on the Kyut. It's unnatural. They're there unjustly. Even this place, built to be bustling and loud, makes better sense the way it is now.

She is careful not to cut her hands as she dusts down the window, sights cast down this end of the temple, and on. One side the desert, the other the rise of Silsalat.

Her sight is distant. Her face straight.
    She asks if he wants to know how she deals with it.
    He says nothing. His silence invites her.
    She breathes that it's all the same. It doesn't matter where you go, it's all the same. That stuff isn't destroyed, she means- it just changes. The same building blocks always remain. The man, she says, as she looks his way, he is made of so much more. Of crushed stars and cosmic dust. Planets, torn apart an age ago, whole galaxies ablaze, their pieces sent far and wide, bunched together and reused. Reborn and reborn. Those swirling colours, like milk and oil in water, curling space.
    He has been things so much greater, she tells him, blue glowing. What he is now, it's just another state. He'll be here, and gone, in a flutter. She says it's fine for him to feel as though he isn't home. He isn't. By coincidence, the celestial remains made him man. This isn't his natural state. One day, he'll re-join the extramundane fray. Everything and everyone will.

She says it's fine for him to feel as though he's not home. This isn't his natural state. His natural state is not life, its death, but she says this with far too much ease. He spends a lot more time like that than he does alive.

She catches him with a faint smile, glancing toward the ground. He mutters, mulling her words over, that that's an oddly comforting thought. She smiles too, and says she guesses it is.
    Even now, she continues, he's still changing. Things dying, they're replaced, things once suns and worlds. By now there isn't a cell left of him that was born. Not a single fragment of him named by his mother, let alone birthed. He must ask what he really is. If he's the same thing at all.
    His home has been a trillion places, beautiful and swirling. The paint of the stars. He won't be here for very long, she tells him, wind brushing against the curtains.
    Reborn and reborn, whole renditions of himself have already fallen. Soon, as it is meant to be, he will be relieved of this burden.

But then he frowns, wavering upon an inference. Brow's furrow, he looks to her, head cocked.
    He says that all the stars are gone. Isn't that why there here: there

isn't anywhere else? The few remaining worlds beyond are running out of resources. Time is slipping by. They need the wealth of the Kyut, this diverse paradise of so many habitats. Their godsend, yet one crawling with machine demons. That's what the Fauschenherst are doing, what their Rautbergen armies and Klernsteiga are doing. Once they're dead, there are no more stars to go to.

Pescha nods. And that's what makes them special, she says. The end is near. The cycle of rebirth, again and again, is coming to a close. They've been left with no alternative, their worlds stolen. The rhythm, offbeat.

But still, a thought mumbles. The sequence lingers. Holds on, for dear life.

She looks up, back to the man, resuming a smile. She peers up the corridor, seeing it's stairs at the opposite end, more false curtains streaming by their carved viewpoints.

In voice, she asks for the way out.
In thought, she asks for Emile.

- *FAUSCHENHERST TERRIROTY* -
NYAYA MATSUMASI

He says it was Mehimu Heshimawa, a great boar Humeda. Once, its tusks ruled this savanna, the long streamers bound around the hog's ivory the remains of banners, that flowed with the winds the beast roamed. Four great teeth protrude from the machine's skeletal head, tapered with sprawling lengths of cloth, but they sway only with the breeze now. Pescha and the boy stare across the savanna, overlooked by the corpse of Heshimawa, the boar's body splayed out on one side. A building, detonated from within. Now, the vast mechanical swine lays from afar, figure wavering with distance and heat, observing the land taken from it, ribbons orchestrating the plains flow.

    The Nyaya Matsumasi is what awaits atop Silsalat, a grassland of dried fields and few trees. It lingers before the now low light, its setting making all things the extremes of evening shades. Those cereal tones, of high, parched grass and patches of sun-baked dirt. As they stand there, watching the veld ripple with oncoming gusts, the only noise that of the approaching breeze, what captures Pescha is the sky. It stretches over the flatland, in burning sun-down orange, the only things in its way the spars silhouettes of trees, and the mountainous remains of the boar, golden streaks of cloud consumed by the light.

The ghost Nomad says she has no more than an hour left of daylight, but he wouldn't camp on the ledge. The limit of Humeda wanderings, she would better sleep if she ventured as far inland as she could. In the dying day, the shadows cast by his hair are strands of their own, so making his face cuts of illuminated features, loose shawl adding to the shapeless illusion.

    She thanks him for the help, asking where he'll go from here. Looking out, tracing the line of Silsalat, he shrugs.

    He says his friend would have been forced to go this way. Keeping to the shoreline, probably. The way he speaks, the impossibility of there being any other prospect, it defies mere confidence, but Pescha only nods. He stands there, an image of contrast and distortion, shawl hiding a plethora of killers, the tools to get him to this place, in whatever bombs or cables, systems and components. The many methods of his work.

 He stares, awash in evening winds.
 She smiles, and walks before he turns back.

Under the watchful gaze of Heshimawa she goes, heading for the setting sun. Hands trace the dried grass, watching the day sink until, after only so long, her advance stalls, and she holds atop the Matsumasi.

 It's a machine, pawing at something on the hardened dirt.
 A feline automaton, but like Masago it is made of man's parts, cast in steel. No taller than her, its attention is rapt by a grounded thing, the digging motion slapping against soil. Red cable tendons span its digitigrade legs, remining Pescha of those worn by Constant, and she sees the beast even has ears. The whole image is a quivering black outline, so she cannot see the thing on the ground while she walks, striding against the cooling breeze. But she knows, as a hand reaches for her pocket, her attention set on the cat which rakes and rakes and rakes. It is so mechanical in motion that when the Humeda looks up, the sudden pause of surprise almost goes unnoticed, as a trick of the blanket warmth.

But she does not miss it pounce, bounding low, every step condensing its form.

 Her hand flares.
 She does not miss.

She looks down on them, the butchered party. Like wood splintered, blown out and twisted. Picked apart with a hand of knives. Her blue sight wavering, fatigue oozes through her limbs.

 She walks to the closest tree, collapsing at its base. It feels like the only one for miles. Weariness mounting, she rests her head against the bark. She doesn't remove the Pack from her waist.

 She dreams of nothing.

Birds.

 They squabble a few feet away, leaping for one another, flashing ragged wings and cawing in competition. She isn't scared by their noise but awakens to stare, sunken and dreary. Impassive features watch them flap and peck, pulling with hooked beaks and struggling in arid shrub. Laying there, in the cool of early morning, she listens to their efforts with half attention, slumped amid the sparse grass. She rises only when her thought wake enough to inform her of their meal.

Pescha stretches, glaring at the raptors who do not flee from her, but slow and move attentively, leaping with her every twitch, their feathers slick and matted. For a moment, her hand lingers over a pocket, but she lets the arm fall. Behind them, she can still see the cat Humeda, a mound of cables and machinery rising above the parched underbrush. When she stands, she looks to the sky, the familiar blue enduring before the harsher heats stake their claim to day. With the breeze still cool, tumbling over steppe toward Silsalat, Pescha secures the straps of Pack One and walks from the buzzards, into the Nyaya Matsumasi.

The plane is expansive, spanning the bounds of view, but where she was once confined to harsh, blinding weather and low waterlines, or the infinite emptiness of The Frown, now she can see where infinity leads. With the rising light the temperature swells, but the rolling airflow keeps her going. She drinks, powder shaken and shade used whenever she brakes, to eat food already dehydrated, so making her drink more. The concept of taking off her jacket brushes against her exposed face and hands, but she feels the wiring system looped within the fabric and the bombs within her pockets. She wipes her brow, and presses on.

The curse of clear vision torments her- a distant tree wobbles into view, and comes to her side an age later. She can't run, or else she'll bake and loose water, so she walks the dead and malformed pasture, its shades roasted and its vegetation either eradicated to dust-like dirt or climbing to her waist. She considers the birds, how they came to roam the Matsumasi. Someone's pet, or scouts, even something to eat, escaped from their cages. Maybe, but time has passed, so to now create a new avifauna. When everyone dies, Pescha thinks, the Kyut will be home to machines and birds.

At some time, at some point, she reaches the remnants of a camp. Canvas pitched and improvised equipment set, she looks upon the ash and empty cans of a caravan, crossing the Matsumasi with direction unknown. Pescha figures distance and wonders whether she knows who once slept here, thinking of those the feline mauled. She stands there, the centre of the ringed bivouac, the abandoning of the camp standing only to one reason. Bags and supplies still sealed, lain across the site, she sees too much for those she found torn. In the panic and in the night, she thinks of them running.

The wind rustles through high grass, trying to draw attention, but she doesn't look. She can imagine it, the furore as firelight catches a stalking automaton. Some manage to disappear into the dark. Most make it only beyond the limits of their fire. Upon open ground, against the machine cat. She didn't see anything else on the way in, but she won't check.

Something catches her eye, drawing her even in this incongruous place.

A thing of reverence, a small table stands, embellished with the pieces of respect. Trinkets in decoration, she walks to the board, seeing a cloth marked with scripture she cannot read, although she recognises the insignia.

It's a shrine, to Small Hand. The other components lay in order, but she knows only the cloth underneath, one of many associated symbols painted as a banner. She sees his razor whip, fashioned from the corpse of an Humeda. When he walks, they say the staff rises high, way over his head, a cloth bound around the top to waver, creating a silhouette reiterated across all the touched Kyut. A symbol some Klernsteiga better rally toward than those of the Fauschenherst, who sent them here. None more so than those of the sobriquet Clan Kamakara[12].

The Nomad's awarded the highest decoration offered, of Kites[13] rising to that of the fabled Kite of the Kamakara. The best incentive the Fauschenherst can offer, in prizes demanding selfless commitment of implicit suicide.

There are four in Clan Kamakara now. Small Hand is one of those four to receive the most venerated of medals. The other three each have one Kite of the Kamakara to their names. Twenty seven of those Kites have been presented.

---

[12] *Clan Kamakara* : Referencing the recipients of the Kite of the Kamakara, the rarest of Fauschenherst medals. The four honoured have no true loyalty to one another, and have scarce ever met: Klernsteigas Taifunschneider; Mincemeat; Yubokumin; and his greatness, Small Hand.

[13] *Kites*: The medal system of the Klernsteiga, bestowed by Fauschenherst command. They are scarce given, and oft overlooked, but such accolades afford luxuries in larger cities, and cement names otherwise lost.

Her time becomes that of blind advance, like time spent upon the Kodakame Wetland although here she must walk. The only gauge of distance is the corpse of Heshimawa, which slowly turns her way, a sideward glance becoming a direct stare. She sleeps and drinks, conscious of her water but not worried, keeping pace, in observance of trees evermore sparse, horizon evermore bare. Something is changing as she proceeds, but to an end she doesn't know. She should have asked the ghost.

Pescha knows she will reach rising hills of forestry, a woodland ascending along a mountain ridge. The Shae Doken, scaling to another icy flatland. Like Dodtohmet, maybe once a continuation, had the many habitats connecting not carved through. She just doesn't know what is in between.

She isn't sure what is beyond, either. Into Kenidomo Country, beyond the bounds of Fauschenherst maps. She'll have to find a Nomad to guide her.

She wakes before Heshimawa, the boar's great tusks framing her as she ambles from slumber- it is some machine deity in waiting, streamers drawn toward the sea. Out here she couldn't find a canopy, the trees lost and forgotten to an evolving Matsumasi, so she stands in a place equal to that all around, direction dictated only by the rising sun to her back and the wind which approaches. Flat savannah, Pescha and Mehimu Heshimawa stare at one another. She continues into the plateau.

Then the ground starts to mound, rolling to block the horizon. Steady heights and downlands form, so that she must check the light to make sure she isn't lost, that same day of Heshimawa's sole attention also seeing the machine slip from sight. The image of forest mountains makes sense as Pescha advances, but they're not there, and this draws her speed, unease growing. A new skyline, she should see them if the ground here already rises irregularly. A predicate of a ridgeline, she walks through a rippling steppe.

She stares, blinking. Up here, she can just see the dead Humeda behind her. It has become insignificant to the spectacle she approaches.

It cannot be crop, not in this quantity, but it looks as such. Like tumbling cereal plants, grass of that grain colour spreads, flowing to the bounds of vision. A new sea, of wheat sprawling, Pescha looks back at the Matsumasi, the parched grassland wobbling off one way, and then forward, to a blonde field spreading anew.

She walks to the plant, running a hand through the mass. It is just grass, no seed or grain growing, but the quantity is mesmerising. A vastness uncountable, it is a golden fur blanket lain over what must still be the Matsumasi, although Pescha has never heard of this place. She wonders if that's why all the trees went. There is so much here, what little moisture present is consumed entirely. The sky also changes, blueing that better heavenward shade, and the Nomad on the fringe stares out, wondering what exactly it is she sees.

Leaving isn't feasible, and she has no reason, she figures, to fear this stretch. If those mountain hills do indeed wait on the other side, then the enormity of grass here makes sense, as water drains down to the limit of the Matsumasi. Gazing over the fields, she gives one final glance at the open Nyaya, a flatland chasing the ocean, before she looks to the crop-like grass, lapping as the waters the other way do. She is insignificant, a dark protrusion from torrid earth, facing the wavelike gold, rising near her stomach. The embrace of the cool breeze and the noise of it, the gentle stream of tender gusts. Pescha wades in, her path parted in her wake, the only imperfection visible against the grass, as a single line to cross this wheaten earth.

Out here, there is no guidance save for that of the light above, apparent hours spent wandering with her neck craned to the sun. Fingers running through an endless mane of golden hair, the bewitching immenseness makes time truly a thing of the mind. Not a tree to figure distance, not a storm to lie about it, she ambles, her own hair fluttering. A single line of communications cables comes into view, the length of the horizon, but once she passes them no more come. For what feels like miles, she walks with her eyes completely closed.

As the camp had before, an oddity swells from the flats. It spires from the other side of a crop mound, a spear protruding over the opposite face. A rod dressed in knotted cables, Pescha watches it rise, a sky-fallen bayonet. She wades to meet it, climbing the rolling wheat to overlook the scene, for all intents the centre of this infinite farmland. Alone amid the wheaten grange and unbroken blue above.

A skewering pike, she sees an Humeda impaled. Thrusted down upon, by a figure who lays upon the machine corpse.

Both are dead, piled against one another, their efforts of murder so draining that they now rest together, watching the grass sway. She looks down on them, the Nomad's lance driven through the automaton's head and deep into baked mud, a dislocated and bent mechanical jaw barely affixed to its hinges. A brutish, heavyset Humeda pinned, she walks down to its side, seeing to the Klernsteiga sprawled above, a sword shattered, and cords draped. She tries to figure the Nomad's kit, beyond the pike and blade now discarded, but they are so intertwined that she cannot figure the trail of machine remains from the elements of the Nomad, who's hair still curls with the wind.

Pescha wonders if it was a chase, if one pursued the other, or if they would both wander from their summits and stumble into each other's sights. How far the Klernsteiga walked amid this cereal flat, to be ruined atop the golden stretch.

She stares. She leaves them be.

Pescha sleeps like some bird, fashioning her nest from wheaten reeds. She flattens a patch atop the highest mound she can see, to stare at the starless sky. While the days here maintain their warmth, comfortable with the oncoming gusts, at night a cool swells, making noise and chills of the corn plateau which flutters and sweeps around her. It builds to a constant ambience of that dry, brittle rattling of barley, reverberating like a fabric drawn across the ground for miles on end. In the dark, her azure is the only glow, a lone world in the dark above, a blinking blue which observes the nothingness overhead and the rolling meadow with the idleness of late lassitude, her sleep building. Upon hardened earth and amid the bittering night draughts she sleeps, comfort amid the cool stolen by the hardness of her rest, sore and stiff and aching. She wakes to the grass picking at her face, her body stricken with cramp.

With the winds sometimes building to a gale, unrestricted and free atop the plains, she instead walks through the dark, hair snapping from one side to the next. Pasture raging around, until her exhaustion near knocks her from her feet, mouth dry and legs pounding. Existence confined to the rhythm of that cereal level, and its endless berating of the lone blemish upon its perfection.

Because of this, when she should find relief, thoughts of sleep would come first, her pain relieved of the baked mud and incensed night windstorms. But this will fade immediately. So quickly, that the idea of slumber coming first seems stupid, as the Nyaya Matsumasi figures its final form.

The sun has set the sky alight when she arrives, smouldering cloud and an ether of bittersweet sunset overhead, as a hand parts the corn, and she looks to the resumption of life. The grass is short but green, viridescent and flourishing in so many forms, bubbling and teeming. A carpet that leads the eye to the settlement ahead, similarly blanketed in flora.

Brick and coloured plaster, crumbled and patchy, where people have left the plants have moved in, pluming from any space they can. They turn the buildings of all muted colours into a frame for the foliage, scaffolding upon which vines and shrubbery spread. Windows smashed in place of encroaching wilderness, the untended town lies under a webwork of cables, too many to track and too entangled to divide. They bunch against their posts and host the verdure too, which hangs upon the wires in clumped moss.

A line of buildings, an outer wall of houses, she approaches, leaving the wheat and walking the garden stretch. Her feet fall from parched fields to brief pasture, then the settlement that divides the Matsumasi.

Tired and beat she comes to the closest home, peering through a half-shattered window and seeing the abandonment within. No lights, the green has made its way well inside, crowding to the single settee and stand, an end table askew and pushed aside. Suddenly, looking upon that pleasant familiarity, a place to truly curl up and rest, she feels the shiver of satisfaction and shatters the glass, sweeping it aside and hauling herself through. She breaks in, stepping onto shards, rug, and moss, looking over the dark interior. It leads through to the rest of the house, the stillness within stifling as she comes to stand. A breeze follows, night descending fast. The distant end of the sky, away from the falling heat, adopts bluer shades like her own, her own which sweep the building, eyeing with suspicion, which peaks through shadows and doorways. She draws her sword, angst pretending intuition, yet she is calm as she walks, wandering the house made a garden haven, looking from room to room.

There will be nobody here, the trinkets of families and friends still remain, clumped and undisturbed vegetation mounting and climbing, playing forests upon counters and against corners. She stands there, the subtle ruin silent and sleepy, her mind drawn to memories of Glermvender, like some odd parallel to where she now stands. The same sense, of a room so large yet so confined, and so different from the last. She sheaths her sword.

Pescha tries the water, taps turning but coming dry, a pipe strangled by the vines or rusted with neglect, so she collapses onto the settee. She runs a hand through her hair as the evening deepens, oil spreading over the liquid sky like the night leaks. Drowning day with a fuel its flames cannot ignite. The breeze creeping from her broken window rolls, grass making waves as she watches.

She stands and takes to her jacket, undoing the straps from the top down, feeling the cables of her kit against her arm and the many stuffed pockets bunch, opening the clasps and then the wrappings on her hands. Tugging the ribbon end and then twisting it free, the priming swich on her palm comes loose, the imprint permanent against her grip. She releases Pack One, the straps undone, the cumbersome implement dropped.

She dumps the jacket in her chair, bear arms rolling in just her black vest, a sleeveless underlayer tucked into her pants of many more compartments. They sound their explosive elements as she walks, jumping the window back out into the field.

Like the cosmic pillars in records, kicked and scattered in every colour. Indigo behind luminous cloud in rippling tones, shifting with every passing second. The cold is furvert now and she holds her arms against the chills, all noise confined to the current which has so many instruments with which to muse, in the leaves and distant wheat, on hanging wires and in slight passages between buildings and their wounds. She will stand there, her sights bright and firm on the theatrics of the setting dusk, until curtains of black, true black, aside from the residue of day, fall, before she turns, making for sleep. She stares and is still for what feels like forever, all things loose fluttering, staggering against the retreat of light.

Pescha wanders back to the window and, taking the lantern from Pack One's compartments, she sets her lamp and sprawls across the settee, listening to wind and staring at the roof.

From wet marsh to grass and the hull of a boat, she lets them all slip with her breaths as she sinks into cushioning, letting the breeze play upon her bare arms and hair. For a moment, she may sleep with a smile,

even if only upon the corner of her mouth.
   Then she thinks on where she goes.

She huddles herself into the creese in the sofa, curled against the breeze.

- FAUSCHENHERST TERRIROTY -

BASE OF THE DOKEN

Her skin has never browned in the sun. Emilia, her home world, one of the four remaining planets, is a place of storms, of white upon white upon white. Snow constant, so that even most mountains become great dunes, piling the cold up as a frozen wave against the sky. Forget the lack of resources- away from the city's life becomes so hard, the deficit in food and supplies forces all outside of the big settlements to cut from computers, crashed but still storing data. Existence becomes that of wandering into the chills, to hunt for monoliths of steel against the colourless skyline, to dig and chip and burrow until something, anything, is hauled free, and then towed back to a port for sale. Always glacial, wintry, and sharp, any sunlight to colour the skin is offset by the vast bitterness of her gelid world.

Throughout her time on the Kyut, she has confined herself to sibling habitats. Not homesick, she never could be, but the cold is where she works. Away from it, the heat always bares on her mind. It is reading of some place, and then actually appearing there. She had never truly known heat before this place.

It is the sun which wakes her, managing to find an angle through the panelled windows to blare against her sleep. Her rest smoulders until she rouses with warmth, draped over the chair with her jacket and kit lain amid bundled greenery, moss pluming from breaks in the floor. When she steps into it, moisture squelches under her sole. The workings of this place are strange- an abundance of fauna, upon the fringe of an arid wasteland.

She dresses and eats one of her snack bars, the pocket notably light now, and she leaves from the front, as a pose to breaking in the back.

Like floodgates, day streams through as she hauls the door open. She struggles against swollen green until the gap is just wide enough, and she slips through. Pack One is fastened tightly, and she abandons the dank lawn within.

Consumed, she thinks. Swallowed by plant life, it stretches as a street from right to left, the sinistral way slipping over the beyond the hump of a mound and the dextral spanning further, branching into more roads a way down. Like a weird corridor, it is an Eden of crumbled plaster and damp sky against the flourishing, climbing, ruling verdant sprawl, a place turned into a playground for the plants. Their home now, as cables become bridges and cracks in the walkway sprout, vegetation bubbling from the undergrowth. Where the savanna had dried the sky, it now sags with moisture, building and overcast, and when she walks out into the road and looks to where she came, she can see the clouds ripped to an open blue.

Not there yet, but the Shae Doken nears, its wet draining down to the lower flats.

Apart from her and the flora, there is only one thing in the street. The sunken road leaves it stuck, intertwined, and made part of the shrub. A car, wheels deflated and sewn with the bush, its glass is dirtied and smashed and all else is rusted. She sees tanks upon its back. Containers, busted open now, the worn symbols against the hull suggesting their past contents, as water drums mounted atop the vehicle.

The street covers from both directions, so she goes right, a lone figure amide the tones of damp, flourishing moss, and dank brickwork below peeling plaster. That humid cloudiness, she feels as though something terrible happened, but she sees no carnage of the machines. Their chaos isn't here; the steady and meticulous redesign of the Kyut instead of the destruction of its automatons takes the town and makes it its own habitat, stolen from her invaders. There aren't any bodies, nor blown out walls or great Humeda carcasses- there is the subtle reclamation which persists all around, an ongoing task to tear the town apart, and force it back into the ground. She walks amid this cycle, a spectator of progress. It is a beautiful place of that perfect neglect. Like this road and its buildings and cables were always meant to be fashioned in leaves.

She walks for the crossroad, going slowly for it feels odd to rush here, such gentle devastation starting long ago and enduring still. When the offshoot to her left comes, a lane driving deeper into the town, she stops, central amid the divide, staring down each path.

Despite all charms of this consumed ruin, there is an eeriness here. Maybe it comes with the decay, that it has not yet fully spread. An uncanniness, growing with the vines, still hiding against windows and behind wire-tangled posts. Like the green unfurls every time she turns her back.

An alleyway to the next street, the offshoot opens out to a main road, one wider yet similarly devoured, great breaks in the paving made pocket forests. With such prosperous conditions more colours should arise, but Pescha walks amid no flowers, save for a few white petalled blooms, sparse and concealed atop roofs and within homes. Shades are maintained to those of this damp, post-human idyll, of civilisation made a mere scaffold for the shrub, and as the greying sky churns with threats of rain she sees, approaching from the left incline, another, who intrudes on the verdant.

    A cattleman and his beast, Pescha watches a boy walk alongside his animal. Like some buffalo or ox, the great cow is led by rope bound around its neck, although the tether is lost amid the coils of cabling and antenna mounted atop its back. A bull made a radio, the communications cow hauls the burden of so many wires and rigs. Slow, so to not drop its cargo, the tangle of fibres hangs from tail to head, wound and draped from his horns like a veil of power lines. Its russet and speckled coat is protected from the weight by a shawl, worn and frayed as a cover between fur and wire, and the fall of its hooves tap as a distant pen against a desk, echoing their approach.

    The herder is obscure until he comes closer, for he barely rises above the buffalo's head. He does not break from Pescha while he wanders, as she does not for him, each watching the other as the cow ambles in pursuit. When he does near, a boy of bronzed olive skin now faded to cooler realms, and hair as matted as his cable's nods, drawing the beast to a stop with a hand on its muzzle. The buzz of his radios is soft and twitchy. His expression is without expectation, held in a regard of constant disappointment, his cow picking through the sprouting vegetation at its hooves without interest.

    Oddly, her blue fits this place well. A colour bright and strange, yet it complements the flanking tones. An insect amid the foliage. A firefly, hovering over the remains.

Pescha asks him what happened here, looking out to a ruin without people for years. Turned away, she waits for his response.

    Instead he speaks in a dialect alien, words short and clearly a statement of his incomprehension. A rehearsed verse, that despondency in his face is clearer than any words, and she can only look back, a slight similarity forming between their two expressions.

In response, he gestured a cup, forming a glass in his grip and drinking, watching closely when she nods and pulls her canteen from its pouch, tending to the power and shaking. This process intrigues him, sights set as she works, but his stillness is uncanny and when he takes the bottle, he swills the contents and ponders upon the liquid. Trying to figure something, he wonders words which he cannot ask, but he looks to her kit and shrugs, lifting the flask to his cow.

Brushing aside loose wires he waters the beast, careful to avoid the cabling as his buffalo drinks. When it is done, he has some himself, glancing around as he takes but a mouthful, passing the canister back as he wipes his face. His soft uneasiness in the act does not go amiss to Pescha, but she can make no comment.

For her efforts, the cattleman tries to offer her information. The look in his eye is telling, as only the minimum can be conveyed, but a straight hand and sharp directions point her the route through and out the town, as he drives his arm through imitation roads. The fastest path to leave, told without any indication of her purposes here. He does not hesitate, making as close to an order as can be given, assuredness peaking his urging request, and as soon as she nods, he roams on, tugging the rope to draw the buffalo up. It follows instinctively where its herder walks, the receivers atop murmuring their quiet buzz.

She stands there, canteen still in hand. She pockets it and takes his advice.

His suggestion draws her through similar routes, of alleys swamped and streets torn apart and pilled upon themselves, rubble made makeshift homes for the herbage. Like a child's bughouse seized by damp vines and shrub.

She breaks through to a square, a courtyard beset by the crumbling homes, a net of telecommunication cables sagging high overhead to create a box, separate from the vast sky of an impending wet. Enclosed, cut off from everywhere else, a fountain resides. Trying to hide itself from the flora, it is a large stone basin with a rising centre, becoming spherical at the top, like a pawn. Any flow has long since ran dry, but a stagnant pool remains, a conglomerate of grass and greening water risen to the rim. Those small, pale flowers peek from the moss.

It must have been the water. In some capacity, somehow, the

water ruined this place. Rarely has she seen somewhere as potentially prosperous as this fall. Even the Timber Isles has the liquid stretches to fear; compared to this place, the Kodakame Wetland would be unfavourable. And she cannot shake that boy, asking for something to drink. Walled in by the verdant, a swelling haven of plant life, and then to ask for water from another. Dried out taps and basins hauled by car across the town. Maybe a single incident drained through all the pipework. She cannot be sure, but she passes the fountain without taking what would otherwise be a welcomed resource and leaves the stone basin to the green.

The town runs across its roads, built along paved stretches so that, when she passes, she moves through the shortest length. More elsewhere, Pescha weaves backroads and alleys, walking into a sprawling street and out the opposite house, crushing rotten doors underfoot and busting through overgrown backroads until the buildings subside and she steps through what had always been, even before the age of vegetation, a vegetable garden. It is fashioned from wooden sheds and plastic tunnels overseeing unearthed soil. Allotments, it is a ribbon of food that she crosses, seeing no further homes past the tangled fence at the opposite end. She notes the oddities of these plots, as Denkervung server systems are huddled against glasshouses, their wires between weeds and the remnants of farmed crops. Like an all-purpose yard, she heads for the final line, the wall opening out to what she hopes to be a view of mountains. The shrub and slatted timber barricade is caved in at the point to which she moves, a collapse made an exit.

    Pescha steps through, eyes high for the hills.

For just a second, she thinks she's found water again. A pond maybe, where the blanket weed has lain itself over the ripples. Making a mini mountain-scape of its own, divided by flat pathways between the little hills. She sees lanterns swallowed and small shrines buckled, and when that second passes her step hovers, and she blinks at yet another scale mesmeric.

It is the largest graveyard she has ever seen.

    The impression tugs at her. Rarely has she seen a cemetery as great as this, for such circumstances of precise and careful burial never arise. A village is torn apart, mauled by the machines, who are slaughtered or chased away by Nomads and Rautbergen, or just leave of their own disinterest, and abandon in their footprints true ruin. Either no people at all remain, or there are nowhere near enough to establish a place as kempt as this. Normally if this many people die there stands no possibility of survivors, so few in number to dig these many pits.

And there mustn't have been many survivors at all. The mounds are unmarked, save for the odd and unarranged accumulations of lamps and prayer tokens, so she cannot easily figure scale. But she looks, and she sees them wobble on and on, like someone somewhere sits at the edge of a lake and systematically taps the water's edge.

The whole town, buried neatly, for they did not fall to the Humeda. Whatever strangled this place did it slowly. Slowly enough that the people could be dug and dug and dug, until the last of those willing to remain died, and the rest fled. Or everyone died, and a single townsman remained to bury their last friend, before collapsing into their own pit. If she wandered, she figures she could find them. The last, poorly covered graves, or corpses only blanketed in moss.

It is truly like a lake, shuddering between the walkways. She passes through, careful of her footfall to avoid the weak and brittle remnants of respect, lining the path. The wind picks up outside the town walls and the clouds overhead darken, their storm impending. Pescha's blue scans over the yard, damp green churning around and the grey above doing the same.

At the end, she passes under a wooden arch that marks the resolution of the town. She watches it as she crosses, dark and weathered timber creaking as lanterns once lit flap with that higher wind. When she looks down, she sees the skeleton at its base.

Lying against a pillar, young creeping plants intertwined within the skeleton's ribcage, its rocked back head has partly disconnected from its jaw, as vines plume from the mouth. Dead a long time, as long as it takes for the green to eat the flesh and plaster, and find the brickwork within.

She looks back, over the now stormy scene. That sky to give those below shivers, the wind and the bustling flora. Rage, waiting for something to slip, grass quivering, all things loose flitting in waves.

And the other way, she sees them. The mountains, a forest

climbing to the sky, and the trees which already, even here, rise from the shrub. A ridge of hills, ascending to the borders of Fauschenherst territory. The edge of hospitable reach. Where the names cease, and Kenidomo Country begins.

The Shae Doken rises, and Pescha walks to meet it.

- *FAUSCHENHERST TERRIROTY* -

THE SHAE DOKEN

The flat between town and treeline is short. When Pescha glances back she can still see that wooden gateway, the entrance to the graveyard, the surrounding green trying to tear itself apart with a gale sent rolling down the mountains. When she turns it is to an ascending pass, a path carved through the canopy, such an abundance of trees and shrubbery swelling along small streams that fall from the heights.

She had woken on the towns border and crossed quickly, she now has the day of light ahead of her, yet she does not slow to admire a diverse flora. The clouds threaten chaos, and she starts toward the Shae Doken.

In name, the mountains do not start until the corpse. This intermediary, of a stormy woodland upon rolling hills serves only to bridge the space between the Matsumasi and its neighbouring climb. Here, she wanders amid a forest with so much at its disposal. Conditions to carry seeds far and so much water that it flows seemingly all around, the noise is constant wherever she walks, wind and water rushing.

She knows where she is when she summits this forest slope, breaking the woodland to another open stretch. But this one hosts what she knows as the symbol of the Doken, in the vast Humeda body sprawled at the base.

Dai Nakari is a location, more than a machine. Once it wandered these ascents, an automaton so tall that its footfall could have levelled hills and raised new ones but now, it is ruined, a gaunt and leering thing. An impression of humanity, it stares as though the one who felled it stares back, an animosity of revenge impossible gaping in dead sights, with a jaw like that of a skeleton, loose, busted, and unhinged. Head like a skull although with great, seething eyes, globular and hateful, constantly swollen with uncontained intent. Now, it has been floored, long since slain by Small Hand, chunks of steel left strewn and made props for the field- a stretch like a firebreak, a divide between the vague foliage of the last climb and then that of the next. Of harsh pine and twisting pathways, safeguarded by the machine relic. She walks through this field, open ground between two faces of leaves, the spearing pine a wall of dark teal. Heavy cloud exemplifies these shades, hanging over Nakari and its conifer world.

The wind doesn't waste this opening, it is a tempest wild between the two timberlines, but she pushes through, a hand raised before her face against those dark blue-green tones. The giant head watches, so furious and so disturbed, its body blown out from the ribs so that, like the great boar corpse of the Nyaya Matsumasi and its horns, the bones protrude high and wide, machine organs splayed and ripped. Nearing, the enormity of the corpse just becomes larger; if she were to not look to the ground upon which the cadaver lay, she would think it forever receding with her approach.

Pescha stumbles behind the cover of Nakari's bones, a windbreak which ploughs deep into the pine, relieving her of the gale. She composes herself and glares into the woods.

It is a place naturally sinister, besides the soul-peering machine eyes which mark an entrance. As though trying not to wake the Humeda, it whispers, wails softly with branches stiff and bladed, matted locks of roots which curl over stones and moss parted only by vague tracks, trodden bare by things much worse than any relic. Uncanny, yet it would be evermore so if tempest and tree were not found in these conditions, which awfully flatter one another.

She stands there, listening to the eldritch Doken murmur, the remnants of Nakari's bones strewn and gnawed around, and she does not fail to notice, the gale irate and raving, that something watches her from a fragment of the colossal ribcage. A figure against the corner of her vivid eye. A thing which, although perceived with half sights, is unmistakably shrouded as it stares, and looks to be crowned with, its cloak flailing enthusiastically, pointed, branching horns.

Pescha gazes emptily, hand twitching.
The tempest howls.
She turns to the figure, with a smile bright and greeting.

He has no legs.

They're rods, pikes protruding from a poncho like Sartska's, of worn red frayed although his is larger, falling to the shins and beyond the arms. Like a sketch of animated proportions, his hands are hidden within widening sleeves and the single garment skirts at those needle limbs, the fabric churning fiercely, a faded embroidery of gold decorating. For a head he wears a ram's skull, pointed and pale, great horns twisting from the primal mantle, worn as a helmet with his skin covered by an underlayer. It would be something revered by a tribal people, a carving against walls or a deity of war.

The demon Klernsteiga looks down on her. For a moment, Pescha wonders whether it really is a Nomad or just a statue, like some scarecrow mounted atop the bone, but he responds to her kindness. He nods, and drops from his perch, falling in a way to hide anything concealed by cloth. His pointed legs spear the grass, sinking like pegs, so that he must pluck himself from the ground when he rises.

His body shifts airily, a preternatural walk which makes his ghoulish appearance that much more disturbing, as he moves with a slight hunch but an energy to each step. Like a skull and material sheet made humanoid by nothing but the breeze, a puppet with caricature stick-like feet and unseen grips, he stands before her. Small holes carved against the skull allow him to see, but let nothing in, so a truly dead expression gazes with cumbersome horns, both figures hidden from the brutish winds yet still touched by their weaker gusts.

She asks if he's going up the Shae Doken.

He says he is.

She asks if he wants to climb with her. He glances at the woodland, a twisted mass of knives playing trees.

Why not, he shrugs.

He says he is "The Ram Burbles", but that he has forgotten his Klernsteiga digits, as they introduce themselves and ascend through the pine. The trees rise so high overhead- the tempest cannot reach these walkways, but its wake still shudders through, the noise roaring way up above as the blue-eyed woman and the cloaked ram skull walk. The sun is completely lost to cloud now, making her reliant upon her aide, who knows the path through his own endeavours. He walks these mountain roads in pursuit of a rumour, he tells her, called Kakabi, but he's in no rush. He has only a name and speculation, a request from ruined villages speaking of the serpent machine, although he wonders how he is to fight something which retreats to these pointed forests. Whatever would find its strengths here has such a multitude of possibilities, and he cannot figure a single one good. As they go Pescha tries to guess his kit, but without an inch of skin showing she doesn't even know his face, which wears a black cover under its helm. He's tall, but then upon legs which aren't his, and while the garment he sports is beautiful, it is one well aged with use.

Regardless of Humeda and Klernsteiga, the Shae Doken is home to the trees. They conquer, their roots giving life to the blanket moss which curls over all things and itself too, pilling alongside the road and against whatever else intrudes within the woodland. As they rise, they see prayer shrines and litter, the remnants of camps and caravans usually swept away by others passing although, left here, for few would venture into this place with any alternative. Pescha looks at endless trunks and imagines someone fleeing here, in the hopes of tangling their machine pursuer as they run, but this dwindles to whatever else lurks in here. Glancing up, she has joined The Ram's concerns. It is too easy to imagine something snaking overhead, bounding from pine to pine.

The camps are swallowed, consumed in a way different to that of the Matsumasi bordering town. She wonders if it is ever truly light down here, as tents are disembowelled by searching roots or plastered in patchy green, the moss ruling the lower levels as the pine claims the sky. Their hights are tormented constantly by winds which creak and moan. Totems of intricate carvings and offering houses are desecrated, homes of spirits cursed, their small timber and stone stools bent and toppled. What horrors to think, when it is the place below this which was eerie and haunted. When the empty houses and wavering shadows are at the bottom of the hill, and she now ascends through that which made the nightmares. This place's simple existence choked those who hoped for salvation at its base. Pescha strides alongside The Ram Burbles, her guide, and wonders just how much he can actually see out of those near unnoticeable holes.

But he knows the Doken well. As they climb, his route streams between the trunks and small shrubs of pale berries, although when he sees them, he but gestures, never points, or takes. They both know the others awareness, as Pescha collects the fruit with an eye to his sleeves, searching for hands never revealed as he scans the treeline, breeze playing with his figure. She asks if they're good to eat and he says they are, so she drinks from her canteen and chews through their ascent, these pale morsels reminding her of those white flowers below, bright and keen against a tongue dull with her pocketed snacks. What they must look like, she thinks, her chewing from a handful of berries alongside that fiendish depiction. When she holds the overflowing hand out to him, he declines anyway.

As a poor excuse for daylight starts to slip, he asks where she's going, voice bumping into itself inside his mask, echoing slightly.

To answer Kenidomo Country would be dense, she thinks. She changes to ask for his help, saying that she'll need a place to stay, upon the border of Fauschenherst territory. Where she can group up and restock, but even without a face she feels his brow raise, turning to her while they walk.

He asks whether she knows where she is.

When she just stares back, eyes alight and mouth full of fruit, he says she is on the Fauschenherst-Kenidomo border, but not just some random region line.

She approaches sector Zero, Double-Four, Nine, Three, Five.

Our Last Limit was built upon the wreckage of a monumental Sect One ship. A great carrier, descending with hundreds of thousands aboard, enough power and equipment within to establish civilisation upon the Kyut.

Enough to build a city. Like the rest of Sect One, it would be a disaster.

Everyone inside fell with the craft as the machines swarmed and it crashed into the mountains, a wreck part buried against the rise. All those encased were made pulp by the impact, squashed by the Humeda, or starved. It is well known that the Fauschenherst does not reveal statistics, not even the number of Klernsteiga in operation. The number will only show that so many serve with so few results, or so many are dead, and the same. Their policy continues with the crash. But the very few who survived, and those to later come and glean from the ruin, saw the mush.

When Sect Three landed with its Nomads and Rautbergen, they sought to reclaim their ship, so crammed with power and information that to leave it idle would be too great a risk. They were right to worry, for when they stumbled from the treeline, they must have been amazed. Even

Pescha, who knows of this place as well as any Sect Three Klernsteiga would, gazes spellbound at the grand city built atop.

    Our Last Limit was raised from the ruin, a mass towering on the back, a megalopolis over the entire upper hull of an enormous ship. Tapping into the energy and data locked below, it was a mass of steel and cable, and everything needed to build a home just sitting there, so vast that not even the roots could make it near the top. What they were thinking, those first people, when they stood on a roof which seemed to stretch forever, and figured a city. Pescha cannot guess, but the great metropolis needs no consideration. Where so many dream of what could have been, the eyes are well rewarded. Now, The Ram tells her it is rapt with protest, dissent over its independence from the Fauschenherst. On a rocky outcrop the two Nomads stand, a break in the trees, the wreck made a metropolis distant yet of a scale to make distance meaningless. So large that it both feels so close and then impossible to reach. A colossal airship of four wings, all hosting more city, the nose is buried into the Doken. The Ram tells her if she wants Kenidomo Country, that is where she will stay. Its starboard upper wing bridges over the mountains, and onto the flatlands beyond.

Night falls and they continue, The Ram reassuring that she can reach this frontier soon if they keep pace. His needle footfall sounds like pennies dropped, clinking with a weightlessness echoing as windchimes, reverberating, bouncing from trunk to trunk. The onset of the dark builds under the clouds, but The Ram does not turn or search the forest as he walks. His manner may be misinterpreted as overconfidence, for a while, but that falters to his airiness. Not some trust in an indominable strength, but simple neglect. He sways and drifts, and Pescha watches him the whole time, slightly behind and letting the scarecrow wander.

    Eventually, he notices her unease, glancing back at the bright blue which bobs in his wake, and as they pass shrines and unknown forms swamped in moss and root, he asks how long she's been out here.

    When she says she came with Sect Four, his skull cocks.

The Ram Burbles asks what people are doing, still flying out here. He mumbles, for he does not need an answer.

    Gazing into the wood, Pescha shrugs. She says he doesn't know what it's like, back on the planets. Four worlds, one moon, one station. There simply isn't enough left. There wasn't enough a hundred years ago. Even less eight. Now, there is nothing. It's gotten way worse. Most who can leave do, to the big cities if they can, but then they cannot be much better off. Some come here. At least here, they may change that.

But The Ram says this isn't a reason. With Sect One he can understand, they were wishful and desperate, but now, after Sect Three, they must know what awaits, in machines and ruins sprawled. Why would they want to come to this, to flee safety, however uncomfortable. To fight those who do not care.

Pescha chews absently. Maybe it's just the right thing to do, she chirps.

The Ram makes a great nod, voice harsh in retort.

Ascending toward Our Last Limit, he says she can't argue morals. He asks what morals are here, what morals she has seen. The Fauschenherst won't be victorious upon the Kyut; morals cannot kill machines. They can kill people, he mutters, lots of people. But not the Humeda. Klernsteiga cannot trick themselves into believing their own goodness when their goodness comes from fighting things without morals, and that amoral cannot be beat.

Still a little behind, peering at the pine canopy overhead, she asks then why he's here.

Without pause, The Ram says for a second chance. Whatever was before this, it put them here, it made their pain and suffering. He knows the machines are made, that they now have what he's lost, but they're just the same. He hates them as much as whoever put him here, so he hopes to do what they could not. Love of morals, journeying for home and people; suddenly, he says this is what threw the last of life into this hole.

She glances at him. She asks him what he's saying. When he's silent, she smirks and prods- she asks then whether the worlds should just be abandoned. They'll only need more, birth more, sending more Klernsteiga, again and again. A constant cycle, because it's what they're used to. Even if it doesn't work. Why not let them starve, she asks to the back of his skull. Leave only the strongest out here, to try a different way of life? That last system didn't work, so desert it, and live that life he so loves out here. She does not amuse him, but he cannot respond, left to shake his head as she follows. Her azure like firefly friends, exploring the hillside.

Then he sighs.

He asks why they're here, what they're doing. It's like a religion;

how he craves for reprieve. A reason to go on. Because right now, right here, he's got nothing.

He glances her way, and sees her grin. Again, he shakes his head. He guesses she's come to the same conclusion. That everyone has.

She just keeps on staring at the back of the skull.

Pescha yawns. She says this age is different. To any other that has ever been. She says that he's right; the same will not do. Now, without their grandiose past, they know what they are. They have no divine right. Watch them, she whispers, without purpose. They know what they are, just a clump of cells- a figment, of an unimaginative imagination. They weren't made, they didn't evolve, they grew lazy, and they grew slow. The Ram Burbles thinks he suffers? That he is so very sad? He is no more in control than the cobbles of the stone path he now walks. He thinks himself so profound, in his superior thoughts, yet he dangles from the brain's string.

To all she has said, he grunts, and mumbles that she sounds about right. But he adds that he had enough control to force himself out here. To face abject discomfort instead of submission.

She tells him to bite off his finger.

If he could blink, he would.

They have the medical capabilities to reattach it, no problem, and he has the jaw strength to snap the bone, she knows this. What stops him, from proving her wrong. Pescha holds a hand to her mouth, digit between her fangs. It would hurt? There is no hurt, yet this is not what stops him, for when she holds her finger there, clamped in her teeth, a blankness hovers, as though her mind turns a dial, and stops the motion. She knows she cannot bite, not unless the mind had to save itself, and by then, it would hack its body to shreds to save itself. Doesn't it make him angry? Doesn't it make him furious, she asks, hand pressed against her bite, to be stuck like this. There's no such thing, she goads, slowly creeping closer. Rising to the tips of her toes.

What does he see. What does he hear, she grins, or feel or want. His whole reason to be is a formula. He wants to save the universe, but his thoughts barely have the energy to power a bulb. That wind against him, right now, his mind and being, they're nothing. Confined to the bone around him. Their morals are primordial ramblings, worm thought.

Does it not make him despair. If he were to fall, so what if anyone cared. Their care is electric, a primitive impulse. The people and the planets cannot survive here. Their system bleeds. They are pathetic, without reason, and then not strong enough to take even. One. Single. Little. Finger. Strung up by their own emptiness. Emptiness of emptiness, receding on forevermore, born and born again, and again. Until someone breaks it. Breaks the cycle. She whispers this, smile wide, right into where his ears should be.

The Ram Burbles turns to her, facing a voracious light, the twin insects fluttering, incensed. Wild, and bright. An inch from his head. He stares his osseus expressionlessness, but she can feel the sights within, as he gazes into hers.

    Vivid and intense, the mind can but power its dim bulb, yet her madness burns so bright. Smoulders, in its bone cage. And who knows what he would have said, had his figure not suddenly stiffened. Facing the woman whose brow rises, his shoulders squaring as the skull cocks to one side. Like something places a hand on his shoulder, cold and taloned.

    Cobbles?

    The cobbles of the stone path he now walks. That's what she said. She looks down, to rocks arranged as a walkway. The night makes them texture underfoot, ascending ahead. For a moment Pescha stares, glaring at pebbles, but it takes just that moment for her to look back at The Ram, who's hidden hands reach for his dress. She even remembers his description; of the serpent machine he pursues.

Because who's on the Shae Doken laying a cobbled path.

    She sees The Ram draw his blade from the folds, pulling the steel through his collar and raising the sword high, point to the scales. He holds it, not with hands, but with copper claws, like delicate metalwork linked with bronze ligaments, no skin or flesh in sight. The Klernsteiga braces himself into a slight stoop, adjusting the angle, poised to stab. Pescha tries to ask directions, moving to back away but he is enthralled, faceless yet wide-eyed in his coming strike, as Pescha turns from the-

He grabs her wrist.

    She glares, a spindly, burnished grasp holding her arm.

Pescha looks at her fellow Klernsteiga, surprise glowing. The Ram Burbles stabs the floor.

The moment his blade pierces its scales Kakabi unearths, from the head to the tail, breaking like an eruption from below. Trees are torn up, roots snap and the ground buckles, bending as the machine squirms, like splaying sheets with a wave. The noise is deafening; the Nomads would have fallen, had The Ram not leant on his anchoring blade and she on him, as ahead the automaton drives skyward, more like an insect than a serpent. While it is snakelike in face and body, there are frail, spindly legs, like stiff strings with joints, like The Ram's hands, that make the beasts limbs, which shoot for the night. Kakabi hauls its slither of the Doken with it, pines rattling like a nest enraged, wind lashing as the two Klernsteiga rocket up.

The sword stays firm, and The Ram does not break either grasp, so they whip up together, Pescha struggling against his claw. The ground falls like its supports snap, the sky taking everything in their sudden rise. Rushing up, the cool races against them as their fabrics twirl and The Ram clings tight, not even turning as she bashes her fist against his. The churning tower of an Humeda scrapes the sky as debris collapses, stones and twigs cascading. Her legs strike the metal plates and his grip is too hard, her beating turning from desperation to anger, for she would bite him if she thought he'd feel it. Crushing her palm into the frail implements of his clasp. He has to release, but she does not fall. As soon as her hand is free, it darts to the other, both meeting with the flip of a switch.

Pescha blurts past him, a rocket which bolts up the machine spine. The sheer vertical ascent forces her to plough herself against its frame with every burst, her blue chasing the fanged head atop in her scrambling dance, acrobatics impossible guiding the ribbon of smoke. She spirals up the new monolith, the distant lights of Our Last Limit alongside, revolving around the figure of Kakabi who opens its great jaws high above, its hiss bleeding through the sky. Like all nightmares of the dark are punctured. Its spindle appendages catch the city light, featherless wings flying the machine, stretching far like webs cast across the black. The gusts are stronger here and her plumes of smoke drift quickly, but she revolves with them, following the current at speed and then swinging around into it, so that she propels herself on, corkscrewing higher and higher.

Yet Kakabi feels her ascent and veers, twisting at an angle from vertical to horizontal, its twiggy limbs spearing into the forest way down below. Reaching even when it's this high up. She cannot keep to this change, cannot follow this curvature or else she will soar up and past, unable to control her descent. She growls as she throws her legs forward, but she has no choice. She kicks off the Humeda, unfurling and outspread, twisting as Kakabi crawls across the sky. She falls backward, considering her crash.

Her sights are snatched as The Ram churns past, still gripping that blade as he rises toward the curve.

He does not shy from flight. When the twist comes, he releases. Letting slip his sword and continuing on. Floating up, the machine below etching itself through the night. But then it turns, considering its chances, and Pescha watches The Ram overhead face Kakabi head on, as the massive snake rotates against the clouds. She cannot guess what he will do, the fabric dot uncontrollably gliding toward the vast, world-tearing automaton. Her eyes are fixed as she plummets, Kakabi weaving through the night.

There is a spark, like flint struck. Against the wind, The Ram's sleeves flutter back and, where his metalwork grasps make forearms there are more mechanics, a nozzles and vents and they glimmer, firing up.

Like engines they splutter in ignition, a generator blurting into life. They gurgle, whirring up as The Ram flies. As The Ram burbles.

Fire clicks, spits and quakes and it flows like liquid, streaming from his grasps, enveloping the dark and streaming, blurting into the black. If Kakabi had his thin wings of moonlight then The Ram's span the sky, running from his dress and streaking behind. As though the thing within melts, bleeding from its garment confine.

Then it bubbles, expanding, bulging into fluid flame ready to explode. The Doken sees day, Pescha is illuminated and twinkling as the dew of the pine glitters, sparkling with its new light. The Ram Burbles draws his judgment, letting it leak and spew, throwing himself into Kakabi.

Like dawn, the sound hangs back to the spectacle of false day blooming. The blast cracks way above, like a million things smash into one another simultaneously. A sound like a tree exploding thunders and the burst hits her, sending Pescha spinning as the pines approach, and she covers up. Like when she fights, she cannot be kept central, her figure spinning in and out of sight. Firing without anchoring herself is near suicidal, she may rip herself in two, yet she cannot hope to catcher herself at this hight or speed. She waits, until the trees which shudder and sway are just below before she shoots. When she does, it is to send herself rolling, to curl through the branches which knife and spear, so many noises and so little to see echoing, as the detonation rings and the green snaps. She waits until she is within the forest before she fires and she fires wildly, like she plays with some instrument rather than her life.

Pescha holds an arm over her eyes and sends a burst sideward, a whimper escaping pale lips.

When she wakes, it is to pulsing fire. She has not slept long, for Kakabi still struggles, grounded and ablaze, screaming. Her vision toys with every shade of heat. She forces herself up, fingers laced with intricate cuts. Leant against a trunk, she lets her thoughts resume, lets temperature and sense soak back in. Her eyes flutter and see the forest ablaze.

Through the treeline, Kakabi squirms. Writhing against that which walks its stomach. That which approaches the head across its own body, smouldering in its outpour. Pescha watches The Ram Burbles, seething amid his storm, magma oozing from his dress and burrowing itself through the metal scales. The flames plume and the Humeda screeches, every attempt to snap met with a face full of fire, the snakelike appearance melting to the bare scaffolding and cables within.

He walks, needles making their way up the terrified machine, ram horns gleaming as the robed silhouette stalks, embittered, and burning. Savouring his devastation, which smokes and splutters, such hate in his figure.

From her shadows Pescha watches, blue fatigued, before she turns to Our Last Limit. Without even a backward glance, she slips into the forestry, disappearing amid the pine, flicking her bleeding fingers and then her hair from her face.

- *FAUSCHENHERST TERRIROTY* -
OUR LAST LIMIT

A face of steel, it is a wall so high. To look up is to see civilisation against a moon, a distant world of lights, yet should she reach out, she will fell the metal breast of a fallen ship, long dead and drained of its innards. This postern entrance, a backdoor hatch once for insignificant personal now winks, a faint red ebb drawing her attention as she stalks through the undergrowth. Now she stands and admires the lights far above. Even here, against the greatest of shelters, the storm harasses her, drawing the bush in battering arcs but she works on the way in, figuring its mechanics while the dark wails amid its pines. Eventually, she draws her blade and thrusts through the slit, levering with a shove, lacerated fingers stinging but still she barges, until the door cranks open, and she hauls herself through. An abiding grimace holds to her expression. This morning, she awoke in that abandoned town against the Matsumasi and Doken. She grumbles to herself as she slips in.

The Ram Burbles had mentioned dissent and protest and she had heard rumours herself, so she is cautious, as she turns corners and peers down corridors, unaware and coming in the dead of night. If she wishes to see in these dark avenues, she herself will be seen, her sights brilliant even under the hardest of squints, and she is careful regardless. This is a nether of walkways and exposed mechanics, pipes busted and, even as she prowls deeper and deeper, she finds creeping plants and pockets of shrub, swollen under dribbling tubage, this derelict zone long since dredged and now abandoned. Flights of staircases and hull wounds allow her to pass easily, although to where she is unsure. Her vague ascent heads for streets she has never seen, but as she rises quickly, spurred by the throbbing ache of too many wounds to consider, she starts to hear noise above. The clatter of shifted weight, reverberating through vast, empty hangars. Spaces designed for the masses, now made gardens of the struggling verdant and debris. Their roofs collapsed, and organs splayed.

This craft was designed for transport. She can see it in tramways and storage haulers, built to allow people and equipment to be hurriedly manoeuvred from vessel to Kyut at pace. Now, sound carries across these vacant spaces of the interior, bouncing throughout. Vents blown open by copious green chime and when she nears, clarity brings question. From a vague churning she now hears haulage, things dragged and feet dragging their luggage, the resounding clamour seemingly spread across multiple levels. She ascends, sword sheathed but fists balled; within Fauschenherst territory, Pescha scarce hears of anyone openly retaliating against Klernsteiga. Openly retaliating and winning. She reaches an unfastened and half open hatch, hurried footfall and muffled voices audible from many on the other side. One hand brushes the other, a slashed digit against the switch, but she imagines Pack One in this place and lets her touch fall, instead pulling her horizontally stored blade forward so that she may slip through. She holds the grip a second longer, and peeks inside, blue peeping into the corridor beyond.

Like a child's den but of harsher, tastefully garish lights and colour, they have set up a supply line within the sublevel. She has heard only loose radio chatter of nonconformity, yet Pescha knows she now looks upon Our Last Limit's protestors, as they walk boxes and improvised carts packed with the apparatus of their dissent, a trade of rebellion bustling amid the gutters. She steps out, letting the hatch swing shut behind, having to step back to allow the protestors through, hands laden with cans and bottles. Their attentions otherwise taken.

  They wear masks and goggles, like the gadgetry of chemical and industrial work, but those who have set up shop here talk and exchange, their respirators hanging from their necks and shelves as they organise the chaos above. It drains as sound through momentarily open compartments and pathways, sealed when not in use. She can see, at the far end of this stretched but slight corridor, a grid onto street level- it is hastily pulled aside, someone collapses in, and they replace the frame and hurry to their nearby comrades. It is busy, speed a weapon as crucial as any tool they cradle, and while she may not have emerged into the thick of battle, she can still hear things dulled by distance. The pop of canisters, and loudspeaker callings muffled, ever present.

She needs a guide, into Kenidomo Country. Through sector Zero, Double-Four, Nine, Three, Five and on, deep into the Kyut. If her quest was vague until the Doken then beyond, she has but the name of Relief Ukibiki, the Nomad hotel where Emile resides, and the sun. she cannot turn to one of these dissidents, the opposition to Fauschenherst control, and ask, standing there amid their cluster, for another Klernsteiga. But she stands on the cusp of known dominion, and with nowhere else to go. And she cannot ask any random Nomad, one just passing through, or aiding the Rautbergen here. She'll need the best.

She will not risk defeat. Better then, not to ask for a Nomad of rioters, but for a Klernsteiga of their sibling Rautbergen. First, she must find them.

A quick hand snags the collar of a passing demonstrator, his eyes bulging against the throttle, a low croak choking as he turns to blue-eyed solemnity. Not giving him time to see Pescha's kit the Nomad asks for the Raut's line, dazzling bar-lights suspended overhead to illuminate the passage. As another rioter passes, oblivious but with bags stuffed, the throttled tells Pescha to follow him.

She tails the man with the backpack, pockets filled with makeshift equipment and head encased in a helmet and breathing apparatus. She stalks until he reaches the rear of that commercial underground stretch and pushed a grid aside, hauling himself up and into the dark. She keeps close, at his feet when they disappear and she does the same, jumping to catch the rim and lifting herself through.

The breeze meets her gently, sweeping the hair from her face, and she looks up to a street, deserted. A main road, one built for a stream of vehicles although somewhere they have stopped, disrupted by the night's terrors. So desperate and sudden is her solitude, so abstract, an individuality uncanny, that she looks for the man who dashes the open stretch, stooped low and darting for the backstreets. He makes to an alley and slips through. She watches, half submerged in the sublevel and half observing this emptied avenue. She heaves herself up, all things that same midnight indigo as a great commotion elsewhere channels between the buildings, like a diversion to assure her loneliness. She can see faint lights flashing and hear those same calls down the road, vague silhouettes dotted amid a swirl of colour and distant noise. She stands in the middle of that city street, shops and stalls shuttered, with signs powered down, the symbology of a foreign dialect hanging. She can tell their messages, of food stands and stores. She would expect them intense and radiant this late. There are so many, suspended on outstretched struts and bars, but even the fabric banners, colours bright and scrawl enthusiastic, seem hushed here. Like wavering too wildly or being too obvious may upset those causing chaos afar. Her sights have stolen the lights for their own, and she casts them up the street, to indistinct discord raving. She wonders where a Rautbergen officer would find themself amid all this.

A construct that grazes the night sky, he stands by the window of a superstructure, overwatch for the defence below. The room has been emptied, once an open home unit. Now it hosts only a few and their computers, the man of rank watching with his assistants at their screens, muttering against the disorder beyond. Colours to catch the eye, of warning and offense flashing against those of fire and gas, cracking at street level, they make his space their own. Bouncing off blacked out windows and glass shutters, the opposite tower reflecting the scene of madness.

The captain looks as almost every Raut does. Like some apocalyptic condottiere, their freelance attire is always adopted, in great coats of worn shades, luggage hauled in their immense packs, their equipment often improvised, always ramshackle and well used. The man in command leans against the frame and stares, gaze careful, but reserved. His hands hold behind his back and they tell of a desperation, for now, out of reach.

Just behind, she opens her eyes.

Maybe he thinks it's the opposite window, for he squints with sudden alarm, but he sees a reflection and spins to her, the whole room pulsing with that sudden start. His staff call out- they've been staring at harsh monitors against the dark room so their vision is dim, but she points to Pack One and the sword against her waist. Their fear of assault wavers, a slight bitterness of surprise lingering. They mumble and frown back to their work, stares holding.

The captain addresses her as Klausch[14], the honorary title of both armies of the Fauschenherst. Klausch Klernsteiga and Klausch Rautbergen; the common Raut and common Nomad do not outrank one another. Pescha smiles in greeting, the reflected shades of disarray flaring against pale features, and asks if he commands here. His personnel speak through radios and add to charts, busying themselves as the wanderer and

---

[14] *Klausch* : An honorary title bestowed to all Rautbergen and Klernsteiga.

the captain talk.

He says he does, for now, and asks what she needs. Hopeful in his words, he seems eager to give direction, but she is not here to supplement his line.

Brows waver when she asks for his best Nomad, his backup maintained at request. His pause proceeds only a nod, and he waves over her shoulder to a passing Raut, who looks from his tablet and approaches. The captain asks Pescha what she needs him for, their point Klernsteiga. He says that Kausherm[15], a name Pescha doesn't know, has ordered he remain within the city. Pescha shrugs, looking to the summoned Raut when he nears. She says it's just radio chatter someone wants him to hear. Reports. She'll be out of their way come morning.

The captain tells the Rautbergen to take her to L eight-double zero-one, offering them both great hooded coats to move through the crowd unseen. It reminds Pescha of the one she had taken from Glermvender, that torn place flickering against this high-rise megalopolis, as she angles her sword to rest inconspicuously and follows her guide, who descends the stairs with just a nod in address. A few others dot the lower floors, but they serve only as auxiliary, watching the violence outside with their rifles perched against the sills. It does not pass her that they carry Humeda killers, the standard GE. Twenty Three Lautreisgefer[16], the Raut's Laut, instead of anti-personnel arms. Tracer sluggers, meant to cut through the machine hide and be easily visible in flight, their shots glow, for the recoil of firing such a projectile can rip a shoulder apart. It could be considered a testament of escalations, but she thinks otherwise. The Rautbergen here are simply undersupplied for their task.

On the lowers floor the makeshift garrison is barred, a shuttered and locked door guarded by a group in silence, listening, waiting for someone to just fall against the block. They see her, her guide, and they move to open up, quiet in their preparations should a rioter try and force

---

[15] *Kaurscherm* : Commander of the Fauschenherst O-Third Wolstbattallon and a senior figure in the Fauschenherst. He now commands the garrison at Our Last Limit and orchestrates the drive into sector Zero, Double-Four, Nine, Three, Five.

[16] *Goritekaga* : The primary supplier of anti-machine weaponry to the Fauschenherst. Situated in the Heimatus of Alexada and competing with K.A.G in weapons production, their specialised slug-style rounds and bulky rifles have armed practically all Rautbergen since Sect 2. The company's head, Gher Vatachinen, is a senior supervisor in the Fauschenherst, and his company's designs are rooted in blueprints salvaged from the Fauscherin. The G before anti-machine firearm names is the company's stamp.

through. Pescha's escort turns to her and pulls over his cowl, as she does in unison, the throb of vivid anarchy pulsing its crazed shades through the gap underneath the door. Pulling her cover closed, he tells her to keep close, not to interact with anyone, in her case, not even to make eye contact, and to keep her blade and kit hidden. They make sure they're never far from where the Nomad she seeks is staying, so it won't be far.

The mayhem takes so many forms, it is difficult to walk in a straight line, for something seems to occur between every person. Gas canisters and bottled fire, weapons fashioned from construction equipment and masked figures running, the two coated shapes move from the Rautbergen blockade, pushing against the stream of rioters who flood as though orchestrated, falling back and pushing on in waves. The lights intended for night remain inactive, but it is brighter here than any day, with burning pools and improvised illuminations of those neon tones blaring, the noise both a constant approach and retreat of battering and shouts, dissidents calling out and loudspeakers blaring. She stays behind the Raut who shoves through the mass and brakes for the clearer rear, supplies organised in pursuit of the main assault. Debris scattered, only the odd or injured rioter remains at the back. Like her sights, a brilliant blue is cast against hard reds, bold and bright and catching fumes and spilt fuel.

As they cross, she looks at the chaos, a cloaked figure with her azure eyes, gas like its own fog which chases the breeze, framed in the many colours of dissent. Protestors run at and from the Rautbergen, masks cracked and holding bruises. Her guide calls to her, waving her on, and they slip into the backstreets.

It started with the CUPD. The city's College of Urban Power Distribution, when they noticed the self-sufficiency and possible opportunities of Our Last Limit, should the restrictions on its power consumption be wavered by Fauschenherst generals. To ensure the security and longevity of this forefront, constraints were placed on what power the people could access, given that they only used power which had already existed within the fallen craft. The students proposed a withdrawal of these regulations, to allow the city to better grow and become prosperous. According to the current protestors, the proposed meeting was declined, the Rautbergen tells her, as they traverse the alleys, on the grounds that the ship was Fauschenherst property. There was no discussion to be had at all.

It got worse when the Fauschenherst presence increased, as the city became evermore the forefront for the push into Zero, Double-Four, Nine, Three, Five. A force previously for general governance became a military presence, sapping additional power from the people. A point of interest, the Fauschenherst could drive into Kenidomo Country here with this stronghold to its rear, so more and more soldiers came. Inevitably, there were more Humeda sightings, and commotion within and around the metropolis. Pescha must understand, these people hold no allegiance to the group which abandoned them upon the Kyut, as that first Sect One, over a hundred years ago.

One day, an automaton attacked. The Sinne district, he says, and what would normally be acceptable casualties proved a threat, in the eyes of the generals, against their new thrust. It prompted the construction of a military base, located off the Liue-Gho district, physically on the ground of Kenidomo Country. The equipment and resources used were unpaid for, and the CUPD was forced to redirect the power specifically, without compensation. Already, the Raut mumbles, students started to rouse.

The Rautbergen are not an enforcement organisation, he tells her. They are not equipped to build bollards or hold back protests, yet they could but watch even those most peaceful of demonstrations, held before the base construction, Quiaxin Jiipan. Placards and banners, the threat of dissent was just as much of a fear to the commanders as losing Our Last Limit any other way, so its lead officer, Kausherm, made his own proposal. The Fauschenherst would provide construction resources, things needed to physically build complexes and housing, in return for the people's cooperation, until the Fauschenherst could better advance and fortify a position deeper in this new frontier. A plea almost facetious, for those of Our Last Limit knew the Rautbergen would be here a while, their ever-growing base the predicate of a prolonged occupation.

Still hopeful, the CUPD students again requested a dialogue with Fauschenherst officials. While not immediately turned down, Kausherm and his staff stalled, in the hopes of having Quiaxin Jiipan complete before any talks began.

Her guide stammers, pausing halfway up a backstreet staircase, glancing wearily at her. His theatrics are drawn, his history spoken passionately as she follows, hand on the railing.

Two incidents will follow, he breathes, both intrinsically linked, with consequences unimaginable upon the city.

The Red Mangusha Crisis honours the day when a colossus attacked the Liue-Gho area, the right forewing of the ship which mounts Kenidomo Country. The edge most buildings have sights upon the Rautbergen base. A tower block is levelled and one hundred and thirty die, he says, to an automaton named for its bright colour and a word, in the tongue of Our Last Limit. It means something like a startled awakening, or having your eyes opened to the obvious. Red revelation.

To the people, the Red Mangusha Crisis revealed the apparent ineptitude of the Fauschenherst, the Raut states, despite the death toll being relatively low, for the risk. Once the machine was at last repelled, increased protest spread into the streets. Targeted personnel were directly harassed. Once again, the students plead for a dialogue.

Kausherm responded that the Rautbergen expeditionary force would not withdraw, and power would still be needed to finish the construction of their vanguard post.

That was it for the CUPD students. Days later, within the fourth block of their main campus, an attempt was staged, to manually cut the energy supply to Quiaxin Jiipan. An attempt now fabled as the Fourth Block Incident.

Other pupils, recognising the attempt and the inevitable response, transformed their academy into a fortress of its own, turning the place upside down and barricading the complex before the Rautbergen arrived. They set the precedent of using the construction equipment offered to them by Kausherm in their skirmishes, great bollards as perimeters with rods and bricks made weapons.

Escalations of escalations, the small Rautbergen team came underequipped, thinking they came unexpected. They were ordered to push into campus anyway, their commanders citing a threat of Fauschenherst information and logistics possibly falling into student hands. Those students, technical pupils, wore the masks used in the study of their home's underbelly, and fought against the Rautbergen force, which slogged to the fourth block and rose the floors. They found eight students, still struggling to cut Quiaxin's supply, and then were put under siege themselves as they tried to haul the pupils out. The subsequent, and ignored, ultimatum sent by Kausherm, the counter siege of the Rautbergen to save their fellows and their eight students, and the use of chemical deterrents against the pupils, became a city-wide incident. What started as unorganised retaliation in the Kenidomo Country-bordering districts spread to most of the youth across Our Last Limit, who saw their little and wary luxury under physical assault from the Fauschenherst, those who had made such things commodities.

The eight students became living martyrs, symbols of the ignorance of the Fausch, the attacking of the CUPD campus and the Fourth Block Incident, along with the Red Mangusha Crisis, creating what has become, her guide proclaims, an effective state of war. For the Fauschenherst, an ignorant and dangerous separatist endeavour, spurred by students drunk on the stability of Our Last Limit, unable to comprehend the threats facing their home. For those inhabitants, a rejection of Fauschenherst authority, consumption, and expansionism.

Her Rautbergen escort states, as they sweep through into another deserted road, just she and him, both still hooded under their greatcoats, that for some upon the Kyut, the Humeda are not just the enemy. Some revere them, and some here within Fauschenherst zones have never seen the machines. Some, they cannot even comprehend. Muttering, he wonders if this is what they're dying for. An example, the fruit of their efforts, Our Last Limit stands firm against the border. Yet they throw bricks and stones, and act as though this city shelters only themselves.

She asks him what he thinks.

He just shrugs, and says that, for him, the difference between this place and being out in the wastes is that here, there are walls to hide behind. He will not let this place fall easily, or else be forsaken to shooting tracers into storms again. Seeing the round fly and smack against something, to watch it turn his way and leer.

By now they near where the captain foretold: the storehouse of their lead Klernsteiga, a high-rise cubic and modern, the image of dystopian sophistication in architecture. It is clean dark walls and great windows, spanning an entire side of each level. Flats, apartments of luxury, and where in peace it may glow as a black marble obelisk of opulence, even from far below Pescha can see it has been made a battleground, occupied by the rioters. They string their banners, and throw firebombs from the lower levels.

Its entrance is upon another main street, clear of conflict now but they can see the remains, that the CUPD-lead protestors were the victors. Pescha and the Raut approach, burst canisters and broken glass strewn atop the general debris of dissent. Litter and abandoned bollards, a few pupils sift through, establishing their supply line as more climb from the underground- a relatively new tactic, her guid whispers, although one quickly becoming an essential doctrine of the student methods. They cross with heads low, keeping to the pavement and keeping quiet, passing by the protestors whose opinion seems to be that if they aren't attacked, then they aren't near opposition. Nobody stops them, each too occupied in their mischief, but inside Pescha can hear commotion and she ascends close to her guide, keeping her sights to herself, following the Raut's heels.

There is no fight in here, but as that last building had been made for the captain this complex has become an observation point too, as students lean from windows and cast flaming bottles into the streets. Calling to their comrades in opposite towers while they fly their allegiances, loyalties painted against fabric steamers and thrust into the night. They pass an elevator; it has become a stockpile for whatever floor is in need, so instead they rise the flights. Each level is occupied by revolutionaries, who bust open locks to already fled homes, pilling their arsenals against the glass walls, smashing with that repurposed equipment as they light their bombs to drop. People pass, masked and covered, identities a veil of anonymous invulnerability. The energy is a constant, pulsing mix of furore and caution, so thick that Pescha can slip by unnoticed, rising higher and higher.

And then it's quiet. Absolutely silent.

Like her ears have popped, they reach a floor unoccupied. She can sense, even before the Raut speaks, this purposeful avoidance by the dissidents. Not a scrap or flag, he closes the door softly behind, the noise below barred. The melancholy welcome of a murmuring air-conditioner is all to be heard. As it was meant to be, this level is untouched, a long corridor of ice-white lighting, cool and clean, doors at either side to follow the stretch down. None blown open, each unscarred by assault. Yet there is only one which she watches, as her guardian walks her down.

The only flat with lights from the inside. Soft purple, catching dark varnished pinewood, an entrance fashioned in that which ripped her still stinging hands. As though someone with sights like Pescha's but pink spies their approach, through the gap under the door.

He tells her, keeping his voice low, that there are lots of Nomads who pass through Our Last Limit, as the most prominent border post between Fauschenherst territory and Kenidomo Country. But finding one willing to stay, let alone one willing to aid against the city's people, and capable of making an impactful difference, was a task the generals here simply did not have the time, or the resources needed, to assess. He stresses the significance of this place, that it should not be forgotten. He thinks that this city may be where the Fauschenherst has its eye most favourably, and the number of generals involved gave them the authority to haul in the man best suited for this work. That doesn't mean he wants to be here, the Raut adds, or that the officers on the ground wish to work with him. He says that a Nomad who kills people over machines is one thing, unusual but necessary. A decorated Klernsteiga of this calibre is another.

Pescha frowns, looking his way, and asks if he's medalled. Her pathfinder, through these unknown territories.

For a second, he pretends not to have heard. But he glances, sees her staring at the side of his head, and says she should know this Nomad, to whom she is delivering her message. When Pescha doesn't respond, he says yes. This Nomad has been awarded.

They stop outside that lit apartment. Door unlocked, slightly ajar.
He says he's a Nomad every Rautbergen fears, fears falling under their command. Tales tell of his sibling disregard for all life, disregard of any allegiance. His calling here by the generals is of twin reverence and dismay, as a testament to both his strength, and mercilessness, for he has no plight in his work. Offset, amid even the aberrant.
Aberrant and abhorred, yet these are the woes of Rautbergen. To a fellow Nomad, there are synonyms evermore cruel.

The air conditioning hums to itself, like a butler in waiting. He knocks and pushes for her, standing aside as the door swings open.
He introduces Klausch Klernsteiga L eight-double zero-one the Kamakara "Mincemeat".

She blinks, unfocussed, as words take sight. One of four. The Kite of the Kamakara. Each of the clan has met Small Hand himself. Is of Small Hand's clan.

    Fuck, thinks Pescha.

He's so tall.

Every blink is a slap. Every breath a crushing weight. His gaze a choking hold, which turns to meet her stare. His apartment is the image of that dystopia high-rise, window wall to frame a Nomad who perches centrally. A great screen is hung on one side to project the churning colours which tint the space. Dark, yet laced with hues of faint, bordering lilac.

The Klernsteiga sitting there is a monochrome fanatic, black and white like Pescha, but his is styled and ruthless. Hair thick and sheered around his cheekbones, it is so white it adopts whatever shades are nearby, and as Pescha's skin speaks of home amid the snows so does his, yet it is of a harsher, crueller breed.

His features are slight. Like a knife's edge or a hound's, very much like a wolf's, sharp and cutting. High cheekbones. Eyes thin but wide. Malicious. Neck too long, too thin. His mouth a wound, broad and vicious.

Harsher, for against those frozen tones is cut black, joined to already edged expressions. Prosthetics, half a jaw, like someone ran a finger from his bottom lip and down, to the neck, so making the left side dark, of mechanical ink. And it is a carnal replacement, skeletal and dogged, of blackened bone and sinew. Like the skin was stripped and what is below metal plated, matte black and evil. Machine teeth sharpened. The pinnacle of Fauschenherst prosthesis work. Pescha sees the same for his right arm, ligaments and claws, a false replacement from the elbow. Left of the jaw, right arm from the joint. His profile is rough but angular, scratched insignia and make-do attire combined with that designed, fitted, and bought. Pescha has never heard of a Nomad with money, for none needed, so none wanted, pay. None she's ever met.

Mincemeat's head falls to Pescha, the woman of vivid blue staring from the door to him of cold white. The fear he induces is crippling. His lips remain part parted, his sleeves rolled to expose the connection of his dextral limb, joined faultlessly. Both look side on, Pescha's azure through a slight squint, Mincemeat's slaughtering look like a sneer without the mouth. He doesn't look built to smile. His mouth is too big for his face. Pescha has never wanted to run so badly.

Because he's that character of mania. Before he speaks, stands, Pescha knows she should turn. Predatory and seething, to snap and slash by impulse. Danger, painted as stark as the tones he adopts.

A disregard of others, for none other could challenge him, yet he may break and let that bleeding lust loose with equal cruelty.

The Rautbergen leaves, not bothering to mask his instinct to go. Mincemeat doesn't even glance at him. Pescha steps into the room, slowly, so cautiously, lowering her hood. The Kamakara Klernsteiga cannot take his eyes off those of his guest, which look over the room while she closes the door. Night breeze draws the faint echoes up from below.
    Pescha turns to the white-haired Nomad. Now not a single part of her wants to move.
    She asks for a favour.
    Mincemeat remarks how beautiful Pescha's eyes are.

The Kite of the Kamakara. Not even the Auberherst, Klernsteiga generals who command Rautbergen Brigades, possess this accolade. Its criteria are so crude. Where medals have their affiliate, suicidal demands, the obligation of this most revered token is ambiguous, a qualification vague. It's for when commanders meet and see a field, and there are no words for the brutality they witness. Small Hand's sole survival of Sect Two, alone and abandoned. His rescue of the otherwise similarly doomed landing of Set Three. His plight, to forever be immortalised amid so many honours. None can compare. There may be a fourth and then a third, and a third and then a second, but the difference between that forerunner and his kin is crushing of so much steel.
    Yet, there are a few. Their Kite demands that crisis be averted.
    They cannot be prospects, for if Small Hand fell then so would the Fauschenherst. That clan of four has never had a set purpose, it merely aligns names of unnerving records. They, of the Kite of the Kamakara. The greatest Klernsteiga to fight.

And this one is so high. Infamously so. Mincemeat stands, a danseur rising, that faultless figure of strength. Seven foot tall. He must be. Towering over Pescha, his hair fresh and choppy and wild, like the scruff of a mut. He does not entertain question, and Pescha does not ask again, as the prosthetic Klernsteiga looks out over Our Last Limit. The city fluctuating through its spectrum of shy building lights, hiding from the pounding thrum below.

He asks if Pescha has eaten. He talks like he's never feared. So direct. So callous.

Pescha says she has not. It is like a shroud surrounds. It demands submission.

The Kamakara turns wholly, and asks for her sobriquet.

Pescha, says Pescha.

The white-haired man says he likes Mince. Then he tells Pescha to eat with him. Pescha surveys the room, there is no kitchen here, but Mince gestures to the open, sliding, wall-length window which drops onto an adjacent rooftop, and beckons that she follow. In that moment there is no question that Pescha will come. Out, onto the heights of Our Last Limit.

She has never seen a place like this. Feats of engineering, Pescha knows constructs of such scale only in the machines. Mince's tower overlooks the spectacle and the two walk in silence, watching the chaos laced upon webwork roadways, pockets of lights bursting and shifting, flowing like bright energy through a motherboard. The noise is aethereal, of pinprick war raged against the ear, speckled to dapple the city in every area. It feels like each district is gripped by turmoil. Frenzied and brooding, a state of faceless violence, the people of Our Last Limit have no sense of pride in their home. Set against the mountains and the flatland atop, these citizens only know what will happen if they do not protest. The students here can see what is being made of their home. What this Kyut is. They balance atop their ship, a float above the waves, and see that this place is not made for civilisation and colossal constructs. The colossi will not abide pretenders.

They are alone up here, but they walk the pathways of raiders, the protesters having done to the heights what they made of the subsections. Construction equipment, promised as compensation is made weaponry, bridging rooftops with a presiding mesh, impromptu lattices to connect the city both above and below. Tents pitched against rows of vents, lights established upon desks lined with bottles and pikes yet there are none to see, and Mince does not worry, guiding his new company at ease. Hands in the pockets of a shaggy, waist length and loose coat, a worn pattern printed, he takes the lead, crossing thin wooden boards made bridges between tightly packed buildings, far disconnected from that below.

They head for the tallest spire in sight, a timber hut propped atop a tower even taller than Mince's. A faint prick of light from afar, when Pescha asks what it is Mince turns to walk backward, addressing it as a restaurant for passing Klernsteiga, built in a place only they could reach. Beset by modernity and steel, the cabin looks a Nomad itself. Like something from the Timber Isles, Pescha thinks, that stands up here to watch the city work, admiring design from its perch.

    Mince doesn't turn back. Citypeak, he calls it.

This is bad, Pescha thinks, for she scarce listens to his words. She cannot venture with Mincemeat. He of so much renown. Stationed, given orders to remain. Pescha could have never thought of this.

The consequences of this mount against her mind. Mince knows him. He has met him in person.

    Keep quiet, Pescha tells herself. Eat, and then leave, regardless of what the white-haired man says.

Citypeak rounds into view, and they ascend, slipping through open glass and rising what appears to be abandoned, sky high flats, still under construction. Mince walks as though alone, stepping out onto the bar rooftop, wood hitched with bolts and rope. Made for a lakeside, Klernsteiga built this place and now it serves them, soft amber and the call of comfort ebbing through slatted windows. A tavern and a temple made one, the smell consumes her, for it is of a scent which alone rewards their walk. Sunken and part buckled, the Nomad restaurant greets them, indifferent to the violence between their admirers and their allies underneath.

    Old filament bulbs hum and crops grow against sills, crammed in overfull window pots. The interior is a Nomadic mass of tables and characters, the likes of which Pescha has scarce seen. Such a crucial crossing point, from the doorway she observes a mass of people from many climates. Knights of every order, they talk and eat as a conglomerate drunk on the foreign pleasure of company, some resigned to chew hurriedly and in silence, but all at tables packed. Already Mince has abandoned her, disappearing into the crowd. All who notice the half-jaw come pretend they don't. Parting his way like an invisible force pushes, they maintain absolutely that there is no one there. It's strange to watch, how suddenly and fervently they stress that they must move. It's innate. As inbuilt as breathing.

She knows she should leave. But she will not go before daybreak, and when food steams at such mass she must eat. Only eat, then leave to find her sleep. Amid this crowd none may single her out, the complexity of things strapped to so many wonderers tangle all sights, but she keeps hers low still. A counter makes meals and lays them atop a bar, for passers-by to collect- supplied by the citizens, she guesses, it is evermore a divide between the Rautbergen and the Klernsteiga, as those foot soldiers below are berated while their sparse, ambling counterparts feast. Their title of Klausch exists for a reason, it may be easy for those many to fall beneath those few and far ranging. It is a custom for passing Nomads to assist, if not lead, any Raut crew in need whom they cross.

The food is that of the Kyut, in grains and vegetables but it is warm and fragrant, golden as this place is in its soft lighting. Designed by those of the wastes, Citypeak crowns an architectural masterpiece as an odd amalgamation, a mix of so many comforts. Pescha stands at its centre, herbs and produce spilling from their pots; a warm and relaxed place, so cosy that it is unnerving, for shivers to her have always meant but one chasing cold. She walks for a chair, benches and stools made seats and she crosses that open entrance, doors strung always open. She glances out, a plate of rice and dressings and adornments piled high in her hand.

A single building, looking on from the dark.

Quiaxin Jiipan, its lights few but defining. The fenced structure to mark the true end of Fauschenherst territory, where beyond Rautbergen march. Civilisation and settlements unrecognised, unoccupied, but communities, whole super cities, built by those of Sect One descent.

And it is to Kenidomo Country she looks. Not that Fauschenherst instillation, but the darkness encasing, a plateau maybe once just more of Dodtohmet, had it not been carved with the contents between. Within these borders the Humeda still roam, crush and tear. Hjordiis, annihilating Glermvender. Masago, ripping Islanders apart. That unnamed feline whom she slew in the dying light of the Matsumasi, beset by corpses. Kakabi, who would slice a forest in two, and burn for its trouble.

Yet out there, she does not know what she will find.

No, she corrects. She does.

Mincemeat appears at her side.

Looking out also, into night indivisible between land and sky. For a moment something plays over Pescha's brows, a tint of expression that Mince tries to catch, but when he turns the azure sights only stare into darkness, black framed by well-lit and warm woods. To say it is as though the shadows stare back at her is needless, she does not doubt that a Humeda may watch the city now, stalking the drop from flatland to forest. A titan could stand, a behemoth overlooking Our Last Limit, and she would not know. Even still, it is not to the automaton she looks. She sees through, and into the storms. Still so far. A way to wander. Yet she does approach.

A machine finger taps her plate. Overhead, she is told that'll get cold.

Mince leads to a table and they sit, five Nomads already eating but the Kamakara barges room and none of the Klernsteiga notice, shuffling to make space with mouths full and conversation maintained. Pescha can imagine the stories told in this place, one of the few yet sacred safehouses offered to their branch. Still clad in their kit, she sees rifles and gears, the equipment and appliances to facilitate their destruction. The most infamous of their table is the only one vaguely dressed for a meal. If Pescha's plate was full then Mince's goads, an insult to all other so-called dinners, and he eats from it ravenously, not sparing for courtesy or conversation as it continues around. Twin wooden utensils are ripped from their paper and used to shovel his food at mass. Pescha notices that all others eat with forks, none here will remain long enough to learn the art which Mince has, ruined by his voracity. Pescha watches from the corner of her eye as that half-and-half jaw devours what that half-and-half-arm feeds. Pescha eats quickly too. She knows what will happen. Their intrusion demands conversation, and as all erase the mere notion that there are seven at their stools, it isn't long until one Klernsteiga looks over, smiling to blue-eyes.

He asks if she saw Dai Nakari, too. If she passed up that portion of the Shae Doken. As though she'd been listening.

Mouth bulging, she swallows hard, wiping her lips alongside Mince, stooped over his plate, only a few stages of reason from opening his jaws parallel and sweeping the food into his face.

The clicking of sticks is rapid as Pescha says she did.

This conversative Nomad, he wears beads around his neck, and remarks how impressive it was, but wonders how it walked. He says that during his ascent, he saw no great craters to mark the wake of that beast.

For a second, Pescha is completely blank.

She says she saw Mehimu Heshimawa too, the boar of the

Matsumasi.

    He with the beads nods, telling her the boar was felled by Small Hand, long before Sect Three landed. Someone else to his left murmurs, their mouth full, that the same can be said of Nakari. At her side, Mince just eats, lost to any discussion. He nears the end of his pile, and glances over shoulder toward more.

Their conversation condenses again as Pescha is left to chew, thoughts melting amid the warmth and hospitality. She wonders what Relief Ukibiki will be like, when she finally reaches its door. Fables and a common perception, the image of the Nomad hotel is one so alike to this in her head, and she knows that building was similarly made by its hosted Klernsteiga. Already half constructed, when the Nomads came and heard that it was theirs, they took to aiding the build with the furore of a group who never had a home before, bringing their scraps of wood and torn up sections of Humeda and bolting them to the scaling tower. She has heard of a beautiful conglomerate, banners of Nomadic groups and territories suspended against corrugated steel and plaster walls, wooden frames sagging with the weight.

    When the others start talking of destinations, she hears them speak of where they must wander. Some into Kenidomo Country, some into Fauschenherst territory. One speaks of The Frown, how he will hug its coast in search of machines, but when they pause, she throws in her remark, and asks what they know of Ukibiki.

The hotel is run by a boy, the Nomad opposite says. Migimidian, he's called. Not a Klernsteiga, but when he appeared and started construction, Nomads asked and then spread word of a house, being built for those passing by. Like this place, he states, it is built where only Klernsteiga can reach, but when they did, they came in droves, and these are not the Nomads one may find keeping to Fauschenherst land. They ventured to the stone base and brought with them the enthusiasm of something to do, save for walking and fighting. They took to the project in aid of Migimidian without his request. Their narrator says he's never been himself, but he's met Nomads who have, and they tell of Klernsteiga who have defected to work the complex, hanging their kits for aprons and brooms. It's a big problem, she's told, and it's not hard to see why on either side. A sense of home for those fighting to secure it, open and welcoming. It's why the Fauschenherst doesn't recognise Migimidian, or

Relief Ukibiki, as allies to its cause. The illegal Seven-Seven[17] server there stolen from Faurscherin[18] ruins doesn't help. He's harboured every kind of Klernsteiga imaginable, Migimidian has, and many would defend the hotel better than any Fauschenherst command.

The man with the beads asks Pescha if that's where she's going, to Relief Ukibiki.

When Pescha says she's headed out that way, a sudden frown befalls he who told of Migimidian, and he asks why. He looks her up and down, clad in coat with hands bound and shins booted, fingers still stained and marred. Maybe he suspects her of Fauschenherst order. Sent to exact that very bounty on Ukibiki.

Starting to eat again, she will not let this conversation wander. She says she's going to someone there, someone ill and stranded. He of beads asks if it's a Nomad but she shrugs, and says he's just a child. Again, worry flares and the Klernsteiga opposite stares straight, as though he tries to figure whether she's joking or not, Migimidian still lingering on his lips. Hurriedly, Pescha tells that it's nobody they'd know.

It's a boy who has fallen very sick. He stumbled to Ukibiki for aid.

The boy's name is Emile.

Pescha remembers the day she came to the Kyut.

A Nomad escort, the ship she flew in on was a detail, sent to guard a craft of supplies down to its designated landing sector, for the Sect Four effort. She'd never seen the Kyut before, nor the machines. None of them had. She can remember, amid sidelong rain, when they were hauled from the sky. When the Humeda leapt and tore their descent apart. The feeling of it, being thrown as though they were a stone, bound

---

[17] *Seven-Seven* : Referencing servers hooked into the Faurscherin main machine system. The technology was originally developed to give farmers on The Orbital access to Faurscherin agricultural records, and to allow them to instantly communicate with the Fauschenherst. Their anomalous access to Faurscherin data records lead to their confiscation and strict outlawing by the Fauschenherst. Owning one is a treasonous act, and greatly compromises classified Faurscherin documents and machine systems.

[18] *Faurscherin* : The vast ship (see *Kantenlaufer*) from which all that's left of mankind traces its lineage. Its remains are the hub of the Fauschenherst and the last bastion between the Kyut and the Fauschenherst worlds.

by a string and spun. When they crashed, when they were stomped on and torn open, like things hiding in shells, when claws carved through mud and steel. She will always recall when they first saw. Through a brake in their hull, amid the storm and burnt-out ships, fireballs falling from the sky, a colossus striding through the mist. A sick interpretation of mankind, wandering through carnage. Distant, so aethereal, but it summoned imagery and words forever engrained. What she remembers is not the machine. It is the Nomads.

Their faces, as they watched the Humeda. That which they were supposed to fight, simply walk, as though it stumbled from a ship as they would. She will always remember those faces.

As she sits there, as the other five nod and resume their idle chatter, that which seers against the side of her head reminds her of those faces. The faces of those who would have no home, receive no supplies, or hope of respite. Who would fight those things, those behemoths, until the day they died. Would never retire, save for when they were ripped and flattened and had bled out.

Mincemeat stares at the side of Pescha's head, and it reminds her so. Dilated, sights knifed, frozen and quivering, hunched as a cat about to pounce, to see its prey turn, a horror of fangs and scars. Like he stares upon that machine and is condemned to death with them. Faces do not move like this. They cannot conform to these proportions, yet none other notices save for Pescha, who does not turn but eats, eats faster than she ever has. The Kamakara looks at Pescha in a way without a word, for so few to witness such have ever lived. An expression experienced only once, for whatever invokes such a response would surely force them to tear themselves apart.

On hearing that name, Mincemeat sees the misty titan for the first time too.

Then he grows, abandoning his utensils to sit straight, slowly, never looking from Pescha. He nods to himself, hands in his lap. None other addresses, for they have noticed and now will not associate themselves, even at a glance, with she who provoked such sights from the Kamakara. A world away, their talk comes but is not heard, there are none at that table beside Pescha and the thing at her side. She, who cannot even finish her small plate, for her wild appetite disappears.

Pescha also tucks her hands atop her thighs. Intertwined, a finger rests against her switch.

She waits for Mincemeat outside, watching the streets rage while Citypeak murmurs just behind. Its warm light catches her back, but it is dark out here, and the wind circles these hights ravenously. As though it waits for her to come too close to the edge, that it may throw her over.
    When Mince meets her, neither speaks. His expression is a devouring emptiness, dead to a solemnity so sobering, Pescha cannot look his way. A Kamakara Klernsteiga, bored of wandering Our Last Limit, so made sardonic and dismissive, yet now he looks to the war below with an expression of such monumental dour.

Mince says he will take her.
    The wind, faint industrial cloud, the pulsing colours below, then him. A greyscale figure, heads taller than Pescha, hands pocketed as his hair snatches at the empty space in front. Poised. Absolutely focussed on that, and only that moment.
    When Pescha opens her mouth, Mince says he doesn't care. That's why she came, right? To find someone to guide her through Kenidomo Country. He asks it, and Pescha is still. This is all the Kamakara needs.

Mince sends her back to the apartment. Pescha can sleep there, the Kamakara says. He has work tonight. They walk back separately, unspeaking. When they slip back through that window, Mince tells Pescha she can use his bathroom. It's clean and of that same dark modernity, black marble and edged. She removes bloodied wraps from her hands, fingers quivering with the effort, body bruised and worn with inanition and fatigue as she slips from her skin. The shower is built into the ceiling, a square of dots high overhead beside a screen of translucent black glass. The turn of a dark marble dial releases steaming warm water, the grate underfoot matching the holes above. It sooths strained muscles and wounds, washing away blood and dirt and decay, relieving her of a filth which has clung for weeks in a spray of easing heat and cleaning humidity. It soaks through her chest; she feels it against her heart. She looks over Mincemeats luxuries lined on a tall shelf. Soaps and balms, creams, products for hair. Razors too. She takes them all, tending to her battered form.
    Steam and condensation against the mirror catch her shades, blue

flecked against her vague silhouette. She stares at herself, her hands like the fore edge of a book. Wounds as pages, slightly opened.

She steps out into the apartment, footfall slick as she dries herself. A cloak of steam follows, drifting over the floor. She sees Mince, about to drop from the window once more.

    He isn't human. He's the thing that creeps into Pescha's dreams and startles her awake. Striders like Constant's, Mincemeat's legs become blades. Predatory adaptations, swords supported with springs and struts, the tips protected by pads Pescha presumes can retract in an instant. With them on, the Kamakara is a giant, stooped so low to fit through the glass. Concealed under a layered coat, hooded and grim. Something to make you faint should you see it similarly climb through your window; he carries another sword at his waist. Tri-bladed, all that can be made under his cowl is that half-jaw. A matte black metal skull and deathly thin limbs, swords and shapeless coat. He is framed against the night, glancing back as Pescha walks out. Like slender bone shrouded, a monstrous skeleton perched on the sill, his height raised even more on two narrow, slightly arced blades.

Pescha wears nothing. She holds the towel at her side, hair hanging over her face.

    Mincemeat watches from his cowl. He falls into the night, a ghoul slipping from sight.

    Pescha walks to the window, towel in hand, looking over Our Last Limit. Breeze brushing damp skin.

    This changes everything.

She takes some of Mince's nightwear from a wardrobe of decadence. Labels read Lizensbur[19] and Maika Kokoro[20], elegances from beyond the Kyut, and she falls onto his bed- a bed, staring up at the roof, as the soundtrack outside plays. A record broken, it is just the constant cycle of wind, blowing curtains and odd interjections, as vents steam and sirens wail. She wonders how much of the night is left. This morning, she awoke

---

[19] *Lizensbur*: Fashion brand based in the Heimatus of Alexada, prevalent in all capitols of the planets. While fashion on the Kyut is an alien concept, both due to necessity and that such luxuries must be imported at great cost, such garments are sometimes sported by city officials and officers of note, as a demonstration of material wealth and social standing.

[20] *Maika Kokoro*: Fashion brand based in the Heimatus of Alexada, prevalent in all capitols of the planets. Their attire is based off of ancient Faurscherin designs, replicated at great costs, with many pieces of clothing featuring materials from either most or all of the remaining planets.

in that abandoned town against the Matsumasi and Doken. She wonders where she will next fall into slumber. Shredded fingers rub the dark silk throw which crumples at her touch. The window breeze brushes her nose. She has rolled up the cuffs and hems of Mincemeats clothes into bunches for them to even remotely fit.

      She sinks into rest, spread over fine bedsheets.

She must sleep only a few hours, when she stirs day has barely broken. That pale morning of cold and mist lights the apartment as blue slips from stirring sights, and she looks up to Mince, still clad and towering. Staring down at the woman unfurled across his silk. Rubbing her eyes and yawning. The Kamakara says he'll meet Pescha at Quiaxin Jiipan.

      The streets are empty. She and the daybreak fog are all that wander, roads empty of commuters who do not dare to walk, even when morning has come. Their concerns are clear. Visible, in scorch marks against shop walls and litter piled high, broken glass and strewn construction equipment lain bare. She knows not which district she walks but she doesn't think it matters, it is quiet at every bend and crossing. She doesn't understand where everyone is, stalls still shuttered and the lights sapped of power. She doesn't understand how this place can function. In many ways, she guesses it doesn't.

      Pescha follows the memory of Quiaxin's glow, the roads becoming thinner and elevated- she knows she has reached that risen wing. She ascends past homes, away from the high towers and barbarism, where that equipment now made weaponry would have been used. She crosses a suburb, of mass telephone wires and carefully closed curtains, where the gusts truly start to build, asserting themselves as the makers of those lower clouds. Upon these draughts, Pescha can smell the cold. She is back in the coat the Rautbergen gave her for she can guess the conditions she is fast approaching, her dark grey greatcoat lapping against her calves. Pack One now sits on the exterior, slits cut to allow its mechanics to feed through, sword strapped atop. She knows she will wear this coat for a while.

      She left the frozen wastes in a similar jacket, her brown one taken from Glermvender. As snow had chased her there she sees it comes to greet her now, fine flakes like ash blown high overhead. She approaches once more, wind catching, building fast, the city shielded from the coldest of gusts by its elevation. She reaches the end, a grassy park built upon the tip, light frost draped over the lawn. There is an unsteady staircase down, like a fire escape, rusted and burnt with frost. A metal staircase crisscrossing to the ice below.

At its edge, she can scarce look up. Bracing herself against what is, here, a hurricane. Kenidomo Country. Sector Zero, Double-Four, Nine, Three, Five. Bleak and boreal. A gelid waste, this steel pyramid on which she stands mounts its cusp.

Ahead, the dreary station, Quiaxin Jiipan. Wire and barb fencing, antenna high and blinking within the storm. Inside its confines, figures stand, shawled to survive their vigil, like statues draped in cloth, unmoving and observant. Turmoil, grief, and anger brood in their city, yet even from afar, she can see not a single soldier looks its way. All sights are to the plateau, watching the white curl.

This storm is not as intense as that of Dodtohmet, but it aches in a way much deeper. Colder, less idyllic, and of what the mind dreads. Barren, lost of its intimacy. Distant, and Pescha, who stands at that peak and stares, does not doubt this storm will soon rage as strong as any other she has crossed. She can find no comfort here. Not even familiarity to Emilia, that frozen heritage of hers.

For as she descends and steps onto thin, plastering skift, the horizon so bare and vast, she sees her aide.

Mincemeat's blades are retracted, tips touching his Achilles, swords stored parallel behind, as though they are thrust into the ground at his heels. He watches Pescha approach, his long and layered coat open, a dark mass shifting with his handheld sword poking from the cloth. His hood is similarly great but in this bitter light Pescha can just see his face, hidden from the winds within its folds. When blue eyes arrive the Kamakara but nods and deploys his striders, the blades extending to raise him from the ground. It is a mechanical action, twitchy and unrefined. It only adds to the horror of his design. At ease, he already stands so tall. Up above, where his face can no longer be seen amid the shade of his windbreak and the harshness of that white sky, he must pass ten feet. Yet he stands naturally, bred as much for this form as he is for his other.

There are no words to say, as Pescha pulls up her hood also. Her coats collar rises to the bridge of her nose, shielding her face, so only her sights show, as bright and blazing as ever. She feels her kit against her hips, bound exterior, free in use without heeding her overcoat. She looks out to the desert, breathing air raw, and scathing.

She of vivid azure and he of such bladed height start, side by side. A giant of skeletal, bowed limbs, a hand jutting from his grim cloth to grip his blade's handle. A woman, pressing herself against the foray, blue flashing like a signal within the abyss. The noise, of wind and Mince's footfall, a mechanical march plodding at her side. Lost to the modernisms in their wake, for Pescha can feel them wandering into a truly forgotten place, of corrupted depravity. A change in tone, a warp in their senses, for it feels almost like the medieval encroaches on their progress. What an eerie sight they are.

  The two Klernsteiga walk, specks against that abandon.

They named them, those undiscovered lands, after a fable; a beast which sought to slay gods and prove that the mortal could win over their sculptors. The last of his species, the Kenidomo.

In Kenidomo country, time has lost itself. Great symbols of vague religion lay below the boots of dead machines. Grand constructs of the then ignorant, but soon to be so harshly awoken, speckled between ravenous, inhospitable wastes. Empty, and one could fill it with people, and it would still feel empty. Regardless of familiarity this place is strange, uneasy. The terminal minds set loose, desperation unrestrained and sorrow flowing. My Rautbergen's ecclesiastic hymns are most befitting of this place. I feel as though if I were to die here today, upon the Kyut, I would walk through some god's gates and find this same place waiting, the remnants of creation consumed. No good to be found. The very concept itself alien.

As an Auberkemein, I command a Wolstspitzer; two hundred Rautbergen. They are ruined, and desperate. Human history, once known as objective, made that of myths, yet just the same they cling to it. Stories of the Museishingen, of belonging. Their old Emperors are deities now, even when dates and names are forgotten. And to all this is a sacred place. Where the aspiring once landed, built their superstructures, were annihilated by the machine. Lost amid storms, great ruins scattered far and wide.

My Rautbergen are undersupplied and underequipped, yet they will fight like dogs. Xenophobes of the highest degree, against all who would not war for the restoration of mankind in its many forms. As for the Klernsteiga, beyond Fauschenherst watch, their true nature shows. The nature of those with nobody coming for them, no victory to end their struggle, but those who board a ship and know that they will spend the rest of their days without comfort or hope until they're a stain in too short a time. They say to fear the Kyut-Born Klernsteiga, but it's more than that. What would make anyone do this is surely horrid. But all meaningless now.

  Watch what Kenidomo Country has done to them.

It feels so lonely. I'm doing the same thing every single day and I don't know why anymore. The people who told me to do it are all dead, and the situation is just as dire. Maybe worse. I can't shake the feeling that command can only be traced so far. The funds so far. I can't remember why I'm here, or what the end goal is. We remain either close to chaos or in it, and I don't see how that can change. Out here there are no rules. No morals or laws. No command or cost. Just perfect abandon sweeping off out of sight. I wonder if it's always been like this, and I've just never noticed.

Haufenmensch Hellegeneid.

-An Auberkemein

- KENIDOMO COUNTRY -
UNRECOGNISED TERRITORY
"The Cold"

This storm is a sickness, surpassing all she has known before.

Her concept of the cold delights that which circles her, a challenge feverously accepted- she knows snow and chills well, but nothing like this. It transcends temperature, taking on a new meaning. Parts of her body she didn't know could become cold freeze, like frost forms a film upon the mind. She is smart amid the boreal, nothing is frostbitten, but then parts of her are iced through, parts possible only in death. It is a disease, making where weather is not considered, where any thoughts of winter were before irrelevant. Her fingers and face, limbs and chest should shudder, yet she feels her heart beat to both its own pulse and that of her trembling, as though it shakes against its cage. If she were alone, she thinks she would curl up, hug herself with wide, frosted arms, but alongside that monster plods, trudging through thin white, and she keeps pace. Follows the Kamakara, inhuman, and grim. Images conjured of such a reputation as Mincemeat's may envisage what Pescha saw in Our Last Limit, yet to fulfil such a sobriquet, this form is what blue eyes envisaged. Not a person, someone who can be viewed as better than their peers. He is a breed apart. Even bare, not all is simple flesh.

There are no days here. The idea is meaningless, these winds twist any previous notion of light and dark into a constant, rushing mix, indifferent to where the sun is. Anyway, what days would there be to remark. Yesterday, she walked, as she did the day before. And the day before that. She does not know for how many days she walks. She doesn't want to.

There is no name for it, the affliction of this blizzard which works upon body and mind. Ripping at both and screwing the pulp into one mass of blind, aimless suffering, no end in sight. No progress made, she thinks she could walk for years and claim the same success as now. Years more. She feels she has already walked a few.

The only reassurance is that of her guide, he who does not waver from his path. He who walks for an age then turns, shifts to follow a new route amid apparent similarity, a pointless turn yet he makes it anyway. Pescha knows they must progress, and that to dwell on anything aside would warrant absolutely nothing. What is there out here to note.

When the cold darkens and the Kamakara stops, he pitches his stilts as struts. They lay their coats over top, a tent formed atop bladed limbs thrust into the ground. They lean against each other, back-to-back, listening to the rage which searches for them overhead. They eat, passing rations over shoulder, Mincemeat telling her to not let them touch the floor. Even with enough garments to fashion their canvas, still he dons a figure-concealing coat, one which hides what he carries as they pretend they rest. Pressed spine to spine, they suffer together. Listen to each other breathe, learn each other's scents. Mincemeat smells like unwashed hair and laboured musk.

Here, Pescha knows Klernsteiga earnt their bynames- defined Nomads, they wander these impossible places. At least Dodtohmet's snows sunk underfoot, she could understand the seeping cold, but here it is shallow, grating, the winds are so strong they do not let the white settle. She can scarce breathe every waking moment, and even within their shelter, she finds no comfort. Just less pain. Not much less.

After three, maybe four sundowns', she thinks no more. Just walks, the aching cold becoming her settled state as fatigue numbs the torment. She stands in a cold room and stares at the wall for days on end, blank-faced and blinking against twisting coils of snow.

Staring at the walls of a pale room, sleeping against them in nightfall.

Day after day after day. Not a word spoken, no eye contact, yet when Pescha does scarce see the Kamakaras features she sees discomfort, distaste in the storm, but no doubt. With his machine fingers he drums a rhythm against the hardened cold floor, mechanised half-jaw crushing through dried grain bars as the two eat under their canopy, mumbling to one another in thanks of food. To make noise would seem odd, uncanny, and uncomfortable on her throat, but even if she were to talk, Mince, who leans against her spine, would not hear. They use their swords to weigh down the sides of the tent, and do not embrace sleep so much as they let their senses rot, with no progress to note, and no achievement to savour.

She cannot think a description apt for her first days within Kenidomo Country. The people to experience it rarely walk from its gale, it is their norm, their everything, yet she knows it must end. Mincemeat turns and shifts, stops to gaze from his stilted perch into the storm and then spin, Pescha close with greatcoat fastened tight and fully, so that she may hide behind her collar and hood.

It could have been a week. Less. More. Time long enough without rest nor warmth, but it feels forever. All she has to consider is what they look like, those two walking figures, her with coat and Pack One and Mince, striding with the grasp of a waist bound blade protruding. Ready to draw, all other character hidden atop edged limbs.

She thinks; how they must look, but considers who will watch. Thinks them ghoulish but thinks what would see. It crosses her mind for a moment, one of the few thoughts to do so, that she truly has no concept of who she may find out here.

- KENIDOMO COUNTRY -
UNRECOGNISED TERRITORY
"*The Raft*"

It trundles, motion junky and strange. From afar, it looks like rubbish piled atop a podium, like a place for passing Nomads to dump their junk. But as the silhouette starts to take shape, it becomes more. Pescha can make out a misplaced stage and the man at its side, as though a counter to her and Mince, and similarly he is taller than reason. As they come closer together Pescha makes out more and more, and the oddity of what she sees pushes aside all decision, until she can make sense of what exactly comes.

Like the chassis of an armoured tank, flat and large, stripped of its hull to make a tracked flooring, it pulls itself across the white. Engine powered with high pipage for fumes, what has been built atop is nothing short of a collection, of every peculiarity stacked in great heaps atop the land-bound barge. An abundance of servers and radios, Trivi[21], Ubess-Koss, even Geseschaus, and Pescha sees that base marked with the insignia of Inieriin[22], the carcass salvaged an age ago from some Sect One craft. The vehicle is lit with string lights, suspended between scaffolds where armour had once been bolted, now made supports for the illuminations. Faint yet obvious amid the storm, draped between the bars to cast over the produce below. And it is a commercial vessel, made into a travelling sales cart. Cabling, crates and cages stacked upon the sides, climbing even to what Pescha thinks are herbs, dried and suspended alongside the bulbs, and spices ground within their bags. The number of things is baffling, all towered atop that crawling, churning chassis, the

---

[21] *Trivi* : Velt Veit Veiden. A radio company no longer in operation which supplied most of Sect One with their telecommunications equipment. They are cumbersome and immobile designs, but their simplicity has ensured they are still in wide and primary use by the communities of the Kyut.

[22] *Inieriin* : Aeronautics company situated in the Heimatus of Alexada. The company outfitted the Fauschenherst with its Navy during Sect Two, however the catastrophe led to an irreversible loss of confidence in the company, which fell from public favour. It now supplies the Fauschenherst only with landing craft, to ferry soldiers from its larger ships. The company attempted ventures into vehicular designs, however these efforts proved inefficient in reviving the company.

piles almost swaying with the barrage. For the first time in a while Pescha hears something that interjects against the wailing, with that heavy throb of pluming exhaust.

Everything is subject to the winds. Pescha keeps an eye on the lanky figure, as tall as Mincemeat yet without any visible extensions, more organic and natural in his motion. While she maintains sights on the giant until they are closer still, her attention is then drawn to the centre of that stripped-down tank. To a parting between the surplus, and the figure who owns this open space.

A young woman, younger than Pescha but swaddled, a wrapped-up bundle kneeling. Like a baby never removed from its first dark cloths, now made a hood and cloak which drape from that sitting form, to curl like fabric hair between the produce. Upon sight, Pescha thinks of tribal idols, that folkish deity revered from youth who ran away, hidden from her peoples amid the emptiness. And she is well hidden. Her face concealed, masked under her draping, but glimpses can still be caught amid fluctuating gusts, and Pescha sees it adorned with lines and dots of worn gold paint. She is festooned in inked decoration, detailed across her features. Her posture fits with this, she is straight and loose shouldered, and even before she speaks, greets them or nods, a sense of conceit is woven into her slight smile and deep, plush, but wind-faded textiles.

But any fear in her apparent arrogance pales to the sense of her friend, that thing which walks at her side. He is not mechanical, yet he exudes that same sense as the Humeda, of a wicked portrayal of humanity, ill and malnourished, hunched and awkward. The image of misanthropy, there is something both mistreated and then cruel itself in the figure's form, as long arms sway heavy, burdened by hands which could take Pescha from stomach to throat in one grasp. Grips bound out of frailty and infection, like those of a burnt lepper. Mincemeat crosses behind Pescha to align with him, never trying to rise but keeping that blade clear, handle pointed to their company. The lepper supports himself with a staff, like a complex antenna ripped free, which holds him upright. Only when both parties draw to a halt, when the tank sways and stops with spluttering smoke, can Pescha see the ill giant's mask. A timber and peering thing, carved to the expression of intrigue in some erring pleasure, as though he observes with an outward show of vague interest, but could not look away if he tried. Slim sights, eyes calm yet caught, lips tight in a soft smile of carved and streaked dark wood.

When close, the girl raises a hand, although covered, in greeting. The shudder of her breaking vehicle makes her wave and as Pescha and Mince stand in address she speaks out, leaning a little into her words. Slow and pronounced, to project over a storm that interrupts even thought, let alone speech.

She says this is The Raft. That smile prevails, one of polite courtesy for she addresses customers, nothing more or less, and with a wave she gestures to her stock, piled high between those hanging lights. She proclaims herself Costermonger, the man as Brother, and she welcomes them with rehearsed but still genuine enthusiasm, body shifting under its covers with an eagerness to her words. She speaks of what she can offer the two Klernsteiga. Of her herbs and radios, she even proclaims meat, shifting to one side to allow the duo to see a cage, draped in a blanket to keep its captive warm.

The two Nomads stare at the box, before Costermonger resumes that refined seat. She best flaunts the thing beside her, a reach rising from that liquid cloth to lay a decadent arm atop what is at first just another radio, old and busted. But she points to the sequence of emblems marked against its side, and Pescha sees that of the Faurscherin, still baring the Museishingen crest. An apparent survivor of that original craft, ripped from its harbour with cabling crushed and splintered, yet clear in its symbols. Costermonger, even with only her lower face visible, raises a brow.

Pescha says nothing. She is but her coat and lights, and amid these storms her glow must flare against each passing flake, taking hints of emotion with them. She leaves all else to Mincemeat, who surveys the offer from his perch. After another glance to he named only Brother, he says that they need nothing. The girls grin cracks, as though it were a painting on glass fractured with a blink. She does not protest, drawing in that arm and giving a little bow, accepting a distasteful apology over a refusal. When blue eyes look to the Kamakara, they do not miss that he has not even a vague sense of the unnatural, no degree of surprise as he gestures at her for them to leave. Without even intrigue or shock, for he has lost interest in Brother now, who seems to not witness a single second of interaction through his timber veil, motionless in waiting. Pescha watches Mince walk and Costermonger near grimace, her engines firing back up, professionalism keeping something more vicious as simple displeasure.

But when Pescha moves to follow she still speaks, calling over the cold. She warns the two Klernsteiga, thick smog coughing from their pipes, sights straight but voice clear, that there's a bigger storm coming. Pushing aside distaste, she says that Brother almost fell over, gesturing at the inert bystander.

Pescha thanks her and looks to the Kamakara. Mince waits for her to follow, his head cocked, but Costermonger says no more. She bows again, facing ahead, tracks firing back up, overlooked by her most devilish Brother as they trundle once more. Slower than footfall, shuddering into motion, back toward emptiness.

Pescha turns to the Kamakara. He moves on, stalking without a backward glance.

- KENIDOMO COUNTRY -
UNRECOGNISED TERRITORY
"Sinew Machines"

They are tossed and blown, even the cold steps back to the pure force exerted against them- the snow makes a maelstrom, pulling them to the ground. Pescha can barely stand, struggling to stay upright as Mince somehow perseveres, looking back to make sure he has not lost his companion, waving and pointing as though they near salvation yet unseen.

And they do. Those two distant figures stumbling, arms raised as braces with heads turned away, they drive into the cold until one stops, blades skating upon hardened snow in his crouch, a mechanical hand dug into the cold to keep him there. When Pescha comes close, she almost falls over the Kamakara, blind and lurching, but she follows his gesture. Blue peering into a tearing blizzard, and she does not hesitate to follow Mincemeat, who trips and claws his way forward.

A mangled shape. A silhouette, losing form as it forms.

Pescha feels like grasping at the tail of her guide's coat. She wonders what they would do if a Humeda came, but she figures she could just let go, and slip away a mile in a second.

Ghouls forming, the things holy scripture warn of, in machine corpses so colossal, she thinks they would humble even great Nakari and Heshimawa.

Pescha is almost blow over, her hood pulled off and on as the storm whips, back and forth. The moment her footing fails a blade is drawn and driven into the ground, holding her there.

They are things of sinew and papery complexion, a million ribs of cabling made clear through machine malnutrition. Frail and decayed, slumped against one another. Expressionless, features worn bare by winds surging, they are hunched and bony, an amalgamation of forms, like the storm melded many automatons together, searing forearms and bodies into one sick, long dead mess kneeling. Limbs overlapped, intertwined, fused by the elements. As though they ran and fell against, into, the one before.

Great titans staggering, Pescha can define three, maybe more, all one of the same, each of sibling construction in life now redefined in death. As though they were scared and fled, sightless as she is now.

They walk for these slumped things, that scale unfathomable making something so close miles away. The two Nomads drift quick, truly now just pikes in the ground with cloth tied atop, for no clear shape can be made amid the chaos of their raging gear. The occasionally clear arm or leg takes them to the behemoths.

When they near the base Pescha slows but the Kamakara refuses to stop, pointing that they must climb, pointing, for neither can hear even their own thoughts, or else open the way for the storm into their skulls. Mince retracts his blades, starts to rise and Pescha follows. Keeping to the curvature of felled corpses, collapsed and structureless. Rising in aid of each other, hauling their fellow up. Calves and then thighs and then twisted midriffs, the cage of machine ribs like a ringed staircase up. Blades used as ice picks as the ground disappears, yet it is no different up here, to compare sheet white to sheet white. There is no ground. No right way up, for the wind is its own gravity, throwing them hard against frozen metal and then prising their fingers loose, wrapping around the Humeda windbreaks and hoping to rip the Klernsteiga loose. Pescha's grip is so stiff with cold that she keeps firm, holding to cables in deep freeze, once loose, now rigid. The storm works to both push and pull as they ascend in ribbed rings, as though some giant struggles against a locked door. Rattling and bashing, heaving and slamming against the other side.

There are moments when Pescha thinks she's upside down, horizonal, their ascent subject to the will of the winds. They make up down and both left and right a curved route back to where she now stands but she keeps close to the Kamakara, never loses him from sight, and they do not stop until they reach a flat atop the machine, one of the monster's shoulders. When she scales at the hand of Mince, who hauls her up, she crouches on an ice-burnt work of muscled iron, a great neck and featureless head looking out. She does not know how high they are. Like gravity here, it does not matter. An idol, the temple atop the mount, the Nomads approach the faceless head, expressionless yet still looking underfed, if an automaton could ever be so. Alone up here, just them and it, time and light lost as the sun is, a world apart from all others.

Mincemeat moves and keeps to the throat, following it back, looking the neck up and down until they reach the rear, where spine meets skull. A vertebra has rotted and fallen out, been ripped or blow away. Pescha does not care, and follows the Kamakara in.

The silence is thick, like air building in her ears, that sudden quite ready to burst but she knows it won't. She looks back, and sees the storm rushing past outside.

    The cave extends, the far wall of ports and bolts like a cartridge- a whole piece of spine is missing, meant to connect here, exposing wires and fibres unburnt by the chills. An alcove, a little taller than Mince but long, so that Pescha can wander to those vents and screws and peer through their gaps, pressing an ear against the seams to a hush so heavy it is its own object. As vivid sights search, her blue like torchlight, the drop is gargantuan, daylight a rift against the darkness. A hollowed core drops. Not the entirety of the melded machine, but most of it, where one would search for the chest and lungs. It is like looking form a skyscraper window, out to a densely packed but dead city in night.

The Kamakara calls out, suggests simply that she doesn't. He asks for a light, sitting himself atop a looped rubber cable sleeve.

    Mince pulls back his hood and Pescha wonders if she's looked her guide in the eye once since they left Our Last Limit. That half-and-half bite with the left in black, running over his bottom lip and down, carving his jaw, minute rivets and clean join lines flexing in perfect synch. He runs his prosthetic clutch through white hair, whiter than the snows beyond, for it isn't subject to the odd dusk-azure hue of that aethereal timelessness they wander. If Pescha's cold is that of the weather, that allure of the storm from which nobody can turn, then Mince is of human cold, features built to accommodate only half the emotional spectrum. His mouth a broad wound, his eyes even colder, cold in a sense different from Pescha, for while hers are of vivid and beguiling chills, Mincemeats are pale, as colourless as his skin. The emotions he is capable of do not consider fear, terror and fright impossible to imaging upon his face, not unless they are sardonic impersonations, and then they are easily brought to mind. To flow into anger. Like he sorted through all feeling and ripped out whatever would impede.

Pescha pulls her lantern from Pack One's compartment and shakes it to life, summoning light from her palms and laying it centrally. She sits at its side with her back against more ductile cable casing, such sudden and unexpected relief taking her as she rests against something, even slightly, soft, for the first time in days.

She lets her head roll, and that shiver threatens but now she lets it spread, curling up and burying herself against the rolls of rubber, lanternlight flickering. She watches the storm which cannot touch her, cannot rack bone, burn her nose, rip at the roots of her hair, but she keeps an eye on it still, should it try and reach for one last slash. Mince joins her, sitting opposite, collapsing onto the playground-padding surface, the organic mush of the inorganic. He busies himself immediately, clicking and screwing and drawing his feet from their striders, breathing relief, legs outstretched, for he does not walk so when atop his blades. He sits, supported by straight arms planted behind, head back and eyes closed, breathing for a moment as Pescha watches. She is still half hidden behind her coat collar. A child watching from their hiding place.

They both rest there, still cold and aching, but this is better than just being less uncomfortable. Pescha thinks that, for the first time in Kenidomo Country, she is okay. By soft lamplight, they watch the turbulence howl against their gate.

Pescha speaks quietly, thanking Mince for getting them here so quickly.

The Kamakara rolls his neck, slow and gentle, and says Pescha kept up.

They both rest there, listening to the wind.

Mince shrugs out of his coats, disappearing within and then pushing them off like he fights to escape a sack. He removes layer after layer until he surfaces, and draws from the heap what he has carried, his sword and a bag, laying them by his side. He unbuckles the case. He draws out packets, food bound in silver wrapping, his flask and tubs, but does not look Pescha in the eye. He pretends as though Pescha isn't there as he pulls from the sack a K.A.G Neiderkop R-Three[23]. A snubbed, compact submachine gun, the anti-personnel equivalent of the anti-Humeda Lautreisgefer- the standard anti-soft-body armament, tied with a sling.

---

[23] *K.A.G*: Kabreiska Anchen Glachten. The primary supplier of the Fauschenherst with anti-personnel weaponry. Situated on the Heimatus of Alexada, harvesting resources from Trash Ditch and basing its designs off armaments carried on the Faurscherin, where Goritekaga weapons dominate war on the Kyut, K.A.G has armed the Fauschenherst on all other worlds, as well as on the Kyut. Security forces bare their arms throughout cities on the planets and the Kyut. The K.A.G before the names of anti- personnel weapons is emblematic of their company.

The Kamakara acts the only Nomad and pushes the gun aside.

They eat, eyes weary, her ration drunk like a soup instead of spooned. Such a tiredness overcomes Pescha as she chews, like she may fall into sleep with her mouth full. She does not finish before she sets the packet down, rocking back and yawning, while the Kamakara stares. Mince asks, still forking grain from its wrapper, whether Pescha is finished, glancing at the carton she set down. Once Pescha nods, she asks why Mince is so worried about food touching the floor.

Mince asks Pescha if she's ever heard of a Nomad called Befelobeth.

Pescha leans back, closing her eyes and curling up for sleep. When she mumbles that she hasn't, Mince nods, and says that she was a Kamakara too. The only Kamakara to die.

He heard only that Befelobeth was with Rautbergen, when she put something on the ground, then ate it. Not for long, just while she was doing something else. Mince says Befelobeth was no idiot. Nobody had ever heard of Humeda that small, he says. They must have once been a bigger machine, blown apart into individual, tiny pieces. They made her so sick; she couldn't go on. Then they ripped her apart, inside out.

For two days, Pescha and Mincemeat sit there, held up against the machine throat. Watching and waiting, the storm never faulters, not even for a second. It doesn't lessen to its former state, does not even break to figure time, it just churns and churns and churns, keeping the two in their high alcove. Sometimes they venture out, to stand and stare, try to figure if it will ever relent, but there is nothing to see besides that which they hope to go. They talk too. Don't, mostly, but when they are both awake and not eating, they speak. Mincemeat asks for Pescha's name, and says he likes it, Nuxitec Pawasaki. He might call Pescha Nux from now on. It sounds cold, and Mince guesses she came from Emilia.

Pescha stares. She has never heard a Klernsteiga call her by her birthname. It's always been her Klernsteiga designation, picked for her by witnesses of her work, as it is for all Nomads, in the many tongues of the Kyut. She hasn't been called Nux in years. Nux is a little girl.

She asks about Mince.

Pescha knows Mincemeat is a Kyut-Born Klernsteiga, a title given to Nomads birthed upon this plane. A slur, for what may drive those from other worlds can by heroic, hopeful, responsible, yet what would provoke one born here, raised amid all this, must surely be sick. The hopeless, those who see this false plight clearly, taking up arms and permission to kill anyway. By all means, without hindrance.

Mincemeat tells Pescha that he was born to wanderers. Sect One descendants with no home, who travelled with refuge upon their backs, walking from one spot to another in evasion of the machines. They had no customs, practices and culture confined to them being no more than twenty in number. But still they feared the storms. Without guidance, reason or knowledge, superstition became their beliefs. There was a tradition, for a new-born child, and there so rarely was one, for such a birth could not possibly be intended. They would bestow upon their child a horrid name in their tongue. A name so gruesome, so appalling and crude, that if the automatons ever came, they would be disgusted by such a title, and leave the child be. Mince is still in his words, wolfish jaw pronouncing as naturally as any other, then he shrugs, watching lamplight wriggle.

He cannot mock, he guesses it worked. He doesn't remember what happened, he was too young. He has been told all he has said by others. He remembers nothing himself. He spent his youth with a Rautbergen crew, all he has from before is that name.

Sakasuji Fubiken.
Pescha asks what it means.
Mincemeat says he doesn't know. He learnt word and speech amid the Rautbergen, his mother tongue forgotten.
What then, asks Nux. Mince stares, features so slight.

Fauschenherst records remember a young boy, pale with paler hair. Sporadic, he appears in different regions, over the space of years. He joins a Rautbergen crew, then disappears, presumed dead with them. Flutters through distant Kenidomo Country, his childhood and upbringing nothing more than a page of sightings and offhand reports. He eats, bunks, takes clothes. Nobody connects the dots; they would have no reason to. When the crew he was with died, he made it to Hopplostamts and trained formally with Rautbergen.

A while later, after disappearing again, he'd stumble from snows into Mestridoden. Half his face and an arm are torn off, and he clutches a

Nomad's sword. It took time to stabilise and refit him, vague Fauschenherst ties ensuring he received adequate treatment. As soon as he could again talk, he had but one thing to say. A question.

He held up the sword with his new arm, and asked who's it was.

After medical staff told him a Klernsteiga's, the name Sakasuji Fubiken, never formally registered unto Fauschenherst records, would soon be forgotten.

As far as anyone need be concerned, Mincemeat says, that's what. That's it. For a while, they thought he was a Humeda, the way he left bodies cut up. Valderost, Skerkomer, Veiden; the Fauschenherst scarce had Klernsteiga who hunted what they call, and he says the words slow and with guttural levity, soft-bodied targets, not least one like him. Wherever, whenever, one or many. He made himself invaluable, a necessity. He was a dirty secret even before the Shibuta Crisis, but that made him Kamakara. That was the Fauschenherst excuse. They gave him Falmenscha[24] prosthetics and cleaned up his amputations. Outfitted him. Towed him in, but not down. If all else failed, if the risk was too high, then piling requests for Klernsteiga and Rautbergen reinforcement would flatline. A sheet of names and locations wiped, replaced by a single line.

  Klausch Klernsteiga L eight-double zero-one, The Kamakara, "Mincemeat".

  He draws a straight with his forefinger, then lets the machine arm drop.

Pescha hears cynicism, mock and amusement, irony, but not distaste. He never speaks as though disturbed, does not talk of his past with any depth of emotion. He lists his youth from Fauschenherst records, and he considers that all his childhood worth. He cannot remember. The boy before the sobriquet of Mincemeat is nothing more than that list on one piece of paper. Pescha knows no intricacies, but she, like all, has heard of this Kamakara Klernsteiga. His achievements of date as a Nomad may take reems upon almost all others. If Small Hand is most known, Mince

---

[24] *Falmenscha* : Official prosthetics contracted to the Fauschenherst, for use on the Kyut. The company trains Rautbergen medical staff and sends them into combat with a surplus of limbs and artificial organs to aid both Rautbergen and Klernsteiga. The company is based in the Heimatus, was founded during Sect Three, and is one of the few companies under the Fauschenherst considered charitable, even admirable.

is most feared.
> Even still.

Pescha asks what Mince did in the Shibuta Crisis.
> The Kamakara blinks.

He tells Pescha to ask him some other time.

They figure the storm will not pass. Both days slip so slowly by that when they are resolved to leave it is with a dread equal only to that of remaining. Every cable is explored and the sight of that machine inner-city is forever engrained against Pescha's mind. Mince is careful to pack all hints of their camp within his carrier, Neiderkop slung over his back under so many coats. He sweeps where both Klernsteiga sat, coming to his companion's side only when he is satisfied. They stand on the edge, waiting for the cold to wane just enough to descend. Watching white tumble past, leaning against the entrance.

Just before they go, Mincemeat asks something. Glances, but does not hold his gaze.
> The Kamakara asks what Museishingen means. He saw Pescha's reaction when Costermonger mentioned it on The Raft. He saw, even amid the storm, her raise a brow. Pescha stares, halfway through raising her hood.

She says it was an Empire. The one which sponsored the Faurscherin. The reason they're all here. Founded thousands of years ago, for mankind's sake.

None of what Pescha says means a thing to Mincemeat.

- KENIDOMO COUNTRY -
UNRECOGNISED TERRITORY
"Ozwald"

She feels insane. Before, fatigue and loneliness drove her, inspired a sense of purpose to change such harrowing things, but out here it seems impossible. There is nothing else, there never has been, all memories an illusion to cope with this torture. She eats, but hunger and tiredness and thirst all meld into one, a discomfort so impeding on the body that she could be shot, and she would not notice, or would but think it the least of her troubles. The storm is weather no more, it is a new element, undefinable and sick and through it she stumbles, snows skating thin over bare ground and battering against her hood. Dreamlike she follows Mincemeat, a snapping mass atop twin stilts who, and no degree of madness may change this, cannot possibly know where they are, this place of nothing but vague sun, truest only when it falls and marks their sleep. When Pescha tries to work the mesh of coats, hands blue without the light of her eyes.

They'll rot out here. Have skin peeled while they walk and fall off in their sleep. They'll be left as cold-charred bones, still walking on. She does not hallucinate, cannot cry, or speak, for what makes her plight evermore a horror is that she knows it's real, every second of it. She has done the same through Dodtohmet and her home, Emilia, and so many frozen wastes between. She knew it was real ever since she first opened her door and felt the gusts rushing in.

When she sees the pulsing light, she knows it is no delusion. For just a moment, she thinks this is it, it flashes before her eyes, and it is pale and empty, for she has always been amid these snows, but Mince sees it too, and a Kamakara would not fall here. He slows, both watching the light flare from their distance.

Like a group taking pictures, cameras flash, yet before Pescha sees anything she knows it's from one source. A sudden, irregular, winking light, they see shapes form as they approach, a collection to one side and someone alone at the other. One facing many, but the flash comes from within that mass, that lone figure unmoving as the light sparks, each blast coming from a new individual amid the throng. With each flash, someone appears beside one in the group, and by the next, someone has fallen, as though one watches while the other kills, felling with slashes visible only in snapshots. A reel of photography barely readable, each passing glow depicts fewer and fewer, until the shape resounds beside the last of the assembly. They are too close together to make one from the other, the only thing clear being the cloaked watchman, overseeing the executions. Unmoving, through to the final glare.

There is no sound for the event, but Mince could yell and Pescha would not hear.

They watch while they walk, but stop at its conclusion, staring now at the blank stormfront.

They wait, garments blustering.

He who walks their way shows no worry. Nor even attention, as he adjusts his cloak, playing with the cuff of a sleeve. From afar he is as any other, that fabric mess, a scarecrow billowing, and they are the same to him, yet he doesn't even look up. To him, the concept of them attacking isn't even considered, is worth less than that which troubles his wrist as a thicket of dark blond scruff whirls. It is only when he nears do they see, amid many boys who would fib and lie and sneak onto the Kyut, the youngest Klernsteiga Nux has ever seen.

Skin blonde; maybe olive, maybe anaemic, it is the same shade as his hair, an unmanaged whipping froth, cutting at the air. It is as though his features do not feel, for they do not react, do not squint or sneer against the winds. Wide, and of an almost puerile greeting, yet even this imperviousness fails to his most beautiful feature. Apt to rival even Pescha's, his oversized sights stare.

His eyes, they are near mirrors, built of the natural composition but colourless, like pools of clear water inside his head. Globular worlds of crystal floors and thin lakes below, his iris takes every colour presented and plays it through a thousand angular spectrums. Not as harshly as oil, but it's evermore mesmeric, and they're disproportionate to his head, too big for such a small face. He stares with that childlike observance, either completely disinterested or seeing something amazing for the first time. When he stands before them, close enough to talk, Pescha can see the glittering streaks of fibre cables, running as faint veins over his liquid gemstone eyes, implants which would shine without a light of their own even in the darkest of places. Aside from this, all else is hidden, and this is meant to be, a burdensome cloak draped from neck to shins like a clerk of old. A royal attendant or steward, who would have walked rococo castle halls with lace cravat had he not resulted out here, amid the cold, hair wild, sights glistening.

He meets the Klernsteiga as though this is his job, they should expect nothing else of him, or that they summoned him and he awaits instruction, staring up at hooded stilts and blue lights the same way he would look at any other. He glances up and down and then around, gazing over the cold from which they walked, a storm more intense than any he has seen in a while. When he returns to the Nomads it is with a nod, like he hears a request unsaid.

He asks that they please follow him. Pescha doesn't see him once blink.
    She looks at the Kamakara, a thing aside from human or Humeda. He watches the boy turn and walk back the way he came.
    They walk.

When they reach where lights flashed, Pescha and Mince see what the boy did. A Sect One caravan, a trading or simply struggling community lays ruined, sprawled as though they stood together and were blown out, a streak atop the white. Their footsteps show no worry, nor an attempt to flee. They are stumbling, confused, yet not afraid, they mustn't have known what was happening until it was done. But the boy's footfall, they see speed in this, a straight from body to body. Those ambling dead somehow didn't see him cutting their way.
    The wind rises as they pass, the storm crashing into itself. The boy leads the way, Pescha close behind, but Mince stops to stare, turns, looks over the dead. Behind him, azure and crystal sights pivot, awaiting his return. Already, the snow layers, but there's over ten, over twelve bodies there. The blizzard kicks and for a moment reveals the setting sun, repainted in its boreal tones. Framing where they head, ever in pursuit of that late-day light. The giant atop his twin blades, Pescha afar and the boy further still, sunset breaking the storm for an instant between them.

The only thing constant about time here is its irregularity. Beyond the restrictions of day and night, but what could be called evening nevertheless begins its descent, shades deepening as the trio struggle on.

The winds do not intensify, they couldn't possibly improve upon what they have already mustered but they do cool, the cold alone becoming the true threat- regardless of whatever tent could be built, whatever shelter established, if the force would not blow them apart then the ice would murder them in sleep. The boy does not hurry but neither does he slow, doesn't turn to check that they are close, and he walks straight, heading somewhere specific. As though he came out to find them and now brings them back. He does not raise a hand, his figure that of hair and cloak and legs, arms tucked within, and while he cannot stand above Pescha's shoulders he is unwavering, again seemingly careless to that which makes her grimace. She does not question. She stumbles after him- she cannot possibly know where they venture, but she feels that it is close, and whether a trick of the desperate mind or not she hurries, Mince just behind.

The night is of such a deep and heavy cobalt here. She thinks she must never see another colour again, snowflakes like chipped paint crumbling, a stroke of dark Prussian blue coated over vision. She didn't think real places could reach such a shade, navy thoughts spreading before.

And then, slowly, as though they were bugs upon a grand desk, the house seems pushed toward them. A building of dimensions massive, an oblong perceived as tabletop insects see a box, pushed from one colossus to the other, except it is of bevelled roof and high windows, running the circumference of the construct way up from the ground. Beyond reason yet emanating what Pescha knows to be the only light, in slim slats, of miles, save for those of her eyes. A storehouse, made in those hopeful days for a city never built, or one to crumble so leaving all efforts used to reinforce that single surviving structure, for this place could house enough food to liberate the Planets' resource problem. A granary of insulting scale, what a king builds to humiliate his neighbour, but by some means it operates, shards of light glowing like stitching around the hem. So tall that it looks to always be falling toward those approaching Klernsteiga.

  Further they walk, speed taking footfall now for they see their respite and a hill emerges, crests as a rocky ridge into which the storehouse is built, its back end disappearing into stone to an unknown depth. It may be a mountain, Pescha cannot be sure, for its scale is recast alongside that of this madness building but like an Humeda backbone it cuts the horizon, making what has been blank for days that of texture and stone. She doesn't care. She can look at it when she doesn't worry that her sights may be torn by such chattering winds from her face.

Yet, there is something to draw a stare, even against the bewildering heights ahead.

The entrance is that of queuing grounds. Where people would line up amid weaving rows formed by rope-tied poles. Ticket booths and two-toned striped fabric canopies now angled by pilled snow, they were once painted, their hues now whisked away. Even still, as the three Nomads slow, letting the one behind catch up, Pescha can make out stands once selling food and boards once filled with events and she looks to the boy, stares at the child who is not tall enough to step over the lines of corded bollards. Orbs atop, maybe golden and polished once, years ago. She waits for Mince to come, without features yet in body also intrigued, turning to trace his surroundings of toppled stalls and barely connected awnings, flailing now like torn banners, all that similar shade amid this brotherhood of blue nights. They would think it so strange if they had been given the time, for as they step ever closer to the half ajar doors, reasonable in scale although somewhat more bizarre against this building than the building itself, a noise faint and echoing from within permeates. Swaying with the impulses of the whipping storm.

Fairground music.

It is different, apart from that naturally conjured by imagination, for overtop a woman sings, softly, almost at a whisper, an uncanny twist to that supposedly wild and childish. Of bells and violins and xylophone, remade for this place. Pescha thinks any happiness here would sound unnatural, ever more so when faint and vague, but the woman's voice makes the song appropriate for the Kyut. Against such charm, there is a woe in her foreign words. Pescha and Mince watch the boy slip between the doors, and they follow him. Into the ever-falling building, music growing as they come.

The song is made ambience, a soundtrack played from the rafters above. Ahead hangs a gargantuan red curtain which divides the entrance and the within. A heavy stage drape of deep crimson on that ridiculous scale, making the distance between it and the door a mere few meters, then that to the roof a few hundred. As though the trio are backstage, she can recognise a thousand things from its chorus, each as insensible as the last, in laughter and merriment dispersed on the other side.

Away from public view, like the extras of a play, they shake themselves of snow, pulling back hoods to sights, even in this ribbon of space, remarkable. Signs and notice boards, like those outside however not ruined, and they foretell a timetable of amusements, the events of a theme park. Pescha's face runs so many expressions at once, yet they all resound confused, as she reads over games, banquets, new features in galleries, restaurants. Attractions impossible.

She looks back through the door, and still sees the blizzard snap outside.

The boy walks for the draping but Mince grabs him, puts a hand on his shoulder as his striders decompress, taking him to ground level. He holds him to turn, staring at those huge crystal eyes. He asks him who he is.

They called him Ozwald, he says. "Ozwald of Odd Places". I nine-one-twenty-two.

This place, he nods, is called Casse Monvi. It's a theme park, for the crippled.

He draws back part of the curtain, beckoning that they step through.

- KENIDOMO COUNTRY -
UNRECOGNISED TERRITORY
"Case Monvi"

Everything is senseless.

All the same shades, of plumb and crimson, royal reds and purple, the interior must surely stretch miles, miles more. And while what is open here cannot be even a third, if it were not for walls and ceiling and the colour, they would feel they were outside. Upon a world none would recognise.

The entrance to a park, a pathway carves straight through, forming a cross centred at a fountain, the grass around fenced with fine white barring to the waist. It keeps separate the immediate trees and park fields, lined with benches. Beyond those trees rise the attractions, away from the central walkways. To make a Kamakara stare, Pescha and Mince see towering things depicted in transcripts, images, and data they had shuffled through when they were young. Of a time before their fall. Ferris wheels and distant slides, illuminated in those regal tones, everything a distorted haze amid a faint smog, described only in the colours of unnatural decadence.

When the trees and fairground end, of noise she presumes when she thinks of luxury and indulgence, grass flats span an equal length and reach a row of buildings, grand structures yet from this distance no larger than her smallest fingernail. Pantheons in construction, they are testaments of power through architecture. She sees an acropolis, high domes making theatres, vast galleries and museums carved of marble and stone, as though someone walked the streets of opulence and thought all should be in its image. Equal strength and grandeur, they are each their own capitol, fit to rule vast dominions. Here, they are crammed, the ambitious designer given everything they needed to let their imagination run. Sprawled, a wall of magnificence.

The parkland is built within the bounds of that crossed pathway, four patches each hosting shallow woodland and then their amusements, the lights patchy through the treeline. Even upon this straight, lined with those noble shades in bunting-strung streetlamps, sweet and distortedly candied, there are wheeled stalls, the produce of sugared richness lining their tabletops.

But everything is senseless. There is a haze, and what the place hosts the faint smell of, Pescha does not know. She sees the rafters so far above, hung with those vast fabrics of wealth, like the curtain against their heels. She looks around, at those stately tones, all dark, a permanent nighttime festival carefully curated. Curated, maintained. And enjoyed.

They are nobility, each of them. As porcelain as imagined, as porcelain as sculptures. In ballroom gowns and waistcoats, they are baroque in chatter and laughter, leaning against one another and waving hands and fans. But they are broken, remade and remade again with exposed machine limbs, worn, even rusted riggings of arms and legs twitching like wind-up things. Pescha does not see one among them whole, they who saunter and joke and sit at their park benches, backs against iron lampposts with hats and fine wigs. Each is at the peak of enjoyment, the apex of the conversation, the height of the quip, for they are all perfectly entertained, on their way somewhere or talking as though they could talk forever. A stage play, spanning forever.

They are all in attendance, the vendors and the buyers, everyone a part in this vast, metal and meat display. All conforming to that sweet, dark prune and crimson, with soft cream and gold dresses and lace. None two the same, in attire or prosthetics, but there is a commonality, in their masquerade faces.

Regardless of their many skins, augmentations and attires, they all wear ceramic expressions. Some with their mouths still visible, some completely behind enamel vizards. Scars and burns creeping over whatever skin remains.

Ozwald, impassive to those who amble and jest with ivory smiles, that song and woman's voice constant, says they may wait out the storm here. They need only seek permission from the Administrator.

It is weird and unreal and Pescha stares but cannot answer any one of her many questions. Instead, she looks to him, he who watches with his indifference, and asks who they are.

Klernsteiga. Once, he says. Pescha blinks.

Ozwald glances around and asks if they're hungry. He's starving; there'll be something to eat by the attractions, he tells, and beacons they come. The music is its own condition here, as wind or rain would be anywhere else. Pescha looks at Mince, who shakes his head. They follow.

The central path reaches a fountain and divides at a cross into four. They head left, toward the row of trees between them and the amusements, lined with flickering lamplight and porcelain facades, leaning against one another. Arm in arm, jovial and chuckling, they dot the way, a feature in of themselves, leading into the wood. It's just a sparse treeline, but it is of great oaks and they're laden with string lights and bunting, like imperial garden grounds where only the healthiest trees may grow. Like everything here Pescha doesn't know how it's possible, only that they can't be real, ancient frozen-wasteland trees. Between their trunks wander more nobility, around marquees and stone rotundas, each hosting a party endless. Each with reason to celebrate in the most elaborate way.

When the trees open out it is to a fairground, the likes of which Pescha brushed dust off, in picture books from Faurscherin ruins. Ferris wheels and carousels, great steel and iron contraptions lined with bulbs, Pescha and Mince stare transfixed, both in different ways. The grass between each attraction is trampled bare, fabulous dresses and boots sidestepping pockets of dried mud as they meander from one ride to the next, pointing and laughing some more. The sound, of machinery churning alongside cries of glee, feels so strange. The helter-skelter, as Ozwald calls it, captivates Mince. He stares at it like a critic stares at a monstrosity, unable to think of professional words. Like everything about it is off. Nobody who passes him rises beyond his shoulders, yet they are all equally blind to his existence.

Mincemeat turns to Ozwald, who stares at a confectionary stall with his massive eyes. He says he has never heard of this place- how can that be?

The boy turns his head slowly, prises his eyes from the cart then fixes them unblinking upon the Kamakaras. He says it's very difficult to reach. The storms haven't subsided here for decades. But he knows hundreds of places like this, hundreds of places you'd think impossible to exist, let alone hide. He says it's those places that want to hide the most. He sees Mincemeat's expression, distrust, and distaste in a half sneering scowl. Not unease, that is one of his impossible features. It is a grudge against his ignorance, and an indignity to admit. But it fades quickly. A passing distaste, like he knows he can make others talk later, remembering the insult instead of feeling it.

Ozwald tells him it's just one of those things the Fauschenherst likes to pretend never happened.

Mince says nothing. Silently, he watches the park, blankly

staring at the tops of ornate and passing heads. Ozwald glances at the nearby stall, great gaze lingering, then asks Pescha if she'd like something. He talks to them like they've been friends forever.

What did happen, Pescha asks. Here, to this place.

Ozwald ignores her. He doesn't even turn. He mumbles that something smells so good.

Pescha looks at Mince, who shakes his head in unemotional disbelief. Then he nods, his agreement is a jolt, like he tells something to leave. Like he gives permission for his dog to play. But it isn't offensive, where fear is unnatural on him, this fits, this is how he should say yes. Pescha stares a moment more, holding the Kamakaras eye, before she turns.

The stall is a cart, awning plumb and sugared red, manned by a statue in an apron. He offers them something in a bun, handing it with a smile and asking for nothing in return, a treat taken speculatively by Pescha and gluttonously by Ozwald, who is animated in motion for the first time she has seen. She recognises the flavours instantly as she takes her first bite. Compound dried mushrooms, the same as Klernsteiga are rationed, bun made of repurposed grain from their snack bars. She chews slowly, silently, looking up and down the strip of amusements, bustling with more stalls and celebrants. Pescha thinks to her last good meal, back through wastes so empty that there is nothing to remember but the crawling pace of time, spent staggering through. When she reached Our Last Limit, she thinks of what she ate atop Citypeak. She remembers first her apprehension, and her immediate loss of appetite. Standing there, picking through the bun, she figures her last decent meal that dried seaweed, on the pier of the Timber Isles, back in the Kodakame Wetland.

She blinks, remembering the sky and waters, grass rippling as a wave of its own.

She feels Ozwald stare at the side of her head, and takes another mouthful. She asks again, still chewing, what happened here. Who all these people are.

Ozwald asks if she wants a go on one of the rides.

No, Pescha tells.

A group of Nomads hook into a Seven-Seven radio and loop through old Faurscherin records. Illegal under Fauschenherst orders, they start digging, reaching into data stores, riffling through information. The reason why they broke in, Ozwald says as they walk, is still unclear. But those who know the tale figure they did it for the dying, for someone amongst them ill or wounded and unable to heal. Sick and beaten, the team of an unknown number plunged, fixed into the system, and tried to make contact. Find a remedy. A map. Anything. What they found must have broken already ruined minds.

  Old world records. Tomes and logs of pleasure and beauty amid the wastes of disease and fatigue and war. They must have stood there, trying to shield the screen from snows with frozen hands and seen it plume before their eyes, diagnostics and blueprints and stories. Descriptions of music and fashion, art and culture, decadence, and vision, to those who had never heard of such. Pescha has to image, he says over the theme park's songstress, footfall on gravel as the jovial pass; here they found reason. Enlightenment, maybe. The restoration of humanity, the return to comfort and safety, the restructuring of everything- it is what they fight for and here they saw it, had it glowing before their eyes, the things they needed to rebuild. If they had a cause before, they cast it aside for this. If they had faith, then it was apostacy. Now they had something they could follow. The group abandoned the Klernsteigaship, defected and struggled on, wandered the emptiness still. But with a newfound purpose, an eye tracing the storm. Amid the cold, they started looking for perfection.

  A giant storage facility, a granary, warehouse, a place of worship. They found this house buried against a mountain from the days of Sect One, a hillside bunker which the enlightened busted into. With heads full of prophetic art and the imagery of their plight, with what was here they started to build.

  They had little, the sick and weary. But they took their thoughts of greatness to that Seven-Seven and to the frequencies, shouting their newest beauty with a furore to silence static.

  Deserters and defectors, their words were crushed, but they had been heard. The location of their sanctum blurted, for just a moment, into the many ears of the hopeless. They salvaged this place, and what now spread as a promise of their work, the work of Nomads finally rewarded, came to them, in stumbling dregs.

Theme parks, ball rooms, restaurants, galleries, Ozwald says, pointing every which way. They preached the art and decadence of old and the Klernsteiga listened, their search for purpose and meaning, hope and salvation, all intrinsically bound here, through concepts like dreams in which none of them had ever indulged. Others came and the enlightened healed their wounds, sowed, and fed and sawed. It is thought the Fauschenherst term for backstreet prosthetics, Bleiy Totter[25], was born of this place. The only safehouse for days, the Nomads who came stayed, their injuries of body and mind too great- wounds of skin and flesh were mended, wounds of thought were ripped open. A place for the disenchanted, who found meaning in making this place whole.

When they're done eating, they return to the path, making for the central route. None turn their way as they walk; anomalies amid the bizarre, it is as though the blue eyed and monochrome Klernsteiga are not there. When they reach the cross section, they stop to watch, looking up at the fountain which marks the parkland's midpoint. It is but a fraction of the whole complex. A gothic masterwork of stone and water, Ozwald says no one knows what happened to those first deserters. There are no records concerning Monvi itself, but Sect Three came only eight years ago. Maybe they buried their ill friend here, he says, gesturing to the cascade between four pathways.

But what is best known is the amusement park's so respected monarch, the overseer of Casse for years. The Administrator, she elected amid her peers for her beauty and artistic skills, is unnamed, in rejection of her now lost Klernsteiga code. He says she is the only one within Monvi with a title at all. All others, they are so blind and deaf and drunk on pleasure, pumped through their veins and inhaled constantly, spluttering through wires and circuits that they no longer hold names. They're more machine and porcelain than human now.

They'll need to see her, if they are to stay, even if for only a night. Ozwald tells them she's at the other end, in her Auditorium.

It was her dance, he says, and her song, that so raised her above all others.

---

[25] *Bleiy Totter*: Back-street prosthetics spread across the Kyut. Makeshift and unrecognised by the Fauschenherst, the term is a collective phrase for all prosthetics fitted to Fauschenherst forces deep in contested territory, where recognised medical treatment is unavailable.

When the trees stop the open grass levels. People eat, all blankets and baskets- they lounge between the carousels and lights and monuments, the dividing line of wonderous architecture preceded by that single, central walkway. They look up to the constructs, of so many cultures and peoples. They are each magnificent, the peaks of every civilisation, and Pescha asks, in awe at buildings unlike any she has ever seen, how they can possibly be built here. How these shattered idealists could make such a thing, of theme parks and houses of government, of art vast.

    Ozwald says that, if they didn't, they'd still be on the Kyut. Amid Small Hand's ruins, the same as when they'd started. Sick and injured, their dreams of war dashed, she must see that they will cling to whatever is left. Does she look upon something corrupted and false? He asks her whether she thinks it deceitful, and cruel. He tells her to look again and see the fruits of her labour. For those here, this is all the Klernsteiga have to show for their years of suffering. Is this not what the people and the planets wish to restore? Even if false, he says; it is all they are worth.

Monsters of splendour, the places from which age-old deities would reign, the streets form between the buildings, not the other way around, lamps hung with their sagged bunting lining. The trio walk amid few others, heading from gallery to gallery, crossing between pillars and high staircases. It is random, a place not built to be occupied, just built. The streets follow the structures, each building made in sudden and untamed furore to fit somewhere, anywhere, wherever there is room. Those first enlightened who would create this haven, wild in their vision, given something to believe in for the first time, who made everything they could dream of. A roadway will end suddenly at a theatre entrance or be cut in half by a stone embankment.

    The music persists as ever, sweeping through these impromptu streets walled in high on either side. Marble, then carved rock, then wood and brick and sandstone, a museum in of itself, besides the many contents. Through warm windows they see interiors just as refined, dining halls amid pillaring and glass fittings, great drapes with everything still in that dark sweetness, of psychedelic sophistication. While food is served not all can eat. While paintings are hung not all can see. Yet they act as though they do, immerse themselves in worlds they have never, can never, know. With throats and eyes long since ripped free.

    Art making art, observing art, she stares at it all in wonder. Everything is beautiful, everything, even the exposed and jittery mechanics of those who wander past. They are mesmerising in their ignorance, of another time and place and situation, as though the universe outside is not there. That they didn't once walk it, fight for it. She can hear faint laughter and a hundred instruments, concerts, and orchestras, plays and cinemas all within these grand walls.

And then, slowly, it changes.

Starting to slip, the libraries and amphitheatres begin to truly lose sense. Roads lead nowhere- the three of them turn a corner and while Ozwald knows this place he still gets lost, stares at a high, pillared brick wall and frowns, his gemstone sights wavering.

The buildings are incomplete, but not in the sense of construction. The very process behind them is twisted. They merge with one another; columns disconnect with the disease of eagerness, not disinterest, and it worsens as they walk. Rooms empty, stone half carved; back here, the architects didn't have the pressures of constant observance and instead found insanity, running from marble to marble without hindrance. Within, Pescha can see floors end and restart someplace else, hollow buildings conjoined with curling messes of dark wood staircases. The tools of carpentry lain alongside; fabric strewn over that not yet finished. Never to be so, song presiding over all.

The same can be said for the people.

Back here, they are lost of pretence, without their false fulfilment. Garments ripped; mechanics bent. So few of them linger, but they see them still, in shapes behind drawn hangings and enamel faces motionless, watching as the trio pass. Caught in a cycle of drug induced malfunctions, having stumbled to a dead end but never having bothered to leave. Some jittery, heads against glass, some completely, utterly still. Their exhibitions are unattended, food served to empty tables. Back here, Pescha hears less of the song and more of the woman, who sings so longingly over top, for while they may have walked Monvi for hours, trying to figure its aimless backstreets, it has not taken long for the façade to scratch. They are the only ones who walk these roads and alleys. The decay has seeped- always here, merely in a different form, the Kyut forever commands its domain; the beauty becomes meaningless.

Then they turn a street end, at the apex of this disorder, and everything changes once more.

The buildings end as abruptly as they had begun, but there is no grass or fielding planted here. Bare sheet steel of sanded bolts and join lines emphasises the sheer scale, distance changing shade at the extents of the walls and roof. She feels that she has been swallowed by one of the grandest machines.

From these plates rise poles, standards climbing in neat rows. Banners, each spire peaked with cloth, flailing to the breeze this sanctum produces. There must be thousands, each high and swaying. The direct path from before the insanity of that cultural maze resumes, cutting straight on. A line through the many flags.

They are of deepest mauve, slow in their fluttering, like they move in waves to a radiating heartbeat, each painted with the same insignia. Of white carefully layered, and while she cannot read their tongue, she does not know the text, she recognises the symbol instantly. Flying, in so many sibling iterations.

The three walk amid these characters for Small Hand, a flared and ink-stroke emblem redone by maybe each individual denizen, for they have formed a fabric garden from their works. It is captivating to watch, bewitching to walk between, the lampposts forgotten to lights against the ground, like cats eyes illuminating the gravel. They make the standards all equally the highest things, save for the ceiling, impossibly further still. Pescha sees them waver, enough cloth to cloak an army, and wonders why they're here. She glances sidelong at the Kamakara, who admires them also. To that song the trio crunch over the pathway, looking and listening to the many sails. A forest of them, perfect in their neat rows. High above, Pescha sees that window stitching, sewing the perimeter of the wall to roof seam. Keeping them from the furore, belting.

She does not mistake their haste. She stares at the back of Ozwalds head and sees that he will not slow; even when they wandered into a dead end, he would turn as soon as he knew. She doesn't need to question this. She saw the same thoughtless husks as him. She looks back over her shoulder at the cultural mosaic of palaces and halls, a maze of a million entertainments. She wonders if anyone ever experienced them all. Just how long she could wander, to sit alone in an empty restaurant and eat plate after plate served solely to her. The parkland, ferris wheels turning, blinking lights and laughter. She knows that if every Nomad in here had not come, then they would each be dead.

But then she focusses, and sees Mincemeat close behind. Such an expression now holds to his face; it is of abhor below the skin, a disdain which does not twist a scowl or force him to squint, but it is such that if even one of those broken dreamers had spoken to him, he would have crushed them in his own machine grip. Expressionless, and he is devoted fully to keeping it so, straight and careless and he returns her look, his pale grey loathing. Despite the storm, Pescha too is uneasy about this place.

The banner garden levels to a flat, a field of steel sheets. A plane of metal, empty but for the pathway, its recommenced lamplight, and where it leads.

The Auditorium of the Administrator. The capitol of capitols. It looks kilometres away.

Modest against its offspring, the building isn't even complete. Scaffolding and timber walkways, it is more of a support than anything, a cradle, for the dome central to its structure. Ozwald points, the path empty, a scene devoid of characters, the space spared by the impulsive artists behind. He says that they will find her there.

Of everything, this place is the oddest. Pescha thinks of the park and city and flags, glances again over her shoulder and sees them huge, amusement attractions reaching over the rooftops, an assault on the senses so vivid and sudden, but it is here that she is most uneasy. Like the storm outside could be turned on or off with a switch, the scale of this metal and fabric box makes her head hurt. An illusion, she could have been walking this space for all those days, false wind raging, and the scale of this prison would've been enough. She cannot tell how long it would take, to run from one edge to the other. It is a thing of nightmares; to turn to one side and imagine something runs her way, a speck at distance, to grow as it comes. They could test Humeda in here, she thinks.

Marble and pillars, the Auditorium is a children's toy from afar, alone and without disguise in fabulous dress or beguiling architecture. It can sit atop Pescha's finger, but she doesn't groan at how far they must go. The song endures, and she is free of snow.

It is aethereal, they walk in the presence of something higher. There isn't enough metal on the Kyut to build this place, there never was this much in the whole universe. Pescha marvels, all things scarlet and plumb, lamps like a procession, Victorian and iron. They are mainly aesthetic, the high rooftop overheads illuminate this emptiness completely. But to state their existence is only for appeal would be a strange thing to say here.

From the Auditorium itself, all that is lit is its entrance. From an open doorway a faint glow escapes but all other rooms are left dark, light kept to the central dome, inviting outsiders in. There is a garden to greet them, ploughed earth shovelled between the opened sheets of steel floor, flowers poking through. They are an excuse for a hobby, something done so that it can be said it is. They are unattended, enthusiasm long lost, but they are not yet dead. She wonders again where they found all of this, as steps rise, a chiselled flight of smooth, pale stone ascending. The boy is anxious, apprehensive to make sure they are welcome, but Ozwald does not knock or wait for address. He climbs without slowing, like he is short of time, and offers them only a backward glance. He slips between twin dark wooded doors. As though he hadn't sought them out, and they had clung to him instead, but Pescha follows. Mincemeat steps to her side. The sudden lunge to keep apace makes Pescha look, blink over the Kamakara beside. Mince is so much taller than her- she peers sidelong into pearly grey pessimism, which looks back down upon her, Mincemeat's left hand clutching the scabbard of his blade, aimed ahead. A second before they peak Mince steps further still, taking the lead. He barges through the unfastened entrance, his retracted striders clunking against a rug and stone floor.

It's only a corridor, a cinema hallway straight between door and dome. Unlit in of itself, brackets with bulbs long broken or busted hang and other openings peel off, but they are all shuttered, no way to wander save for through the tunnel, threadbare crimson underfoot. For a while the singing softens, muffled in this intermediate space, footfall reverberating as Pescha's blue glows. Mincemeat's pearly sights catch the inward light, the Auditorium illuminated within. Ozwald waits for them to catch up.

Into the mind of the architect, they step past dreams and memories and into the core. A theatre-in-the-round, a middle stage is made an island, a podium surrounded by rising seats, like the ground at the centre sank. The same regal tones, the docks are left in darkness, the edges of seats lit faint, all lights directed the same way Pescha looks. The Nomads stand up above, where the dome starts to curve, and follow the stairs down; they level at the base of a dais, upon which only the Administrator could kneel. It reminds Pescha of The Raft, the volume of machinery stored. Higher even still than what Costermonger could, gloat it is a mountain of mechanics, climbing and slipping from the grandstand, a cascade of metal ligaments and systems. It is the same above; where a chandelier once hung, limbs have been thrown, draped, a stalactite misshapen and twisted, of elements of anatomy overhead. Wires and hands, straining to grasp at the woman who works underneath.

Kneeling, she tends to a corpse. Her dress is the most beautiful, a ballgown of gold and cream and pearl like her hair, endowed with lace and colourless gemstones. Skin pale, kept of sun for years. Her delicate attention loops wiring and screws with tools pilled around, the noise of her work reverberating against the song outside, cranking and connecting with components sprawled.

Her porcelain is delicate and carved, feathering and flowers of enamel, and it is mounted with a thin metalwork system of spyglasses, magnifiers to give her sight within the complexness of machine innards. Interlocking lenses, she switches intensity while she works, focussed but with eggshell features unchanging.

It is a sight which feels wrong to see. The wonders outside are for the eye; this place is kept back, hidden, at the furthest edge where this woman, the Administrator, half machine, half sculpture, toils. She does not notice them, the three who watch from high in the stands, but Ozwald leads them down and they follow, seeing the dome rise, its rafters draped with machine guts and those regal cloths. There are no windows, all light confined to those of the stage by design, so leaving the surrounding seats and their occupants in darkness. Pescha sees, as they descend, bodies, slumped and gazing also. Like Nomads who forsook their last piece of flesh, made themselves automatons, lifeless and staring, dead but then without a single inch of them left having ever lived. Buried in the shadows. Gravestones in the grandstand.

When they near their host turns, a bride in masquerade. A mother tidying her child, she stands in address and brushes herself down, slender hands interlaced with bronze implements, fingers interlocking before her waist. The centre of attention, every piece of her is so delicately intricate and ornate, she must have spent years on herself before she even turned to Monvi. She, who pursued perfection, sought to make herself the first standard, to prove to all else that it could be done. A testament to their fantasy, it works, Pescha thinks, following Ozwald from stairs to flat, leading to the island stage. Pescha is transfixed, by the idol so graceful in simple stance.

At this centre the lights are so bright, a full audience could watch and Pescha would not know, dazzled by beams pointing inward only, so forcing of her the same. She can look nowhere but to her, the Administrator, before whom Ozwald bows, kneels upon the uppermost step of the podium and lowers his head. A gesture unasked for and unaccompanied by the two Nomads behind. They remain a few paces back.

The Administrator nods, familiarity in how she beckons Ozwald forward, like he always does this, and she wishes he wouldn't. Her hospitality extends to the others, as she offers equally polite bows, stepping aside and welcoming them onto her dais. Up close her dress is evermore lovely, of so many layers each laced and floating, yet like her limbs it is only maintained to the best degree, never repaired. Faint breaks and tears, ripped openwork scuffed with such long use, her tedious work may have chipped at cloth and meat but never at heart, for with a refined etiquette unobserved for hundreds of years she stands, straight and somehow smiling, even though it is only her porcelain face on show. Like a bridal veil she pulls back her lenses, resting the apparatus atop her head, like spindly twigs of gold and petals of glass- her vizard of a thousand flowers, of enamel made liquid, imprinted with roses. Sweeping vines curl from mouth and eyes, forever set in graciousness and marble-statue ascendancy; the face of she who knows herself wonderful, to be forever set in stone. So delightful that she must have been designed, and then she did design herself, and she belongs so precisely in this space she has made. Of royal draping, all lights on her, a mind remade by the sole concept of delicacy, the Administrator may say that the first thing she thinks of herself is beautiful, and none could scorn. Yet it is in her flaws that the artistry shows, in prosthetics carved and scarred skin swaddled with gold. And when she speaks, leaning a little to Ozwald's level, calling his visit an unexpected pleasure, it is that same longing which sings outside. The single track unchanging, which pines with undertones of yearning hopefulness.

Ozwald asks that they may spend the night, looking up as though to his mother, and that they might pass through the mountain tomorrow. For all her intricacies, the Administrator's eyes are lost behind her ivory veil, a thin mesh of that same enamel barely visible as a visor between her two faces.

She nods courteously again, and says this place is a sanctum for every Nomad, each equally welcome. From a ruined mess to the giant slayer Small Hand himself, her doors are open to all.

Then Mince speaks from behind, a monster in the room. He is of such opposites, but then too similarities, to the Administrator. To see them face pries even Ozwald's gaze from the architect. He stares at that half human designer, handle poking from his many robes, and asks that the Administrator was a Nomad.

There are no silences, the song presides, but she does pause, this sculpted sculptor, her own speech in unknown words languishing high above. As though as lord of this place her thoughts reign vocal. That uttered in her mind said to all. She mulls that question carefully, even if only for a moment.

    She says that she was, once. A long time ago. But not anymore.
    Mincemeat nods. Then he asks what happened.
    The Administrator shrugs; nothing in particular. It asked too much of her. For too little in return.
    Mince frowns. He asks if there's too large a price for survival. For safety. Happiness, even.

This stirs something, Pescha sees it in the Administrator's neck. For a second it rises, and then the next it falls, like for that instance she is reminded of that which she thought herself free from.

C-eight, H-eleven, N, O-2. C-ten, H-twelve, N-two, O. C-forty three, H-sixty six, N-twelve, O-twelve, S-two. C-one hundred and fifty eight, H-two hundred and fifty one, N-thirty nine, O-forty six, S.
    She says it as a recitation, terms recalled time and time again. For a second Pescha thinks them Nomads, that she may call every convert under her roof, but that isn't it. Nobody interrupts her, but then that grand dome above could cave in, and she would declaim still, spoken from memory so well learnt that it is said as one continuous word.

Happiness, she says. The Administrator stares at the Kamakara and asks if it is happiness for which he fights. Happiness for happiness' sake? Happiness for the people, the planets?
    She gestures behind her, to the pilling debris overwhelming, and

says that she has a few vats of it left, before she must cook up another. If the Nomad wants, she can get him some vials. How does he want it though, the statue asks, head falling to one side. The Kamakara says nothing.

Does he want it liquid, or gas. He can smoke it, inhale it. Drink, inject, mix it in with food, whatever; she has gotten good at making her people think it real. She would joke, she murmurs, but she figures that the Klernsteiga may have actually once fallen to their knees at the sight of decent food. The Administrator shrugs again, as elegantly as the gesture can be done. If the Kamakara fights for happiness, he may lower his weapons now in victory.

That isn't why he wars. It never has been. He belongs here, the architect murmurs, head turning to Mincemeat's prosthetics. What has all that hurt won him.

Mince stares. It makes Pescha think, how little she knows of her guide. To guess whether Mince would dare, to draw and cut the Administrator down, or that her words mean nothing, the Kamakara ever indominable, as the Administrator is wonderous.

Mince says being a Klernsteiga didn't do this to him. He gestures to his own augmentations.

The Administrator, unwavering in her passiveness, nods.

Yes, she says. It did.

They sleep in the stands, sprawled over plush crimson, layering their coats over themselves as bed sheets. Such relief takes the blue-eyed Nomad as she sinks into her chair that she hears Ozwald laugh from his seat, somewhere in the row behind. This far out, the song is so quiet, the Administrator's desperation becomes a lullaby, her yearning soft, as though she wishes her weeping child to sleep. The woman herself though does not stall in her toil. Even now, as the three Klernsteiga sit there, bundled in overcoats, she works on, playing with the animatronics of her creation.

In warmth and faint melodies, Pescha feels her azure slip behind heavy lids.

What exactly wakes her, she does not know. A nudge or vague draft, it is a moment of half consciousness, the mind disturbed yet knowing it will drift again soon. A moment forever forgotten in fatigued slumber. Eyes watching but seeing nothing, she is drawn to a humming. That perpetual song remade, murmured in rhythm with that high above. Confined and echoing here, within the dome.

Amid her rubble, Pescha watches the Administrator dance.

Hand in hand with one of those crumpled things; she holds their midriff, fingers interlocked with its, a machine corpse her partner as she purrs to her own tune. It is the most decrepit of her things, a decayed skeleton in machine form, but such is her footfall, so meaningful and resolute that it is like she dances with another, leaning and swaying with him. She is so synched in motion that she can balance and counter with that dead weight, spinning in a way impossible alone.

Dazed and rapt in her stupor, her sights follow the Administrator around the stage like a child watching something from their car window. Locked without fail, on she who drifts below. Woken by that so soothing and pleasant, she starts to slip once more, rising chest heavy and slow. The rustling of the architect's dress is like leaves, blown over the podium floor.

Pescha's head falls to one side, and she just sees Ozwald, a row behind. He is deep in rest, rocked forward with lips apart. She looks the other way, so sluggish as she turns, to Mincemeat, a few seats beside.

The Kamakara sits huddled, legs tucked in, watching the woman whirl. Fully focussed, straight faced, even in that weariness Pescha knows Mince has not slept a moment, staring from the shadows at the artist's dance. At that angle he is without his prosthetics, complete in face with skin pale and grey sights tinged by those most splendid tones. He doesn't notice Pescha, or doesn't care. He Just sits there, back true, and attentive, amid an audience watching the prestigious. A demonstration of etiquette from both performer and spectator. Whereas in Pescha's near senile observance, the Administrator's waltz has the Kamakaras' complete concentration, and while the rest of his body is as slumber-still as Ozwald's, his eyes follow the woman wherever she goes.

Pescha watches. Maybe, if in waking, she would say something, for words hover over her lips, sleep trying to form speech. But they slip and she rolls into a yawn, exhaling question.

Her firefly blue dims, a bulb losing strength. She breathes, sinking into her seat, a baby lulled to rest.

- *KENIDOMO COUNTRY* -
UNRECOGNISED TERRITORY
"*Worm Hill*"

Like machine worms burrowed through the mountain. A tunnel system once of trains and carts is torn, decayed and empty, its tracks rotten and bent. The passage of grain and resource looks like a war was fought within, and those in retreat ruined everything in spite. The underground network of tubes blown out in places, caved in at others.

When they do find their route blocked, they venture out, climbing through the wounds in the walls and into the hill itself, part-hollowed through years of harrowing. Excavating stone for their world within steel walls, these caverns have long since been forgotten by the enlightened, great quarries cutting into the rock deeper than sight or glow can figure. Distance is made only by the dim light of the tunnel's lamps, humming softly in different hues. Like the electrics failed and fire the shades of warning and permission alongside gentle warmth, echoing down the pipeline. Like the subterranean walkways of Our Last Limit, refashioned by the students there.

Even in this work, Monvis architects let slip to their minds. Took chisel and chipped into outcrops and walls, made sculptures of what they couldn't haul back. When the Nomads look out, they see arms and torsos, craning to be free of their moulds, in a hundred different proportions. When they must, they walk amid, watched by faceless rock giants. If the vast openness of Casse Monvi was once where Humeda were tested, then this is where they were built. Where the automatons were dreamt of and fashioned, in forms perfect beyond living conception, ruined by conflict- these figures, straining against their bonds; they are the work of those who so loved humankind.

    Ozwald tells them it isn't much further. Pescha looks down the burrow of iron, framed pink and blue by caution lights.

    She asks how he knows the way, amid these tunnels of neon and their sculpted overseers. The chasm is barely illuminated by the resonance reaching from tube wounds. These watching stone formations, edges caught, vivid and defining, observe them. Some at eye level, and then some towering from the walls, clutching with fingers colossal.

For just a moment, she sees Hjordiis, hand plunging through the cold.
    Too many thoughts pluck her mind in concert, before the boy speaks.

He says he's been this way before; besides Monvi being a bastion, there's no other quick way through the mountain. These tubes stretch for miles, rising and falling with the hill. He thinks they were to build a city, on the other side, or something big. Maybe a dock, where vast ships would have resupplied. But he likes them, he says, glancing up at the woman alongside. These high stone peaks of storms and their systems below.

    Ahead, Mincemeat strides, leading although not knowing to where, a space apart from Pescha and Ozwald. They watch his coat drift, blades drawn in, but he walks still in strength, swaying with each step. Hood pulled back, hair beyond blonde, truly white, the freshness of their first meet has gone, his hair scarce dissimilar to Pescha's save for in opposite tones and shorter, a mouth-length mass, choppy as it falls. He does not speak, has not turned, or remarked. The two Klernsteiga behind pass the time watching his footfall.

Pescha asks Ozwald if he was born on Gardner[26].

    He nods, their talk slow and unconcerned, and he asks if she's ever been. When she says she hasn't, he shrugs; a world of rock, mountains and gorges, the climates swaying from dense sandstorm to blizzards. Like those outside. He says she pretty much has.

    Noise is but their walking on steel, and the whir of the lights in their brilliant shades. The outside darkness and twisted figures are outlined in this luminescence.

    She asks if he left from Pit Fortress.

---

[26] *LL. U. 13 "Gardner"*: A stone world of dust storms and rocky spires, falling into deep valleys and caves and creeks. All settlements are built on the highest peaks to avoid the worst of the weather, which makes accessing the mineral rich crust hazardous, and the honeycomb geology of the planet exacerbates this issue. The "Five Trench Crisis" ended most industrial mining operations and drove many from the major cities. Now most of the planet's population lives in Pit Fortress, a bastion against the storms, and a trading hotspot for whatever metals can be extracted from the ground.

He says he did, but he never lived there, few people do. It's tough to sustain cities, he tells her, unless they're above the clouds, and there is scarce space left that high. Most live in small wayward communities, keeping from the worst of the storms, always on the move. If a group was strong enough, large enough, it could maybe find a cave system, and build a settlement underground. But it'd need to find food and water, resources enough, and even still it isn't safe. After the Five Trench Crisis, they favoured the surface. His people, and many others; they gave all their children to the Fauschenherst. Kept their numbers and needs low but gave what they could. Hopeless enough to give their family, but not hopeless enough to give up.

From the corner of sight, she watches him walk, a blonde-brown mass and then that cloak, glow presiding. She says he must have been young when he left.

Again, he shrugs, the motion a heaving for his arms are forever hidden under his cloaked coat. He asks why he would wait; he'd only become fearful. He remembers little before the Kyut, has little to reminisce, but he knows they were terrified. All of them. Deep breaths and faces stricken, they weren't old enough to make reason of what they were doing, old enough only to know what it was. What going would mean, not what it could. Ozwald, he knew neither. What fear would he feel. He knew not the horrors of the Kyut; fear was what he felt when he took a step, and worried that the winds might haul him away. Fear was sitting still and thinking nothing. He fled, even before his people considered him ready, and made the journey to Pit Fortress alone. Stricken with terror, just as he was wherever he walked. The same as any other.

He looks up, the tunnel burst open overhead. A vast stone grasp reaches down to the pink, as they pass below.

Pescha asks when he did that to his eyes.

His great crystal vision, twin lakes of rose and teal, watches Mincemeat stride.

He asks Pescha what she did before she came. If he were any other, she would push, ask again, but it is with that constant, childish awkwardness he urges a change, wide eyed but never blinking.

Sidelong, she tells him she mined data. Studied and sold information from the Faurscherin ruins. She watches him nod, a quiet setting in.

Ahead, Mincemeat stalks, blades withdrawn yet still pounding against the tunnel floor. His footfall is so spaced, strong, heavy, that it is as though they follow an Humeda, or one of those sculptures, free and now making with them.

        Pescha asks him if he knows what a Kantenlaufer[27] is.

In the age before, great ships chased reality.

        Testaments of science and modernism, humanity built boats to pursue space itself. Grand corporations with sprawling colonies, they fashioned whole civilisations within the confines of steel and oil, made to support generations on end. Ships, the size of worlds, fast enough to stalk the very growth of the universe. For a thousand years they could churn, alone in autarky, self-sufficient and rumbling, the edge of existence at their bow.

        For glory's sake they sought what was next, watching the dark for lifetime after lifetime. Technologists and explorers alike, ships of business on a cosmic scale would trace that final frontier in waiting, ready for aeons.

For something to pass through. For reality to collide, and something from beyond to travel within. The ever-expanding cosmos, growing and growing, but of what and to what end.

To claim the first things truly alien, the first thing truly from another place. What more could mankind and its many denominations boast, aside from breaking that barrier themselves.

        Behemoths, capable of sustaining life for a millennium or more, financed by single buyers or massive institutions. The height of engineering and technological development, amid times of Compressed

---

[27] *Kantenlaufer*: "Edge Runner", generation ships designed to support life for prolonged periods at the edge of space. Usually corporate affairs, to monitor deep-space exploits. Designed to be entirely self-sufficient for their life span.

Light[28], vast gyroscopes[29] to make ships soar, and great breeding programmes, to bring together the many disbanded factions of human exploration[30]. To breath the air of thousands of worlds, and share their blood in unity.

Amid all of this, these ships were the pinnacle of humanity. Its greatest statement, to flaunt at all corners of the cosmos. Maybe, one day, to whatever was beyond.

They called them Kantenlaufer. They developed, with time, their own histories, cultures, dialects, and faiths. Their magnitude, in all meanings of the word, incomprehensible. She speaks loudly so that Mince may hear, hands clasped behind her back as she strolls with the boy. Ozwald, sights glittering, looks up to her. He asks if that's how they got out here. His voice is like the high keys of a piano, words made music in his boyhood.

Pescha nods. She tells him it was a Museishingen Kantenlaufer. The Faurscherin. Mother of the Fauschenherst. Mother to them all.

But he responds in reiteration, like she misunderstood his question. He asks that this is why they're out here. That they're here; them alone. They're the only ones left.

Again, she nods, looking down to his wild mass of wheat for hair. Like harvest grass, she thinks of those golden crop fields, between the Nyaya Matsumasi savanna and the abandoned town at the Shae Doken's base. She says they were just far enough. Far enough to bare the blast.

---

[28] *CLG*: Compressed Light Generators. High-powered engines that revolutionised their time, impacting all departments of science and engineering. A small module which refracts light until it becomes a physical force, able to function perpetually from its completion. Highly valuable, as the technology is irreplaceable by the Fauschenherst. Their modern applications are exclusively military.

[29] *Gyroscope Compensators*: Micro-structure engines comprising millions of counter-levering gyroscopes, designed to suspend vehicles within gravitational fields. The most powerful Gyroscope reportedly countered forces up to 28 m/s². The rift in physics lead to the first great breakthroughs in large-scale interstellar travel, and the basic design was modified to suit theoretically infinite loads.

[30] *Eine Atmen Breeding Programme*: A publicised and species-wide push to encourage crossbreeding between the many divided nodes of the human genome, after thousands of years of assimilation to specific climates throughout the populated universe. The programme was designed to enable all of humanity to thrive in a multitude of atmospheres and habitats. The programme led to a plethora of genome defects and anomalies down certain genetic lines, but systematically unified the collective human spread, symbolising the unity of the period. It lasted some 450 years and solidified a firm and stable human dominion over the stars for the age to come.

They approach a great wound, a burst in the tunnelling like a gash, stone keeping to the edge of luminescence. Ozwald stares as they walk, out this rupture of a mountain vein.

He asks then what the Kyut is.

These could have been those luminous student subsections of Our Last Limit, made underground passageways. Now the Kamakara walks them, and they are ripped and empty.

Nobody is sure. A piece of whatever blew up, maybe, Pescha says, whole worlds impacting against it as it rushed. Some great invention of humanity, like the crust of a hollow world colossal, its beauty safe inside. But it's why they survived. It shielded them, and these four worlds, from what made all else void.

Whatever Ozwald thinks, staring the length of the passage, he keeps it from expression. Then he calls out to Mincemeat, and gestures that they must pass through the wound. The forward way is blocked further down. The colours play so freely within the boys' eyes, and upon Mince's white they make their shades, against hair and skin.

The Kamakara nods, turns and retraces to lead them through.

As he passes by, Ozwald asks him if he had any hobbies, when he was little. Mincemeat must stoop to fit and when he does, he glances at the boy, brow level.

Stepping onto stone, he says he's a Kyut-born Klernsteiga. The light rolls over his machine hand like glowing streams, slipping between the blackened steel seams of grasp and jaw and he speaks with his back to them. He asks what he was supposed to have done. He looks at one of the sculptures, and mumbles of making snowmen.

Ozwald follows, clearly light footed but oddly reserved in step, waiting for Pescha to join him. He looks out to shadow, and says that there's lots to do on the Kyut, if you know where to look. One can walk in one direction and never truly have the same experience twice. Exploring different zones. The history of the lands around them. Studying the architecture. If more of them could write, Ozwald figures the Klernsteiga atheneum would be endless. And in the big cities there's loads. Things to eat and listen to. Libraries as well, he can't read but he likes them anyway. And parties, he tells; there were no parties on Gardner, not like these. He went to one in Fyorfastin and Snackombst once, the great double city, it was amazing. He asks Pescha if she's ever been.

    To the city, yes, she says.

    He nods, walking by her side, and says that Mince would know. The Kamakara must've been to hundreds of parties. He'd be a sure invite. Then Ozwald leans in a little, and lowers his voice, that only Pescha will hear. He says he's heard stories, about Mince. At parties, he means. When Mince was younger. A Klernsteiga, not a Kamakara, but still one so powerful.

There's a legend. That once, madly inebriate, Mince took a girl to the toilets. In some cubicle, out of his mind, he strangled her without noticing, choked her to death by accident.

    Pescha blinks.

    Kneeling in this four-foot space, he could hear everyone outside, oblivious, music blaring. Intoxicated beyond reason, Ozwald whispers that Mince had to decide what to do. How he could dispose of a body and walk free, surrounded on all sides beyond drywall and a flimsy plastic door. He chose to eat her, Ozwald tells; to break of little pieces of her, chew them up, and spit the pulp into the basin, flushing it away. Pescha glances at the boy, at infinitely large crystal globes gaping up at her. For hours, he says. Hours and hours, he broke this girl down. A nightmare space, a single overhead light. Blood everywhere. They say when the door was kicked in, he'd gotten through her whole head. And both arms. The boy tells Pescha to imagine it, this alcove horror. Imagine the Kamakara rising, giant. Insensible. Matted with red.

    Pescha turns her head fully. She asks Ozwald, keeping her voice level, exactly how much of that he thinks is true.

    The boy gazes at her, glow refracting through his globes. Then he looks ahead, drawing Pescha's sights too.

    Mincemeat waits, turned back to watch them come. Light and shadow play against sharp features, his expression empty.

    None of it, says Ozwald. He says it loudly.

What he means is that everyone has something. Even if they just sit in a blank room they must still sleep, which means they must dream. He knows being a Nomad, being here, has certainly given him much to think about. He says it with half interest, looking up at the rock giants, neck craned so that he misses Mincemeat's glance back. He murmurs that the Kamakara has always been here, upon the Kyut. Lawless and free. He must have had something before the Klernsteiga.

A testament to his own fallacy of youth, Pescha watches him and then the Kamakara, his canvas skin adorned in colour against black prosthetics and grim garments. One hand so pale and the other so dark, if he wore his hood to hide his hair, from behind, one would think him divided by greyscale in two.

Mince states that if Ozwald's talking about a childhood it won't pass. They all know this. Despite the boy's bravery, he says, people will forever distinguish between child and adult. He is in the same place as them, no safer or far from harm, yet still he is a boy. That counts for something. Something more than age. No matter how harsh, how cruel, he tells, he had someone. He must have, or else he wouldn't say such a thing.

The stone figures observe, like they wait for all three to turn their backs before they lunge.

Ozwald steps from the goliath, wandering to Pescha's waiting side.

Mince was a child too, he says.

Expressionless, unconcerned, like something snags at his coat, that catches his attention enough to make him turn, as though he looks for what hooked him. Gazing at the boy who pulled his jacket.

He looks Ozwald up and down, neat cloak closed, boots clean. When one would always settle on his eyes Mince instead looks down. To the boy's shoes, laces tied into a bow. He glares, then he looks at Pescha's, then down to his own. He calls attention to boots just as clean, scrubbed by snow water and wind. They both stare, and it is Ozwald who speaks first.

Frowning, he asks why he's done his laces like that. Cord bound once and then looped, tied around the ankle again and again until there is no thread left. Now when Mince gazes at them, he gazes with expression, and at that angle and that light it is difficult to discern. Maybe agitation, but for the first time Pescha sees a break in Mincemeat's minimal and constant display, in embarrassment peering. He rocks and shifts from one side to the other.

He looks up, lips tight. Almost a grimace, pink and blue against white and shadow.

He says nobody ever taught him.

Regardless of all things, they always had someone. Not parents, they had people. Lots and lots of people. To love and admire, impress with achievement, and complain to in crisis, but it's more than that. Standing there, the Kamakaras shoulders sag. To hate in anger, to distrust. To fear enraging, to worry that they may find what you hope to keep secret. Not just to know they are always there- to fear that they may leave. Fear that they may not be there when you look back. A trivial thing, the Kamakara knows, shrugging to his rocky audience. But that's the point. They learnt. Fear: to worry their mother may never again embrace them.

His fear was made of steel and cable and crushed his mother underfoot, long before memory could make it a nightmare. For all others, he didn't need them. What happiness. What sorrow. There was nothing between, there was only what was. He knows nothing. Understands nothing. All he had was fear, and he hated it so. Sought to make it a stain as the machines had made his love.

Then he stammers, thought picking at his machine half-lip, prosthetic twitching. He turns to hide it, looking up to one of the colossi.

Ozwald wants to know him, Mincemeat asks.

He stares at that thing which looms from the dark, like he dares it to move. He turns to the boy, hair drifting, hanging free, strands before his features. The expression within is stagnant.

He asks how much further.

- KENIDOMO COUNTRY -
UNRECOGNISED TERRITORY
"The Rautbergen March"

Cold and wind and dread build with each step, they hear the storm call. Vibrant shades wilt to that impending, waiting for them to come. The light at the end of the tunnel, it is dark and heavy, deep indigo and scathing, and they expect to turn and face the wild once more. Instead, they find their way blocked. Round the bend, they draw hoods tight and clasp layers closed, to see an ensemble sitting, crammed against the tunnel walls. Maybe one hundred and fifty, hunched in greatcoats, stoves and lanterns splayed, the blizzard raging at the end of their camp. For a moment the trio might start, frown, and reach for their waists, but when all eyes meet Pescha knows them as friends, evermore so when theirs reach the Kamakara. Such a reverence takes their gaze, that they may bow and weep.

These Rautbergen, they are different. She walks between them, returning nods and smiles, and they are unlike those of Fauschenherst territory, within its jurisdiction and resource. She remembers those of Our Last Limit, of Fyorfastin and Snackombst, they who patrol cities and are summoned to Humeda outbursts, but here they are at war. Amid their packs and cloaks, they sit, rest against crates and the curvature of the tube, but for each who is idle there is another in practice, and she watches their ritualistic discipline from behind Mince. They murmur, eyes tight, and scan over scripture.

Incense is burnt and symbology fastened to standards, propped against the tunnel walls. What they read is in great books with text fine but bound in tapers and inscribed cloth, fastened to thick leather detailed with intricacies of virtue and faith. Around lanternlight they gather, talking, eating. With nothing but welcome do they greet Pescha as she follows Mince, who leads to the foremost point of the column. She does not miss the many oddities happening around. Neither the Kamakara or Ozwald much care, seeing but unintrigued as people clad in their gear, faces from every world and every descent, pray, with beads wound between fingers over rifles and blades. Flags and streamers decorated in the symbology of ages lost, but dedications eternal, wound in their faded shades about barrels and stocks, totems and tokens tied within the binds.

This is a modern practice, besides her learnt records and histories of reality before its collapse. She looks over worship with wavering brows, those of Sect Three around her melancholy with their many years here. Still, she recognises things, against fabric strips and emblems knotted to their bags. Sees the marks and notes of that Museishingen age, those days of human unity now lost with their Emperors, detailed upon cloth and tongue.

She peers over shoulder, to Ozwald, who follows close behind.

He does not notice, rolling a strand of hair between his lips.

They head for the exit, snowfall curving the tunnel lip and slipping through, wind and noise building. The flakes claw at those within as they drift past the tube's end. By this drop, which falls to a rocky slope then the flats below, sits the head of this party, watching the cold curl. Skin dark and weathered, the eyes of a man much older, he is distinct from the rest; an officer's coat over his shoulders, plain epaulettes and buttons worn, high-peaked visor cap by his side, with service jodhpurs and boots battered. His uniform is tailored, fitted before his descent or upon bravery and promotion, a declaration of rank. Like a cloak his coat rests with his arms free, and even still she can see it a little too large. He could have lost his, had it ripped or stained, and had to take another. Maybe he just lost the weight.

When a Raut calls and he turns he is slow and so weary, if it were a machine which approached Pescha thinks his face would scarce change. But when the Kamakara comes slack features straight, although forever numb with cold of body and mind. He rises to greet them, boots clicking on frozen pipes, and he gives Mince a weary wave of a salute. Upon his shoulders, the insignia declares him an Auberkemein in rank. In command of a Wolstspitzer, equal to five Wolstkader; two hundred men.

Pescha turns and looks down the tunnel.

He's missing a quatre. And the way they are sitting, in such a diversity of groups. Most weren't always his.

For all formalities, the Kamakara nods, looking to pass without word, but instead the officer speaks.

He asks where they're headed.

Pescha glances at the back of Mincemeat's head.

The Kamakara, monstrous, asks why.

The storm twists beyond, grasping at the tails and empty sleeves of the officers coat, his steel insignia of shoulder and visor cap catching the frozen timelessness; he is a silhouette against the ripped end of the tunnel, and the blizzard so close.
    He asks if they've listened to a radio recently.
    A pause.
    The Kamakara says they haven't.
    He nods, glancing out to the storm. He must watch for only a second, but with that screaming wind it feels forever. He asks their destination by gesture, pointing to know if they walk this way.
    The Kamakara says they will.
    He nods again. Tired and beaten, he addresses Mincemeat solely.

He says there's something he needs to know.
    He suggests they join his column.

If Pescha didn't know her records, she would think those better times myth entirely. It is a sight so medieval, so ancient, to see them trek through the wind. coats and hoods and bags larger than their wearers, they walk in double pairs, hands raised as they lean into the storm, each individual billowing in one turbulent strip. Most carry their rifles in hand, cumbersome Lautreisgefers, with their disproportionately long magazines clutched or buried within the folds, scarce stowed. Those who have packed theirs away lug with them telecommunications or more bags, clutching antenna which whip like cloth overhead, tied with fabric emblems and marks. As though an invasion went wrong, but this is their common march and none talk, none eat or fiddle. They slog on, pushing through, stretching from one end of vision to the next.
    In marching, she cannot think. The noise, the cold, of banners fluttering and footfall so hopeless, constant, little comes to thought, and less still is welcome. Their straight, advancing and receding from sight; she thinks of the power lines of Dodtohmet, wavering overhead.
    She thinks of where they lead.

When they must rest, they pull from their packs canvas and canopy and stick their rifles upright, leant against one another like bonfire timber. Huddled, bunched around whatever heat they can muster from wood and flint, nurtured so carefully by shaking hands. Most must sleep in the open, underneath their high spears of reception towering, made like the aerials into flags. The snow builds against them, cold soaking but the storm does subside, if only a little. Enough for them to talk, pushed so tightly against each other as they are.

Mince leads with the Auberkemein, lost in the storm before Pescha and Ozwald, who wander some unknown midpoint. They could be a few from the rear, could mark the halfway, but they walk in pace with the Rautbergen and when they stop, labouring to build camp and warmth, the soldiers share with them their goods. Pass bundles and flasks to the two Klernsteiga with smiles and curt bows, and although they do not talk, it is not so much a welcome with which they are included, it is gratefulness. Like the Rautbergen are obliged; feel it the right thing to do, beyond simple manners and kindness. Pescha thanks them, blue lights within a cowl, and shares with the boy pressed against her side, steam rising from things fire warmed and tough to tooth.

    They sit against tenting and snowdrift. Camp light brushes their side, and they face the abyss. In their marching and such a horrid freeze, they think nothing, but when it is just the cold, some things do poke thought. Try to distract, but she is there none the less, and it twists the mind. What she considers makes her shrink into the folds. She wonders if, should she stand now and walk straight, she'd find anything. If she strays from this preconceived route. If anything would wait in that uncharted inner space.

    She stares, hood drawn so close to her collar that she peers through the slit of a knight's helm, watching the wastes sheet and splay, a bundle watching the white whirl.

    She stares, the gusts clearing all thought. Maybe, for just a moment, she even sleeps.

They sit against the outside, of a column of canvas and radios and banners and huddles. Lent against a snow-piled tent, she hears Rautbergen talk, their voices fluctuating to the pitch of wind.

    One holds his weapon up, gesturing to it loosely with sharp jabs. He speaks to a mass which scarce listens, eyes cast to their boots and firelight, snow whipping. To distinguish them as humans seems odd, they are in a place inhospitable, with figures burdensome and hunched, and here their voices are aethereal, muffled and indistinct.

    He bears a K.A.G Neiderkop R-Three, the armament carried by

Mince, the standard anti-soft-body of the Fauschenherst, but in its long-barrel configuration. That is the point of his scrutiny. He holds it high, a compact gun without the stock of its common counterpart, instead with a lengthy bore for better accuracy. He waves it like it isn't a gun, drawing muted concern from his fellows, who watch him preach.

He asks how they ended up with this.

The blueprints and designs of the Museishingen, he says, they who sought to and most certainly did conquer the stars. Who laid out for them the foundations of a new age of exploration, in their hands, and now they bare this. Over one hundred years of war upon the Kyut, from Sect One to Sect Four, leads to this?

Someone at his side, fatigued and half asleep, moans that it's a good gun; that they're all good guns. What is he even complaining about, she grumbles? He brought both a Neiderkop and a Laut.

That's not why, he says, and anyway, she knows the Lautreisgefer is junk too. A whole new frontier, and they've got guns with twelve-round magazines, and too much kick to shoot while holding to the shoulder and moving. But that's beside the point, it's this, he says, while he waves the long barrel like papers, that gets him. The Neiderkop long barrel "configuration", he calls, emphasising the word, and when he goes to next speak, half of the camp around him interjects, grumbling for silence or joining in, like he's said this a thousand times.

He asks how they can call it a configuration, when they've just used the metal of the brace for the barrel. It isn't a configuration, he says over them, it's just a different gun, and they don't have enough material for both bore and stock. He turns the thing, words lost to the commotion of argument and storm, showing them fittings designed to bare the brace now replaced, but they kick at him drowsily and flick empty packets, begging for silence.

They argue for some time, words lost to Pescha's frozen stupor.

When their rambling subsides, he collapses back into his stoop, and grumbles that it doesn't matter. Cradling the gun, he says they give them Humeda guns for people and people guns for Humeda and they still fight; they could give them sticks and the Rautbergen would march on.

Until the last human being has fallen on the Kyut, he speaks, and what he says next is reiterated throughout his circle, mumbled and slurred, but without cynicism, devoid of humour and mock. They say it

with complete conviction.
>Haufenmensch Hellegeneid, they say.

Pescha stirs. Her eyes feel like they've a film of ice over top; when she blinks against the storm it is as though she works to melt the frozen sheen. If she slept it couldn't have been for long. Few others in the column rest, eating from tins and huddling around their many fires, the bombardment constant and whining over the flats. But it is quieter, as the Rautbergen drift into deeper numbness. Like her, they do not sleep so much as they watch, curled against themselves. Weary, in every sense of the word, rifles propped in snatching piles or against their sides, in hoods and scarves, always with one eye open. They've been here for years now, the same thing day in, day out. What's the point in sleep and dreams. What are they to dream about. They've nothing now but this.

She turns from the noise. Her neck is so stiff that it may snap should she spin too fast.

The storm rages always.

Ozwald lays against her arm, watching the cold twirl. They are both swaddled in many coats, now a pile of frozen cloth.

This close, she can see the mechanics of his sight, fashioned into eyes from glass and fibre. A system of mirrors, layers upon layers they are liquid gemstones, fluid but also automated, like thin sheets of transparency within water. Shaped into the systems of vision. They twitch and revolve, forever in flux. But not once does he blink.

He looks up to her, skin milky and pale yellow, waxen, and tinged, surely beyond reason of ancestry. She pulls him in closer, snow building against their sheets, banners beating above. Under his layers and cloak, she feels the metal framework of his unseen kit, steel against his arms.

They stare, unthinking. Minds of ice.

They stare at the emptiness they'll die for.

Ozwald mumbles something, blanketed head against her shoulder. He asks her to get him out of here. To take him someplace else.

He will die here. Or he will win, either way he'll never leave. He doesn't know if there's anything beyond this. Anything worth this. Worth this much, or worth this little. He knows there's nothing better. That's why he's here. But surely there's nothing worse.

He wants to hear a story, he says. She knows of worlds before this. Because he doesn't want to fall asleep. He already knows where he'll go if he does.

Pescha feels him shuddering, tucked under her arm. Loose strands of his corn hair grasp at whirling snow, illuminated in her headlight blue. In the middle of nowhere they sit, bones stiff with ice. This whole camp could die in one night, drift away without a voice of commotion, and the Fauschenherst would come only when they knew their Kamakara missing. If she were to pass herself and him now from afar, she would think them dead. A boy cradled by his machine, its glowing conscience wavering with each second.

She can think many things in that moment. They twitch over a brittle mind.

The Museishingen Empire, a fable of scale and greatness. Few care to learn its enemy. Few know the Museishingen were born to meet them. Few know which came first.

Amid the horde of disbelievers, a champion of their sickness fought. She was everything, all virtues of courage and strength but with such blind hatred, fed to make her vile. Of these cynics she led, modest in rank but in command of more respect than her position could ever imply.

She had hair so white. When Pescha first heard of the Kamakara Mincemeat, she thought back to this age-old fable.

Pescha shivers. She wonders if this is a story best to tell.

She thinks of the child trembling at her side.

To a battle unrecorded, a place long forgotten, she brought her war. To take a Museishingen world by sky. Tear them apart from flighted wings far above, so quick and indiscriminate in her assault as to force capitulation. To make the Imperial fleet obsolete, in the face of her severest overrule. They rumour the world was a harried one- beat by constant cosmic storms, battered by stone and debris. To survive they built a barrier, a wall to shield the planet, in great sheets of armoured steel. One with a single gate. One way, in and out, open between collisions.

When she came, she thought that place so important. Thought to snap morale, by making of a force sworn to death prisoners, hauled from her new frontier. When she and her fleet swarmed, there was no resistance. They were to flood through and trap those of Mu in with them, they would let the gate shut to their invasion and open to new rule. She led a fleet through those doors to a world undefended.

Lured in, she realised too late, ordering a retreat. Fooled, she charged to flee, to evade trajectory, but she knew herself caught. The gates remained open.
    Those of Mu, they would sacrifice a planet to watch her fall.

Like a bombardment incapable of mankind, whole crushed worlds slammed. Making of everything more ammunition for its great salvo. She raced, watching her friends get blown from their cockpits, shattered and ripped. She, the fastest, the strongest, put everything into her engine. Fired with all the power she had.

Pescha is unsure what it was, exactly. What sent her so far. A fragment, which punctured her thrust perfectly, or a wing clipping the gate. Whatever it was, it struck her at precisely the right moment. Caused such speed in the explosive dump of fuel that she shot herself, her corpse, at a pace that outran death, in a freak of probability and chance.
    The Museishingen Empire thought her dead. They would never report of her again, and saw their efforts and knew the results. Her allies thought the same.

Ozwald rubs his face. He asks how she lived.

Pescha's brow twitches.
    It isn't known. The science behind her endurance. By all standards, she should have died the second her ship blew, and stayed that way; the only true, empirical evidence anyone ever had that she remained was that they saw her. Spoke to her, many years later. The only story known is what they heard, rarely, from when she once explained to her

closest partner.

    That she was cast like a stone, skimming to the bounds of reality.

    Flung at speeds impossible, went so far in the blink of an eye, on the perfect course.

    And like the Kantenlaufers of old she reached the bounds, but there she did not stop.

    A corpse, in flux between the two states, which found that seam and passed through.

    Broke through to the other side.

She feels Ozwald look up at her, cold breath drawn by winds as though on a string. She watches the snow, blue unwavering.

If her tale were well known, she would have been invaluable. Indispensable: truly the greatest achievement of humanity, for in her transcendence she may have met that which could change all things. That which she never spoke of, left as blank as all had though the beyond.

    She slowed down. In some form, outside the bounds of reality, she met matter, enough to ease her pace. It slowed her down, so the universe could catch back up, reeling her in.

    For a second, she was all. Was creation itself. She saw the beyond, before reality caught her and the planets raced past, surging as colour and light bloomed.

The world which crashed into her, it was a heartless place. A stone hunk, empty of all things. Food, drink, life. Or air to breathe.

    Ozwald sniffles, wiping his nose.

When she woke, she stared at darkness. Sat up, cold beyond cold, and tried to inhale.

    Clawed at her throat, dry and heaving, and choked there, scratching at dust and rock.

    Suffocated, gurgling, wide eyed and writhing.

    Just the same as she had for days on end.

Whatever happened to her outside the fold, when she stepped back into creation, it did to her the unthinkable. Beyond the anomalies of distant species. Some are with lifespans fixed, until death is forced on them. She couldn't die no matter what.

    Fingernails would snap as she dug into the grit, she would scratch and bruise herself as she collapsed, lungs burning as though aflame, and moments later she would wake, to suffer again, wholly renewed.

Again and again. Waking, choking to death, froth and bile foaming, and waking anew.

Trying to kill herself, breaking and breaking, hoping that she may curl up and stay dead.

Ozwald rubs his hands within the folds of his cloak, tired and sluggish in motion.

For seventy years, she told.

For seventy years, without respite, with nothing besides, she felt her eyes bulge within a swelling skull. Felt skin itch, insatiably, and her bones arch. Unable to take a breath, clutching at emptiness. No sound. Nothing but suffering.

She walked, ran, crawled, it didn't matter. She could pound her skull against the stone and awake moments later, blood pooled but not a gash upon her face. She could snap fingers, rip skin. If she could keep conscious for long enough, she could watch it crawl back into place. She didn't eat, had no energy made. She just was. Forever, she thought.

Imagine that, says Pescha. Thinking this will, without doubt, never end.

Ozwald asks what she did.

Pescha nestles herself deeper within the folds.

She herself said seventy years. For seventy years, without stop. But she couldn't possibly have known. She was out there for much, much longer. Long enough to erase herself, as a hero, from record. Long enough for a renowned name to slip all tongues.

It must have felt like forever. So, she trained. Her body remade itself, renewed time and time again but she saw scars, would pick at wounds and see their marks remain. She broke her body down, ripped muscle like bread. For common strength she worked a hundred times harder, forcing herself until she collapsed, choked, gurgled, and sat back up. She sprinted. Ran, without rest, for years on end. She learnt control, to its furthest extents. She could stand, straight faced, seconds from death, and not waver, until the dark descended and she rose once more to meet it. Until she could stand forever. Not even death could floor her. Until, of body and mind, she became infallible. Unbreakable. Until she walked

every inch of her planet and felt nothing.
She could no longer feel death.

And when a venturing ship, some convoy on the bounds of space stumbled upon her world, she must have still felt nothing. As long as it took for this vague and random clump of stone to be landed; this is how long she waited. How long she suffered.
The snowfall is the sequined shawl of a great Humeda, ever drawn across the flats. Ozwald asks what happened to her.
In the end, Pescha tells, nobody is sure. She turns to the boy.

But she was there. This woman. There, at the end. There is record of her, in the closing moments. When everything fell apart. She saw it.

Under her wing, she feels Ozwald turn, facing the storm. His legs are tucked tightly to his chest. He asks why she'd tell him this. Or is this truly the happiest story she knows.

She shrug; because, Pescha says, laying a hand atop his blanketed mane of hair, maybe she survived even that. Somehow, she endured the worst of all things. Maybe she does still, here, amid the remnants of where the collapse occurred.
Imagine that, Pescha tells. The worlds of which she could speak. She waits out there, in the dark, in a state between states. She must remember still. Maybe she's here, she never left. Encased under impacted stone for years, just finished digging herself out of rock with raw fingerbones. They both stare, wind like someone flays the air and draws razors across ice. She feels his knee, rested against hers. Over her shoulder, the trails of Rautbergen chatter swirl faint against spitting campfires. She looks up the line, to the extent of her bubble within the storm.

She draws him in close and asks if he wants to know something funny.
Against her hooded cheek, she feels the whisps of his hair nod.

She tells him that, before she came here, she was sure the Kamakara Mincemeat was that woman. Upon Emilia, while Sect Three fought, when she heard of the white-haired Nomad, she swore them the same. She didn't think much of it, it meant little to her, but she thought it still.
When she joined the Klernsteiga, she learnt that Mince was a man, and of his prosthetics. They didn't make any sense, if flesh and bone

would just regrow. Then they met. He was so tall, and she saw Mincemeat's hair in person. How much shorter it was than the accounts of the girl before.

Ozwald asks what the haircut means. Pescha glances at him, his head against her chin.
      She says the woman couldn't cut her hair. It didn't change alone; it stayed the same length forever. If she tried, it just grew back.
      She cannot see, but she thinks he makes a face.
      He says he didn't know hair was alive. Pescha blinks.
      She says she isn't sure the woman was, either.
      She moves her shoulder, and feels building snow slip.

They sit. They will sit for as long as the Rautbergen do. Despite all things, with her back to malleable canvas, draped and huddled against that boy, she feels her sights droop once more. Feels that weight unstoppable. Feels her blue roll around inside its sockets.
      Ozwald shifts, fidgets under her arm, and whispers her sobriquet in question.
      She says his back in response.

He asks what they're doing there. She says nothing.
      With the Rautbergen, he means. Why are they following their column? Mincemeat knows it's slowing them down. Why would he hold them here?
      It occurs to Pescha that Ozwald doesn't know where she's going.

She says she doesn't know. Their voices are so close, an inch from each other's ear.
      She says she'll find out when the Rautbergen march.

- KENIDOMO COUNTRY -
UNRECOGNISED TERRITORY
"Befelobeth Revelation"

They pray. Foreheads against the snow, breath of word melts the cold at their lips. Rifles are oiled as though baptised with trembling hands, and the storm resumes in all its distaste, fighting to swipe them away, swat the insects plaguing this timeless place. The Rautbergen make no complaint. They are silent in their work. Restrained in their food, eating little, but they all look from their cans, lift heads from packets and flasks.

They watch the blue eyed Klernsteiga pass, greatcoat snatching. Her blue steady, kit and sword strapped at the waist. She walks when none other stands, headed for the snake's head, and in that low light the snow is thick, pluming and bursting like smoke against her side. She can look out, to the shape of white waves, and know they tower so high. Like an ocean of sea spray, and they are in its deepest trench.

The heading tent's streamers billow, mounted on standards far reaching. They flag the party's head. A tepee preceded by but more kneeling shapes and supplies; there is nothing beyond the officer's hut but the expanse, which watches its invaders first wake, then immediately look around. To make sure they're still there. That everyone is still there. Pescha doesn't bother to look for Mince.

Guardsmen watch, not an inch of skin offered to the ice. They turn to her but say nothing. She pulls back her hood.

From within, firelight flickers, but any rising smoke is snatched before notice.

She steps through the drapes, near hard set with frost.

The instant she looks at them, she knows this is important.

They pour over sheets, diagnostic prints, and a map the size of the makeshift table over which it is lain. The moment she enters Mince looks up, his striders leant against the pile his coats form, as though there were another Nomad crouched aside. Their fire is dim, dying and unrenewed but the Kamakara has his sleeves rolled high to the elbow, where his blackened steel meets the palest skin, fingers splayed over the chart. The Auberkemein glances up, tending also to the papers.

Mincemeat smiles faintly. He stands straight, shirt creased but tucked in and fashioned against his form. It makes Pescha stare. She thinks of the Kamakaras apartment.

Mince says he figured Pescha would be impatient. He gestures the Klernsteiga come, waving over his chart and he takes from the table a small, cabled screen, holding it in his machine clutch.

It is no map, it is a schematic; the layout of a complex, six stories high. Like a large, broad air traffic control tower, rising to a hub at its hight, it is its own superstructure, as though the tall obelisk was crushed, squashed down. Square from above, its control cab protrudes the circumference. The diagram is unannotated and unmarked, and she doesn't recognise it. She sees nothing of significance. Her sights trail, brow unsure, until her surveying hand sweeps over the adjacent parchment. She stares at it, grasp hovering. At her side, the Kamakara rests his fists atop the desk.

The Iron Driver, he tells Pescha, is a train which cuts through some of the densest stormfronts recorded upon the Kyut. Who built it and why, in those days of Sect One, nobody knows, but its range and its stops at key cities throughout this sector, and beyond, make it vital for Klernsteiga support, where that of the Rautbergen march would be impossible. Nomads can cross some of the most inhospitable regions, quickly and safely, on a train not needing crew or fuel, running constantly on a circuit.

Pescha mumbles that she's heard of it.

And these, the Auberkemein says, are the people threatening it. He points to the complex and says it's a mere few miles from one of the Driver's stops; an old observatory, probably built after the Humeda revelation by some scattered band of Sect One. Now, he tells her, its crawling, wayward wanderers making it their home, safe from radar in the tumult and from the machines at its high, precarious altitude. It's a vital vantage in of itself, he states, coat once more draped like a cloak, vapor permeating his words, rising to flow around the peak of his cap. But Klernsteiga on the train have seen them venture down, taking interest in the tracks, and leaving when Nomads make their presence known. Now, they're pitching camp down the slope.

Pescha stares at the papers, guise unchanging.
>She looks to the Kamakara. Her expression asks for her.
>The Kamakara hasn't looked from Pescha since she entered the hut.

Because she's near, Mincemeat says. Because she's closer than she realises.
Once she's on that train, it'll take her from the cold of Zero, Double-Four, Nine, Three, Five and through, to where the snows fail to rain. And on, into a zone they call Summer. There, she'll find sandstone pillars; huge towers of rock, climbing with their heights flat, overgrown, with greenery flourishing.

The Nomads have a name for these, too.

They call them the Ukibiki Pillars.

The Auberkemein glances their way.
>Mincemeat's face, it is a stare unchanging. An unnamed expression, a midway between sympathy and something cruel, like wavering derision. Even contempt, cut as a grin against the Kamakaras features.

The Kamakara asks Pescha if she knows what this means. She still must get there, must ascend through this constant winter, and reach the Iron Driver. Even then, she still has a way to go. But it won't be difficult once she reaches that train. At least, nothing to compare. The Kamakara rocks back, arms straight against the table. Whatever it takes, he says. Whatever has driven her here, whatever she has felt along the way. She ascends. If she can beat through that base, she can reach the Driver, and then…
>With his hand, the Kamakara gestures a clean swoop.

But it'll all mean nothing if she can't clear that compound. She'll rot and freeze if she tries to cross that stretch on foot, she needs the train. And for the train, they need the compound. And for that compound, Mince slurs, pushing from the desk and striding to Pescha's side. She'll need the Rautbergen.

Mincemeat holds out that cabled screen, not to take but to see. Upon it is what reads only as a list, but Pescha recognises the layout. There are multiple teams, all converging on that one point.
    The Auberkemein talks from behind the Kamakara. It's a cathedral, he says, on the hump of a huge snow dune. That's where the teams will meet.

From there, Mince tells, pocketing the screen, they'll fall on the complex. But until then, Pescha has an actual mission. A genuine order, from her commanding officer. Mince looks back at the Auberkemein, who rolls and stuffs the papers into his bag. The wind hammers their canvas.

The column must endure, the Auberkemein says. Under no force can it break. He ties his pack against his coat.
    Protect the column.

Haufenmensch Hellegeneid, he calls.
    Pescha nods, and is first to leave the tent.

- KENIDOMO COUNTRY -
UNRECOGNISED TERRITORY
"The Gelid Cur"

It's a song, to which the Rautbergen salute. The Haufenmensch Hellegeneid. A composition of a hundred languages, it is a psalm made for the illiterate, the uneducated, who may wish to fight under the Fauschenherst banner. Many cannot read, cannot write, but through this muse they learn the words of command and war in all the Faurscherin's tongues, the ethnic mass and multitude of that Kantenlaufer ever expansive across the Kyut. But what was born necessity soon became emblematic, symbolic, for a unity the people and the planets can rally toward. One voice, for all of humanity.

In full, the psalm may take a whole day to chant. Pescha knows, beside Common Tongue, only the words of a small cultural group on Emilia, close to where she lived. It sings; we are skulls and eagles and church steeples- we are war, on a holy scale.

Most Rautbergen know it word for word.

They are the flanks of the advance, Pescha and Ozwald, the wings of their march. She cannot see him, keeping pace on the opposite side. They watch the storm as the Rautbergen struggle on, but when the wind picks up, both Klernsteiga peel out, to the extents of vision. They walk as far from the column as they can, so long as they keep it in sight, eyes fixed on blanket cold the other way. Waves and arcs of white come at her so fast, she feels they may cut her in two as they lash, but she doesn't look away. She keeps her sights fixed on the tumbling snow. She doubts there is a noise like this anywhere else in the universe.

It is hard to figure how much ground they cover. As they walk, knee-deep and heaving, they focus only on each step, each individual motion. She cannot know how far they have come. In a minute. In an hour. Sight tells nothing and she is so numb, but when she forces herself to count their steps, to see how far their footfall reaches, it is at a laborious pace that they march. It demands such focus, such effort, that she cannot let her thoughts wander, or else she would slip or loose the line. She doesn't daydream, she thinks nothing. She watches. She walks. She eats from packets stored in Pack One's satchels, but she does not stop and when the Rautbergen halt, the Auberkemein and the Kamakara far ahead staying their charge, she stands vigil. To the soldiers, she is a vague shape, beset by clutching white. Barely visible, facing the storm, but when she turns, they see her light. Like some ghoul of this endless winter, watching over their course. Ever present, the same is said the other way, of the boy with the wild corn scruff billowing, out of Pescha's sight.

What worth could they make of this, she manages. What implement could make use of this place. What people could live here. To send their children, to send themselves, for this. Ice, they die for nothing; if it is won, the Fauschenherst could use the bodies for fuel. She thinks on what the Kamakara said. Looks ahead, into the furore, and knows that somewhere, there is a wave. A great swell, the crest of a frozen tide, mounted by temple and fortress.

A Nomad's duty is to take the Kyut. To relieve impossible suffering, that is their purpose. The fable of the machines, it is a common enemy, inhuman and cruel. Mindless, it stands between the people and their salvation. But a Klernsteiga knows their undertaking, better than anyone else. Missionaries, they require nothing, ask for nothing, for they know their charge and what it demands. To relieve suffering, to make space for resource and the colony, the new territories, free of threat. All threat. Any threat. Machine or meat, combatant or not, they must be destroyed. All know; the Humeda cannot be herded. They are not moved, they are removed. Unfortunately, this attitude is applied to all who would halt the Fauschenherst march.

Her last hurdle. That between her and Emile.
Of course it would be human.

She has never heard of the place Mince calls Summer. But she has dreamt of Relief Ukibiki and its warmth. The Nomad hotel, respite beyond danger. Impenetrable, forever protected by Klernsteiga, and they are the Nomads who wander these far reaches of Kenidomo Country. Not by direction, by choice; the territories under their authority. Self-sufficient atop its stone plinths, a ramshackle safe haven.

And just like that, with a gust it is gone but she isn't. She trudges on, fumbling with the column alongside. Cold unbearable, she feels the hilt of her blade knock against her elbow, and she thinks the brass cap would burn itself to skin, immovable. She wonders if she could even

draw.
           She lays a hand upon the grasp. She looks out to the storm.

Armies of automatons, she has seen so many here.
    Each she remembers; from the scale of Hjordiis to the speed of Masago, each is different, so each cling to thought with differing dreads. Each form of fear, fear in the unknown, in strength, in intent; for all terrors, she knows a machine. For all terrors, she has blown them apart. But there is something to make all shudder in the way this thing just watches.

A hound, it stares. The size of a house. Maybe bigger. Like a dead dog sitting it slouches, as though part bowed but attentive, a mongrel sick. Motionless, as far from her as she is from the line it haunts, a mut watching from its window. A wolf dishevelled, its great mane plumes like a fur coat, the pale scruff of arctic hunters but made of ribbons of steel, a thousand blades soldered to the beast's hide.
    She would rather it charged. Rather it prowled or loomed from the white. But it watches. Sits, perfectly still. Mane ruffling. A silhouette, wind racing by, snow stealing vision for seconds at a time but even in these lulls, it does not attack. Like it waits for command. Sidelong she stands, staring from the corner of her eye. Just as still. She supposes, in a way it does.
    The column cannot see, they are too far.
    She doesn't move an inch. She must draw it away.

Then the snow starts to shift.

Like long carpets unfurled in lines they are drawn, layered with snow but now gently towed in. Conveyor belts, they are steel strips cast like a net, perfectly spaced, and emanating from that one central hound, ever still in its observance. Now she watches them, wide eyed as the failed trap is recalled, and she sees those slight metal sheets climb behind the beast, rising as they are withdrawn. They make its many tails, like snakes

rearing behind this wolf. This dog of the cold. This gelid cur.
The Gelid Cur. She has fought icons before. These machines, they are things biblical, which those of Sect One must surely revere. In its slyness, its patience, its stoop and dogged slenderness, she sees this again.

But she thinks something else. For all fear, all talk of eeriness, of its ominous restraint, of its mechanical aplomb in letting the first move be hers, there is something which holds entirely over these. The thought of what she has just heard. Of where she is. She could stand, wait for the column to pass from danger, but she will not become lost. Not now.

And she does not forget what the machine must see. Still, upon the wastes.
Her blue light, staring straight back.

The Rautbergen feels his friends shove against his side, fall and push against one another, but he doesn't care. Instead, the Rautbergen looks, brow high.
The Nomad. She watches something. Something he cannot. She stands so straight, he knows that if he tried the same his iced spine would snap, but neither can he look away, for he is so fixed on her attention. He glances around and nobody else has noticed, so driven in their fatigue that they see only their feet and the cold. But he is set, rifle in hand, reluctant even to blink. He sees her stand, such purpose, with her head held high. Then she draws, slow and exact, flakes curving around her steel. He nudges the Raut at his side. She nudges him back.
The Nomad holds her sword at her side. Not in stance, not even offense, but while it borders on reluctance there is an assuredness in the way she glares, head falling to one side. Whatever she thinks, it fills steadily. Not solemness, not aggression, it must be a determination creeping, for when she reaches with her bladed grasp to the other, she almost drives a finger through the switch against her palm.
He stops. He stares. Behind him. Someone grunts.

She plumes, with a blast like a bomb detonating. Blowing a bubble in the stormfront, as she disappears into arcing wind.

He shouts and grabs but others notice, saw her vanish from their peripheral edge, a row of heads turning at once and calling out, their clamour spreading up the line. They step from formation, raising rifles but they cannot know where she is, cannot know what she pursues, sweeping the cold blindly. They scatter, spinning, yelling, calling for someone to bring the Auberkemein, to bring the Kamakara. They reach for radios and trudge up the column, they cannot much run in this weather, but they come as close as they can. Weapons primed, careful not to stray too far, the Rautbergen disband, commotion orderly but uncertain, for many do not know why they are alert.

But they quickly figure. They hear it, like rolling thunder.

Explosions, barely audible, rumbling from afar.

So loud that even here, at this distance, they can trace motion by ear. As all fall silent, they see a pursuit through sound. Their rifles flex, all redirected to follow that which trembles, and it is so distinct that he thinks he could shoot into the fray and land the slug. Those around him congregate, leaning against one another, forming lines of fire.

She's chasing it, trying to force it from their column. When it deviates one way, she forces it the other, working to block its turns, and the speeds of both are insensible, impossible, they can't be that fast. Who is she, to chase so fiercely in a storm like this, and what could possibly evade her pursuit. The straggler, a Nomad they didn't know, a wanderer without words, the figure at the edge of firelight battles- they are used to this sense in Klernsteiga, and the Rautbergen listen, adjust and prepare. Despite the intensity of what they hear, they do not miss the noise lean, fall to one side, as the chase sweeps toward the rear.

Whether she loses it or has to dive, the explosions falter, dim enough for the Rautbergen to exchange worried glances. Each Raut braces hard against their shoulders with steady formation. They hear the detonations ring, progress louder and louder. Approaching.

It is so cold; they can barely hold their rifles. To walk is such a labour, but to stand alone seems harder still, for so many forces bombard. The cold, their tiredness, apprehension, and unease. He watches, sees them rush past, form against one another, and pull back, prepare, for what else are they supposed to do. He listens and hears noises terrible.

They can do nothing but stare. He thinks of what could sweep from the white. This is something more than fear. That which you feel when your brain has figured a danger that you, in your furore, cannot. When it realises the severity and tries to turn you away. He spins and spins, coat billowing, snow skating.

The Auberkemein lays a hand upon his shoulder, draws him from the rushing cold.

He asks the Rautbergen what happened. At his side stands another; he lugs the GT. 22 Ablescheiber, the only anti-Humeda machine gun breed likely seen in Kenidomo Country. To fire it standing without support is suicidal. The gunner wears goggles, a mask, and a great poncho, and rests the armament over shoulder.

The officer's coat flutters; the Raut doesn't think he has ever seen the man wear the sleeves. The snow clings to his high peaked visor cap.

He says he doesn't know. He just saw the Nomad with the blue eyes. Saw her fly into the storm.

Then, from behind the officer, he comes. That demon barges, dark and hooded with blades. In this cold, the Raut's mind struggles to form even a sentence; the Kamakara is already passing him before he blinks, staring, watching so many layers fluctuate. He steps aside and averts his gaze.

The Kamakara offers a turn to the Rautbergen, but it is nothing more than a glance. That boy follows, the young Nomad. Flakes of white cling to his eyes yet he does not care, trudging in Mincemeat's footfall. The Auberkemein keeps close behind.

The Rautbergen joins them at the front, behind a row of rifles. Approaching thunder, for a moment the Raut wonders if it is footfall, but he sees the expressions of those two Klernsteiga. In either knowing of their friend's kit, or in faith in her endurance, they stand steadfast, facing the cold, one unbearably exposed and the others veiled behind his hoods, half and half jaw barely visible. Before them, the line jostles, stomping into the snows at their feet to stay upright, to anchor themselves as sheets roll against. The gunner, he with the Ablescheiber, he joins them. Laying with chest to the ground as others stow their weapons to aid his fire, cleaning his ammunition belt and holding it from the freeze.

The explosions aren't constant, they fluctuate and bend this way and that. It is a pursuit their way but a pursuit still, it twists and rolls yet whatever she casts her shuddering destruction at is evasive, too quick and agile. In their firing lines, the Rautbergen hear both a testament to those things fabled of the Klernsteiga, of speed and determination infallible. Then that which tests such beliefs.

They reverberate, like horns to warn in fog.

Rumble, with such power. It is odd, how he feels both so sure and so beaten at once.

In the expressions of these Nomads, he sees the seeds of this same feeling. He wonders what this is to them, to each other, for where they come from must be afar and where they venture must be further still, because there is nothing, absolutely nothing for them here. Such conviction must drive them. Clutching his rifle close, he sees the Kamakaras stare, faceless but so direct in stance. Coats churning, cloth coursing, inhuman, his machine grasp ready to draw. The boy stands at his side, no taller than the Raut's chest. The Kamakara and the kid, so still, so ready to move. He sees the child lean in, calling to Mincemeat over the roar.

He shouts- all others are quiet, yet only the nearest can hear. He says the Rautbergen are too close together.

Like senseless war drums, the sporadic advance comes.

Under his cowls Mincemeat nods. He reaches for the Auberkemein, his human clutch moving to gesture, to tell them to move or spread out.

Before his fingers unfurl, his head snaps.

Like dogged steel fabric it barrels from the white. A bundle of swords on a string wrenched through the heart of the line. Each Raut feels as though the wolf looks solely into their eyes as it plunges.

The Kamakara grabs the officer's wrist and twists, tries to haul him aside with his step, ducking to evade the thousands of long knives making matted fur. Throwing his weight, around him is ripping. Tearing. The rushing air pulls back his hood.

When he looks, crouching, wide eyed, Mince holds only an arm.

The beast is insane. It moves as though scorched or it chases its tails, which flare and spike like dance ribbons. Bounding, writhing, it snakes and leaps, pale and pointed with slender, snatching legs, eyes cold and colourless. If the thing sat still, none would know it living or dead, but here it is so animated, at some midpoint between a pup's wild vigour and the dexterity and ferociousness of predatory impulse. It scarce claws, instead it dives, all in its way or nearby sliced through. The Kamakara stands, the mess pooling around him. Many in its way, they are not felled but are cut thin and deep with wounds yet to take full effect. He sees Rautbergen stumble, clutching their sides, new dimensions of pain etching with every step as mechanisms within them meant to be connected plunge and poke, severed, waiting to gush.

Amid this carnage the Kamakara stands and he roars for the same, hauling Rautbergen to their feet. He picks them up and shoves them on, kicks to crawling men their rifles. He sees, always, in the corner of his eye, that ravenous hound slash, whipping and whisking in and out of view. Flustered, some of them stagger on, rifles raised. Other lean with his grasp but peel apart, both staring at wounds of papercut blades. The Kamakara moves, taking a Lautreisgefer and aiming after the mut, commanding them to rally, drawing his own blade, hair snatching like the dog's. They follow his order. Even those without limbs try to rise. Anyone would, looking up and seeing him overhead.

And then she comes. Spinning from the white, twirling, stumbling with hands flailing and running to a halt, staring at the streak of trembling lumps and staggering Rautbergen. Her blue is shocked, like she was lost and didn't know the line was here and she stands bumbling, eyes wavering over the splayed bodies, all dying but so few dead. Shots pound. Twitching in and out of sight, something mechanical writhes ahead, while those around hold themselves and work on either their lurching advance, the dead, or dying themselves.

She has stepped from the white, the blank canvas, and sees the worst that could be drawn.

Mince comes to her side. Pescha turns, lip wavering, azure hesitant, unsure what to say. The noise, so many things at once. She steps toward the closest casualty. But the Kamakara doesn't even look.

Mincemeat shoves the rifle into Pescha's arms. Blue eyes see such terrible decision- she takes the thing without a word.

Mince tells her to find Ozwald. Sights fixed on where the Cur rages, he stalks, sword low in hand and while he strides, he looms, blades jutting, assuming that ghoulish form. In the blizzard the storm beats. For moments, Pescha can see nothing. In others, she sees both the Kamakara and that dogged cutter which whips at the snow.

The rifle is heavy and cold and each step stammers, an endeavour made of every motion but as she goes, she sees more, delves deeper into the line. They do not know what to do; the Rautbergen press their ears to radio receivers and aim at nothing, surrounded by bodies as the Cur rages ahead. It means nothing. Most this far up are dead, and she doesn't care what the rear does, they would be mad not to flee as their forefront troops watch the wolf tear. Those who do fire, they shoot but see nothing and the brutal force of their rifles makes even this cold part, tracer rounds burning bright red to let the Rautbergen aim when the force of their rifles would hinder accuracy. She has never shot this before. She holds the gun close and thinks she will fall should she fire. But here, in this way of fighting, she cannot bomb, or else risk murdering the Fauschenhersts finest.

Every step and there are more, bodies strewn. She thinks there can be no rear line, she has already passed more than there were in that tunnel, but they crawn and try to put things back inside themselves. In those moments of impossible injury, they find the wild determination of their bodies writhing, thoughtless as they claw, eyes glazed, at white stained dark red. Even the limbless, they roll and groan but then there are those who are very dead, caught on the Cur's hide and sent spinning, torso whirling one way while their hips go the other. Amid this battle, she sees the bundled piles of soaked cloth and fur leant against by Rautbergen, rifles pitched upon the corpses. If she sees the boy, she will recognise him. Amid hoods and masks, his hair will be clear.

She must find him, she thinks. He must know the way.

Like artillery, shelling and bombardment, Lautreisgefer cannons blare and the Gelid Cur mauls at the wind. She must shrink from the debris, duck under glowing slugs meant to bore through steel, as the white at her side kicks up. She sees it, the storm bulges and the beast thrashes, leaping like a whelp in its first winter. A warzone, this place is chaos, without direction or a front line. This isn't a fight, it's a bad dream. Senseless, and she has no influence.

Of those who stand, none are the boy.

Then the Gelid Cur writhes, suddenly off balance, throwing itself from the storm and Pescha must fall back, slipping, hands buried in the white. Her hair whips, a breath forced out, cold racing. She lays there, propped up by straight arms. She stares, swelling blue bright.

Mince and the Cur grapple. But it is a match of wrestling, not a dual, and it locks Pescha's mind. The words in her head stammer.

Hand to hand. Fist to claw. The Kamakara stalks to the Cur head on and lands a punch to rock the machine's great snout. A paw comes, blades lashing, but he kicks it square on, swords withdrawn, and repels the blow. Repels it. Forces it back. This massive, edged mandible that could crush Pescha whole. He takes it on with equal strength.

Then he throws another fist and grabs the automaton's head, dragging it around like a man's. He tugs and slams and ploughs it into the snow, then stomps from above, driving it into the white.

He makes this great hound his bitch.

Then the Kamakara straddles, extending and treading blades buried deep in machine skin. He holds himself firm with his own mechanical grasp, bound with the Cur's hide, steel sheets ripped free and cast aside while he slashes with the other, sword arcing. When he has cleaved enough of the wolf's ribbon fur he steps forward, impales himself again and does the same, hacking clumps and tearing pelt, punching through the hull, and hauling handfuls of cabling out. Pescha pushes herself up, turning her head from the blown-out cold. Around, Rautbergen dash. The dog leaps once more to the edges of sight. She raises the Lautreisgefer.

The shot feels enough to yank loose her shoulder, kicking back. It is something fitted for a vehicle, not human hands, and she misses anyway, the case flying with smoke whisked by wind. She stumbles after the Cur, its tail trailing, whipping in its wake. She watches the blades catch the back of a Rautbergen's leg and sees him quietly slump to all fours. Everyone else is directionless; some stagger alongside, some flee. All are lost. She passes them, rounds blaring.

The shots build. More and more, pounding past.

She cannot stand straight, by force of storm and force of mind for she knows if she rises tall, she will lose her head. Before her, if not the line, there is something. Coordinated fire, at the dog pinched between the stragglers and Pescha, and the rest of the Wolstspitzer.

She moves faster, carrying the rifle with one hand. With the other, her fingers are primed to activate the switch against her palm.

Her lips are parted, breath heavy. Her azure winces against bombardment.

The tail sweeps, making a Raut nothing more than a guttural thud and in a bulge in the cold she sees the hound rear, throw itself back from gunfire, as organised as it can be. It's the back of the line. Under their banners they have rallied, crouching, trying to hold themselves up while they shoot, attacking with rounds slamming. The sound is mechanical, or like lightning firing.

Amid their front stands Ozwald. He lets the Rautbergen jostle, forcing the dog to move and move back, but he watches in waiting. Intense, for he does not take his eyes from the Kamakara, who crawls like some disease, pulling the Cur apart.

He waits for him to move out of the way.

The Rautbergen gunfire concentrates, lost of their Ablescheiber but firing in volleys, aiming instead for the Cur's limbs, looking to sever its reach and break its mobility.

Mince attacks besides this. He does not shrink from shrapnel or pull from singed steel, he hacks and tears, a swarm embodied in one figure which infects the wolf's mechanics, dislodging cog and fixture, always slashing. The Cur, it has lost its intrigue now, and falls in motion to desperation, wheeling and bucking. It tries to force him from the scruff to which he clings with an unbreakable grasp. Like a tick draining the beast by the second.

Ozwald shouts, calling over the furore. He screams that Mince must let go.

Even amid all of this, Pescha hears the Kamakaras snarl.

Then the dog keels, rises high, standing on its hind legs. Towers, demonic, an idol to some frozen faith. Burnt with cold and gunfire, it is as though time slows, the mechanical rumble like the Kyut itself shifts. Blocking light, shifting the storm. It feels more so that the plateau tilts than the Humeda falls.

When the Gelid Cur tips Mince moves with it, knifing himself to the machine's belly and when it rolls, he flows then too, using his sword at hand as a pick. He climbs the steel cliff face which spins, the Cur ploughing itself into the ground. In its craze, Pescha runs for the line. Around her, the stragglers do the same, dragging bags in their staggered sprint.

Mince pulls something from the Cur's leg, and the limb shudders uncontrollably.

Ozwald screams for him to let go.

The dog must hear, for it looks to the boy. It turns its claw. Pescha moves to snatch Ozwald, reaching for her palm.

Eyes wide, she sees Ozwald blink, his sights glowing.

Everything goes white.

She is blind. Her ears ring, in parallel with the destruction. It is as though an explosion landed at her side and she loses all sense. For a second, two seconds. Five. Ten. As though a camera flashed in her face, and she is numb to all things.

She feels Rautbergen hauling at her, dragging her from the open, things faded and vague gaining clarity too slowly. As soon as she can stand, everything a blur, she pushes them aside, holding a hand to her face. She looks up, searching for the boy.

That is his prosthetic. So stunned is she that it takes her a while to focus on him, walking from the line.

Whatever he did it blinded the dog too, but it didn't think in its rage anyway and it doesn't think now, fit to shatter the Kyut with its pounding as the Kamakara chops.

Ozwald calls out one last time. From amid the Wolstspitzer, Pescha sees a hand poke from the boy's shawl.

When his cloak parts, she sees the rig fitted to his form. A metal skeleton, it runs from chest across his arms and legs, unarmoured, a scaffold over his body. At his wrists are joined ignitions, firing cylinders of an almost flintlock mechanism, and she traces the rivets to the canisters strapped along his arms and chest. It is almost as strange as Mince's fistfight.

Actual bombs. Fuse-tipped missiles, barley longer than Pescha's hand, but bombs still. He stands there, wind rushing, holding out a hand toward the dog. A boy made a mortar system, a short blade bound to his waist.

She stares. So do the Rautbergen. His eyes and sword for personnel, they could reason with this, but a silence falls. Mincemeat turns, sees what they see, steel ribbons wavering before his sight.

Ozwald tilts, and shouts for the line to get back.

Mince, his blade buried, pulls it loose and slashes. His edges aren't designed to fight steel, he is a slayer of men, not machines. It leaves her in awe, to see such an elegant automaton, humbled and dragged into the white by the bloodsucker against its side, half-jaw fanged and growling. He retracts his blades, bringing in his legs to kick off like he swims. He cuts, cleaving down, the mut's chopping fur mottled and ruined. When he lands, he does not run. He pulls his coat up and covers his head, crouching low.

Caps of soda bottles popped; the firing process looks like little more than the flip of a coin. On a rail the bombs shudder down to his grasps and with a jolt they are fired from both canisters. The head of an orchestra, like a conductor, his arms swish in pitch and depth with cloak rippling, missiles so high that he can wave off many before they fall.

When they do, someone blows against her face. Warm air momentary and gushing, surging, light catching every dark drift of tormented cold. They crack but do not flame, burrowing; they are for machines, not people, made to drill deep into Humeda hide, but they do detonate, and do so with such a sound to make the Rautbergen shrink, crouch, each explosion bringing a new wave. Ozwald does not move, fixed in spot, launching and launching, coat snapping with his hair.

The wolf freaks, ground splintering, rising around and it turns, gashed and scarred, twirling to bolt back from sight. Despite the bombardment, even wounded, it glides so smoothly over the sheets, and the boy grits his teeth with a squint. So mobile, so he switches strategy, and with a flick the settings change and when he next flies a bomb it barely rises, pops to eye level. When it turns to fall, he lashes and strikes the thing with a steel arm. He sends it surging straight, chasing the Cur. He does the same again, kicking, slapping, punching, lashing at the ignitions of explosives inches from his face. But does not waver. He sends bomb after bomb, striking with such force, straight faced and unblinking.

Beside her, she hears a Rautbergen joke about not needing their dead Ablescheiber. From the blast radius they drag their friends and their wounded, flinching with danger so close, snow piling against their sides. Each detonation brings a momentary lull, then the winds renew. She stumbles back with them, these dregs of the line, very few left but still they crawl, hurl themselves from the boy as Mince darts, bounding into the storm under Ozwald's cover. Under he, who destroys the white but no longer sees the Cur, bombs sent but hitting nothing.

Pescha, stooped, sees her chance, and runs up behind. She grabs Ozwald by the arm and turns him her way.

She drags him, back toward the clump of surviving Rautbergen, rifles sighted every which way. The severed remains of the line, there are others alive elsewhere, but where and how many, she does not know.

She almost carries him, the remnants making space. In such cold air, they can smell too many things. Amid the cluster, she doesn't see the Kamakara. She puts everything into hauling that boy to the safety of the line.

Her feet sink, breath hard, winter rushing.

A hand emerges from the bunch.

It points into the storm at Pescha's side.

She watches Rautbergen guns wheel.

Holding the boy in her arms, she must look through his quivering hair to see.

The wolf, it limps from the fray.

She watches, its hind leg dragging, loose, and juddering.

Before it disappears, it's snout nods to something beyond sight.

She stares, the Cur slipping beyond the waves.

But its shadow.

It's shadow does not dissipate as the Cur does. The shape lingers, like the beast stands still a hair from open view. As though someone called an insult, and it considers coming back. For a moment more, she thinks it does. It takes her a while to figure that it's the rest of the pack, bleeding from that one dark stain on the storm. Each sweeping their fogged horizon before they settle upon the clump. Machine wolves, great tails trailing. Forms thin, spindly, jagged, and edged.

In that second, every Fauschenherst soldier knows the line is lost. There are no officers, nobody in command, no ammunition, supplies, no nothing. So, no Fauschenherst. Standing there, amid the cold, they have no orders. Instantly, each and every Rautbergen looks at the Klernsteiga, but before Pescha can even reach for the switch, Ozwald grabs her hand.

He says he can't run, not with his kit. The suit, he can take it off, but he'll have left only blade and blink. Pescha stares, feeling his grasp against hers. His fingers are so thin.

She thinks of the boy from Glermvender, watching him wander into the cold.

She grabs him by the shoulders and asks, desperation trembling, wolves watching, if he knows the way to the train. The Iron Driver. She does not need to clear the Rautbergen's compound, she thinks. Without their orders, she need only get herself into those carriages.

As she was with the boy she left atop Dodtohmet, their faces are mere inches apart. But now, they are both wide eyed and wild.

liquid crystal sparkling, Ozwald looks to one side. Looks at nothing, for all Pescha can tell. But his eyes twitch like they shiver. This way and that, navigating obstacles. He envisages the route, expression lost in the effort. He looks up. At plain white swaying. Somehow, he knows where they are.

Yes, he says. He does.

But they can't just go, he states in surprise, his hair like corn waves. What about the Rautbergen, he asks, turning to the huddle at their side? What about Mince?

She follows his trembling gaze.

The Rautbergen stare. Whether they hear the Nomads or not, they await what is next with rigid attention, as frozen as the white underfoot. So closely are they gathered that she cannot make their number, but they are few. No more than twenty, all sights turned to the Klernsteiga. None look at the wolves- they know in who their lives truly rest.

Snow clings to her eyelashes. Her lips are near blue. Her breath is heavy and vapor trails. She turns to the last of the Rautbergen, her eyes vivid. The shade catches the passing cold.

Forgive me.

She shouts it over the tumult.

Pescha turns to the boy and rips free his cuffs, pulling the loop loose and then his arms out. He stammers, wide eyed. The Rautbergen blink, rapt in disbelief. Frantically she unties his restraints until she can rip him free from his kit and she takes his wrist, holding it tight, lunging for the storm. Ozwald stumbles, struggles to keep afoot with his cloak left against the skeleton. When he looks back, he sees the Rautbergen start to flee. Desperate attitudes clash, some demand they stay and are thrown to the ground, those already running doing so from both an accusing barrel and the machines, which shudder with glee at the pungent terror displayed. Drunk on human panic they bound, more and more pouring into sight. Ozwald stares, sees the shots flash. People run, dropping their heavy rifles and bags. He sees the hound's pounce. Sees some looking deeper into the gale.

He turns, scrambling, wading in Pescha's wake. He looks up to her, sights wider than ever.

She scarce stands. Part throws herself, part crawls, ever slipping and pushing herself up. Up and on, frantic and reckless, air raspy and dry but she doesn't slow. She is only shin deep, but they run into wind which catches her burdensome coat and his light shirt and if her breaths are uncontrollable and horse then his are frightful, shocked, cut short by every flux in the blizzard. Now he too clings, grasp tight around hers. He doesn't know what would happen if he let go.

A fairy-tale image, they tumble into the drifts. Hidden from sight, they hear the Humeda run and Rautbergen fire, paws and shots pounding. They hear a slaughter.

Pescha listens, holding the boy near, circling, eyes searching the white. She flips the switch against her palm and primes Pack One. She creeps on, head turning every which way. Catching each faint noise, lost to the churning cold that batters her thoughts. It steals sound and makes things vague, and illusory.

She cannot whisper here, but she keeps him close and tells him to blink if they part, to run and blink again so she can find him. He shivers. Shakily, he pulls free his sword.

It's a nightmare. She couldn't stop, her legs wouldn't let her, but she hears the wolves and knows one of them must lunge. She spins, hears them all around, sprinting the spectrum of her senses; they would streak past and rip her apart and she wouldn't know. Her ideas race, she is as good as dead. Dead if she leaves Ozwald. Dead if she stays. She thinks of splitting up, trying to draw the dogs away. She wouldn't make it and he'd freeze before he got far. Already she feels him wane, but with Pack One over her coat she cannot take hers off. Her mind prods her with a thousand odds, each landing flat. It tries to numb the inevitable, ease her worry. Her body is heavy, tired but still charging, incapable of slowing.

    Ozwald tugs on her arm, and parts his lips to speak.

Again, like a pet's toy on a string a dog darts, low to the snow and kicking up white like water in its strike. It glides, gaze fixed on the Nomads. Gaining tens of meters in a second

    Ozwald stares. The oncoming force sends his hair aflutter. Locks drifting. Fangs approaching. Then a hand nudges him aside, and smoking blue blares.

It's head snaps back as though hit with an uppercut, a gash in its nose showing she shot past and overhead, then liquid fire explodes against its chest, hot air and components bursting from its stomach. Ozwald glares, all his garments billowing.

    More dogs hear. She resounds to face them all.

    She's like his guardian angel- everywhere he looks he sees only her ruin. Every attempt to get close to him is swatted by an invisible hand, flaming machine claws and fangs shattered and smashed every time they reach. He looks for her, standing alone as a dog rears. Then there's a flash, dark hair, bright blue, and another explosion. More come and he crouches, the dogs drawn to the sound and piling into sight. One comes straight at him, they are face to face, it's attention fixed on him, then it's eyes dart just over the boy's shoulder. Its bottom jaw disappears. Tumbling through the air, slamming a way away. A top row of razor teeth lingers over Ozwald. Then the whole dog is tossed aside. Everywhere he looks a machine comes, everywhere it is repelled, its foremost limb obliterated. He is a second too late every time to see, drawn to falling mechanics and smouldering cuts. This great shadow looms behind him but he glimpses her bulbs ahead, too fast for him to focus and she rushes under, disembowelling the mut lengthways then dodging between its whipping tails behind, slashing through sheets. She is more of a dog than them.

Then her gaze fixes, azure suddenly iced. Sudden and desperate. He doesn't have time to change his attention before it is again centred on her, streaking toward him.

Pescha pulls the boy in and fires a plume. She can't control both him and her, but she fires anyway, sending herself sprawling as the hound wheels, unearthing more cold. Like he turns hard in lake shallows.

She plunges, extremities slamming hard ice below the snow. Rolling over it is like being punched all over, beat a thousand times. As soon as she can, she tries to prop herself up. Her arm rings with blunt impacts.

She searches for the boy, hands patting the space around her as the wolf skids.

A hundred cameras, each searching for the perfect shot, bulbs flaring without restraint or control clack. Blare, sudden and deafening. As though after her one-thousand beatings, one-thousand bombs fall.

When she hears a crack, and the sudden quiet, she has no desire to look up. None.

But she does. Slowly.

Expression so desperate. So slowly.

Ozwald stands, cradling his wrist. In shock, he has lost control and blinked, blinked too many times and now those liquid crystals leak. The inner mechanics float in half-spheres, still within his head. Spindly cogs, fine metalwork; they bob with his shivering. When he blinks, sharp glass cuts raw against his eyelids, more chemical lapping free. But he is too startled to feel.

Blind, still he stares at his hand, thumb caressing his shaking grasp.

All the fingers of his right reach are cleaved. Clean and angled, the blood hasn't started pumping.

Pescha screams for him. Pushing herself up, she reaches out.

The beast behind the boy rounds to her voice.

Ozwald turns to where he hears, unable to see, red mixing with his shattered eyes. Barely able to stand, he extends an arm, clawing for her to take his grasp. His good hand twitches out front, he expects to find her with each passing second. The dog shivers. Composing itself, like it ran through cobwebs.

As soon as it lays sight on the Nomads, it pounces. Bounds, attack indirect.

Runs, not to bite or claw. Merely to run, and make of them ribbons.

This Gelid Cur leaps, and crushes Ozwald under its paw. It does so in one step. It could have been an accident, but then for Pescha it springs, flattening Ozwald on the way. It's so close that she can see this one has no mouth, just the fashioned muzzle and snout. She can see every scarred and mottled steel sheet. Every inch of exposed wiring, burn marks black and still searing. Cogs and gears and cable ligaments. The way it bounds, it does not raise its squashing foot. At least she needn't see that.

She feels her pulse thud in her neck.

Hears her heart pump.

Speeding up.

Faster.

Faster.

Like rainfall on a strip, or a rhythm drummed against a desk. Even in soft snow and hard wind, she hears it like the rising beat is tapped against her skull. Bladed footfall, impossibly quick.

Mince streaks past and hops, surging with sword drawn into the Cur's face, impaling three blades through its head. With such force does he impact that the beast is stalled mid-jump, stopped, its steel fur flying forward where it does not, and at full length Mince withdraws his cutter and, in an instant, arcs, scything through the sheets. Chopping every edge like they were truly just hairs.

All in the space of an instant, he remains there, feet buried in the mut's face. Too quick for even the dog to react, but holding there he turns, just a margin, wind taking the freed metal strips with it.

He looks over his shoulder, at the Klernsteiga staring back.

Pescha blinks.

Smoke plumes and Pescha draws, scything into the Cur as she spins past, cutting the length of its side deep and at its back she pivots with the tension. Twirls, doesn't sheath but just let's go of the blade and stuffs a grasp into her pocket, taking all in a handful.

When she rounds, she faces the wolf's hind, it's legs compressed with the pressure of its impact. She doesn't aim, she just twirls and throws. Casts with a snarl the bundled bombs, letting loose so many lights. She thinks of The Ram Burbled, back in the Shae Doken. Thinks of him making a new sunrise of that machine he burnt.

What hits that Cur, surely no single human could muster. It should blow Pescha off her feet, but she carries the spin to stoop and endures, arms barred before her. Her destruction rolls like liquid, the blast like a crashing wave and of bombardments this is the greatest, noise deafening, light swamping. A hole is punched in the storm for such force makes a bubble, even if only fleeting. The wolf itself is annihilated. Of the things left in her wake not one can be identified, beyond the charred and mangled wastes of ruined metal. Once coat and hair settle back to the rhythm of the storm she stands, cold already encroaching again upon the craters she has made. She gazes at the shattered mess, twisted and baked.

She hears other wolves, whipping from beyond sight.

Mindlessly she looks and sees her blade, sent skating with her blast. She shoulders through the winter to reach it, lifting steel and cleaning it of snow. She marches on, holding it tight, eyes cutting through

cold sharper than any edge, manically looking for another mut.
Around her arm closes a black machine grasp.

Mince stares at her, face straight and waiting. Ghostly, of dark prosthetic and wintered skin, the Kamakaras eyes too are tired but, in a way, different to Pescha's. Not fatigued, so much as he has that sense Pescha would feel disturbed for feeling now. That he has wasted his time.

In his other hand, he holds that cabled mapping screen. It is battered, but the coordinates still read.

The look with which Mincemeat stares. There is no question upon his face. No anything.

He turns and he walks, slow and trudging. Pulling his hood up with that mechanical grasp. Behind him Pescha hears still the hound's hunt. Disorientated and lost, she doesn't know where the line fell, or where the bodies piled. Those dead will never again be seen. They are left out here, in this fragment of Kenidomo Country. The snows will but cover them over, and make way for more to fall.

Pescha turns for the Kamakara. Already his massive figure fades from view.

She takes her blade and sheaths it across her lower back.
She pulls up her hood also, and follows Mince into the wind.

- *KENIDOMO COUNTRY* -
UNRECOGNISED TERRITORY
"*Orison*"

How they beg, Orison.

Of the frozen flats here and so many beyond, the Fauschenherst do not name Kenidomo Country's parts- what right have these invaders to name. Foreign, they bestow words dying, spoken from starving throats. But these wandering Klernsteiga, they cannot help but recognise, against frozen sheets of empty white, anomalies to know their way, and plot course through this infinite blank.

A machine on its knees, Orison can have done nothing else but prostrate. An Humeda in prayer, it has never moved, yet nobody is sure of its state- whether it is alive, whether it is active, but dormant, or felled long ago. Fashioned this way, its form is too perfect for this to be random, an automaton too fervent in its faith for coincidence. In posture it yearns, leaning into its devotion. Scale so grand, none have ever thought to ruin it. No Nomad has ever lain assault, none have ever dared to stir such a fanatic from its slumber. In practice, they have done the reverse.

Passing Klernsteiga, Rautbergen, those abandoned peoples of Sect One descent; they have adorned the devotee. Swaddled it, for like the banner fields within Casse Monvi they have driven pikes into its back, mounted with streamers long since frozen in their waves. A hundred colour and shapes, all are set in ice, frosted and pale as his bones are, brittle and thin. Speared, but Orison does not move, it has never shifted from its faith. The greatest ribbons are frozen in time, and most trail from its clasped hands, fingers that image of malnutrition and illness and clutching so tightly. It is as though the Humeda skin has been peeled by the gale, clinging in mass only at the furthest point.

Any face of Orisons was worn bare years ago. Pallid with sickness, a plastic bag pulled over its head, even exposed cabling and innards have been sanded down. Expression blown away, yet still ever devout. The anchor point of fabric once like seagrass, blowing below the surface, now firm set in undulation, a static photograph made dimensional and vast. A moment in time now stiff, unbreakable. Mince tells Pescha of Orison, and they camp in its view.

Under their tent pitched upon Kamakara striders, Pescha pulls back binding and coat and shakes down to her vest, aching, back-to-back with Mince. From when she threw herself, her left arm still throbs, but she is silent in her suffering and when she pulls free her reach, she sees only bruising, nothing broken. She runs a hand over harried skin, cold touch against cold injury.

The Kamakara looks over his shoulder, rolling a wrapper between pale and machine fingers. He asks if it hurts bad.

Pescha feels muscle tense and swelling, but she can reach from breastbone out and straight. She says she'll be fine.

Quiet creeps.

Mince shunts a little, rests his head against the back of hers. He says he can get the Fauschenherst to send a team, to find his sword. Have it brought back to Gardner, to his family.

Pescha thinks about what Ozwald told her, of his people giving their children. She's thought nothing else for a day straight. She says that'd be nice.

He saved them from the storm, the Kamakara tells; without him and Casse Monvi, they'd have been lost. Mince can make sure his world knows.

Pescha nods. She glances over, feels the Kamakara reach back, their hands resting together. They sit there, shuddering, cold a part of them now; the Nomad thinks, if she left this place, she would collapse and melt. So numb, she feels the Kamakaras grasp against hers, and does not know it the machine or meat hand. Cannot sense, for her clutch is frozen and she cannot think, it is like the mind sleeps yet she is awake.

It's not just about violence, Mincemeat murmurs. It's both body and thought. The machines, they are electric; they are made, and so is what hurts the soul.

The Klernsteiga have their convictions. All are just sheep, but theirs is the flock that knows why it falls.

It's about being an example to the righteous.

Against the rage outside, there is such a stillness in here. An openness, yet a reticence too, and a quietness lonely, like they push their fingers to their ears and shut their eyes and whisper within the safety of their skulls. But when Pescha next speaks, her words and firm and rigid, and she draws her hand from the Kamakaras side.

Pescha asks how much further to the cathedral.

A pause, the quiet, then Mince rummages and holds up his screen. A couple of days, not far. He says he isn't sure how many of the Rautbergen teams will arrive.

The glow of his tablet is nothing compared to his partner's vivid gaze.

Pescha says it won't matter.

- *KENIDOMO COUNTRY* -
UNRECOGNISED TERRITORY

"*The Denkervung Spire*"

A great frozen lake, the snow does not stick. It skates and clumps in small patches and is broken to drift on again, the ground a deep cobalt of thick, rugged ice. Upon this Prussian blue tarn she can see far and wide, see the horizon distant and dark, but this flat is barren and void. Like a great, frosted, inland sea trapped between high mountains.

Wind howls, but there isn't as much snow. The white descends, it does not just race her sidelong and straight on. It is caught upon something, swooping up and dropping from afar.

A great crest climbs, somewhere ahead. Like the snows have pulled back, receded in way of a tsunami, frozen. The moment the two Klernsteiga step onto the lake, she notes Mince's look, a glance almost heavenward. Now, careful in step, Pescha looks nowhere else.

Stares at the sky, until Mince wheels and shows his screen, frost chipping glass edges. The Kamakara points at a marker, a blip on his diagnostic; interference, something playing with the signal. Pescha eyes Mincemeat, head cocked to one side, for they wouldn't even bother speech out here, against this. The Kamakara turns and gestures, indicates toward the beacon, and then up, into the gale. Neither sees a sun, yet both understand. While the wind itself changes in their favour, Pescha needn't ask how cold these planes become upon nightfall. She nods. Mincemeat leads the way.

An estate, long abandoned by its family, it is low and angular. Mounted atop an island in an age past, paper walls and timber verandas are deserted, both visibly unused but preserved, maintained by cold, thin walls clean and pale and wood dark, interior in shadow. What would have led builders here, Pescha does not know, for human footfall has not traced the Kyut long enough for this to have been a sea, but those who came have gone, and left their home out here. Single storied, minimalistic, with its sloped roofs and plain sides, Pescha screams to ask the Kamakara what this place is, a solitary manor with its innards, even when looking through crooked panels, stripped and bare.

Mince yells that he has no idea. He's never heard of this. But he knows what that is, he tells, pointing, for this stately home is built square, its centre an open courtyard, and from it rises a spire, knifing the storm. A pillar of radios and servers wired together, a mass of lights and antenna, it is the decoration of some mechanical festivity, with ornaments of receivers, cabling, and signal bulbs; piled computers, towering above. Pescha recognises them as Denkervung systems. The Denkervung Spire.

Mincemeat tells her to watch her step.

Lumber creaks underfoot, whines with their weight and they can step straight from the ocean's edge up onto the veranda, timber beams receding to either side. Like halls each connected by corridors, all of that same construction, the Kamakara leads through the closest open panel and into darkness, both Nomads silent as they snoop.

Inside, everything unessential was discarded, the necessities of this life maintained in low tables and cushions, no chairs, shelves and draws cleaned with the family's exit. Without crest or banner Pescha does not know why she thinks this an ancestral home, but there is a discipline here hereditary. Nobles of Sect One, descendants of note and history; whoever made this place made it to endure, in supreme elegance, upon the fringe of survival. Servants, attendants, and their masters, the Klernsteiga can picture them here, standing against these barren walls. They walk, for the complex is merely the surrounding rooms and then the courtyard within. In some spaces, they see single stools, centred with benches bare, ground lain with thin, dried straw mats. Nobody spoke here; it must have been a house in silence, any noise besides the howling would make Pescha grimace, and she does not say a word as she follows Mince. Her blue sweeps across the Kamakaras colourless hair.

To counter that wailing cold, the Spire's song hums with their approach, the murmur of electronic cycles whirring and completing. Like the heavy sleep of a resting Humeda, sheltered between paper walls.

The courtyard is just open stone flagging, neat and cobbled, never any grass or flowers. If they had faith, the family prayed here. If they fought, this is where they trained, and with their efforts the bricked slabs have slumped and deformed, dipped and risen with years of ware and contact. Now, it is the lair of this machine hunk, computer flesh an obelisk. The

Nomads step from room to stone and out from under the canopy, the spire rising, slumped but bound upright. A mess of radar and lights murmuring words in their tangled, unattended, unmoderated thousands. Its peak, those highest rods, they sway and are drawn and slip from view. To look up is to see it forever falling, always a second from collapse.

Mince stands before the spire and takes his screen, reaching into the matted piles and pulling clumps of cabling free. Untangling fibres, plugging in. Over shoulder, he says he'll reach out to the cathedral, see if there's anyone there. Pescha nods and watches him work.

The Kamakara takes armfuls of snakish cords, colours and markings protected from sheer wind and cold by walls and the warmth of the tower, which steams at its densest points, snow boiling against its edge. He pulls them apart, wiring them up.

He stops, then turns a margin, glancing at Pescha. He says it might take a while.

Like the tower's hair trails, Pescha follows the vast wirework worm of cabling on, hand running over the knots, tracing them into the opposite half of the manor. When she steps up and into the room, the facing door is ajar and through the slit she sees the iced ocean, boards rattling. She sees the sun falling, its light a walkway straight from her to it, blinding if she stares too long. Its blade-edge beam cuts her in half asymmetrically, from her left eye, catching her breath and the frost against coat and collar and lip. Beset, the space around her is empty and dark, nothing there to make the shade, so it is shade in of itself.

Her attention lingers, holding in her bright sidelong view. Sight hangs upon the next door over, its room the scale of a gallery yet just as empty as hers. Through that slight opening she sees into the hall beyond. She hears Mince work, looping coils around his arm, organising the tangle.

She pushes the panel quickly, shunts it aside and stands there, half in the room's view.

Straw mats underfoot and exposed timber beams overhead, an ancestral tapestry runs the length of the left wall. Aged and threadbare, brought here with the landing of Sect One, a relic even then. It is bygone and beautiful, but it garners only a glance, a secondary look, all attention strung on the opposite door. Everything is the same shade, dark and of boreal dusk, her light imbuing the space. She approaches, slow and staring.

Unfastened, the way is busted, blow out from inside. Paper bent and torn, the mats are a mess, unarranged and overlapping, like someone slipped and never bothered to repair. There are no cuts, no shots or burns, nothing to connote struggle besides the disorder. As though someone threw themselves through the panels, and just walked off.

She does not step through, lingering at the entrance to the cube beyond, a square room with its rugs removed.

It's a hole, sawn through timber and then the ice below, drill bore smooth and clean. A perfectly carved drop, falling from sight; between lumber and ocean there is just that open space, the area where the manor is suspended upon its stilts, exposed and unbarred. There are no splinters in the wood, and when she leans, she sees ice shaved, even and sleek.

Worn smooth with friction, or made so slowly that its curve is unwavering, but it drops well from sight, deep blue then black within.

For a moment, she thinks what an elaborate trap this place would be, the Humeda tail a beacon, drawing wanderers in. But she stands there and stares, the hole staring back. From Pack One, she reaches and pulls a packet, snapping the bar within in two and tossing half into the pit.

The other half she eats, listening for the splash. Peers down, chewing as she waits.

She wonders why she so quickly thought this an ocean, one with only its surface of ice.

She listens to the storm. It could have landed instantly, and she wouldn't have heard. She finishes her half and drops the wrapper in, gazing still.

She reaches into a pocket, holding the bomb on her palm.

She pictures a Humeda bursting from the ice.

Chewing, she puts it away, turning from the hollow.

The tapestry is near unintelligible. Made long before the collapse and the era of the Fauschenherst, but she can tell this is an Imperial depiction. Fine symbology and well-worn colour, in composition and sheer majesty she recognises Museishingen inspirations, their banners curling.

It's the Founding Fleet; the first Imperial ships of invasion. They span the stars, crossing galaxies, whole solar systems rendered as single stitches. They come in restoration against the heathens who they think rule. The result of so many years of isolation, of so many worlds consumed in silence, concealed, in the corner of human dominion. The work of the Hidden Emperors, condemned to silence and secrecy, secluded from the universe until they were ready to advance. She runs a hand over the fabric, recounting her tales. Of an Empire shut away, blind, so enthralled in their hatred that they would look upon others and see fabled chaos. Strike, hunting an enemy they didn't understand, and which had never existed on the scale their bedtime stories told. Generations, remote, on the fringe of expansion. They called their great arrival the Hecatomb.

This piece, it does not shy from its depiction of subjugation. A family, of history stitched with pride and no need to pretend otherwise, the many varieties and forms of human existence are forced to kneel, rising in arms, unaware, confused, facing a Museishingen infinite fleet. Guns shred, its shots are straight streaks of thread like light beaming, slicing the scene apart, golden and severe. She cannot read the text, and intricate threads have all merged with time, but if she had to pick an adornment for this place, she would not have strayed far from what she now sees, its symbology and tone eternal.

She looks back, into the cube with its burrowing. She wonders if something came out and scattered the mats, or those here hurried to uncover the pit, casting the rugs without care. She hears the Denkervung Spire whir, something previously dormant now active. She turns from tapestry and pit, gaze lingering, breath illuminated by her blue.

When she turns the corner, Mince stands in cabling pilled to his shins, face straight but attention wholly fixed on something above, watching it with wariness. Pescha must step out from under the canopy to see.

Near the Spire's peak, a woman clings. The shortest of the three, her attire is that of an aeronaut's; she wears a scuffed and faded orange flight suit, pilot's overalls pulled down, the sleeves and chest hanging around her waist like she has half crawled from her skin. In heavy black boots and a tucked vest, she looks misplaced enough, but it is her headwear which so defines her an aviatrix. Masked and marked with the insignia of her callsign, not an inch of her face is exposed, insectile visor and military headset making set expression; it is like she has just ejected from her craft and landed against the tower. She climbs, again like some bug, so nimble and in tune with her motion, grappling like she mounts a rockface. If she were to fall from there, she would face similar consequence.

Around her hips, where orange overalls fall, there are strung hats. Visor caps, like that worn by the Auberkemein, Imperial and peaked. Maybe five per leg, bound from each thigh, weather worn and battered.

Pescha steps to Minces side. Both look up at the Nomad connecting ports way overhead. Pescha asks who she is. When the Kamakara speaks, he is quiet and discrete, under breath. He barely turns, keeping sights fixed on the scaling pilot.

Klausch Klernsteiga B Zero-four-two-eight "Saltwater Six", Mincemeat mumbles. Then, leaning in, but never shifting, the Kamakara asks if Pescha has heard of her.

She responds that she hasn't.

Even at a glance, there is such caution over Mincemeat's face. Not anxiety, not on a Kamakara, but a sense of the situation, demanding. A sense Pescha does not understand. They both watch, silent as Saltwater Six reroutes and reconnects. The sleeves of her rolled down overalls grasp with the wind and her vest ripples, but arms bare and hands ever dexterous, she seems not to notice, and any discomfort is entirely hidden behind her helmet mask and screen. After a while of staring, Mince nudges her arm, elbowing a bruise Pescha pretends not to feel.

The Kamakara tells her to go up and help.

The gusts race, pulling at all Pescha's garments and with limpetlike fixity she must claw her way up, stiff grasp forced to curl as she climbs up the spire. Cables once loose are set hard, she can keep herself in check, but when she slips, knees and elbows crack against iced steel, and with bare fingers she either grasps machinery frozen or burning, with a boiling mass of messages. She is careful in her ascent not to haul or kick anything free.

At height, she twists, faces out to that setting light, a laceration down the face of the storm. As though far ahead great gates open, the decompression enough to make an uproar over the ice. Like a glowing bead trails down a window, she clings there and stares, squinting over the brim of her coat collar, leaning from the Spire's side. The buzz and whir of its mechanics mumble, like Denkervung radios whisper every shared secret under their breath. A constant, humming drone, drawn and pushed with the blizzard.

When Pescha turns, Saltwater hangs opposite. Masked, but still staring straight back, sunset mirrored in her visor, like a crack in the glass lets light spill from within. Up so close, if Pescha recoiled she would fall. She can see every intricacy of her helmet, nozzles and vents wired with cable veins, and the markings over the dome, numbers and insignia scrubbed rough by the gale. The shade of her screen is more alike to an astronaut's than an aviator's, bronze and for Pescha opaque, but it is scuffed and chipped, etched with its years of use, burn marks and cuts scarring the bowl. Saltwater keeps her stare, bare arms as strong as her gaze. Then she holds out a cable, passing it to Pescha. When the Nomad takes it, hesitant, the pilot gestures in the air a box with her forefinger, then punches through two parallel holes. Pescha nods, and searches for the port.

The two Klernsteiga crawl, looping wires and firing signals; for Pescha she is back on Emilia, digging through Faurscherin ruins, but she marvels at how Saltwater works, wrapping fibres around her waist and scaling the height of the Spire, time and time again. When Pescha cannot reach, Saltwater will descend and offer her a hand, hauling her up with a grasp of muscle as malnourished as all are out here, and it makes the blue-eyed Nomad cringe, how desperately the pilot drags, like upon their lives does each lift depend. Not the aviatrix's dedication, just how much effort she must enforce to mount the tower, and her haste of action. It ensures Pescha does not ask for aid, and ensures her grimace when it drops and grabs her arm.

 Her hats form an open skirt down to the knee, peaks like tufts in a fur dress, of so many colours and crests. The peeled back sleeves and torso of her overall rest atop, scraped of once vibrant saturation so that now all things are brittle antiquity, weatherworn and charred with frost.

 After countless configurations the Kamakara waves, beaconing their descent. Together, the two Nomads abseil without a word shared.

At the Spire's base Mince holds his tablet and with that maintained fixity of expression he thanks Saltwater Six for her aid, already turning to Pescha with screen glowing. But the pilot points, asks of the display, its cable hair trailing into the density of the Spire's wire mane. It looks absurd, so many lines for such a small monitor. Mincemeat blinks, and stands a little straighter.

 He tells Saltwater it's a way finder, synched with others, all heading to the same rendezvous. Before it told him where to go and the vague whereabouts of its links. Now, he can send his signal to the meeting point, so they know of their approach. With such heavy storms, he thinks most crews are either dead or delayed. Now that some survivors are certain, they won't leave before he arrives.

   The aviatrix's voice, it plays over her helmet's intercom, a crackling transmission from another world. She talks with a lilt, accent thick and fluid, resonating with these chilled parts. Pescha cannot take her eyes from the pilot's dress of hats. She asks them for some food. It's payment that both Klernsteiga offer, Pescha giving wrappers and Mince offering satchels of packet meals. Saltwater takes both, stuffing them into overall pockets. She gestures them a final goodbye, returned with a nod from the Kamakara, before she turns and makes for the sunset, mounting the corridor hall and slipping between the same panels Pescha stared through. She has half the mind to ask Saltwater if she'll stay, wait out the night here with them. But Mincemeat's expression holds and so does she, hands frangible and bruise pulsing.

She looks at the Kamakara, holding his screen. She asks how much further.
   Mince stares. He says they'll rest here tonight. Tomorrow, they walk, and rest on the ice. The next, they leave the ice and scale the wave. The cathedral waits atop. It'll be harsh, mounting the crest, and the next day they will march again, fall on the complex. Pescha will probably reach the Iron Driver that same light.
   The Kamakara returns her look and gives a faint smile. He asks if Pescha's arm is okay.
   Pescha nods, gazing back out to the storm through the panel slit. She says it's fine.

They pull together mats and make their bed on the veranda, looking out to a twilight of falling indigo. All shades of blue, they watch the slipping sunlight fall, and see it be eclipsed still far above the horizon. They see it fall behind the great wave, risen miles away and miles high, like some vast Humeda stalks, snuffing day short. Under their coats with backs to the panels they huddle, attentive to fall into slumber while boxed and blind, squashed side by side and watching lace-like snow drift.

Mince tells Pescha that Saltwater Six once wanted to be an Auberherst, the only distinguishing rank amid Klernsteiga. A Nomad who directs a small army. Pulled from the field by the Fauschenherst who see, a rarity amid these roamers, leadership, and teamwork. Command is forced upon them, and they are given their Brigade. Four thousand Rautbergen, under Auberherst control. They are specialists, under the leadership of the bold. The Nine-O-First Fhreidattaken Guard under Auberherst Hangar is known to guard key interior cities. The Nine-O-Fifth Komodo's hunt deep into Kenidomo Country, under Auberherst Shikari, the most reluctant of the Klernsteiga Brigadiers. Auberherst Sawbones glides high overhead, scouting the remains of battle, and her Nine-O-Ninth Messiah's tend to the wounded after the greatest of conflicts, calling last rights and sifting through the bodies.

The Nine-O-Fourth Harpy's is the only mechanised Rautbergen force, with their armoured Ubenpanzas. Heavy gun cars, they are modelled on war machines of old. Unstoppable and unbreakable. Nobody knows how Auberherst Firefly found the designs, but he had competition. Another Nomad, who proposed her own vehicles, in craft that cut through the sky and lay fire on the machine hordes below.

In the end, Mincemeat says, Firefly won. His Ubenpanza fleet required less training, was easily built, but it came down to fuel, and Saltwater's planes cost too much for too little. The tanks can crawl anywhere. What would a jet do in this, the Kamakara asks. It broke the Nomad apart. Everything she'd worked for, years scraping through the Trash Ditch of world Alexada[31]. Her dream of changing all on the Kyut lost, changing the face of war.

So, she came out here. Forever pledged to the Fauschenherst, her bitterness wasn't against them, it was against those who would be sly and false. Call it what she will, Mince murmurs, but call it an inquisition and she won't be wrong. Now, Saltwater stalks radio waves and wastes, hunting desertion and idleness, amid Klernsteiga and Rautbergen alike. No people, nowhere to go, nobody to turn to. If either Nomad shifts an

---

[31] *V. O. FF. 5 "Alexada"*: The capitol planet of mankind, the centre of all human industry and commerce, and home to the greatest city in operation. The world can be divided into two parts: the Heimatus, a mega city of glass and fibre which seats all major human corporations, built on a vast Faurscherin engine which powers the complex; and the Trash Ditch, a scrapyard of ship remains and industrial factories and smog, which covers the vast majority of the planet. The population of Alexada contains most of all worlds, however the spread between the two industrial sectors on Alexada is split by over ninety percent.

inch, they will stray into frozen cloth. They sit completely still, watching the white curl from their folds. But the Kamakara does turn, just a margin. Pushes his voice to Pescha's side. He says he doesn't know why Pescha's going where she's going. He just hopes she's got a good enough reason.

Pescha says that's a silly thing to say. Quietly, she asks for the Kamakaras why.

He's a Kyut-Born Klernsteiga. What reason has he to fight for human sake. Its history, music, art. He doesn't care about these things. Humanity abandoned his people out here, a people he never knew. He is alone.

All but Pescha are blind, she murmurs, half asleep. She may be deaf, but all others are unseeing. She feels the Kamakara stare at the side of her head. Those treasured hallmarks of humanity, its modernity, the arts, yet wherever Pescha walks thousands suffer. Everyone's starving, dying of thirst. Diseased and helpless, and they have nobody to tell, and no way of telling. What of songs and systems, what testaments of human might are these, when so many more rot. So many more. She may be deaf, but he is blind, Pescha says. One day, they may seize the Kyut. Cleanse it of the machines, the greatest show of human progression, of evolution and superiority, of engineering and strength. One day they'll take the Kyut. One day, they'll war for it again.

Unmoving, Mincemeat whispers that he knows who Emile is.

Pescha says she realises.

Mince leans over, resting his head against Pescha's. Hers burrowed against his neck.

He says he's so tired. The Denkervung Spire hums and the wind chases, rattling soft against the many panels.

They wander into sleep, curled against each other.

- *KENIDOMO COUNTRY* -
UNRECOGNISED TERRITORY

"*The Cathedral Dune*"

The snow dune climbs, like the spine of the greatest Humeda of all. A wave frozen in time; an ocean world would not make the waters needed for this one vast ridge. It's scale makes their journey evermore crushing, they think they must surely rise above the storm, but they do not. They just ascend, deeper and deeper. Crawling for the heart of the furore. On either side, there is only the drop; Pescha does not know how high she is, but it is a measure in miles. An endless slope, nothing lost here could ever be found; if there are secrets, this is where to hide them. Atop this edge, of all her boreal pursuits, this is the tallest, the most distant, and alien. She peers over, turns an angle, if she turned more she would slip, and looks down, past where the white sweeps. Down, into the blizzard. How many dead lay forgotten, up here.

Ahead the Kamakara prowls, striders drawn in, his coats billowing to one side, trying to haul him overedge. Dark, hooded, clawing on, he holds up his screen and watches the lights, keeping well fixed on their marker. He brushes away cold and holds the monitor close, sheltering it like he shelters a child. Pescha stumbles in his wake, death walking. She reaches up and touches her face and feels nothing.

This is beyond mental challenge, the bounds of digging deep. This is where the body fails.

Where conviction means nothing, against the raw strength one has brought to fight. Slender, supple; to use Pack One she has made her form lightweight, and relied on will to push her footfall. But up here, up above the Kyut, above the Humeda and their war, above all things, in a place besides concepts of conflict and drive, there is only one law, and it hammers against her so. Pulls hair and dress, she must bundle them midflight in her hands and draw them in, in this psychedelic state of weightlessness. Both of ethereality, everything whipping and curling and floating around her, as the air rises one bank and twists to drop down the other, and then a heaviness, pressing against. Pinning her, but should she try to break its force she would take its brunt on one side and slip. And there is no tumbling here, no grasping at the snow to stop. So brittle is she.

If she slips, she dies.

The Kamakara stops, pawing at his glass. He scrubs it clean and looks from it to the void.

Pescha stammers to a halt, craning her neck, gasping at the sky. Gasping up. There is no sky here.

Like they hang on tendons she lifts her hands, pulls them from the incline up which she crawls. Holds them before her, shaking in a way inhuman, shaking like they malfunction, wild and mindless. She tries to stand, staring at her ice-charred fingers. If she stays here, she will lose them. She forces herself to one knee. The Kamakara plays with his screen, and over shoulder Pescha groans, claws trembling.

Her leg slips over the edge, and she draws her blade, sticking it through the ridge.

The Kamakara turns, looking down at the shaking ball, hunched and gripping her impale. He stoops over, hand raised against the gale, crouches down and lays his grasp on the Nomad's back. His hand blocks the airflow against her face. When Pescha does not shift, he leans in, lifts a slumped head. Her lips are so pale.

Pescha mouths. She tells Mince she cannot go on. She asks for help up.

The Kamakara does not help. He shouts that Pescha follows or gets carried.

Together, Mincemeat's arm around Pescha's waist, the Klernsteiga rise. Ascending through wind and delirium, it is an initiation, the test of whatever faith to which this cathedral atop is dedicated. The trial of consecration, its survivors ordained, for with what human might the Kamakara climbs Pescha cannot know, but limp, hands held to her chest, they creep up. Slower now, but they do not stop. Constant in its incline, they scale the wave.

Bury themselves knee deep and look to the squall, white peeling, a roof of white paint collapsing.

Ever higher, the colour leers. The shade becoming midnight blue. Back in that timeless state, unconfined by day and night, like this is a monstrous bridge, or the ring of another world. Ever soaring, transcending the physical. Maybe the sky doesn't change. Maybe the ridge doesn't ascend. Pescha breathes hard, and holds herself close to the Kamakara.

Like the great wave carried this debris to the summit, frozen stone forms. Wind racing, the snow against its shattered spires and points is swept, the irregular peaks creating a maelstrom. It is like all the cold for miles seethes from this place, this relic of faith. She thinks of Casse Monvi, their masterpieces, but this land is so forsaken that with their understanding, their hindsight as to what would become of all this ancient beauty, this eerie majesty is far better fitting. All was destroyed, but if there was only one ruin left, deep in this emptiness absolute, she would picture here. Such strength of mind and muscle, to make this of nothing, and look what it has become. A cruciform temple of steeple and slope, it's rose window is pulled apart, glass shattered and whisked away, shards charred by cold. Stone blown out, it is under constant assault, yet its details remain intricate, the forest of pinnacles atop and carvings climbing the slabs now burnt with ice, but ever beautiful. White scales its edge, encroaches through wounds and burst sides, trying to dismount the cathedral from its peak. And while brick and glass has been displaced, its bones are unshaking, scaffold unfailing.

It is dark and massive, spiked and glaring, the wind rushing through its webbed stone windows. Echoing into the storm, like someone plays static over a distant radio. An arm around her waist, the Kamakara holds up his screen, glow buzzing, staring at the temple. There is no light from within.

He hears Pescha's breath, raspy and hollow. He hauls her on.

That same senselessness of scale with most things on the Kyut remains, but here it is biblical, for no human could place this here. Above conflict, above human reach, Mincemeat gazes, its moaning hymn lost to the blizzard's call. This must have been what it was like, in the age past, to find a new world and stumble across its ruins. The bodies of those last there. The Fauschenherst has scarce walked the Kyut for a hundred years, this place can be only so archaic, but those first of Sect One walked in the delirium of their downfall. The forlorn, yet blind to their fate. If this is not ancient in time, it is ancient in mind. Those who built this place, they did so with hope forgotten long ago by most.

From a time destroyed. Another system. Another life. He gazes, dragging the Klernsteiga who heaves in his arms. Enormous and spiked, he sees this religion's tenets in its architecture alone. In scale, the faith is strong established, and in its points and high blades of stone, the faith will endure. Even up here, ruined by gales, the majesty remains.

Its door, an ironwork of curls and furrowed vines scales almost as high as the structure itself, made to be opened by procession. Holding Pescha, he doesn't bother to try, passing the door for one of the many holes gashed through the cathedral's stone. He walks the side ravaged by stormfront- if he slips, he feels he will be plastered against the slabs. He shoulders through the racing cold, gripping his sunken Nomad like she is but cloth, snatched by winds.

At its base, the cathedral rises so high and runs so far ahead. Surely, this is the place where judgment is made. Where the souls are dragged, pulled atop this mount, their calls resounding eternal. In his arms, the woman bitten by frost murmurs, hums in tune with the wailing church. Dreamlike, the Kamakara no longer receives a reading of altitude from his screen. For the closest gap he marches, rock gnawed open, and he pushed Pescha through, slipping from the gale with coat trailing.

Lit by its slits, cuts and slashes that would fell cities cleave through the stone, like something ravenous straddled the hall and ripped in frenzy.

Ever immense, of pillars and marbled floors and constant rows of pews, if Humeda had skeletons and kings, this would be the skeleton of that Humeda royal. Ornate, its ribs fall from the spine overhead, arches inscribed with carvings now meaningless in all but grandeur, in splendour. Its vastness alone would be magnificent, but all attempts by the Kyut to destroy human influence here have fallen short. Columns furrowed, edged and leering, these bones are teeth and claws, jagged and splintered, made so by endless cold. The frost cannot encroach far, kept at wounds and holes but its clutch sprawls, frozen disease chasing the struts and pegs of the cathedral's foundations. His footfall crushes the sheets, a webwork spreading with every step, laden with Pescha's added weight. He walks to the central row, and turns to face the church straight.

Ribs lining, a procession of elaborate decoration, like carved stone nails dug into the ground, flags him at either side. Some sick wedding, he approaches the cross, snow whipping through the breaks. Open and packed with benches, the cruciform midway opens out, the left offset collapsed, white flooded through. Overhead, paintings and glasswork have been worn flat. He barely notices the art. First, head cocked, his steps resounding throughout the great corpse, he looks to the altar, and its towering effigy in bronze.

A figure in outstretched prostration, statue arms splayed when he kneels, his hair hangs to hide his features. Ribbons of cloth bind both his neck and arms, and his splayed limbs are laden with censers, once smoking carriers of incense wrapped around and around. His figure, shirtless and starved, is hunched in thought, but while eyes are masked his lips are straight, unwavering under the stress of his burden. Cast of once shining copper now dull, the Kamakara can imagine that smouldering perfume, lights lit in his metal candlesticks. While he holds, behind, another figure looms. Working over top. Winged and veiled, her shawl hides her whole form. She draws, her utensils ritualised and crude. Jots inks against his back, tattooing stressed and muscled skin.

Their prophets, deities, both Pescha and Mince stare as they walk, transfixed on the dual sculptures. Amid bronze bindings and incense burners are more things roped, tied up besides the faith.

From his outstretched arms are stung corpses, robed like she who inks. Nooses bound over their shawls, they are limp and still, feet bare, chewed by frost. Veiled from crown to ankle in red blown dark, rough. The cathedral howls as their mantles flutter.

Below the bodies the Rautbergen sit, camped on the steps surrounding the icons. Weary, beaten, and slumped, their lamplight dots the base, glow catching the edges of those copper models. Like an amber metal tree, branches weighed with bodies. The Nomads count eleven dead. Eleven saints strung up and hanged. From amid the soldiers an officer stands, brow high, his circle of troops rising to follow. They lug Lautreisgefers and Neiderkops and know well the Klernsteiga who stalks the aisle.

The officer steps from the congregation and stoops in address. Ever confused, he sees the shuddering woman in one grasp, then the screen in the other.

They're all dead, Mincemeat says, throwing him the monitor. The officer cannot snatch, he is too cold, so the box hits him and falls into his hands.

Looking down at the tablet, the visor of his cap hides his eyes.

Staring at its brim, the Kamakara says they'll assist. The Rautbergen look from Mincemeat to the Nomad in his arms. She stands but stands keeled. Mince catches their glances, holding Pescha a little straighter.

Like a conversation already midway continues, a conversation they have debated for days, a Rautbergen stood at his officer's side shakes his head, saying this is pointless. There just aren't enough of them to survive. His choice of words is specific, Mincemeat observes. To survive; it isn't a question of whether they'll win. There's only so much difference two Klernsteiga can make, and as he says it, he steps forward, raising one arm toward Pescha.

It isn't a move in malice. A simple step, and a gesture. Remorseful, he begs if anything, but when he takes that step closer, he is flashed a glare so empty and condemning- not aggressive, but a sudden and instant switch of the Kamakaras attention onto him, as Mincemeat steps in his way. A look that he is in the danger zone now, that he must make no sudden moves, and his offense crumbles instantly. His lips seal, his character silent in submission.

Mince says she'll be fine, she just needs rest. He asks if the Rautbergen have anything warm to eat. After a pause, they shake their heads. The entire assembly looks at him.

The officer raises his head. His expression isn't sad, it's just solemn. He tells that they're the only attack group that came. They'll march at dawn. The Kamakara is free to take whatever he'll need. They haven't got much, but the team that made it made it with most of their gear. There's a fire at the base of the sculptures, he can sleep there if he wants. The officer looks nobody in the eye.

The Kamakara surveys the crowd, everyone huddled around pockets of lamplight and leant against their rifles. Each Rautbergen looks condemned. All expressions steadfast with their coming deaths.

Mincemeat says they'll keep watch.

From timber rafters high in the ceiling, Pescha watches the Rautbergen pray. Afar, she cannot hear their words, but she sees them bow in prostration. Beside, others busy themselves with comfort, picking through wrappers and huddling from the worst of the cold, trying to figure how they may warm their frosted flasks. The officer, perched upon the uppermost steps, does not conversate among his closest, he is reserved to gazing straight down the length of the cathedral. In his hand he still holds the screen, light faint against his shin.

Over Pescha's shoulder, atop their little outcrop, the Kamakara lays their coats as a bed. The roof is blown out, but the storm runs parallel, wooden struts snapped, and it doesn't touch them. Mince tries a fire, tearing timber with his machine grasp from running support beams and with matches from the Rautbergen he strikes a flame, bringing in the sticks with his unfeeling hand. Pescha watches him stoke the kindling with his fingers, letting ash run between like water. She turns from the overlook, collapsing at the warmth's side.

Arms unbound, her skin is torn and charred, but not lost. She holds her palms to the heat, flexing digits scarred from her fall through the pines of the Shae Doken and gnawed with chills. The lines run red and sore but hurt no worse than the rest of her clutch. Through them she looks at the Kamakara, who slips from his striders.

They'll do that for hours, Mince says. Pray, he means, drawing his foot from its straps. He murmurs that you'd think they'd give up on that by now. He takes a packet from his coat and passes it over the flame. Dried mushrooms. Pescha rips the bag with her teeth and pours with one hand from packet to mouth.

They're not asking for goodness, she chews. They're not asking for deliverance. They pray that they may war forevermore.

They fight, Mince says. They don't war. They can't tell the difference between searching for resolution and being beaten up wherever they go.

Pescha closes her fingers, looking at the Kamakara over the tips. She raises a brow.

Mincemeat blinks. He smiles, and shakes his head.

They listen to the storm, scraping slate and ramming against church spires. Sitting there, watching it fly, Pescha cannot understand how anyone could walk through; even though she has, it makes no sense. Like shots or running water the snow does not twist so much as it surges, straight and blistering, turning only when it meets the stone towers, spinning free at the last second. Their overhang rattling, Pescha's lamp buzzes alongside their fire, catching corners painted with a film of frost. She has done it, but to think of her ascent seems impossible, let alone living up here. Miles above and miles afar from anything else. She thinks of the suspended, left dangling from their idol.

Below, she hears a Rautbergen conversation rise a moment, then drop the next, echoed through this hollowness. Mincemeat rocks slowly, leaning on his haunches, then falls back, exhaling with breath like smoke.

Pescha asks why they hanged the priests.

For a moment, the Kamakara is unmoving, eyes shut, each breath a silent sigh. When he speaks, he does not rise. He lays a wrist over his forehead, like he checks his temperature.

He doesn't know why they killed them. Maybe they resisted, or tried to keep the Rautbergen out. But they hanged them for the message. They'll leave behind as many Fauschenherst banners as they can too.

Pescha asks why the banners.

Laying on his back, the Kamakara looks over, his hair everywhere.

Because they know, in a hundred years time, when the Fauschenherst has been pushed to a new front, trying to cram itself into another corner of the Kyut, the ignorant Sect One descendants who wander up here will see the symbols, hung from every wall, and think it of some God. It's standard procedure, he tells, again rocking back. When the Fauschenherst leaves a ruin unattended. They call it Antheldesfleck. They perform Antheldesfleck; leaving their insignia to instil a weariness in the Kyut's populous. Reverence, fear, Mincemeat says they don't much care. If the people and the planets didn't stand a chance, they'd make it look like they did, once. Maybe it could resurrect the Fauschenherst. At least in name.

Mince stays lain back, but opposite so too does Pescha maintain her stare. It is fixed on the Kamakara who's chest heaves, face half caught in lamplight. The half with its machine jaw.

Pescha asks Mincemeat if they have enough Rautbergen.

The Kamakaras hand falls to his eye, and in fatigue he rubs vision.

They expected more, Mince tells, but were prepared for none. The firelight wriggles against the rivets and seems of his arm and he sits up, propped on that machine reach. Their small pyre builds itself, ever brighter.

But they never thought of him. He is amid their reverences, he says; pledges of bravery and strength to rival that of even Clan Kamakara, the most fearless of them all. Rogue flakes of white crackle against their flames.

Why do the Rautbergen look so defeated, she asks. Her gaze does not waver as the Kamakara turns and meets it. He stares straight back, slow in his glare.

The Kamakara leans forward, as close to the fire as he can be unburnt.

They'll reach the Iron Driver by next nightfall, he tells. In his prosthetic jaw, Pescha can see the shape of flame roll with the motion of word. Pescha will take it until the rain starts; once it does, she'll depart the next stop. Like a thousand insect colonies, bulbs of moss will roll for miles, beset by blinding fog and thin streams. She won't be able to see twenty feet ahead of her, but if she follows the trail, follows reason, she'll reach a city, the border of sector Zero, Double-Four, Nine, Three, Five. Once she surmounts its hill, she'll be well free from the cold. Then she keeps walking, makes for Summer, its clear sky and vibrancy is famous. Towns, more cities, whole hopeful peoples consumed by the green, a paradise revered. She has seen nothing like it.

That heavy midnight blue fights with the heat over the Kamakaras features, making their shades upon a monochrome stare. Snowfall frames, the hole in the roof letting white in.

When the pillars rise, Pescha will know she is there. Scale them and atop she will see Ukibiki. The Nomad Hotel. It's beautiful; the peaks of rock are laden with grass, sandstone and vines intermingled. Above, the blue is empty, warm, peaceful. Farms, mills for wind and water. The noise, calm.

The Kamakara has never been in day, though. He has heard this only from others. When he went, it was at nights darkest pitch. When the Fauschenherst sent him to haul out every deserter, into that dark.

To cut down the scores of Klernsteiga defecting to comfort. To route the rats nest and cleanse it of cowardice. To make an example of the treacherous, if only one temporary.

He says this with dual meaning. Pescha mustn't think the Rautbergen revere him. Does Pescha revere him. For all the legends, when she first lay eyes on the Kamakara, was it awe which struck her. Pescha stares, unblinking. The Kamakara shakes his head. Then, a frown creeps, his brow twitches. He shuffles a little, suddenly uncomfortable.

It also means that Mince can't take her the whole way.
    Not to the door. If Klernsteiga heard he was approaching Relief, there would be uproar. Migimidian would rally an army. It'd start another war, another faction: the Fauschenherst, the Humeda, Sect One, and Ukibiki.
    For a second, his eyes lose focus. Then he zones back in, but his brow remains uneasy. He goes to speak.

Pescha asks when Mince will leave.
    Mouth ajar, the Kamakara rocks back, straightening up. The Iron Driver, he thinks. When Pescha gets off, the Kamakara won't. He'll ride on.
    Pescha nods.

In silence they sit, not warm but warmer than they've been in days, weeks, since the Auditorium of the Administrator. It makes of their minds fatigue, soothes thought and question, and while the edges of Rautbergen conversation drift, up where they rest is but sputter and wind. Slowly, they start to sink; they know tomorrow is not a day to awake to tired, but they are also so worn and battered that they cannot possibly heal at all overnight. Gripped by a complete fatigue then do they lay back, fall upon their bed of coats, let heat spread from face and fingers down and stare into its colours, between crackling sticks and planks. Rest, both watching it burn, seeing each other on either side, faces twisting, aflame.
    Or Pescha does. When she glances at the Kamakara, he gazes straight back, his eyes fixed on hers. Passively, absentmindedly, his withering gaze falling slowly, lost in her features as he drifts. She pretends not to notice, a gentle, soft smile of warmth permeating her icy and fatigued expression, the afterthought of Rautbergen chatter mumbling up from below.

These frozen winds never started. They have always been, and they will never end. There is no calm before the storm. But here, there is some semblance of peace. A moment in which nothing can be done, and so nothing is. A small space of intimacy, to assuage the loneliness which afflicts everyone here. She feels that weight of slumber. That heat seeping through her face, it warms her skull and melts everything inside.

    Tomorrow, hundreds will die. Her hand may claim more than it has ever before felled. But then that's it. A short walk more, and she's there. Gentle breeze and nice food. She's free. Out the other side. Her whole life, for this moment. Shadow and light dances in the slits between slackened fingers. She drifts off, awash with warmth.

Fire crackles.

     She feels the icy breeze try to push the warmth of their camp, two extremes brushing back and forth against her face. She does not open her eyes- it is that moment where she is unsure what has woken her, for she feels more comfortable than she could ever expect, and knows the Rautbergen must not yet march. She cannot hear their talk; it is silent beyond their smouldering flames and rushing wind. She fidgets, and her brow furrows a little. She doesn't want to look and alert herself too much to fall back into sleep. She tries to reach closer to the flames and finds that she can't. She tries to move her other hand, and feels something between each of her fingers.

     She goes still. Slowly, she opens her eyes, and breathes in. She smells smoke and charred wood, then unwashed hair and laboured musk. Gently, she looks down. She sees an arm wrapped around her waist, the other intertwined with hers.

     As she tilts her head down, she feels heavy slumbered breaths against the back of her neck.

For a second, she doesn't know what to do. She realises that he has carried her, from her side of the camp to his and then covered her with himself, shielding her most from the cold, taking the brunt against his back. His frame rises inches over her shoulder, guarding her completely, and he has undone his coat, holding her to his chest. The warmth, it is like he has pulled her inside his skin. If she was not so heavily cloaked, she would feel the beat of his heart.

     Pescha shuffles a little, and he does not react. Deep in rest, he does not pull her closer as she moves. Knowing then that he is asleep, she relaxes. Softens her shock, falling into his touch. The arm around her waist is the machine one, wrapped over top. The one holding hers is his flesh, her hand atop his. Pescha's entire reach can fit in his palm; his fingers are intertwined with hers, his nails reaching to and past her wrist. She stares at his hand. Runs her fingers the length of his. With both, he could hold her by her waist. Thumb to thumb, tip to tip. It's a thought which sways with the pulsing flame, coming into a leaving her mind.

She stares at his hand. Feels the rise and fall of his chest. His soft breath against the nape of her neck.

Gently, Pescha pushes herself back. Fidgets, into his lap, pulling his reach further over. She tucks herself into his arms, nestled between his limbs.

In another life, she wonders what they would've been like. This isn't something she thinks often; so engrossed is she in her single-minded goals, to picture another reality is a pastime she resents, but she'll indulge it here. She pictures what she'd wear, how she'd walk. What she'd do. Him too. Without his prosthetics, unscarred by war. The mannerisms of a man so great and strong but not forced to prove these strengths every waking day. She knows nothing of ordinary work, before they were all forced out here, but she tries to imagine how he would use himself. A sport, maybe. Or some role important, somewhere where he can lead. His sense of command is absolute, but if he softened, he would be admired too, and she knows he does not fail before a crowd. She wonders what he would think of her if they ever met like this, what the better him would think of the better her. She can think the same of everyone she has ever met, and wonder how things could've been.

She squirms further in, pressing all that she can against all of him.

He is strong. But not as strong as can be. Whether of men or strength as a whole, she thinks there three factors- in the will of aggression, the desire to dominate, and control. Mincemeat has never had any control. Beyond emotional restraint, he knows nothing of the worlds around him, nothing of their history or drive, and this must torment him so. He has no reason to do what he does, and this is what makes him so effective, for it is the nature of his talent to lose control. He lives blindly, doing what he is told. He is chained by his ignorance, and it batters his ability to live. Makes him a doll, big, and nightmarish.

But aggression? Domination? He has these in excess, he is these things incarnate, yet he is incomplete, void of the most crucial tenant of all, for what are his strengths if he cannot use them for himself. His anger, his hatred, all that fulfils him comes from this absolute shortfall in his character, and he will die nothing if it is never overcome. Pescha feels his weight against her, the power of which he is capable, the same hands which hold her now having thrown machine dogs and so many more, and for everything that will happen tomorrow and in the days to come she cannot help but picture stepping from the Driver without him ahead. Listening to the doors shut, and seeing window lights trail off.

She rocks her head back, facing the sky, feeling his breathe against her cheek. His lips are colourless, the machine jaw toward the ground, so that from above his face is whole. She wishes his arms would close around her, lock her there. She wishes she could cling to him like this, and that he would carry her all the way to Ukibiki.

She shuffles her leg under his.

She wriggles, stuffing herself into the space between the boards and him.

She curls up, that she may loop him around herself.

He starts so suddenly, she blinks and he's atop, her arms pinned either side of her head. More reflex than conscious, he seems to wake when he's already up, hanging hair shielding all but his mouth. He heaves, stirred suddenly from slumber, his attention gradually forming on the wide-eyed girl underneath. Her blue startled, frozen on him.

She's sorry, she says. It was only her. His breathing starts to settle, his figure relaxing. She says she didn't mean to wake him.

He says nothing. He just stares at her, thoughts coming to him slowly. Like his body is alert, and the man inside is still waking up. For a moment they are like this. Suspended in a second, her watching him blink and ease back into consciousness.

When he's there, when he's back, what he says, he says it slowly. Like he isn't sure he's the one saying it, or why he is, or whether he should.

He needs to know something, he says. She gazes up at him, his fists balled around her wrists.

She remains silent.

This whole time she has followed him. Abided by his every rule and instruction. She has followed him without question through stretches which have claimed legions, and not said a word in retort. He asks her why. Why she's done this.

Pescha's brow furrows. Because she has to reach Relief Ukibiki, she says.

The Kamakara shakes his head, this isn't what he means. He asks again, why.

She pauses, lips parted, uncertain. She starts that she has somebody there to reach, but again, he shakes his head, wolfish glare locked on her.

Why.

This whole time, Mincemeat says, Pescha has walked like there is no possible flaw to her plan, or alternative, beside the path she follows now. Such certainty, he has scarce seen it in a Klernsteiga, never seen it in anyone else before, and he has toppled giants alongside fanatics. There isn't a way to describe it, the absoluteness with which she strides. It's not confidence. The subtle and constant knowledge that every second, she will devout toward her goal; every Klernsteiga knows this, every person knows this, it is what drives them day to day, but not like her. It's like she believes in nothing else. Like there is nothing else.

Her blue is dazzling and fixed, unshaking. She lays below him, defenceless, but when the shock has waned it leaves no fear. None at all.

She looks at him. Looks into eyes untamed and vengeful, but ignorant and blind. Angry, but he doesn't know what at. Remorseful, but he doesn't know what for. She sees a desperation so innate and carnal that he wouldn't know it longing, he would think it his natural glare. He wouldn't know he was missing something if it weren't for her.

She looks, and sees her own blue glinting back. Sees an emptiness, an unfocussed void, her glow hidden deep within.

He says he cannot understand. Cannot fathom what is here, or what she has in there, and he gently gestures with a nod to her chest, which can drive her so. Others have it. He does. There are other Nomads who have it too. Small Hand has it tenfold, and for each of them Mincemeat knows why. How long they have fought, the tragedy they have endured. But not Pescha. She has might to rival the highest, and yet she is unknown. She is a mystery to all, her page even blanker than his.

Mincemeat ruffles his hair with a shake of his head, like a wolf would in frustration. And it makes him mad, to see her so. To walk alongside someone for so long and through so much and to know their mind by snippets, whispered proverbs that leave him racking his thoughts. To see her determination, blunt and unapologetic, in the suffering it has caused her, and in the lives it has cost. He has never had anything like this. What she knows must be so good, so worthy of her work. All he has had is heartache and misery, and the knowledge that it may never change, so that he may be ruthless and spiteful and gruesome, and it'll account on him to naught.

That isn't true, Pescha says. Pretending he doesn't care; she struggles a little under his grip, and he releases her left arm with a glance, like he hadn't realised it was caught. With that hand she reaches up, holding it against the side of his face. The side that is whole. Her thumb caresses his cheek, touch soft and caring.

He leaves it there a moment, expression still.

He slams her arm back down by her side, leaning in. There's something wrong with her, he tells. Something unnatural, inhuman.

It starts in some school on a mining world called Jiro Basaal, Pescha interrupts. Mincemeat blinks, pulling back a little. Where kids dig for and build machine components, she continues.

What is she talking about, he asks, but she quiets him with a shush, relaxing. Exhaling completely, that her body may be as exposed as can be. She invites him to listen. She sees his tension slack, features vaguely attentive. She sees him ease and sees that he is hers. She says they are mules, slaves, digging and digging in a pit, miles deep, with no chance at a future; they'll die here, there's no question about it. It's nothing unique, nothing special, and nothing new- It's the same way it's been for thousands of years, cursed by birth, bound by land. For one of the many schools there, that of Senmei, more boarding houses that raise the children for work, the solution to this burden is simple; if they cannot live, then make living seem such a foreign and false pursuit that it holds no desire.

Mincemeat glares at her, disconcerted, but following. She gazes, blue sharp and piercing.

Let science relieve their charge and soften their pain. Tell them that their sorrow and discomfort is no different from joy and pleasure, that it's all just chemical and electric, the same as everything else they perceive. That they themselves are a hundred parts, made of a hundred parts, made of a hundred parts; that all which makes them was there in the beginning and will always be, and that they will soon be allayed completely of their strife. So they can abandon conscious and torment, and return to sweet oblivion. The words are spoken with such assuredness, no snow or smoulder or stare could disturb. But the houses who ruled these mines would not abide such blatant disloyalty. An easy example, they did the unthinkable.

When someone is burnt, Pescha tells, they pain for only so long, before all nerves are singed. She's seen the footage, she tells, unblinking. She's seen it here too. Then, they sit- lament in flame, senseless, unable to feel the agony anymore, just smoking away until they're ash. Children, empty, despairing, blank and wretched; kneeling and burnt, when the other urchins started to eat, it went unnoticed at first, as unfeeling and incinerated flesh was gnawed. They felt eventually though, unable to move. Like a plucking at their bones, as teeth found meat not yet charred. Mincemeat is still, waiting for the point in all this. Pescha shuffles a little, finding comfort.

Yet one did survive. Crawled from that pit.

A son of Senmei, a boy like Small Hand, a genetic mystery unable to age[32]. And in their panic, the houses became crazed; they feared a diplomatic incident cataclysmic, the spread of fanaticism through their mines, through their worlds. They overestimated the threat and feared its potential. In response, the four strongest houses united under this one common, secret cause: those of Sei, Gen, Mu, and Shin. At first, they quarantined their territories, enforced authoritarianism, and broadened their search to neighbouring worlds. But the potential of their cumulative resources, their military might, the power that ensued birthed a new order entirely- they became obsessed. Cut themselves off from all others. Through their single, common, detestable enemy, and their devotion to its destruction, they became a people of power unimaginable.

But when a uniquely militaristic and isolated mind, bent solely on the purpose of annihilating a heresy in mankind, looks to the stars around it, that mind no longer sees other cultures. Compared to their own, the Museishingen saw degeneracy, blasphemy. A sickness in mankind's myriad of ways.

Pescha breathes what is next. Recounts it as though she were there. Mincemeat abides her zealotry.

The Hecatomb; a mass sacrifice for a single cause. That's what they called it, when the Museishingen unleashed terror from their corner of the universe. After thousands of years, an armada capable of eclipsing a sun from every angle came, an army of the virtuous, the unshakable, legions in rows, stony faced, generations bred for this moment, this life.

---

[32] *Eine Atmen Genome defect G-Fifty Three* : An untraced genome defect discovered during the later stages of the Eine Atmen Breeding Programme. Individuals with this specific genetic mix achieve a seemingly random age of physical fixity, wherein they may theoretically remain forever, so long as they maintain their general health- outside of external factors, natural deterioration of the body stagnates, and an individual can live for hundreds of years while maintaining whatever physical age at which their aging ceased.

Millions, dying in silence, working from birth to death to build this army, in complete faith of its ideal. The saviours of humanity, they made what they sought to destroy; with their invasion they forced their imaginary enemy into existence. Against a foe unbeatable, odds unsurmountable, and the threat of total submission, Senmei was reborn. But they too were as twisted from first reason as the Museishingen. Unrecognisable from their original state.

These words. She says them like they are holy.
The Iconoclasm, and its Iconoclasts.
As fervent as the Museishingen, the enemy they had always craved. Misanthropy infinite, heartless, murderous, reborn in that aggression which first gave humanity dominion; that aggression which obliterated all hominid competition and made mankind supreme. Both sick of human idleness and insolence, and apathetic to all morals and rules.

The greatest war in history, she almost groans this. All other things were meaningless- religion, politics, race, resource, nation, money, revenge, all insignificant. Complete fanaticisms clashing, complete opposites locked in a holy war, of total human salvation, or total annihilation. The inevitable war- a testament to human evolution. When all of mankind would at last unite, or rid the universe of its curse. The one thing someone could commit themself to wholly and have no regrets. The one thing someone could die for, without a shred of doubt.

She glows at him. His expression is lost, in every sense of the word. Lost to the sacred knowledge which floods him and lost to why he is told.

It ends the way it always would, she tells, voice monotone. In annihilation.

They called it the Humiliation Syndrome. The spread of the Iconoclasm through vast swathes of Museishingen and neutral territories. Millions at a time, whole worlds consumed by their indignity. Each time they would be cleansed, purged in mass to eradicate the spread. Culled in their billions for their heresy. Eight times the Museishingen survived, obliterating massive numbers of their own population. Eight times, they massacred so many of their own, ignoring all please and prayers. By the Nineth Humiliation Syndrome, there was little left of mankind, both numerically and individually, to preserve. By the Nineth, the Museishingen had slipped back into their little corner, fingers in their ears, unable to fight an enemy capable of crippling all allegiance with whispers.

Instead, they sent one last army to fight. In their dying moments, they released an army impervious to this disease, deaf and blind but savage.

Mincemeat glares.

Relentless in its cause, and remorseless in its assault. An army that could fight for a thousand years more, long after the Museishingen were dead.

Mincemeat's face relaxes, understanding gently released across his features.

An army tasked with genocide, merciless and unwavering. Machine demons, dropped from the heavens to plague worlds for generations on end, until every little thing that still claims itself human was devastated, and they wandered the wastes afterward. An unimaginable punishment, laden upon all mankind.

Then more weapons, tools of devastation to eradicate all worlds sullied by heathen footfall. Objects to ensure this cancer could never survive, to ensure there was not one left who carried its rotten core. Objects in the hands of the helpless, the humiliated, and the aggrieved.

She doesn't know if it had a name. Whatever went off. Whatever the Museishingen built after millennia of depression. Millennia of killing themselves for a single cause, now beaten. How they must have despaired, she tells. How hollow their thoughts must have been, to forsake humanity to a fate worse than death. To forsake the whole universe to total obliteration.

Mincemeat says that doesn't make any sense. The Museishingen did their enemy's work.

Pescha shrugs. She says if they hate something to the core, it's very ideal, then they create an ideal they themselves must live up to. Two enemies; mankind couldn't be what they dreamed of, and that was just as bad as defeat.

So, what, Mincemeat interrupts, shaking his head; he asks that they blew everything up. Just like that.

She sees the immense weight of his self-loathed ignorance, and how deeply he detests asking so innocently. They meant to, she says. Maybe it was Compressed Light, or something new altogether. Either way, they never intended this, she says with a nod. To leave a little segment of humanity and their ancient war, out here. They meant to burn everything, and ensure nobody could ever return. It's a thought worth thinking, Pescha says, that they bred, without even knowing, their perfect soldiers. Created an environment in which mankind can obtain its true apogee, where it may fight a crucible of the machines they left behind, or endure the motivation of complete poverty and hopelessness back home.

How can she know this, the Kamakara again interjects. He slams her arms, unresolvable aggression growing. Nobody, he growls, nobody here understands anything. What she's saying, she cannot know. She- her, of all people.

She's the same as everybody out here, Pescha tells. A nobody. She is not dumb enough to fake blasé, but then she doesn't show any emotion at all. She welcomes the Kamakaras raw, uncontrollable response. He is of the disposition of complete power, and he knows this always, no unease or hesitation comes to his voice. But he is aware too that he knows nothing of the woman under his arms.

But she'll tell him, she says. She'll tell him everything. Her blue is like a bottomless space of light, and with the cold of their breath it is like the glow reaches, bright tendrils clawing for the Kamakaras face. His expression, so flooded with revelation, she thinks she could tell him he is pale, and he wouldn't comprehend. She feels his grasp tighten around her wrists, so harshly the blood flow is cut off at once. She doesn't react.

There's more, she says.

The Kamakara grips harder. They hear her skin crinkle and twist. Neither flinch. Her eyes are still but visibly wider, yet they both know that has nothing to do with Mincemeat's grasp. He stares. Like he wants to crush her skull, but he isn't sure why, or what would happen if he tried. Like he isn't sure of anything.

She revels in it. This whole journey he has known her, he has never seen such intensity in her face. Not when she scaled mile high machine sides. Not when Ozwald was crushed at her fingertips.

A boy runs, skin split and crawling. If he touches it, it sticks to his fingers. Body burnt; the mind tells him it is time to stop. Time to die. But of great flaming pyres, nothing burns as bright as his faith, aflame within his skull. Dull and self-absorbed and arrogant and empty, short sighted and so humiliatingly ignorant. Heretics, each and every one. Some throw themselves from heights. Grovel in their worthlessness. Claim that the best anyone can do is to help others, chase happiness. That it is not in their power, or not right, to change. They flee from it. Close their eyes, begging to be ignored. But that same chemical to make them run will force the opposite. Of flight or fight, that same signal controls. Two sides of the same coin. The flip of a coin. Some flee, scared, weep and rot. That boy, his anger is unbearable. Impossible to forestall. Inevitable. Pescha raises herself up, straining against her unbreakable bonds, coming as close as she can. In that moment, she tells, a grim truth is revealed to him. A revelation which all human history was leading toward, and which would dictate history forevermore.

Her shoulders contort, twisting at their limits, in a way only one as conditioned as her could endure. A set of ideals, she preaches, which would form the premise of every worthwhile feud to come, every worthy world or war. Everything- this boy, as he stumbles, he knows this. He realises it, spittle and hate spilling, and decides that mankind must face judgment.

 And if only all knew, Pescha moans, holding herself up impossibly. What a people they would be, they who realise the folly and insignificance of their current ways.

 If only all knew, she whispers, her arms rotated to the point of trembling, her vivid sights an inch from his own. In his gaze, she sees so much aggression he is unable to release. The pinnacle of mankind's thinking. They are dogs, he has pinned her, but she is feral and fears nothing. Let her show him, she snarls, her body at his mercy, his mind at hers. Let her tear at the fabric of his reality. Rip him from his little world and make him more. He will not bow to those false idols of blindness, for his eyes are aflame with faith. Blessed be the believing, she seethes, he will be an example to the righteous. He will be reborn an Iconoclast.

Her hands slip free, and she darts to hold either side of his head.

 He grunts. One hand wraps around her throat, forcing her back. The other reaches down, to the space between her thighs. She pulls him in, lips parting by his ear.

 He parts her legs with his forefinger and thumb.

She is brutalised by him. His strength- he has no need for words, he lifts and turns her whichever way he pleases, she is subject to his whims. She wonders, so high in the rafters, whether the Rautbergen below can hear, as gasps and moans and slammed timber drifts, aethereal from high above. His body is so elegant and long, underfed as are all Klernsteiga, but this is a malnourishment matched in the striations of his muscle and the power of his build; that under everything, his pale flesh was built to dominate. To crush all others- his is a form cruel and devilish, a son of the Kyut.

And all the while, she whispers to it. To a destroyer-form and an empty mind she feeds the blood of ten thousand years of war, groans and shudders into his ear poison which broke the greatest warriors to ever exist. She sees it, sees it overflow his skull as he shakes with chills of revelation. As his arms tremble and his head twitches. As she rips apart everything that he knows and fills the space with rage. With humiliation, the indignity of this existence he has ignored.

Everything he has harboured, all his resentment and pain, he takes it out on her, and she fills the space that hatred leaves with her faith in nothingness.

- *KENIDOMO COUNTRY* -
UNRECOGNISED TERRITORY

"*The Rautbergen Fall*"

The Rautbergen assemble Yaybahar; the cultural instrument of the Museishingen, played on grand renditions during the Hecatomb. The strangest of sounds, a harrowing call reverberates through bombarded atmospheres, dual vertical strings tied to twin coils and frame drums, played with a wooden bow. It both rumbles and leaps, like overtone singing that grumbles or glides, and splits the ear at the musician's whim. It is constructed with a risen neck and twin feet, like a snapped slingshot as tall as its player. They would have sung across the stars, the voice of massacre and decimation. Those who do not build pray, bowed in rows and ranks, inscribed cloth and smoking thuribles intwined between their fingers, words whispered quickly over revered guns. They plead that they may be graced with that same foresight of the Imperium. Of patience and precision in their planning, but supreme fury and hatred in their attack. That for battered and makeshift armaments, they can make their victory through fervour eternal, and a hunger for war ravenous and apocalyptic.

The Kamakara watches over them, crouched on the bronze statue's plinth. He holds his sheathed blade in his left hand, the other rests upon his knee. Over his back is slung his Neiderkop, bound for him with Rautbergen ritual bands. He is dormant, staring at space. Vacant, lips apart, watching snow drift through the ravaged above.

The Rautbergen officer, his rank and command obsolete within this patchwork militia, asks Pescha for a designation; a name for this facility they will invade. He must log how all these people die, he says. She thinks, standing with him at their exit wound, watching fervent recitations lead by prayer masters who commune in their own tongues. She remembers what Mince told her, of the only Kamakara to die on the Kyut; the Klernsteiga who ate the little Humeda. Bit off more than she could chew.

Befelobeth, she tells.

Their pilgrimage traces the ridge spine, the knife edge of the cold. There are less here even than Pescha found in the tunnels of Monvi, single file and forever struggling to keep to the crest, but they march ever steadfast. She keeps to the front, keeps sight on the officer and the Kamakara, the heads of their line.

When the Rautbergen start to sing, it spreads up from somewhere deep in their following. Mumbled at first, their chords too sore to make sound, when the voices rise, they do so desperately, a choir's pleading. Wishful. In awe of that to which they revere.

But it soon shifts. From desperation to yearning, and you would have to listen to truly know the difference. Haufenmensch Hellegeneid, Pescha thinks; she does not know it's language, yet she feels their tones, wailing to the winds. How they sound from afar, she wonders, their calls carried over the mountain drop. Ecclesiastic, their chant inspires. Rising and falling, it bates the storm in, breath of fatigue quietening them, for a moment, to rise when the worst passes, but it will never cease. Constant, droning, like someone tries to sing with a knife in their neck. Someone who refuses to stop.

They maintain their altitude, following the great wave and its curves and ripples until the officer stops, holding a screen of his own. Pescha passes the stalled line, shouldering through the gale to his side. He holds the monitor high and shields it with his hand, like he searches for something out on the horizon. When he lowers the screen, his shielding hand remains, pressed against his brow. He reaches out and points down the slope.

Carefully, Rautbergen slip and fall, sheets cascading with their descent, rifles used like supports, driven into the white. The slope gives way, and they drop onto their rears, but they are helped back up.

The line splits with their decline, fanning out, spreading over the slope face. Bedraggled figures, heavy set with great coats and hoods and boots and gloves, packs cumbersome, all tones are worn and rugged. The troops of a forgotten army, the last defence, they are without uniform yet uniform in their mood, for their attire is fading and battered, but what it represents is eternal. Outliving even their very clothes, their dedication endures, and when Pescha looks back from ahead, as the snows flat and the ground levels, she sees them trudge from the tumult, footfall crushing. Of all ethnicities carried by the Faurscherin, so many shades and tones, made constant without an inch of skin showing. All people made images of endurance. Besides heritage, colour, voice; only two things can be discerned. That they are human, and that they have fought for every second of their journey here.

They walk level for what feels like minutes, unsure how high their sliding drop has left them. A search party sweeping the white, their rifles scan, officer and Klernsteigas at the centre fore, searching too. The commander has pocketed his screen, and holds his Lautreisgefer level, driving its barrel through the rushing cold.

When the mount drops once more, the pit it forms and the rise on the other side makes a ramp for the storm, firing it overhead. Letting them see the space between, this indent in the snow face.

The squashed traffic control tower hunkers, sheltering from the brunt. They must have dug down in hiding, for its roof is near level with the base of either bank, white skating over its flat top. Keeping the Rautbergen behind, the forefront three watch from their peak, coats adrift with hoods and hat pulled low. Reinforced, she sees a square concrete fortress. Blocky and mushroom-shaped; its upper viewing gallery, which surrounds the highest perimeter, is the only weakness in its walls, and one which allows those inside sight from all angles. No windows besides, scarce any pipes and vents, and all external components are bolted and caged. Sheer and angled, the glass observation is bevelled; she squints, and through it she can see figures move, doors lining their walkway. The staircase must be central, all floors surrounding.

    She leans in and asks the officer about the instillation's schematics.

    He says he doesn't have them. The Kamakara leers unspeaking, fixed on the bunker.

They watch the Rautbergen haul their Yaybahar near the summit, themselves hidden behind the small peak between flat and drop. The riflemen fall into rank, arranged in blocks of five by five. They barely make four, but each looks to the risen instrument, mounted just out of Befelobeths view. It looks medieval, a trebuchet aimed for the compound, but Pescha stands back, observes, as a Rautbergen fixes his stringed bow. Besides her, the officer paces, looking over his troops. She doesn't know how many more he intended to bring.

When he comes to her side, she can see him shake his head, stomping and beating his arm to drive out the cold. She asks for the plan. He glances at her, face tight and forlorn.

It's whatever that says it is, the officer tells, shouldering toward the last wave.

Toward the Kamakara, neck flung back to the sky, watching the white whirl. Arms limp, his machine hand undulates, forming waves too fluid for human precision, flexing in ripples; against his stony stillness, it steals the eye. Pescha watches from behind, wind rushing, her hair lashing. Over shoulder, the Rautbergen rows stand braced, struggling to keep upright.

The Kamakara seems focussed on a feeling, something nobody else can see, concentrated completely in his psychedelic heavenward gaze. Standing like that, he looks like Hjordiis, Pescha thinks. Back upon Dodtohmet, its half-head amid the clouds. She thinks of when she climbed its hand and fired, rising so high, its vast claw pulling at the storm's hair to catch up. Here, she knows she is higher still.

It's like he's trying to stop himself from crying. He's not, but that's what it looks like, the physical effort to control demanding everything. His rolling hand balls, fingers falling perfectly into their fist. Pescha frowns, leaning a little to see better. She takes a tentative step forward, brow furrowed. For her, he is a dark billowing post, vaguely human. An abstract of limbs and slender form, the only thing making him man is his head. His face: she comes to him and lays her hand on his shoulder, asking by touch that he is alright.

He glances down at her, his expression still.

She sees his focus faulter, and the glimpse of subtle dread which brushes him when it does.

She sees his expression snap. Crack: his machine jaw pre-empts the organic.

She sees his prosthetic short circuit with the breaking of his mind.

It forces the rest to twitch into submission. Some broken, bleeding lust, his smile is too large for his face, prosthetic in overdrive; it threatens to split his bottom jaw in two, rip in half down the centre. Malfunctioning, it tries to draw his forced delight, pulling toward the ear, beyond what could be natural, and Pescha sees such discomfort, playing over his brows. Like he feels his bones strain and is unsure what he should do. Like his confusion gives him some grinning stroke.

And desperation, but not for help. Something tearing- Pescha sees his machine arm shudder, quiver, impossibly minute, impossibly quick. An expression of hopelessness, distressed and confused, but mixed with his pale and sharp angles it is scorning. Contemptuous misery, like teary mock. That every second he looks at Pescha, the feeling gets worse. The Fauschenherst need not dehumanise. Mince fights harder knowing that all he fells are the same. For all in that terminal, the universe ends today. Ends again.

While they stare the officer passes, shouldering up that final wave. Pescha watches and so too does Mince, both turning to see the solider rise. Rise alongside the Yaybahar and its musician and crouch, digging his gloved fingers into the bank, to look over at the bunker below. When he glances back, he sees them all, standing there. Waiting. Sees Pescha, leaning into the wind. Sees her uncertainty. The Kamakara turns away, looking back up the dune. The officer turns to the Rautbergen, from atop his snowy mount.

Faith demands that they make things good, he calls; restore humanity to the glories of old. And they must value this over all things. To make great and relieve the bad. But their conviction for this is so deep, they must give their all to its cause. Sacrifice everything they have. That they may give their bodies, he says; surrender their goodness and suffer themselves, so that the people and the planets may find reclamation. Like those Emperors of old, they must cast aside what is right, for the sake of what is needed. To relieve wrong, there is a fight far simpler than the inner search.

And these heretics, he rises; they deserve no sympathy. Their ignorance knows no bounds, their idleness is an insult to their species' name. They make of a grand observatory their cave, from which they may wallow and breed in their own self-pity, and it disgusts him that in the shadows of so much they may hide from the light, that it hurst their eyes.

There is no heroism in his words.

They must be cleansed. Their apostasy redeemed; they must be shown what their heresy is worth, he pines, racing gale playing with his form. It clings to the last crest, like a dark cloth snagged in blizzard.

Pescha looks at Mince, his expression locked in half-and-half glee and indignation, irritation, and the fury this brings. She is so close, on the gusts she pretends she can smell grass and flowers; how long she has prayed for this day. Not dreamt, the mind does not allow. But of curling drive it makes her uneasy to know that this is it. How long has she stumbled. Toiled, through every single moment. Suffering of body and mind, never once at peace.

Because this is it. The final challenge. An army in their fortress, against this bedraggled flock. And it is as though the Kamakara and Pescha are an inch apart, for they see in each other a symmetry, yet of faiths rival. Beliefs totally opposite, but of belief equal.

    All wars are won the same. It lifts Pescha's spirits. Those in Our Last Limit will be able to smell the blood. The stench of faith will bleach their clothes.

- KENIDOMO COUNTRY -
UNRECOGNISED TERRITORY
"The Befelobeth Crisis"

He and Gamilah both carry the crate, each at a handle, box swinging between. It isn't too heavy, but even still he feels her adjust her grip. When they step out into the glass gallery, she pulls her scarf better over her shoulders. The complex interior is like that of a boat, a steel warship of tubes and grey.

It's cold, no, she says, looking out to the white. She asks if there's a problem with the heating.

He says he doesn't think so. Ahead of him, someone kneels and tends to a radio, and further down another couple walk, gesturing to one another. More groups amble further on. It's just the draught from the tunnel, he tells.

They could extend the piping down, Gamilah tells. Nobody really goes there, but if it'd help.

He grunts. He says it's not on the top of his list.

They lug the flares for the signal room, built to fly drones through holes in the roof. From its ports they fire beacons, tied with paper flyers to catch the wind; like little parachutes with lights, they are tubes rolled in bags, pulled by the blizzard when they're flown. Whatever their original use, they now serve to turn away the machines, when the glow draws them in night. The blinking luminescence takes the machine chase, and gives them time to turn off the gallery light. They've been using them a lot recently. Almost every dark, when the automatons stalk the slope; the flares fly up the mount, and the machines follow, getting lost high above. It haunts him, to think of them all up there. Wandering, all sense of direction lost. He's never seen one come back down. But he doesn't want to know where they've all gone. He thinks of them, standing somewhere on the ridge.

Frozen totems, twisted and gaunt. Like rock formations, only up close can shrivelled limbs be seen. It's because he thinks of this that the noise cripples him so. Like the machine's cry, their howls wailing loud even against the storm.

A shuddering of springs like ripples on a lake, reverberating. Zippers and droplets.
    And drums, bouncing the sound. Liquid music, skating, wavering, as though noise is disturbed by a hand brushing the surface. Rolling. Swelling.
    A pause. The song lingers, allowed to merge with the wailing cold, and its resonance becomes like the wind, heavy and low.
    Becomes a song impossible, surely beyond human conception. Organic, but trembling, on the edge of the senses; more than auditory, it tests the ear. Produces sounds unthinkable to minds condemned to the constant roar of storms. A sound alien, foreign, but not just unnatural. It is what the foreigners brought for war. From their gallery, all watch. Bags and boxes hanging from loose grips, unblinking they stare, transfixed; it is like a machine summits the crest, leering down. But all that stands is a man.
    A single Rautbergen, playing his springs and drums. Manoeuvring around timber struts in his lone choreography, to stand at the strings and lay over them his bow. Of the eeriest of things, it is a sight reserved for the day of judgment, instruments calling. He blinks; he guesses today is that day.

And when it pitches up it pitches to new hights, spiking into the truly aberrant.
    Alien ships rising.
    A great revelation. He stares, completely transfixed, completely still, feels his body shudder and he knows that everyone there feels the same. Feels their skin prickle and squirm, their figures tense. That all people know the same. He hears more emerge, brushing through doors, to look the length of the gallery and frown, then to look out and find themselves too, mesmerised. Bodies snatched, the mind frozen.
    Because the brain will gnaw their limbs to save itself, but what can it decide here? What reason when it faces the nightmare? The insensible. It has told itself; the impossible.
    The bedtime fable. Of those wretched dregs, forever slashing. Their armies endless. Senseless and constant, to fight and fight until they have killed everyone, or everyone is dead. The sick half. The lonely half.

The half of want, want of the other half, of all things. It stands there, rattled by wind, and gazes down at their home, its horrid song moaning. Coat swelling and pulsing, the performer unstopping, and his song is so enchanting that even those who stumble from the inner hallways laden with guns and knives gaze. They know of but have never themselves heard this. This haunting call to score their horrors.

But when he lands. Crashes against bevelled glass and stares down at them.
All emotions in one moment.
When he lands, how they break. How the Yaybahar pitches, wordless, its tone says a thousand things. Pining. Longing and lonesome. But certain, too. So certain. It does not bare thinking. He will not look away, but he knows those around look at their guns anew. How they whimper. Clutch at their faces. Shudder, like a breeze sweeps through, ice replacing bone, then melting cold and weighing them down.

In their tongue he is the Shae' Bilaah. Stilts and hood; it is beyond description, it is innate. They eat. They drink. They breathe. They fear him. Dread, inbuilt from birth, they are gawping, teary eyed and numb. They stand by their lovers, their friends, but they don't hold them; nothing is sacred, not when he looks back. They shiver with indecision. Rapt, the mind cannot think command; thought races, but comes to no end. Twitching, chests heaving, they are petrified. If the Bilaah had stayed a second longer, gunshots of suicide would have rung.

But Mincemeat does not stay. As soon as he steadies himself, he arcs his strider, like he would sweep someone's legs from under them. He carves a ring in the glass and thunders a machine fist through. Their fabrics billow as wind rushes in, and like liquid he seeps too, falling between them with arms tucked in. When they splay on his landing, a handful of shards like knives are cast one way, and his drawn blade scythes the other.

People do not move like this. His slashes are so thin, so quick and so thin, the metal flexes like a whip, snapped too quickly for its weight. Like papercuts, for a time they do not bleed, yet figures drop and crumple to cuts clean and inches deep. Mechanical, he can lay five, six, however many blows he deems through a body in a second, making of persons pieces, leaving them half assembled and crude. Animalistic, like a level bird with wings wild, he remains stable as his arm conducts, wielding steel like air. Inhuman, of all virtues, for he stoops himself so low, chest a hair from the ground, then his striders spike and he rises, eleven feet from the floor. Tall enough to raise his bladed leg and stomp from crown through groin. These are people. Human beings. He disassembles them, leaves things overlapping and split that shouldn't be.

When they start to run, he reaches back and offers his Neiderkop. With one hand, he does not fire precise but in volleys, not bursts but torrents, emptying the magazine in one pull, shredding through the corridor. Felling tens in the space of moments, the light of his gunfire crackling, a glow to catch and make motion a film reel. His expression, still fixed to one side, is empty of his grin. It is straight and leering, and while both he and them are wide eyed, his is a look so intense that if bullet and blade break the body then this breaks the mind, that they stagger and stumble instead of fight. He has made a blanket of their corpses, his shells like fallen leaves before anyone thinks to fight back, and when they do, they fire over shoulder or fall into their aim, laying sights while others barge past.

To see it is to see a rock fallen in water, a black and white speckled stone sending ripples in all directions, to splash against the banks and send wavelets lapping. He throws them against walls like they are but the cloth they wear, and he hacks ravenously, pouncing and gliding and shrinking and growing that tall. So many pains all at once, people falling against one another and clutching their wounds, but those in hurt do not scream. They are silent in their suffering, scrambling to make distance, and he will leap on them and skewer them whole, and scarce even grace a downward glace.

And maybe what's worse, what's most crippling is that for the half-sneer, his other expression is annoyance. Not glee, nor fury or even effort, but his struggle with something else. His head whips, sways and jolts against the tugging jaw; he reaches up and claws, trying to settle the throbbing fault. And then anger builds, like he struggles from a tight coat, and he takes it out on those around. Wheels and lunges, dives to snake and leap that he must duck from the high roof. Like he spins in a brawl with his face, and all in his path are cut. Like he tries to get away. Argues quietly, squabbles, and attempts to ignore something he pretends unimportant, but that he is weary won't leave him alone. Won't go away. And with every butchery, each going unnoticed, he grows evermore irate.

Darting and slipping, like a bug pesters his ear. Seemingly without tendons or joints, he can wash over in a sea of cuts and then crush, pound and bludgeon, dropping all in reach before he loads another magazine and makes the opposite way tatters, Neiderkop blurting bullets to rev in his hand like a chainsaw. That single corridor becomes a killing ground, a massacre, and while those doomed but enduring drag themselves into the dark and deeper rooms beyond, most don't make it that far. They roll and blink, blinded in their ending moments, grasping at air, and rubbing their hands over lethal wounds. He walks over them, these things once people. The mind discards personality and consciousness, feels it seep between its fingers. They mumble, chew their lips, all gawking. Limp and fidgeting; in dying, they are like restless babies. Fitful, as his manic strikes rain overhead, his bladed legs flying and sweeping, the speed weightless. Like he dances, his martial art lashing and grappling. For many, he does not even force them to drop; he knows they will die before they fall, and he leaves them severed and reeling, clutching limbs hanging loose.

Then thunder, a detonation rings.

An explosion resounds, and it takes his attention. From the carpet of the squirming, his sights fix up to the opposite end, where concrete and steel blow in from outside, those running there hurled to the opposite wall.

Through the debris and rushing cold a woman flies, curling through smoke. Snow and dust follow her in, tentative and drifting with her embers, all hair fluttering. From her lower hip she draws a sword and points it the hallway length, the one yet untouched and full of rifles aimed at her corner. They awaited their horror's turn. Now a new horror has come.

Her blue is electric and ravenous, the blade glows with reflection. They hunger, but even crouched Mincemeat sees Pescha's discomfort. The slight twitch of her lip; still shaken by cold, she is uneasy in her grip, rolling the handle within a weak grasp, but with such expression does she drive her point down Befelobeths way. Facing those who stagger upright with her, she glances down the adjacent hall, flakes bombarding glass stained and riveted with gashes. To the Kamakara, edge and Neiderkop hanging from his sides. The Kamakara shakes his head.

Infront of Pescha, they raise their barrels. She only has time to nod back the way she came before she ducks and plumes, bursting down the stretch. Mincemeat follows her sign.

The Rautbergen line the slopes, spread over its face. Their Lautreisgefers trace weak glass, heavy laden but raised high.
    And azure sights have deemed the Kamakaras attempt too slow. He stares, glaring down the spot where Pescha had stood. And it boils; a thousand things, bouncing within his skull. Seething within bone. Frothing from the rim. If he has cracked, then there. That is when what's within seeps out.

He races, points stomping between the bodies, building a sprint, kicking like he skates, momentum rising. The flex and spring of his striders and his own strength- in his wake, the streaks in solid ground are like someone strode and slashed the floor from side to side. Over ten foot tall, he throws himself into every step, until he does not run, he glides, this billowing dark cloth atop spindly steel legs. Inhuman. Dreamlike. It is a horror to witness.

When Rautbergen shot's ring he does not stoop, he feels the heat of their tracer's whip by and lifts his coat against the shards. Like lightning strikes or artillery thunders, in seconds the glass panels collapse, and Lautreisgefer slugs pass halfway, even further, through the steel and concrete walls of the complex. Someone rising the central stairs would lose their head. Red streaks, catching fragment and snowflake for an instant, before they bore into the side and dig their way through. The sound, too. Like he stands amid an orchestra of drums. And when he rounds the corner, sweeps like he is carried on wings, he sees Pescha cut, plume and slash against those with sidearms, pistols and shotguns, ramshackle and improvised. Firing through the middle, she has carved a line, leaving those behind to Rautbergen bombardment. And to Mince.
    Stumbling, they grip bending wounds, blinking at hands hanging and bone snapped and he fells them all, a night terror who kills all he touches. Kicks rapid, they whip from the black fabric bundle, form shrinking and growing, untouchable but constant. Gunshots blare and frantically they hobble retreat, but he grabs and rips them in two, mauling whoever he can reach. Lashes out with those edged limbs and catches someone meters away, to pull them close and make mush with pommel and fist. Lautreisgefer rounds smack around the two Klernsteiga, made to ruin steel so destroying the meat they slam. Like they snag with them, as

they pass through, life itself, folding spines and blowing free legs and arms. People crumple, backs severed, their chins smashing against their shins. And if they're hit at an angle, then that side turns while the other remains, and all bones disconnect, the figure collapsing like someone flipped a switch, and all systems failed. Like an impossible force pokes their shoulders, and they are sent spinning.

Mince darts and curls, fixed on Pescha who's smoke fills the corridor and gushes out, tracers making their shades. A raving bird, a cat fighting cobwebs, blue eyes churn, her cutter disrupting, splitting, forcing the denizens to clump, so making easy shots for the Rautbergen who see shapes fumble from the two bladed storms and blow their outlines apart, as that inner distance closes, and the Kamakara invades.

Steps within Pescha's reach and knives, moving in her way and cutting down who she sought. Keeps pace with blue eyes which scowl and roll to another, the two Klernsteiga wrapped in each other's attacks. More and more come, trying to stem the flow of the two Nomads and pull back their trapped and wounded, and when one plumes and other chases, close to her heels.

Competes, each clawing before the other. Elbows bumping, like water they rush down the gallery hall, a wave of swords and smoke and gunshots, so quick that none can turn to aim. A torrent, floodgates opened, a twisting mass of dark cloth and fumes which snaps bone and leaves bodies riddled with bullets and gashes. But their most brutal conflict is between themselves, with their glares and snarls. Surging, arm in arm, eyes locked in slaughter. Side by side, Mince leaps and Pescha flies, fighting to fight, dodging the other's blows and stealing their victims and moving so quick, like a beast charges the walkway, whipping and tearing, a single entity, bright-eyed with swords for limbs. Its exhaust like a cloak of steam, its footprints a carpet of slumped moans.

Ahead of them, Rautbergen shots volley, blocking their path and making of those running there a stain on the steel wall. A horizontal rainfall of glowing slugs, it takes its targets from their feet, but when Pescha slides to a stop, hair lashing, Mince glides on, spinning into the last between himself and the impassable pounding. Some are cut down, some are grabbed and thrown into the barrage, and he is both a danseur and a brute in motion, butchering the final few in reach.

When he turns, his face is still stricken with its grinning stroke, yet childlike he is expectant, vast eyes searching. Breath heavy, he turns and turns, spinning, his coat twirling. A kid, wating for their parent's compliment. Looking for someone who noticed.

But nobody is there. Nothing, but shattered glass and smoke and dying shivers, curled up and twitching. He gawks at emptiness, gaze huge. Like it might fall out of his head. He stands alone, heaving.

He wipes his bottom lip and retracts his striders, so letting himself straighten up. The last thing standing amid devastation. Arms limp at either side, he is slouched backwards, infirm, but those around him are split and pulled to pieces. Now that they are left to calm in their knowing death, they start to bleed, properly bleed, muscle soft and relaxed. He looks both lengths, himself the middle of the massacre, and sees the innards drain, blanketing concrete ground. He looks down, and sees the red pool.

He thinks, they could bring every mother in here. None would recognise their child.

Over the ledge he sees the Rautbergen descent, making for the entrance. They plod and trudge, still steaming magazines left dumped across the slope, rounds emptied into the above. He stands on the overhang lip, watching them advance, smoke curling around him.

Blown central in the concrete wall below is a great hole, exposing the lower floors. Stone still crumbles, pipes spray water made snow in an instant, debris tumbling into the white. A gaping wound, maybe into the third or fourth floor. Mince must lean over the edge to see.

The Rautbergen at the base. Mincemeat from the top. Pescha somewhere between.

And hundreds of people who have done nothing wrong, awoken by a sudden draught. Their whole life, a constant struggle, never a single moment of absolute rest; now they sit, half-propped in their beds, blinking at one another, tense and waiting. Unsure. Unready, but forever prepared, rifles against their headboards. No home. No reason. Always scared.

Meaningless little things, Mincemeat thinks. Empty and aimless. He cleans his sword against his sleeve.

They have nothing, so are nothing. But they've fought; they deserve everything. He is like them. He of nothing. He will give them everything he has.

They sweep with torches, for there are few bulbs on this lowest level. Submarine innards, piping, and thick steel doors, they shuffle their way through, listening for someone to shoot first. Shoot first down here, the officer corrects; the sounds far overhead are monstrous, and thumping. A Rautbergen, face pushed against his rifle, asks if they're really doing this, if they're really going to kill everyone inside. What even are their orders, he questions? They stand by their busted open entrance, seeing the last file in. Cold light illuminates the backs of many. The officer turns to him and stares. His expression is like that of someone sworn to silence, but who will speak anyway, and with the barrel of his Lautreisgefer he indicates upwards. They listen.

That's a Kamakara, he says. A Kamakara, and whoever makes friends with a Kamakara. They hear gunfire and doors slammed shut, then slammed open again. He adjusts his cap and follows close to the last invader, white creeping with them.

He's The Kamakara Mincemeat, he tells. There won't even be an inquest. But this is hideous still. A gross summary execution, and everyone will call it what it was.

The Befelobeth Crisis.

They're all going somewhere, somewhere down. Pescha thought it was because of Mince, but like ants it is instinct; there is something below to which they retreat.

Her fumes fill the corridors, a gas attack which the fearful watch seep under locked doors, a fog creeping between the cracks. Hunkered low she keeps to the stairwell, circling the descent, waiting for those pushed down from the upper levels to reach hers. Not one ascends, the noise above forcing a squint as she hears, and already she is impaired enough. There is scarce a place less ideal for Pack One than this; a closed off area of tight angles and too many obstacles, tubes and vents poking into her way. Sneaking around her level, keeping an ear to the halls, she remembers thinking a forest her bane, back on Emilia. She now thinks this compound, this intricate hive even worse.

Small groups descend, dropping down ladders and backroom passageways in the hopes of keeping hidden. When they near and see the mist, they are hesitant to walk, but in their tight bands they venture, hunting weapons and pistols probing the fog. Some are hurt, hobbling wounds bound. But the vast majority look to have fled as soon as they knew. Unaware, they make for the bottom floors.

Two men stumble, finding their way through with memory. They swat at the smog and hold shotguns high, footfall gentle and cautious. Weary, not to send anything skidding. These under levels are without windows, lit by bulbs suspended and lining, but not all corridors are narrow and winding; each floor is surrounded by four full-length walkways, containing the interior rooms, and it is through these that they stagger, keeping to the lights. Trying every door, in the hopes they can slip though, but they dare not speak beyond whispers. Calling each other on.

They walk a slow and steady pace. Continual, one looking forward, the other back. When they reach the corner, they see the smog dissipate, fade to stomach level, lapping over the concrete. Both turn to look, more hesitant now to step from the cloud than they were to enter. Uneasy, they stare the hallway length.

Behind them, twin blue orbs apparate, confused to hear them stop. They hover, gazing at the backs of their heads.

When one man turns, Pescha closes her eyes, listening as they mumble. They ask if there's a vent they can fit through, or if they can somehow get down from outside. There is no inclination that they may ascend. They are both equally built; a little malnourished, but far from easy targets. She stands completely still, a few feet away, sights shut. Waiting for their move. If one sighed, breathed hard enough, he may clear the fog to her face.

He's had dreams like this, the one closest tells. Everywhere he's ever loved was a ruin when he came, and a ruin when he left. Here, this is the nicest place he's even been. It's like a nightmare; to sway through halls frozen and frosted once more. The one furthest starts, treading lightly down the open walkway. What he mutters in return, Pescha doesn't hear. Something about dreams ending and waking up. She is unmoving, invisible in the centre of the corridor. Straight and patient, letting them both leave. She tries to imagine what they're thinking, those walking backwards. In motion, she can sense their anxiety. With every step, they pause. They seem ignorant to the fog still at their chests.

When two azure bulbs peer around the furthest arm, like a child looking from behind their parent, both blink and stare. But it too makes her stutter, the way they just watch.

Maybe they don't think her an assailant. Maybe they're petrified. But the smog drifts and a woman gazes, gazing up at them from her crouch. Chin length hair black and damp, straggly and hanging, she looks at them like she's been caught, but isn't sure how they'll react. Like the door was opened on a friend stealing.

She slashes up, blade gripped in reverse, cutting into one's thigh, then almost through his arm. She draws back in and plumes, bursting the width of the hall, skewering him in her burst.

Clumsy and physical, she pins him to the opposite face, but

withdraws when the second aims. His shot is one to clear her, to try and make space, but pellets streak way past and she cuts, trying to get close. Swipes and lunges but he fumbles for fog and she must race, careful not to give him room as he racks the next shot. Behind her, she hears her first victim cry. She glances back, to see him push himself from the wall and level his weapon on her. He must tuck the stock in his armpit- his slashed arm cannot support the weight, it'd snap.

    She growls, lashing out one last time before she spins, drifting back to the wounded. It's such a task to stop herself from grinding raw against the ground, and she won't use a bomb unless she must. She doesn't know the range of the amplified blast. Pescha skates low like she slides, Pack One and her heels grating over the floor. Ever rapid, the speed with which the gunner must correct his shot bends his arm the hurting way, and his face bulges with the odd angle. She comes in low, cutting the burst and leaping, slamming against him, crushing the gun against his ribs.

It's brutal and barbaric, the way she must hack. So close, her sword is too long to well stab, so she hits him as though she wields a stick, battering his defence. Whacks from above, straddled on his chest. For a time, he tries to guard himself with his forearms, shielding his head, but her chopping doesn't stop. Eventually, he lets them fall and works to push her off, tucking chin to chest. Forcing her blows from his face to his crown.

    A man of ribbons and flapping skin, he shoves her off, and crawls. She might have blinded him, or he's concussed- he crawls against the wall, like he'll climb it vertically, so she rises to one knee and falls on him, bayonetting through the back. Piercing again and again, sword in two hands, forcing through as he rolls and claws up, snatching out of reach.

She pulls back and swings, sticking deep, sawing at his shoulder. Pinned in that corner, her violence has somewhat parted the mist. Making for them their own little world of hurt, walled by fog. She grunts with her cuts and struggle, hewing away. Digging deeper. The sound, the feel; it's like fighting a wet tree, she thinks. Splinters of damp bark. Weak and wet innards.

    Peeling. Her sword a woodwork draw knife, shaving him down. So engrossed is she in her carving that she only moves in time because of the barrel, poking sight a few feet away. Moves before the second sees her.

She crawls frantically, leaving her blade, shuffling over the concrete, fixed on the sweeping end.

Before he can step from the densest smog she reaches out and grabs the gun, yanking it from his grasp and casting it down the hall, watching it skid into the mist.

He veers into view and kicks, slamming into her chest and grabbing at her coat.

She knows her weakness' because she knows her strengths, and her strength is the part inhuman. A body powerful, tough, but made so around Pack One. She is light and flexible, she can take strong impacts, but for a very specific reason. She has quick reactions, but for a very specific reason. Yet when stripped of her kit, of bomb and blade and boost, she is then no different from those she now massacres. Slim and sickly, forever hungry and worn. As fit as a body with no food can be.

Except she is even lighter, and evermore starved.

He ploughs into her like a Humeda strikes, like the Iron Driver slams through the haze. She scrambles to stand in the second he wastes staring at his friend, bloodied but not quite dead enough for peace of mind, for still he twitches and rolls, curling up against the wall. She flips the switch against her palm, but he has her sleeve, and he keeps her near enough, kicking and kicking, slamming his foot from out of her reach.

Eventually she breaks his grasp, but he doesn't care. He hits her with a punch to break that tree she thought in half. Then he does it again. And again.

Pescha covers up but she can't stop the fall and when it comes, the impact against the back of her head is like another swing, sunken into her skull. The best she can do is bring up her arms as he stomps down, trying to catch a bug with his heel.

She's like this place against the Rautbergen Lautreisgefer's; they are guns powerful enough to fell the great machines but against weak flesh they're worse than the pistols they face. She isn't made to fight people, Pescha. Bring Mincemeat's swords, or those pistols.

Or the anger of someone who has all reasons to detests what he hits. Has every form of hate. She twists to take the blows on her back as she crawls, but he grabs her foot and pulls her in. Then he takes a handful of her hair and hauls, tugging her head back, yanking in fury and not knowing what to do. Blind with rage, he tries to pull off her head. Out of impulse he plants his foot against the nape of her neck. Pulls harder, heaving in a way she can do nothing about. When he next stomps, it grinds her throat against the concrete. With his fingers still intertwined, she cannot free from his clutch, and her hands can only flail aimlessly ahead, unable to reach around. Maybe it's the blood rushing, or the sudden severity of this, but she can't ignore the thought; she hasn't seen this one before.

He pounds, surely trying to descend the levels simply by kicking out the floor he's on. It is agony. Colossal, his boot forces her windpipe to protrude, and she gargles with each impact; there is no exaggeration or expression, a bat to the neck would feel better than this. He stomps her throat into the floor, and she cannot make him stop.

On his tiring he groans and lets her head fall, hard against the stone, stepping back with a stagger. He wines and shuffles, but she cannot see; she lays there and shivers, pawing like a hurt dog.

His moans become a snarl. He would take her lodged sword, if it wasn't stuck in his friend, so he must hobble back and fall by her side, fists balled.

She imagines firing Pack One and grinding her face off. She imagines screaming; that thought is even worse. She holds her arm straight, trying to keep him back. He swats it aside and she tries to roll, feeling bombs press through their pockets against her chest. He grabs her wavering reach and keeps it aside, kneeling closer. She takes one of the thrown explosives and stabs a point into his thigh. It does little but anger him more, and he drives another fist down. She pulls up her own in defence. With his swings, she tries to kick the metal star deeper into his leg. He ignores her attempts, throwing blows apelike, pounding on a door instead of a person. Their fight devolves ever further; scuffling, one with adrenaline wasted, his appetite after his outburst lost, and the other scarce able to breathe. A primal battering, palms pushed against faces. Knees and elbows. Childlike, rolling amid the mist. For a time, she thinks they may both give up; just sit back and stare.

But when they hear heavy footfall pound down their way, she sees his emotion furrow and curl. His grimace, as he glances over his shoulder. Then his defeated anger; his head rolls and his expression twitches, becoming sick and grudgeful. He slams against her, primitive and thundering. One of his shots falls through and crushes against her cheek. She rears against the ground, gouging for his eye.

He takes her wrist and hooks into her still bruised forearm, from the Gelid Cur's attack. Like a tree. The bark splinters.

Then he rears and reaches for her sword. He has time to stab only once, so he raises the blade high to drive through. But Pescha endures, lifting that battered arm alongside.

At the point's fall, it slides over her forearm. Lacerates deep, grating into bone, but with it she leans, pushing the sword aside. Instead of skewered, her forearm is slit, her blade half impaled, thrust into the floor.

When the Rautbergen emerge, he scrambles back and raises his hands in defence. If he hopes to surrender, he hasn't even the time to gesture fully. A Lautreisgefer slug thuds through his hand, fingers spinning, into his chest, and splays everything out the other side, blowing back the smog. His muscles seize with arms curling and legs straight. He collapses instantly, a long and droning exhale wheezing free.

Eyes unfocussed, gazing up, she listens to his dying moments. Laying there, lips apart, she lets her own sigh pass, hair bunched around her face. She does not rush to rise.

Her head rolls to one side; she looks to her left arm, still dexterous, but already her brow wavers. When she forms a fist, something pokes through the adrenaline.

A Raut crouches by her side, looking her over. A scarf muffling her voice, she asks if they arrived just in time.

Pescha touches a thumb to her pinkie, and feels things shift. She would say no if her throat could form words. Instead, she makes a syringing motion with her good hand, and the Raut nods.

Pescha is told they'll find a doctor. The Klernsteiga can follow them up.

But Pescha whines, voice breathless and small. She may suffocate yet, but she manages to shake her head, climbing up to sit. The Raut cocks her head, coat still layered with brittle cold. Pescha leans back, trying to force her throat open. She can manage only one croaked command.

Down.

Their shots sound like rockets, missiles launched down the halls. They fuzz the length, their glow burning, blowing through all they hit.

The fighting is brutal, confined to either those long straights or tight interiors, room to room with fist and blade in ambush. Behind crates and corners, all make for cover, a tug of war of pushing and pulling, trying to force the other around the bend, but the Rautbergen are winning. Weapons unsuited or not, there is nothing for those of Befelobeth to hide behind once they are known to be there. They pitch themselves on the turning angles, and Lautreisgefer slugs puncture through, ripping apart those down the adjacent way. The residents are forced to fall back, always; the Rautbergen are in pursuit, but they don't yet know where to.

It spans multiple levels; they take Pescha down, descending to the lower bowels where the officer and his close staff command. Radios hurriedly linked and stacked upon one another, he asks if she's okay and she nods a lie, holding her arm close. There is not a place in this facility quiet, every hallway echoes. But the tenants know this place better. Down backrooms and ladders, they are making their way here, to these deeper levels. Even if it's where most of the Rautbergen are.

The man who treats her does not talk, his lips are in the constant flux of prayer, blessing the bandage with which he adorns her arm. Sleeve rolled back he stems pumping red with stitches and sealing ointment and her skin is yellow and blue and very red but still straight, swollen but not snapped or chopped in two. The first layer of swaddling is sprayed with something, and it seeps through the pain. For her throat, it is something hot and sour. She cannot see the bruising there, or on her cheek. When redressed, she is offered a sling for her arm. She takes it but stows the suspender within her coat.

Clear speech is impossible, but with the hurt reduced she can force words. Her voice is like churned gravel. She tells the officer that there's some way out down here, some way besides the main doors. It makes no sense for everyone to ascend, there is no escape above, but neither does it make sense that they would so fervently drop, yet they do.

The officer says he's noticed; the Rautbergen aren't really pushing up, not in waiting but because there are so many flooding into these levels that they haven't been able to rise. From what he's figured, of the six levels, the Rautbergen still scramble over the bottom two. The third and fourth are rabid in fighting. He hasn't sent anyone up to the top two yet. Or the roof.

Pescha asks if Mincemeat knows about the resident's descent.

The officer says he couldn't. While he stands straight and looks unhurt, Pescha can see the misery in his eyes, as he throws the disassociated dregs of tired Rautbergen crews into this storming for the sake of a Kamakaras bloodlust. He is upright but unfirm, and his shoulders hang. His radio operators listen to the channels, and tally on their report. Pescha thanks the officer and turns, making for the stairs.

She says she will find the Kamakara and bring him down.

Before she can ascend, the officer calls, stepping forward. Pescha does not look.

He asks that she does not leave. Not while the Kamakara is here. He knows the command, but with Pescha there too, there's a chance. He almost begs.

Don't leave them here with the Kamakara. For both the Rautbergen and the residents' sake.

Pescha feels her mauled arm swell. Just the ulna bone, she thinks; not snapped in two. Her hand shakes if she focusses on the pain, dull but not silenced, only quiet. She feels it pulse and her blood flow throb, all vessels thumping. It is dizzying when concentrated on.

She says nothing and climbs to rejoin the Rautbergen.

All Klernsteiga are offered swords before the Kyut. Each built to order, it is the only thing they are given; the Rautbergen get their gun, the Nomads a blade. Part of the experience, and a wonderer learns to recognise their make. The smiths live on The Plinth[33], the last whole remains of the Faurscherin carcass. The hub and castle of the Fauschenherst, the final thing between planets and Kyut. Pescha's Teke Saiga is of draw cuts and thrusts, light and simple. Famously, Teke's smith was born of Sect One, but for his craftsmanship was flown up to the fortress to work. So few are those descendants who leave. He even remembers Ozwald's, a Naulerkisch, made by multiple masters. They're the group for shorter blades.

Mincemeat has never left the Kyut, he stumbled into Mestridoden with half a face and half an arm and leant upon a Nomad's sword. They told him it was a Hagaburi, of Hagaburi Dagadarah. His swords are longer, to chop and impale, but he was old and took an age at the forge, so his pieces are odd and rare. He forged over a mesh, inlaid into the blade; they were tougher, could take more strain when others would chip and bend, but when his swords had endured enough, they did not snap. Long after another would have failed, his works would shatter. Mince no longer has the original blade. It broke long ago, and he lost the pieces, but apparently Hagaburi no longer works, so he keeps the handle, and replaces the edge.

After the Gelid Curs, he thought this set was lost, striders too. Chipped and frayed, fighting their bladed ribbons was suicide.

---

[33] *The Fauschenherst Plinth* : The in-tact remains of the Faurscherin, now used as the hub of the Fauschenherst between its worlds and the Kyut. All who land on the Kyut pass through- it is where all war resources are collected, where the seat of power is, and a revered site of mankind's fortitude. The construct itself resembles a space station, a webwork of tunnels and docks which houses the Fauschenherst armoury. For many who pass through, it hosts the first and last comfort they will ever receive.

Ever sharp, they're slightly serrated now. Jagged and notched, they split bone in one draw. A clean angle may skate over the skeleton; when faced with so many, it pays to do as much damage as this with a single strike.

Rooms sprayed, some sick depiction. Red everywhere, arced and burst, blown out. Trickling like a punctured bag does. Bodies twitching, stiff in sudden death. Cradling themselves, moaning in that dull acceptance, resistance failed, a state between sleep and weariness. Rolling and clawing at nothing. Eyes unfocussed, flaps and segments.

Whole corridors in this state. One wouldn't think a blade and a gun could make such a mess.

They never bleed as much as he'd expect. In bursts, pulsing for a moment, maybe, but it doesn't last long. They crawl to their corners, senselessly pile atop one another, a twisted mass of limp limbs. And the blood they bleed doesn't stay red for long. It goes dark and dries over. Muddy and browning. But all states cover him. From slick and still wet to a paste, clotting over his coat. He walks amid them, vacant glares following. They watch him pass, making strange noises, groaning and waiting. That's the part that sticks. Brutalised bodies, they wait to die.

It's carnage. They hear his pointed footfall and scurry, quiet and fearful, making for the centre stairs but most are trapped, waiting in the outer halls with guns tracing the innards through which he cuts. They want to descend, but fearful, they hear him stomping around within and they hunker down, staring at the rows of doors, pitched behind crates in their hurrying bands. Between some, he can figure families, holding hands as they run. He stoops to fit through the frame or rounds the corner staggering, a hooded and stilted mass unfurling, half-grin lolling from his cowl, hunched against the roof. Their friends hanging from his sword. The looks on their faces when he steps out, seemingly so slow and clumsy, yet they run like a tidal wave gushes, or they hope that by turning and sprinting he won't see them. Whole rows of rifles, running without a shot.

But people like this, people abandoned in the middle of nowhere, they follow the strangest fables. It's like their Shae' Bilaah cannot fall to gunfire, and those who do dare shoot feel this furthermore, for they fire at a liquid menace, fast and folding. Abstract and inhuman, they slip over the mess, bumping into each other, trying to keep themselves as far from him as possible, muttering as they race from where he is. Like children, running from it.

       When he catches them, they do not scream. Eyes wide, they scuffle and slap, trying to break his grasp as the rest flee, insectile in their mass mind that as soon as one is taken, they are lost, and they all disappear back into the cracks.

Such violence shouldn't be so quiet. People yelling, shouting, calling to their loved ones; it isn't like that at all. It's gory and sickening, that he plucks the one at the back and mauls them. Saws through, gouging. Levering with a mechanical hand and splitting ribs. They don't all retreat, some stay with their friends, but they know their cause a lost one. This traumatised, they see no reason in fleeing if their closest fall.

And their resistance is as such, petty and weak. An excuse to die well, and in hopes of dying quickly, and not being skewered and bashed and left frothing, paddling amid the piles of soft bodies. He cares not for this. He hurts them until they no longer fight, and leaves them patting their great cuts, dazed and drunk.

       Then he reaches into his drape and feels his face, strained against its malfunction. The skin is sore and tight, if he prods more, it will surely split. Crouched in the corner of some dark and bloodied room he fiddles, trying to right his head, for some sneaking group to stumble in and see him turn their way, stained and steel claws poking. He sways, a caricature of madness. From room to room, devouring everyone within. Almost too big to fit, then he ducks and dodges their blows, shrinking and rising at will, slack as his blades lash. A ghoul, everything from his chest down drenched. Dragging bodies from doorways and slumping through.

       His pale grey eyes, they search the halls. He doesn't know what floor he's on and he doesn't mind, there are still so many hiding. Below, he can hear the Rautbergen climb- it is the highest and most violent peak that is the quietest. Corridors chewed, glass blown in, frost and snow already building. Heaps of dying.

Even in form, he can no longer be called human. They name him what they will, to numb the fright. When they see him, at the opposite end. Plodding their way. Hooded, half-mouth leering. His stare icy, seen only when it is too late. Lax, but unflinching. Limp, but invulnerable. Kamakara. Seen as sick, but ill with the most human emotions.

Truly, few have been more human.

They decide to draw their line, cut off the descent from the upper levels and make sure nobody else can drop. Pescha follows, keeping close to their lead. She dares not burst, not with this damaged wing, and even to keep up she feels her throat heave; she runs like she has a stitch in her neck, holding it with a squint. But she stays by their side, and heads them to the interior. Where knife and sword rule tight corners, even with one hand she may reign.

In the corridors around slugs fly and by ear she can trace their flight, each roaring like missiles from behind, thudding into the opposite end. She follows the outside push, keeping with their advance, flushing out those barricaded in their rooms with rifles pressed against the entrance. She zigzags, bouncing with her inner team of Rautbergen from side to side, kicking open corridor doors when they're reached. Her foot busts through and she looks to those hunkered behind their crates, Lautreisgefer's propped atop, showing her progress. They nod back.

The fighting over the central stairs is the fiercest. Those there hold out to death, making time for those trapped under fire in the hallways to retreat, all efforts in keeping the descent free. Whenever she or a Rautbergen steps forward, makes for the middle, those on the other side blare, pistols red hot, or if they're out of rounds until more come they charge, throwing themselves and their blades in the way. A small open space, connected by every wall to the rooms beyond. Anyone who enters is blown apart. So instead of pushing, Pescha waits. Any of the denizens too close are similarly destroyed, and she listens as the surrounding Rautbergen advance, squeezing the residents toward the centre. Until three of the four halls are theirs, and those in retreat have no choice but the drop. They build, seeping into their small cluster of remaining rooms. Reloading. Cleaning themselves. Blue eyes cannot peer around, when they do a thousand rounds roar, but she watches through sound.

She looks to her Rautbergen, each leant against a wall. Walls peppered with Lautreisgefer wounds. She tells them to stack against the resident-facing side.

The second the corridor fighting quiets, they shoot. Empty their magazines into a steel sheet with rounds which burn maybe to the opposite complex side, and they burrow deep through the resident mob. Stumbling on all fours they fall from their doors like they were piled high and Pescha grabs the arm of a Rautbergen, and the others follow, blowing apart those crawling for the drop.

When she looks up to those dappled barriers, she sees how weak they now are, rife with still singed holes of bombardment.

Crouched, slugs thundering overhead, red light and whipping hair, she pulls out her bombs, pivoting out of the way.

She casts a handful through an open entrance, turning to cover her head, still low.

The explosion rattles the complex; so many sheet steel walls, it is like the inside of a drum, bouncing the force around. Even outside its containment, she feels the force, splaying her coat.

When it settles, she hears rushing from the opposite end, as the Rautbergen round to close in on anyone left. The shots become few and far between, they must have all been in those closest rooms, ready to sprint. She doesn't look inside. Instead, she and her small team make for the stairs, resting against the railings as more Fauschenherst enter the centre space, from all sides, lowering their rifles at this level's conclusion.

 One asks what floor they're on.

 Someone just entering says the fourth. But the conflict isn't as linear as that. Below, Pescha can still hear gunfire, spread amid the lower levels, as hiding groups meet Rautbergen and chaos erupts, sporadic bands of both factions clashing. No more will come, but there are so many trapped between. The Klernsteiga peers around. She wonders how many are left here, huddled in the corners.

 She leans over the railing, looking down. The sound simmers, distant but clear. She walks from the ledge to the ascent, glancing up.

 She blinks.

A body lays. Pescha can see the notch in the crown; someone descending, stomped on from above. Skewered, from the head through. Behind them is another, one not so lucky. Ripped open from shoulder to heart. Dried red awash, like they spurted and slid against the side, making a messy arc.

     Pescha looks to the Rautbergen, telling them to clear this level and drop. Help those below in their clearing. None see what she does, but they know anyway. They were all waiting, and none protest.

When she starts to climb, someone says good luck.

They feel with their eyes closed. Three of them, scarce children but not yet adults, hand in hand. The one in front touches along the wall- a boy, then a girl, and then a boy, sights shut tight as they shuffle. They refuse to look, and while they grunt and whimper when their feet hit bodies, they do not stop. The lead will lurch and grimace when his fingers roll over wet red, but even then, he won't see. Mincemeat stands still and watches, coat flapping, in that upmost level with breeze floating. It's a painting, he thinks. Those three, inching along. Ripped up corpses sprawled, blood long since dried with the wind.

Maybe not. He's never seen a painting anyway.

Wherever they're going it leads down, but not by the stairs. He retracts his striders and follows on foot, stepping between the heaps of cloth. He wonders if creeping's worth, if there's anyone left up here but them to hunt.

But they'd ask the worth in any of this.

The boy who leads, his hand drops as he rounds the corner, patting at stomach level. When he reaches the handle, he breathes and shunts, careful to keep quiet but eager to escape the cold, pulling the other two in and closing the way behind. Mincemeat sways to the barrier but holds, ever silent, listening to the three within. He's been in there already. He's been in every room, and he didn't see a way out, but he hears shifting boxes and grates; hurried and scrambling, they must open the way before he closes it.

Inside, one of the boys prises loose a panel, and exposes a vent in the wall. But when Mince tries the door, it doesn't open, lock juddering. He shoulders again, and it stays firm.

What happens within, he cannot tell. With his machine hand, he pulls free the grip and with forefinger and thumb grasps the mechanism, slowly prying it loose. He hears them whimper, someone stomping their foot, and the boys must decide who goes first for the girl tells them no, almost laughing that they should think like that now. Steel and iron bend and warp as the Kamakara pulls, like he eases a splinter. On the other side, a child presses themself against, bracing the door. In response, Mince starts to kick.

All he hears then is what one of the boys says to the girl.

Woeful, he says that it's fine; he speaks like he holds her. They wouldn't have made it this far if it wasn't for her, and they're so grateful. But she's got to go. They need her, underneath. She knows best. So many have already died to keep her safe.

She knows the tunnel better than anyone else.

The Kamakara stares.

Just don't look back, the boy says. Whatever she does. She mustn't look back.

The Kamakara rams his hand through the lock, sinking fingers into steel. Slowly, like metal was butter or clay, he tightens his fist and squeezes through, pushes until his grasp is free and he snatches, reaching up. Taking the handle and pulling it off.

When he bursts in, the girl is already half through the gap, legs and waist in the wall. A chute, she squirms, leaving the two behind who stand tense, for a moment unsure what to do. For a moment, completely petrified. Mincemeat lifts his Neiderkop in the motion of rising from his stoop and shreds, spraying the room, both bodies crumpling as he darts for the vent.

He reaches in after the wriggling girl, finding a handful of hair. He grabs and pulls but the girl does not yell- determined, heavy breath, she struggles, writhing around the pipes. The Kamakara feels her tug. A crawlspace, he doesn't think the boys could have fit.

He would have asked what was below. But feeling how fervent she is in her escape, Mince doesn't think she'd talk. She seems willing to rip loose every hair on her head to break free.

The Kamakara hauls and lifts the girl as high as he can, then let's go and plunges, claw diving, driving through her mouth, breaking teeth; he holds the girl by her upper jaw. Before she can scream, Mincemeat wrenches.

Jerks back, pulling with all his strength. Then again. And again. Yanks the girl up from the duct of tight angles and tubes. The process must break every bone in her body.

What he lets slam against the floor is jointless and still, a boneless skinsuit ragdoll. Mincemeat looks at it, a vegetable sack of a person.

In the wake of that sudden outburst, he hears running and more doors. People rushing in the opportunity of his preoccupation. He hears a hatch slam, and a ladder pulled from above. In his daze he turns and casts one last glance to the three dead. Shot to pieces, the boys are stiff, muscles tense. The girl couldn't be less so.

He tries to roll his jaw. His eyelids feel on strings, pulled past his face. The Kamakara grunts to himself.

Mindless, he slips back into the hall.

Each floor is a new world; they are different dimensions, not levels. The circles of sin and evil, although here they rise, evermore morose with her ascent. A journey through time, passing the higher she climbs. Flourishing in the depths, communications fly and people flee, rushing for their escape. But the further up the tower you go, the more skewed your perceptions become. Soldiers lugging rifles in one hand, sifting through the bodies. The dead, lain in ranks. mankind, now bundles of sodden cloth.

Up here, she transcends human war. This would be where the soul goes, the halls of the after world. Improper. Unholy.

She has never been so disgusted. Its sacrilege, a violation. She walks though those passages gaunt, mouth ajar. She feels as though sick clings to the top of her throat and that if she span, she would hurl. Desecrated; people aren't supposed to see these things. All ideologies, all faiths. What she sees breaks each and every one. Nothing can stand sane in the same place as this.

So disrespectful, she must stop and hold a hand to her mouth. It is hideous. Rabid and primal. One cannot do these things to another; their humanity surely would not allow it.

Criminal, she thinks. In that moment, she forgets all things. All convictions. The animal within stares in awe. Laps at the corner of her vision. Swells and distorts, trying to block sight.

Tears. Great fat tears brimming. Not of sadness but involuntary disgust, they glow bright blue in her light. If she went outside, her eyes would freeze. But she stands amid a corridor of molestation. The weak. Feeble. Innocent.

They were wrong, those scholars of old. Hell is cold, she thinks. Hell is here.

The stairwell from fifth to sixth makes her groan. Bodies stacked up and lain over the railings; it is a way made of corpses, not steel and stone. Her ascent from the mortal place, made of those mortal dead, like they have collected here and packed themselves as tightly as they can, or the submarine crashed, and this was the last place with air. There are so few places to step, she hugs the bars and creeps up, hands at either side in balance. She dares not rest them low.

    Floor six is little different, but the breeze curling through cools. All bulbs up here are dashed, blown, and slashed from their heights; she sees by that chilling blizzard light, creeping through the rooms like she does, reluctant to illuminate more for it knows what it will see, that there is always more. Pescha steps out onto the gallery, shattered and jagged, a long waiting room for the fallen, and stares its length. Still, she can hear vague fire below, but it is no longer sporadic; condensed, she listens to combat deep, fought on the lowest floors. Closed in, she even hears Rautbergen descend, echoing from those dreaded stairs. Flooding in.

    Then shots overhead, too quick for Lautreisgefer or pistol. Sound carried with the wind, rushing the rooftop.

The hatch is in an empty room, an offshoot compartment, ladder perched against its rim. At its base, Pescha looks up and sees the maelstrom, pale and furious over this timid dark within. Like the scene is broken, static, a piece missing, but lone flakes flurry through, traversing the two dimensions, falling, and becoming azure at her sight. So close, she hears nothing but the gale above.

    Halfway up, she holds her hand out through the gap. She feels it may be ripped off; through the moving window, travelling impossibly quick. The sudden change in light, atmosphere, temperature- if she goes up, she'll be whisked away. Taken from this place to another world.

    She stares, the tips of her hair wavering. But she breathes, and the shuddering cold sooths her throat. She leans into it, letting it fill her body. Leans in until she mounts the ladder and climbs onto the last level.

The true summit of Befelobeth. Flat, smooth concrete slabs, a landing bay, square and uniform. Beside the rooftop rim and antenna, faint golden lights line, whipping. Like a city lost in the clouds she can barely see the edge and all around is aethereal; like when she and Mince climbed those anaemic Humeda to hide from the storm, at its shoulders and now, she is in a place apart, a place without the Kyut and the disasters. Already, day starts to fail. The storm is the colour of smoke. That final dais.

    And Mincemeat.

There are far fewer here. She could count the bodies on two hands. She could count the living on one, her open palm by her side quickly closing to a fist as she watches. Raising that hand to shield, as a maniac whirls.

He does not run, he glides. For an instant strong, stronger than anything, unbreakable and tall and then he is whisked like his body is gone and he is just cloth and stilts in the wind, floating across his stage. Loose, shapeless, forming from nothing before the final few, chopping limbs.

Pescha stands afar, one arm high, the wounded one drawn in, sheltered against her coat. Struggling with the current flung up the compound face, surging like water. All things are grey but her eyes, and even these are tight and upset, for she struggles against the fray, barely able to stand.

The Kamakara rushes in, spraying rounds with one hand like he throws the bullets, callous and with a flare, then he leaps springlike, drawing in his blades and when he is atop another he opens, swords driving down; he crouches on a man's shoulders, his twin edges spiked far through his bowels. But it takes too long for him to fall; with his prosthetic Mince hammers once, crushing his skull, and as the man collapses, Mincemeat retracts, falling with him and stepping off, landing right. Walking on, arms swinging loose. Like he just skipped down some stairs.

He spins, looking over his work. Their jackets fluttering, you couldn't tell who was alive and who was not, but none stand, all huddled against themselves. Curled up or sprawled, they are so slashed that they couldn't. The Kamakara surveys, careful to see that none merely play. A sword in one hand, Neiderkop in the other.

   Pescha forces herself to straighten. Hold both arms low. Steady herself.

When the Kamakara turns he sees Pescha and slows, dancing to a walk. His hood is blown back and he glances at blue eyes like he sees an old sour friend, pretending they needn't talk. Stalking, his hair snaps around his sideward slight-sneer, face still pulled in its grimace. He glances at both Pescha and someone over her shoulder. Azure looks around and sees the officer, climbing from the hatch into the gale.

   Mince does not wait, neither does he hold eyes with Pescha; when they come to pass, neither looks at the other. The Kamakara only leans in, a little, both Nomads staring level the opposite ways.

   He says, barely in earshot, that there are more below. He sweeps

by.
        For a moment, Pescha is unsure.

When Mince is past, Pescha turns. She tries to call out. The rasp she produces is enough to make anyone stall. Even him. Mincemeat stops, hearing her all broken up.
        He glares at her. Lost between the indifference of his slaughter and the sudden unease at seeing her hurt. His eyes skim over her, discerning all wrongs.
        Gently, Pescha shakes her head. Wind chasing.
        She beholds up to pale grey.
        She asks which way. The Kamakara flinches, like a fly invades his space.
        The way to the Iron Driver. Mincemeat blinks. His shoulders sag.

Eyes teary with rushing cold, Pescha manages to smile. She tells the Kamakara thank you. She wouldn't have gotten so far if it weren't for him, what he's done is invaluable, but she must go now. Mince couldn't come anyway, it's better like this. The Kamakara is needed here. Pescha can manage on her own. Mincemeat's expression is unreadable because it isn't one. Pescha thinks, gazing- she decides it's like that of an adult, never before told all people die. Which way, Pescha asks. Mince need only point. There really aren't that many people left here, she says. Rolling around in the dark. Aren't they so filthy, Pescha speaks. Never enough. None of them are as good as Mince. So full is he. Full of things. So much hurt. Overflowing. They deserve nothing because he will take everything. Eager to impress.
        Inside, they're all the same. Gross. And empty. Pescha stares, unblinking. She asks the way.

The Kamakara barges on, a grimace shrouding all features, like he despises such sudden affection. Like that she would do this now, here, so quickly, is an insult he has never had to bear. Glaring as he goes, he gestures with a jab the way they would have walked had Befelobeth not been between, and Pescha cannot ignore that it pains her so to hear the Kamakara walk from her like this, striding by the officer who turns, brow high, unsure why one, and which, of his Klernsteiga leaves. Pescha looks at nothing but a parking lot and lumpy balls of fabric. She shudders, unsteady.
        It shouldn't be like this. It should not be this abrupt, but there is

nowhere near this place that could harbour such numbers of the Raut. They will be here for days and so will he.

She regrets her forwardness. She could've waited, even to face him with the matter inside would have suited better than this. Her sights fall- the ebbs of sympathy brush her.

It hits her suddenly that, again, she is completely alone in these barren wastes.

Pescha turns, blue vivid and liquid.

Mincemeat has stopped, staring at the back of her head. He has waited, to call over the storm.

He says he won't pursue. Come looking for Pescha. Mincemeat's hair rages, as wild as the storm. He hopes Pescha wins. Gravelly too, his voice wobbles. Suddenly as mournful as hers. He nods- he hopes Pescha can get him.

Pescha stares, harder than ever before. Someone holds it, her heart; they squeeze it tight. The officer, now decided, looks down at his boots and heaves. Teeters on the brink of hyperventilation, attention flickering over the concrete panels.

Tears fall. Real tears. Her blue refracts around the droplet trail, like neon leaks, bulbs bright and brilliant.

The Kamakara commands the officer to follow and stalks the way he came. Ever inhuman, the coat and striders bend and twist to lower, flexing around the figure, dark save for his skin. The officer, he has lost himself; ever obedient, for ever fearful, he follows him down without word, coat trailing in pursuit. He doesn't once glance back.

  Pescha gazes at the Kamakara, sight untiring. Watches him draw in his blades, sheathing weapons and pulling the coat to let him see his fall. For a moment, the shape changes. Not Mincemeat. Not the Kamakara. Just a boy, scared of what everyone thinks. Scared of his own name. Sakasuji Fubiken seethes, heart shatteringly sad, but he knows it will quickly fade. Already, he feels that boiling. He feels a hatred restruck, and his sorrow is kindling.

He and the officer drop, leaving Pescha alone, holding herself. Arms wrapped around. The snow skates in sheets, cold flowing, trying to pull her with it. Trying to take her away.

Pescha stands by herself. In the middle of that unworldly place, perched atop an ossuary.

All lonely again. And the tears swell, a river breaking its banks.

Because she's so close now. The final hurdle, surpassed. That's it, she thinks; the hard part is over. Lip quivering, she shudders, warbling like an infant. Pescha can go now. She may cry more later. Or maybe she won't. She does not yet know what later is. She is not faint on sadness and relief either, she knows what will happen below, but she may finally turn her eyes from those deep terrors.

Turn from it all, and to that final light.

Pescha sobs, looking back the way she came. Nuxitec Pawasaki looks back, trembling. Then forward, the low white sun peering through. So worn, Pescha wipes her face and smiles. She thinks of a warm train carriage and soft seats. Warm fields, green grass, and soft blue skies. She'll think about everything else later, too. With the crying.

Pescha sniffles, blinking back more, and hobbles on, leaning into the storm.

This can't be happening, they stammer. Holding their heads, they beg and pray or sprint, abandon those beaten and unwilling. Around them, the Rautbergen close in. They have found their hidden exit.

On the lowest floor, a doorway central to the corridor is offset on the wrong side, facing all others. It surely opens to the storm, but those who slam through throw themselves down stairs, panting as more follow. A short descent, a ninety degree turn left leads them down another small flight. Then they're there, in the bunker, a space scarce larger than a garage, underground with dark steel walls and dim, winking lights. Ahead, there is only a tunnel. The tunnel. There were rails there, once. Tracks, like that of a cart to deliver foodstuffs and resources. Now, it is an empty straight, closed only by a thick ascending glass pane a way down, to slowly sink into the ground at the press of a button.

This is it. The last corridor, its odd door, left angle stairwell to bunker and underpass, perfectly square and lined with warning lights- white and blinking, rushing the burrow length and beyond. But the pass; it can be opened only from this side, so closed there too. Crouched and lain around the space are the injured and reeling, alongside those with all guns aimed at that angle, listening for footfall too tight. Waiting, as still more residents stumble, from the thump of Rautbergen guns and feet. They must leave all at once, close the door while they run and smash the console. Nobody has said it; nobody has said anything. But they've all rehearsed this day in their dreams.

Shotguns and pistols, down surrounding straights and inner chambers the residents retreat, holding corners for as long as they can, biding time for more.

The Rautbergen pull together as one, collecting their dispersed groups and sending them all below, Lautreisgefers blaring. Puncturing steel like pens through paper, they bring their best weapons to the fore, leading with whatever anti-personnel armaments they've mustered and their GT. 22 Ablescheiber. Propped over another's shoulder or lain prone, a machine gun shredding. The sound is horrific before its faceless gunners. All Rautbergen, hooded and robed in beaten and snow-charred browns, like sketches of wasteland dwellers, scarfs and masks hiding expression; the invasion foot soldier, uniform in their experience, decorated in their struggle.

They squeeze and squeeze, forcing the residents in, until they fire around the corners of that endmost hall. The second Lautreisgefer barrels poke past both sides the tenant peering through the door spins and screams, yelling to the refugees below.

They're here.

Upon his call maybe ten rise to his side, lining the first half of the stairs. They shoot blind, stalling the Rautbergen at the edges, filing out into the passage and hiding behind whatever cover is left, for almost everything is ripped by gunfire. Behind them, all others pile toward the tunnel, dragging their wounded. A shotgun kept under his arm, a man lurches for the console, a panel against the burrow wall, fingers playing over its dials. He is an inch from lowering the glass when someone shouts, flailing out to him.

He turns, but the woman who called stares down, transfixed on flashing lights. He follows her sight, as all eyes do. All looking down the tunnel. Respectively, all features twist.

At the transparent barrier, a man stands, forehead pressed against the glass. He is illuminated in moments, cast in black the next, but they need only a glance to know. Softly, he knocks his head on the barricade, pressing hard- like he might just melt through.

Emotion pulled to one side, his damp and harried hair hangs over his face. Striders retracted, he holds his sword in sheath, Neiderkop slung over his back. He looks at them with such abhor, with strength like each individual in that room ruined his life.

A woman crouched, a child at her side; her eyes bulge and she raises a pistol, firing down the length. Her rounds smack against the glass, useless, their spiderweb fractures instant.

Another woman tells her it's pointless, nothing could get through that slab, it's so thick. She looks up to the resident at the console, frantic. Like she asks for confirmation she's right.

Overhead, the shots thunder. With every second, the Rautbergen come closer. With every second, the white hair pounds.

The man from the door, he has come down and seen and he asks what they should do, everyone within glancing at everyone else.
    They haven't the time to think.

They must open it still, says the frantic; what other choice do they have? But she of child protests, scoffing, bold in her disgust. She holds her young dear, a hand on his head.
    She retorts thar she'd rather be shot than skinned. Everyone ran down here, she tells, surveying the group, they all saw the same things. You never know, she shrugs, looking down at her infant; maybe they'll be taken prisoner.

And be imprisoned where, he at the console asks. The mother just caresses her tot, smiling down at him. It'd be a death march through the blizzard; they'd all freeze, but they won't be taken prisoner anyway, he tells. They've got stores hidden in the tunnel. From its end, they know where to go.

From behind him, leant against the wall, a boy drawls.
    He says they're not getting down that tunnel, though. There's a monster in the way.

No, the console man says; there isn't. Look at him, he tells, pointing to the white-haired man.
    Mince slams his head against the glass a little harder in retort.
    They need to stop daydreaming; he's alone, stuck in one long hall. There's no way he can get them before they get him. The collective expression is doubt, but nobody speaks. Because however begrudged, they all know they're going to open it anyway. There is no Yaybahar down here, he says. Just the man who killed everyone they love.
    That does bring some liveliness. Heads rise, attentions flickering.
    That's a point, he hears them wonder.
    Everyone stares into the passage, suddenly reinterested.

And while the white-haired man can't hear them, he sees their faces and grins, lips curling. Like he is just told he can eat, he lays a hand on the glass, pushing softly.

Everyone, bruised and beaten; they raise their weapons, makeshift and cobbled, sidearms and hunting rifles, shotguns and for those unarmed their wounded, hauling them from the forefront of the gathering, making room for all those able to aim. A firing squad all looking one way, Lautreisgefer shots coming ever near.

There's maybe twenty, twenty five people in there, total; it's hard to tell of the hurt who still lives, and those who do are made of every age, but they each have their harrowing reason to loath. Quickly, they start to return the hate cast their way. And the man who watches, he starts to talk, words lost behind the glass, but he rolls to a shout, soundless yet soon screaming. Fanatical and muted he pounds, spontaneously roaring incensed insults, his breath condensing on the barrier. It lasts only a moment, an outburst in retort, but his glare does not subside. Like he and them argued, they went too far, and he had to see them checked. Threw their darkest secret right back.

Every free gun is traced forward. So many barrels his way. He stares them down, mumbling. Pale gaze darting between.

The flashing lights are constant and boggling, making him detailed one second, then a silhouette, as the glow ebbs past and into nothingness.

Mince watches the man's hand rise, hovering over the console. On bated breath he stares offset, frozen as the resident wonders. His other grasp holds his shotgun, levelled down the corridor length.

They could never be sure that they'd live. They haven't the time to be convinced. But so sure are they now that they'll kill him too. Such unforeseen determination: it makes him cackle behind his screen. And this display only maddens them more. Still cradling her young, even that mother lifts her pistol, although she does not raise her sights, so enamoured with her child. Knelt on the ground, babe held against her chest, firearm straight.

All resolved. None glance around, not even the console man. The last standing, each with their finger on the trigger.

He pushes the button, pulleys churning within the walls.

Despite the neglect, the system runs smooth; a whirring, then the glass starts to drop. Ever so slowly, sliding into the floor. Mincemeat stands a millimetre from the sheet, ogling the line of guns. Holding for the glass to drop; they follow its descent with their barrels.

Completely still, leant toward the pane. The Kamakara also waits. Glaring at the congregation.

The moment the glass is low enough, in one wave of the lights he leaps, clinging to the rim and jamming his Neiderkop through the gap, holding himself from the ground.

Every resident stares. Mouths drop. Completely shielded still, he points at them his shooter, grin ever leering.

When he pulls, there is nothing they can do. Neiderkop aflame, the spitting sparks catch his face too, flickering between yellow and pale, illuminating his agony. Stacked against one another, the residents are chewed. Blown apart, the bunker filled with gunfire. Those at the edges, they can throw themselves out of view, but most are central, most can scarce walk, and he rips them up, splattering bodies without pause. The woman with the babe bends over her boy, and bullets smack out the other side. When Mince runs empty, he is far from sated. Ravenous, he slings the gun back and forces himself through, contorting between the gap. He must dislocate bones to fit; insectile, he crams himself in. Snatching and biting, squirming.

He falls into a run, springing from the glass. His striders protrude, and his pace only builds. Once the bombardment stops, those remaining have mere seconds. Seconds they waste gazing at their dead friends and family, crammed in that little alcove.

Dogged and primal, he snarls. Monstrous, he dives into the closest person he can reach. Slamming. Slashing. Stabbing. Pulling them apart like food. Spinning and whirling, a tumult of swords and arcs and brute force. Hearing the shots, one of those last outside defenders stumbled down the stairs. He sees them and Mince there, filleting. You would think the brain itself powered him down, the way his posture slumps.

Mincemeat cuts and drives. Cracks people open like eggs, throwing away the shells. Dances around the shelter, manic and free. Like nobody watches; he makes sure they can't, alone in that basement. Almost childlike, he sweeps around the bedroom he never had. Barbaric and beautiful. Careless and brutal.

There is nobody left who speaks the tongue which named him Sakasuji. A dead language, he is a canvas empty; in that underground, he paints himself. Baptised; bathed and born anew.

  He spins in it, the red waters of his christening. His revelation. His fanaticism.

  The blind can see.

  The man on the stairs lifts his rifle and jams the barrel in his mouth.

- KENIDOMO COUNTRY -
UNRECOGNISED TERRITORY
"The Iron Driver"

A railway stop of one platform, its canopy is dimly lit, a small row of chairs underneath. Sitting there, what's ahead is completely flat, snow barely swept. It is like the ocean of the Denkervung spire, now completely coated. She wonders if they were the same waters, once. Behind, the great wave drops, its tail end almost sheer and lost to the cold, ever battering. She huddles up, watching. Out here, the sun is scarce seen but at the dying of the day she may witness, see the boreal dark slip from the mountain slope as this pointless daytime glow recedes, a faint gold failing.

See the onset of night, for so tired is she.

She must rest soon, she can feel her arm throb. She looks time and time again, for it feels like everything within her bleeds out at every beat of her docile heart, drumming as vessels tight and frosted thump in her ear. The train must come; there is nothing to tell the time, but she sees a bell propped on a post, surely set to ring when the Driver is close, and a radio overhead, soft and mewling.

It plays music, and she struggles not to drift to its tune. A piano, classical and sad. Eyes barely open, she buries her hands in her lap, and hangs in a space between frozen consciousness'. Alone, a single entity in that vast cold, train station lights flickering and vague.

When the bell sounds, she does not start. fatigued, she raises her head, azure widening.

Like a doddery, aged Humeda, its headlights trundle through the sweeping sheets long before the Driver is clear. Listening to it come, it pushes through the cold slowly, mechanical, and soft. Bumbling, just out of sight, but she can hear that it stretches far and when the train finally pushes through, it splits the snow with a pointed head, parting the white which cracks and crumbles to either side. Bunching, then bursting, in clouds of snow, illuminated. With a grinding it decelerates, windows alight but she sees their glow only in the forefront carriages, all those behind tightly sealed by great sliding steel. Maybe six carts pleasant, and for her the train halts somewhere between, the entrance directly ahead, doors shuffling open. Frigid and iced, the Driver is worn, but a marvel still; she has never seen anything human made like this and functional.

The inside is not fashionable or ornate, it is a transport carriage with seats, but one lit and warm and made for people; she boards and looks down to a grid, confused for a moment, but she blinks at the white underneath and shrugs. Shuffles and, careful with her injuries, batters her coat, shaking off snow over the mesh.

The train travels right. To her left is only storage, metal containers piled, taking up half the carriage; the other way is rows of two chairs, grouped to four, a duo looking one way and a duo facing, a central isle dividing. Brushing herself down, she glances to a huddle of three; a trio of Klernsteiga already aboard, talking amongst themselves in their quartet of chairs. They each peer over, turning to stare; her azure glimmers and with zipper up tight, everything below her colour is hidden by her collar. She pretends they don't look. Shivering, her sights do not move from the velvety seats, grid heaters lining. She collapses, sinking into the seam.

Her bones melt.

Her head falls back, train shuddering like the great beast shivers. The vibrations rumble to her face and slacken a constant grimace. Massage, releasing the tension; her neck goes limp and she looks out her window to the flat expanse, storm raging inches away, night now well enforced. From behind glass, she is so weak; her gaze slips in and out of focus, and when it does, she struggles to lock onto anything, besides the vivid reflection cast in return.

Drowsy, it's like staring at the sun. Her eyes just want to close.
She wonders what stops the machines from attacking the train. Maybe they think it's a Humeda too.

She is so eager, wants so badly to sleep. But within moments her glow flickers, fluttering behind heavy lids, and she does not know her stop. Her breath is misty against the screen, clouding her own blazing reflection.

she forces herself back onto the Kyut, mumbled conversation resuming.
Pescha sits up and looks over, alone on her side of the carriage.

Those Nomads ahead, they are a pair and a new friend, making conversation with different faces; the two who know each other, they come from the same place, for they are tinged blue and grey, the colour livid, and adorned in jewellery of wooden pendants, hanging from their ears and around their necks. Spiritual and ritualised, their coats are larger than Pescha's, great pale leather and fur layers, of a people used to a cold even worse than this. With hair cropped short, they are a man and a woman, her with a rifle and something akin to fishing equipment laden, him with no obvious kit.

They could scare be more apart from the woman across; a Nomad dressed for the cities, her coat is clean and her attire straight, and her skin is the deepest dark, darker than ink. Where those before wear wood she wears gold, laced within hair and rings. A Klernsteiga of the megalopolis' beyond Fauschenherst defence, dressed for her arrival without bag or supply but fitted with the adornments of her defence, in a screen against her forearm and a multitude of minute devices, organised in her pockets, just poking over top. Pescha has seen this breed before, in Fyorfastin and Snackombst, on the far border to the Dodtohmet Plateau. From an empty room this Klernsteiga may cut all lights, communicate the length of a city, close and open barriers; if the dwelling has guns and garrisons, without connection to a single radio she may command.

It's her who returns Pescha's look, blue so bright that she need only turn, and attentions are caught, a smile shared both ways. When the other two follow, Pescha shuffles closer, scooting over to the next seat, leaning from her row.

Her voice sounds like someone trying to imitate words, grinding their heel against stones. She doesn't talk, she chokes, recoiling with a furrowed brow. It takes her a few tries to get it right.

She asks them if there's a screen. That shows the stops and stations. One of the Nomads with blueish skin, she frowns hard at the crunching tone. The city Klernsteiga keeps her face straight.

She replies there isn't, voice smooth; stupidly, she tells, you're just expected to know. She rests back against her chair, posed with an arm rested vertically; politely, the Nomad asks Pescha where she wants to go.

Pescha stares. The other Nomads watch. It suddenly occurs to her that she isn't even sure. Then the train starts, steam billowing. It does not lurch, it slumps back into motion, slow and heaving.

Moss and rain and fog, Pescha tells. Where sector Zero, Double-

Four, Nine, Three, Five ends- the end of the cold. An abandoned city, where warmth borders.
 The posed Klernsteiga mulls the words, and says she knows the one. The city on the edge of Summer.
  Pescha nods.
  She'd almost forgotten.

She's told thirty, maybe forty stations, she'll know she's close when the snow melts and the rain starts. The best stop for her is the one with the barrel in a wooden cart; a timber pushing wagon on the side of the platform. There'll be a lamp overhead. She won't be able to see far, the downpour will be intense. But she should notice the glow.
 Pescha sounds like Saltwater, that pilot Klernsteiga on the frozen sea. Her voice is like static. Still, she manages to ask how long.
 The city Klernsteiga shrugs. Who counts? But long enough to sleep between.

Pescha smiles. She says her thanks, nodding to the two with short hair, and returns to her window, huddled against the corner of backrest and radiator. Presses herself in, watching the Kyut outside. The powerlines following the track overhead are lined with bulbs, catching the closest snowfall in her passing moment; face close to the glass, cut and beaten and bruised, cheek yellow and neck purpled, she lets the twofold song of the train, in music and machine, lull her mind to rest.
 It feels like a break. Like someone turns the volume down.
 She feels the curtains droop, vision fading.

She sniffs and sits up, eyes half open, turning to the trio. Again, she catches their eye.
 Pescha asks if everyone is getting off before her.
 They each glance, and each nod.
 She asks if the last could wake her.

The city Nomad says of course.

She is stirred by a poking, someone prodding her shoulder. Before she even opens her eyes, she hears the rain against her glass, and a cosmic pounding from afar.

Blue parts like the azure forces itself out, looking up to the city Klernsteiga, now hooded, her hand hovering. She smiles, and says she's leaving, and for a moment Pescha thinks they travel through a tunnel, for in the dark, lights drift way overhead, high in the pouring sky. Pescha blinks, frowning, pulling herself up as the city Nomad nods and leaves her side. Open doors let in the tumult of rainstorm, showered against steel and window, and what sounds like distant thunder, rumbling to the left.

When Pescha sits up, she gazes from her port. Ogles, hands pressed against the pane.

Like meteors or flares, great balls of fire soar in their hundreds. Drift as far as the clouds and further, their shades burning through the overcast.

Artillery or bombardment, she turns and looks to the hill from which they are sent, blaring with cannon shots. Ubenpanzas, she sees; cannon cars, a row of them, lined on the crest, blasting into the night.

It's like the sun has exploded, its shards curl and smoke, trails long and slow. She follows them, the train shuddering back into motion. The beads against her window catch both the high and burning shades and her own, liquid blue and orange.

A monster of a Humeda, it writhes aflame. Gutted, mostly melted away, it stumbled behind a hill but by size she sees most, and it rips at its molten skin. Screams, back arched, clawing at its face and chest. So bright it glows, every droplet within a mile smoulders, a haze of fluid heat. Reflects, that morbid and shining pyre in every puddle and stream of the barren and damp expanse over which it flees.

She watches, a cosmic hate crushing against him. Blowing through his outstretched hands, igniting.

The Iron Driver trawls on, sneaking under the barrage.

- *KENIDOMO COUNTRY* -
UNRECOGNISED TERRITORY
"*Moss*"

Sheltered in the doorway, the light from her carriage permeates, bouncing off a hundred water sources. Her arm is tied in its sling, hanging from around her neck, close to her chest with a loose sleeve hanging free, but while she can feel its throb the pain is under control, and her mind is elsewhere besides. Of the planets beyond, she's been on only Emilia, her home. Staring now, she thinks the Driver has whisked her from the Kyut, and to a sibling world.
That of J. A. Twelve; Moss[34].

Clumps of the plant cover everything, it is the land of moss. Like millions of insect mounds blanketed in soft green, they roll as far as she can see, and she sees only little, for with the rain has come fog also, and it makes all things sodden.

Between the heaps run streams, shallow and bending and running every which way, through their plateau of bumps. Night or day, it doesn't matter; all is dark. So dark, that to live here you must make your own light, and she sees in an instant that first sign that she makes for a place beyond the cold horrors well known.

Little flies, following the thin brooks. On their backs are their own bulbs, faint and small but buzzing in groups, bumbling with the waters at ankle level. She watches them, listening as rainfall sploshes in the barrel to her left, forever overflowing. Like the bugs, she too has her own glow, and it looks over a plane unchanging. Constant and dark and misty, she wonders

---

[34] *J. A. 12 "Moss"*: A wetworld planet of constant darkness and rain, characterised by dark foliage and its people's affinity with lanterns and lights. Most of the surface is low raging seas, and whatever land there is is swamped completely by moss and plant life. The capital city, Shimaschita, is a coastal skyscraper strip of imported steel and stone, but the planet has no natural resources, so construction of the city cast the rest of the world into a dark-age poverty, with all other settlements cutting ties. The planet has a small population, and its lack of economy and tradeable resources has led to many abandoning it for better, but those who remain live a quiet life of rain song and lamplight in endless dark, amid a city of vines and green.

where she's supposed to go. But the Driver is patient, and it waits for her to decide.

She steps out, splashing over the platform. Better rested and at least warmer than before, the downpour against her hood is not unpleasant, and she may fill her canteen. She figures she is running low on everything now, food and drinking powder and bombs. Dropping onto the moss, she reaches back and takes her lantern from Pack One, rattling the bulb to life.

She suspends the light on the hilt of her sword, and walks with it held in front.

Aimless she trudges, keeping to the lowest ground; it doesn't ever really rise, but a mountain could climb a hundred feet away and she wouldn't see, so she follows what has become a riverbank, the pit of the valley into which the little streams drain. Under her lamplight, she keeps an eye to both the stream mouths and humps, careful not to slip, and to the slight inclines on either side, filtering down her way. She is weary of her own blindness here, but she walks amid a realm of insects, and each of them shines too. For anything watching from afar, she will be nothing but two more flies of weird colour, around which the others flock. And they do, interested and circling, hovering before her face to stare at her alien shade. It would be a good trick to ambush someone, she thinks; to wait for the insects to group and then pounce. She looks through the shield of fireflies, searching for her forgotten city.

What emerges first is no ancient ruin. It hangs over the moss, vibrant. From afar, she is dazzled by the absurdity of the sight, for amid nighttime mist and pale amber buds something this bright is jarring. She wonders from what distance she could see it, its shades dyeing the fog between. Pink and blue, neon and foreign, she creeps with caution, sights firmly fixed now. Its colours catch her, fringing her figure vivid.

It's an eye- a massive, machine eye. Still dangling in the scaffold of a face unrecognisable, it is like the optic is under construction, suspended on a rig for access. Taller than four of her, on machine cords and wires it sags, an orb of chemical electricity; she has never seen a Humeda with a look like this. The rain smacking against its curve becomes a haze of bright pigment; she imagines the sight in a glowing city, not here. She looks it up and down, there is no way what's left can fight. She trudges over, the ring finger of her left hand hovering against her palm, itching to flip the switch.

The beast that fell here was stripped clean long ago; covered in moss and eroded by the streams she sees other remnants of its bones, collapsed, and misplaced, but most has been stolen, or completely swallowed by the shrub. Whoever scavenged the remains though, they left the eye intact. Dangling, its mechanical pupil like a massive and luminescent camera lens, an intricate network of inlayed rings and glass domes, she walks to its front and looks up, its own sight pointed down. Staring at the point where she stands.

In its view, she sees the optics twitch and revolve, focussing the lens.

The Humeda eye stares back, helpless. Like a small neon star, crashed into the Kyut. In its complex mirror she sees herself, sees her blue under its scowl, furious rain, and the little sparks floating around. In their passing moments, they illuminate parts of her face.

And behind, far away. Like more beasties, high and distant.

She turns, looking over shoulder. Looking up, up and into the mist, to sporadic and random lamplight, raised from the mounds.

The lanterns of Klernsteiga, camped on raised ground.

The moss does not end, the concrete just rises, but it is no city; she walks toward a stone frame, hollow and windowless. Through breaks in the mist, she sees its perfectly cubic towers; they climb a hillside, the furthest peak summiting the brink, and they are the bones of a metropolis, neither furnished nor finished. A three dimensional grid, each floor is open, no walls or doors, and there are hundreds of them. She climbs toward, seeing their shape in drifting clarity, their bases verdant and coated, their upper faces tall and untouched, flat and blemished with constant rain. It's like they built a city for the Kyut, never intending the structures for human use; she cannot fathom the place's existence beside it never being complete. Or somehow, the most intense fire ever raged, leaving the scrapers barren and lost.

Standing at their bases, she must crane her neck to gauge their height, squinting through the downpour. It reminds her of staring at Our Last Limit, at its sheer steel face, on the edge of a new world both times. She hopes this one pleasant.

She hopes it the last.

Rainfall slapping, she ascends and where the constructs border, she stands level, at the end of a central road; she thinks someone must have misplaced a city model and forgotten it out here. Stripped of lampposts, people, cars; all things are that damp and humid night green- she can make no details, but she sees the avenue stretch, wide and running. Where shops should border, there are only empty floors, square window frames empty, just the shape, never any fittings. She stands in the centre, gazing its length, to the silhouette of the coming hill and the few obelisks to summit.

    Amid the shadows, figures lurk. Even in only the light of their lamps she can see Nomads, and the travellers they corral.

Each busy, they move their refugees; it is as though all the sporadic bands of this region have collected here, now under the administration of the Klernsteiga. Led into the skeleton buildings, to the scale of this city they are few but they are hurried and pointed off, and all Nomads with nobody to direct head the same way as her, down the avenue. On, toward the hill crest. Tens of them, gathered in these ruins. As though of their joint mission too, she follows the few rising.

    Lining the road run small floodgates and grilles, draining the street; through them she hears the waterways of the hill, churning below the strip. Above too, the overspill from flattop roofs smacks against the pavement, more and more liquid building. Nothing here is dry, all who would come are drenched. The line between snow and warmth. Harsh, a border of climates. Of all places to build home, she thinks.

When the road rises, it rises quickly, becoming insensibly steep in an instant. No wheels could climb; as though begrudged, the architect made his highway here for its own sake, to prove the impossible. The buildings follow this trend, ever straight and angled, a geometric illusion. At its base, the Klernsteiga stop. Unspeaking, they inspect their kits, a foot against the slope as they check riggings and cables and gears.

    Pescha approaches, her blue like faint headlights, in moments framing every passing drop. The closest Klernsteiga wears a flat hat with a brim wide enough for himself and her to comfortably hide from the rain; a Nomad of these sodden regions. Completely clad and wrapped against the wet, he could have stared at her sidelong since her distant azure appeared, and she wouldn't have known.

She stands at his side, staring up the slope. She cannot tell the gradient, but she can make it.

Eyes high, squinting through the flood, she asks what's happening.

After a second's pause, a muffled voice says hopefully nothing, not here. It's a safe zone; where they've moved everyone.

Pescha blinks into the shower. Safe from what, she asks.

He turns, head and hat cocked. He asks that she hasn't got a radio.

She says she doesn't.

He shrugs and tells they're not sure. A Humeda, a big one; they were called in to gather as many safe here as they could.

She asks if she can go up. He glances at her arm, bandaged, and hung.

He steps aside, letting her pass.

No car ever drove here, the asphalt is coarse against her hand, and with fingers splayed she is steady, even with her other reach bound back. The wet trickles, liquid veins breaking and reconnecting, roots of water constantly shifting, like droplets finding each other on glass. She does not fall, as Klernsteiga below glance up and nod her way. Without the rain it would be a steep incline, but not one Nomads would struggle to summit. As damp as it is, her boots slip from under her and her knees crunch against the road, but she stays poised and so long as she does not keel backward, she will remain. With every hit, she feels her left forefinger and thumb twitch. Eager to launch, they motion ascent with the inactive system. Something tries to convince her it'd be fine, that she could manage the burst with one arm. She wipes a slick hand against her coat and clambers on.

After a while, Pescha breathes and looks back, down the way she came. A haze of liquid impacts, there is no base. Just a descent slipping from sight, and it is only the inverse ahead. She rubs her face with her sleeve, pulling her hood further forward.

Just Pescha, her rain and slope, caged in concrete. She wonders if it's ever light here. If it's light now; she could stumble through midday or midnight, it doesn't matter, there is no time on this endless rise, as she passes between realms.

But when the ground starts to level, she lets burning thighs ease. Shoulders up, barging into the furore where the buildings lower, a couple of stories at most. Where the moss rules freely. In corners and between breaks in concrete, the bunches of green plume and collect around pools formed in the seams, where the city ends and the Kyut resumes.

Atop, the constructs become sporadic, no longer bound to the lower framework; they dot the ridge, incomplete and mislaid. On this thin streak of ground, an island surrounded by a sea of fog, where the moss makes its own miniature forests, which climb walls and sag roofs laden with boggish tufts, she sees only one other this high. Sat in a partly crumbled two-story, on a stool fashioned from fallen debris. The wall closest to Pescha and the wall furthest have both collapsed, like a cannon blasted straight through. In the room between, everything is a dark outline. He sits and stares, out over the opposite sky. She approaches, weaving between mounds.

Climbs his chipped and crumbled stairs, little woodlands underfoot.

When she steps up, it is a shaman who looks back. Muddy and bedraggled, his face is painted with dark streaks forming symbols, his skin dirtied and clothes in strands, a garment of damp and soiled ribbons, hanging from his shoulders. Hooded, his eyes are amber and foggy; he looks at a thing and sees double, and in his hand rests a staff, a small radio strapped to the base, a rattle bound by leather straps at the other end. Thin wires connect both lengths. A Y-shaped split like a slingshot, with taut strings tied between, timber and stone tokens fastened, to clatter should they shake.

She thinks; maybe he slept- he seems weary and infirm, he does not lock eyes with her. He leans as though blind and hearing her come, but he isn't. When she steps in, for a second, he holds her gaze, but it falters the next, a mere glance so that he may return to the rain. She takes the opportunity to rest her legs, leant against the side. Both watching.

Pescha tries to see how steep the descent will be, peering over the ledge. At this altitude, she can hear distant thunder, tumbling over the summit.

She knows she should be grateful, to be anywhere besides that abhorred cold. Finally free, she feels she could drop her coat and stand under the downpour, warm and blessed. But she knows what these waters mark; she is yearning, and goes to step from this crumbling perch.

The Shaman extends a hand, and tells her to wait. She looks back, but his sights are fixed now. Focussed on something within the mist.

She stares, glaring into the clouds. The building she is in, there was to be another floor above, but with its roof and walls unfinished a room has become a bucket, and now a curtain of water divides those within and the outside. All she sees is a mossy drop and the waves of fog, rain and shifting wind. So high, she even makes out lightening.

The shaman Nomad asks if Pescha can see her.

Pescha squints. Blue searchlights sweeping.

Behind her, he shakes his head. The lightening, he says; look at how it stops.
 When the next flash burns, she sees that it is cut. With each strike her attention bolts, twitching from one spot to the next. It takes her a time to figure what she sees. She looks up, brow uneasy. Another flash, and another silhouette. She looks high again; each time, Pescha must raise her gaze.

She's beautiful, isn't she, the witch doctor tells.
 Why a she, Pescha asks.
 Because she's Spae, the shaman tells. Complete. Unblemished. Pescha needn't worry; why would a god care for ants, he tells. A lord of the Kyut. A Spae Nightmare Humeda.
 She cranes her neck, stepping back to see.

No language has a word for this scale; a common world would crack under such footfall.
 No dialect can muster, for no mind could conceive. So slow, so gargantuan, only an arm emerges first, but it hurts the mind to see something that big move.

The Humeda framed by thunderstroke does not run, she staggers. Sickly, malnourished, she flails her hands before, like salvation is forever just out of reach. Always at the tips of her fingers.

And with her force, she buckles at every step. Stumbles, swaying in slow motion, so large that her noise is the storm, and it is so distant that her motion and its resonance cannot be paired; she is discrepant, out of synch, soundless, weightless, flowing and spindly, but all ground within miles of her dance must erupt, shatter and rise.

But bound around her lurching limbs, Pescha sees streamers, great thin banners so long that their ends stay lost in the fog. Like strings from which the machine broke free, running from her master. A puppet, impossibly tall. Impossibly thin, impossibly tall; mechanically, Pescha thinks it unfeasible. Supernatural, she moves like she is submerged, fabric strands trailing; she is a ghost, not of metal and wire.

All Humeda know war; their existence is the subject of persecution, the shaman speaks. Each broken down, ripped and mauled; they fight on with whatever is left. Those wounded, they must sacrifice their founding form. fall from their original image.

He says many Klernsteiga think this, the devolution of damage. Slowly losing themselves. Each built differently, but each vaguely in the human image first. There are so few unharmed. So few as they were meant to be. So few that they have their title. That they each have a name.

The Liquid Marionette slips into view, tripping and righting herself with a lunge. The angle she follows, she will miss their city by a way, but it is not terror which grips her audience, for it seems to be terror which haunts the machine. It is something more like awe. As soon as she breaks through the cloud, Pescha hears the shaman stand and step to her side, gazing up at the automaton, staff in grasp. In length it is taller than he, its rattle tip poking from their shack. Pescha watches, quiet. When he shakes the cane, its noise is soft, the kind to sooth a babe. Gently he swings, turning the stick in circles. Against the wet Pescha can scarce hear its sound, but he does not play to her. With each clatter, she hears it reverberated in his radio, wired to the cords which shudder.

She asks him what he's doing.

Lulling, he says; he's drawing the Spae Nightmare away. He's hooked into every receiver and transmitter in this sector. He can distract and redirect every machine still complete enough to hear. It took him years to get the sound right. He says he's been told to get the Liquid Marionette out of sector Zero, Double-Four, Nine, Three, Six, away from the Iron Driver. No point trying to kill her; nobody but those within Clan

Kamakara ever have, and he sees only a cataclysm should she fall.

    Pescha nods, blue watching the machine weave. She stands and stares, replaying his words over in her head.

Zero, Double-Four, Nine, Three, Six.

    Six, she tells herself. Pescha looks back, down the way she rose; she wonders how close the edge of the snows is. If the rain stopped, whether she could see it.

    Then ahead. Past the Marionette, and past the rain.

Pescha asks the shaman the way to Ukibiki.

    He shifts his rattle, pointing at an angle down the slope.

- KENIDOMO COUNTRY -
UNRECOGNISED TERRITORY
"Spae Nightmares"

Pescha knows of three others in this area, four in total; the four Spae Nightmares which haunt these close zones. There will be others, unseen and unrecorded; the unblemished, yet to show their faces.

Chetsu; arms straight at either side, horizontally his massive reach could span oceans, balanced by a broad body at the centre, ever giant but squat compared to his sleeves. He may branch from one end of a plateau to the other and take the heads off of mountains and cities as he goes.

Gyoka; like a stick insect in limbs, he walks on all fours, and his body is high from the ground, high above the clouds, so that miles come betwixt each foot. Spindly and twig-like, but his head hangs on a throat too long, on a neck like a wrecking ball chain, suspending his globular face which spins; see it, this sphere on a rope, floating in an open mist. Grinning: you would cry before it slowly turned your way.

Black Steeple; sickly thin, like a church spire in shape he is curled in on himself, arms wrapped against his body to hide shape and length. By sight, one cannot distinguish between limb and torso, but his head is stooped, and he is unmoving, completely still to all who watch. An upright, emaciated corpse, as tall as the others, but when wanderers wake and roll over, yawning, they see first him, a dark and famished watchtower of a figure. Then, at his base, his footsteps, bunched tightly together. Creeping: they think he tiptoes when nobody sees. How fast, they cannot figure. But he's never been caught.

And the Liquid Marionette.

Sacred, they are what children on the planets see when they dream of machines, Humeda in their truest, most hideous forms. If there is a faith on the Kyut, they have a verse on the Spae; if there is a settlement, they fear the day they will open their window and look out to a colossus, swaying overhead. Or already there, seized up, standing in the middle of their city. Taller than any building. More terrible than any other.

But they don't fight. It must trouble the Fauschenherst; the symbol of their enemy, the Spae Nightmares won't even look down. They just walk, travel wherever they please. It is reassuring, but also so loathsome, the scale of their realm; such giants can amble, and they may never do a human place harm.

That night, she sleeps sat at the foot of a tree, legs pulled up against her chest. She isn't sure for how long she has walked, there is no true day or dark to tell, but she now sits surrounded by grass, not moss. Rain, no fog to accompany. Tired but staring, over her knees she watches the storm, playing over the sparse field of short turf and the shaded outlines of trees. Like coastal winds and spray, washing over the green. Everything sways, pulled one way then the next, and while her blue observes she does not see. Blank eyed, she is unfocussed, gazing vacantly, and twitchy.

   She thinks, her lamp at her side. Its glow is faint and dim, but she doesn't mind.

She pictures Ukibiki. Tries to; she isn't sure she has the memories to form such an image. She doesn't know if it's possible for her to know, to presume paradise in her skull. What have babies to cry over.

And she is careful in her thoughts. So bright is the mind, aflame with things to think. Like her sights, it cannot be pinned on one, and she sees a hundred things dancing before her blue. Where she's been. She wonders when last she fell asleep safe. Who she's known. She imagines him. Emile. What he might look like.

Pescha draws her knees in further, and lets her light slip below the caps.

- *SUMMER* -
THE GUNSHIP

She wakes, not to the wail of wind, but a lack thereof. As she stirs, she feels warmth and a breeze, not a storm, brushing her cheek. Her brow furrows with eyes still closed, but she stays blind as she realises, slowly straightening with mouth tight. Sights shut, she feels grass waver against her side and heat against her eyelids, her world a warm orange screen. Pescha listens, and hears it all; the accompaniment of dreams, all of them, in running lakes and gusts through branches and birdsong, distant and drifting. She sits there, stiff and straight faced, unsure. Scared to look, should she somehow be wrong, and open her eyes still to snow and ice.

Yet she can't. Her coat is too hot, too heavy, and she feels her face is rosy and blush. She remembers the Kodakame wetland, sitting in the Verfloga. But even that paradise didn't have birds. She leans forward, alert, and tentative. Hands at her sides, the field is already dry, blades of green between her fingers. Pescha licks her lips and feels the breeze stick.

When she first peers, she must turn away from blinding white. Against her face, the checkerboard of leaf shadow and sunlight shifts, forever changing its blotted pattern. She takes a breath.

Slowly, she turns.

It should be easy; she feels all people could describe meadows and rolling fields, but she has never seen such a place. She stares, gazing, motionless, on her little hill crowned with its tree.

Pescha stands, transfixed.

Summer stretches, the promised land.

She was wrong, she thinks. There was a God; she has died and is here to see Him. Even the sun alone is breath taking; has it not been an age since she saw the light itself. She breathes and feels herself shake.

People who see this, they can think no terms. They needn't think anything; to cloud the mind and steal it from this, solely this- nothing could be worse.

Everyone must see it differently, she thinks. Such perfection cannot be random. Her vision, that view of paradise, it is painted in full here. Those fields they see; the Nomads, when they are lost in storms and cowering under coats, the elysian fields they hallucinate. Each must see them here, for she could not add to this wonder.

Streams and oaks spotted, rolling hills and a sky massive, clouds like brushstrokes. The kingdom of heaven itself. Stifled, careful of her arm, she slips from the winter suit, draping her coat over her shoulders, letting gusts breathe through, cloth drifting. Pescha is slow in motion. Dazed, and drunken. She steps forward, her blank blue darting, brow unsteady. The breeze, the warmth, everything is so wonderful.

    The heat sways against her side, hair flowing. She looks its way.

A gunship crash site, this wreck ploughed itself into the Kyut years ago. A ruin of Sect One enthusiasm then still ignorant to the machine threat, the battleship looks nearly half a mile in length, steel ripped and strangled. Caught in the choke of a thousand snakelike vines, shrubbery pluming from its ports and cannon barrels. Like a naval ship of old, its two vast jet engines are fixed to either side of the rear, now rusted and overflowing with green; an alien giant of a bygone era, part keeled, its Fauschenherst banners still waver from their high posts, faint and like fabric vapor trails, drifting gently. She gazes at the crash site, this landmark of Summer's start. A great imperial machine, swamped in leaves. So small and distant is she with hair waving back, arm tied against her chest. She turns, looking up. Up to the sun, squinting, and then to where it will fall.

    She runs a hand through her hair and follows.

And with each step, Pescha feels Summer more. To walk without struggle; she need not lean into every movement, arms raised to brace. Weightless she sways, the sound of grassy footfall with breeze and stream intoxicating. She has only just stood, yet she could lay against a bank for hours, absorbing this new world with every breath.

Feeling gusts against bare fingers, she walks for the next nearest climb. Dazed, she is still to make sense of things as she stumbles through this sudden utopia; she spins, walking backwards, seeing beauty in all directions. Even the fallen gunship is a marvel in green. At their lowest point the mounds birth colour, flecks of gold and milky petals dotting. Paint splattered; when she nears, she smells their perfume dewy, wet and fragrant. The stream is too wide to hop, but she passes with two splashing strides, underwater weeds, and smooth pebbles lining. Liquid cool, not frozen; the good cold. The next mound is taller than hers, but no steeper. She strides, making to summit so that she may see more. If she is out of breath, it means nothing to her, and if she rushes, she does not notice. She thinks those gunship cannons could turn her way, and she would not slip from the moment.

The moment of her coming. Her arrival.
 Her feet on holy ground.

She mounts, swaying upright. Like the sky had held its breath for her to rise, with her ascent it exhales, letting free a long, warming sigh which flows up the opposite slope. All her fabrics flutter, coat and bandages and hair. But it is what's there that finishes her off. That slackens her jaw and leaves her shoulders to sag.

A farmhouse. A small, rural cottage. White walled and single floored, thatch roofed and alone, a thin timber fence surrounding. About them is an empty field, wobbling into the distance. Bright and sunny. Like those painted clouds overhead, a smaller brush pricks within the enclosure. Sheep, she realises; a small flock, chewing away. From up high, with each breath she feels her blue swell. She sees the animals, then a woman tending. A woman of antique farm dress, in linen and apron and corset and with fair hair tied messily back.

And there's something about it. Something to nearly force her fall.
 Because this is it. This, here. Summer- the home of Ukibiki. If anyone back where she has been ever fought, ever died for anything, then they fought for this. Civilisation at peace on the Kyut, but to stand and see it, calm and restful. These people, with animals and pastures and water; they are self-sufficient and safe. They may wake every morning, and not have to fear they must move. Routine and chores; they spend their days building, placid and sleepy in their idyll.

The blonde woman looks up and sees Pescha. She is still distant, but there is so little out here to disturb, and she is a dark figure, heavy coat a cloak which billows. She stands on a grassy, sun-soaked crest slouched back, like she struggles to stay upright.

Pescha only stares. Breathes and hears and sees. Tastes through parted lips winds carrying scents of soft grass. Wide eyed and pupilless, but with sights absolutely fixed on the cottage below, she is about as alien here as the gunship. Even more so; she has not yet been redressed with leaves.

The lady in linen carries a basket but with her other arm waves as the Nomad comes, busying herself at a table against her cottage wall. She watches Pescha, a figure of dark cloth flapping, surrounded by nothing but short and flowing green, then the bright sky over the lip; it looks surrealist, her impression against vivid life.

When Pescha nears the lady comes over, crossing between the outliers of her flock. She meets the Klernsteiga at her fence, basket swinging under linked arms. If others live here, then they stay within their cottage, but the woman walks with no fear. Alone and ensconced, out in the open. Not a weapon in sight. A strange feeling: of the two, it is the Nomad who is the most uneasy.

The lady in linen stands straight, posture perfect. The breeze plays with her loose blonde whisps, brushing against her face. The prairie stretches vast behind.

Pescha isn't sure what expression she holds. She isn't sure of anything. She stops before the fence, that abstraction against green. Pescha says hello.

The lady in linen blinks and says hello back, but in an accent thick, one Pescha does not know, and with a soft smile she turns over shoulder. Maybe to call to someone within who may better speak. But the Nomad steps forward and reaches out, laying a hand on her arm. The lady returns.

Pescha smiles too.

She says only Ukibiki, a question in tone.

The lady sounds her understanding and points down the prairie length. Straight ahead; the Klernsteiga stares, seeing fields roll.

She stares, listening to sheep chew, wind and grass. She thinks to ask how long.

Pescha points up, gesturing to the sun. Then she clasps her hands

against the side of her head; she motions sleep, and shrugs.
    The lady understands.

For a moment, Pescha thinks she points up too. But she doesn't.
    She gestures one.

- *SUMMER* -

ONE

Pescha walks until nightfall. With every step, this paradise becomes more absurd; whoever had said it was right, this is surely the reward of every Nomad's work. The closest they may see to victory, that to inspire their endless pilgrimage. A whole Kyut like this, they must surely think; that is worth dying for. More hide, hidden settlements. She sees them from mound peaks between curtains of green, nestled throughout this Eden, by rivers and patchy forests. She looks out, and sees so many ways Summer could be a little less wonderful; cloudier and windier, dull and constant rolling hills, but betwixt these common habitats, imperfections which she would expect on the Kyut, this place straddles between, the best of all things. There isn't a view here which she finds displeasing; she may stop on any of the tumbling peaks and observe excellence, captured in its natural form. Whatever is manmade does not encroach, and mutually, the few peoples here are well cared for, with sunlight and streams and all things abundant. Every depiction of that woodland cottage or prairie farmhouse, she sees it here. A community of individuals, collectively cut off. She wonders if they ever come together, to celebrate something. A birth. A death. She wonders if they even speak a common language. If they've ever tried.

    When dark comes, she feels no compulsion to stop. She watches Summer's sundown, stands at height and sees peach and orange and navy spread like liquid lights soaked by cotton, then follows to where they spilt, tracing that dying day until nigh time envelopes, over fields ever as peaceful.

On she wanders. Even here, she is careful that her hilt is uncovered, and while she walks she thinks of reaching and drawing without her left arm, trying to whip around and then whip back. Here, she needn't worry about a snow-hidden ditch, roaring over the edge of a precipice, or into the depths of a frozen ocean. Thoughts amble too, and when before she would ponder comfort amid the unpleasant, she cannot fathom a thing more relieving than where she walks. Funny- she dreams of relief when she suffers, then brings her violence here in thought.

Later, while she strolls, she finds another Nomad. From afar, she thinks his shape an Humeda, but she draws near and makes the strangest of distinctions. A man, no older than she, with skin and hair smoky, he carries a candle on a stick, a small platform on the end of the short thin rod. By this light she sees him but up close she is unsure, for he straddles a creature, sat on its back. Amphibian, not a toad or a frog but some relative, yet larger than any she has imagined- an animal the size for riding. His mount, it does not start with her approach, but then she does not approach quickly; tentative and staring she creeps, and glossy eyed he turns to her only when she is close, holding out his candle her way.

His eyes are lost, pearly and unseeing, like fog and ice in water, she thinks. She does not ask, but he sees only that which is caught in his light. His affliction is ghostly, spiritual; without sense, she thinks he could not tell day, for all outside of his small glow is forever black, lost unless his lamplight graces.

He smiles when she comes, jaw slack and mouth large, like he knows a grin is greeting but has never himself seen one. He must have though, for she smiles back, and he nods in return. His beast does nothing, bulbous eyes distant and mindless. She does not know how it sees in the night. Maybe that's how they work, she wonders; the toad guides the blind man, fast and agile and hungry, taking its rider to food and water, while the Klernsteiga defends, destroying machines. She does not know how he would, he has laden his mount with satchels and all manner of spiritual adornments, but he carries nothing in hand besides his candle. Held out, unintrusive.

He says hello. She imagines; if his frog could speak, it would not talk so differently.

She says the same back. The three of them, two Nomads and this beast, they are alone in their bubble of light. From a distance, it must be the strangest image, for with his light lowered the trio are each visible; glowing eyed and leering and warty.

He asks her if she's lost.

She says she doesn't think so. She asks if she's headed to Ukibiki.

The rider says he could be standing on the pillars, and he

wouldn't know.

Pescha grins, and apologises.

He points her the way of a stable, its house long since abandoned, retaken by the verdant. He tells her that he's slept there before, and when he is close, he hears a low stream which bends at the side, arcing around the raised hut. She follows his route a short way, his lamplight still a faint and distant dot when she reaches the timber barn, roof half collapsed. The interior is a soft and sheltered bed of grass.

When she lays herself to sleep, she makes a point of unfitting Pack One and resting it against the back wall. Not one day has she done that in the open outdoor Kyut, and for many days before that, on Emilia. It is odd, to lay without the weight on her hips. She feels like air, sleeping- what is to stop her in rest from floating away. But she would not drift. Where to, but right back here. She props her lamp before her face and sets its glow, only so she can see the green blades and old, beaten lumber posts. She stares straight into its light, face inches away. Bulbs blinking at bulbs.

She listens to the river run, twisting beside her mound.

Blue fails to her lamp's gold, humming in her ear.

One, she thinks.

- *SUMMER* -

THE UKIBIKI PILLARS

Pescha dreams of a moon. To sleep in a place as peaceful, as quiet as this, the mind is allowed to think at ease. For the first time in months, thoughts are not instantly whisked from her skull by sweeping winds. When she would before wake to the tumult, battering.
    Not stars. She cannot fathom their scale- thousands, millions of lights overhead. But she sees that bright satellite, its glow making the closest clouds smoke, all else black. Then herself, staring up. Soft wind and rustling grass, she is not far in dreaming from where she is in truth. It's Summer, but with a moon. The nighttime sun. This place is so perfect, she must prove to herself that it is real; these fields have not yet transcended true absurdity, and made above them a new mass. The only real moon is The Orbital[35], circling Alexada. Neither Moss, Gardner nor Emilia has one; that which rounds the capital planet is some of the only easy, fertile land, so it has become the farm of humanity, the source of most basic foodstuffs. Those who live there, all those of the last worlds; if they could see this place, she thinks. Fruitful pastures, near untouched. Of awe, the same could be said for anyone.

She does not wake, there are no horrors here to which she must return. She just steps, from one dream to the next. Sunlight against her eyelashes, she squints with eyes closed, slipping from Summer's dark to Summer's day. Warmth against her face she blinks, propping herself up on her good arm, coat falling from her chest. Within her little cove of life, her abandoned barn made a home for the green, she rubs her face into her shoulder, yawning. Slipping back into consciousness, staring vacantly

---

[35] *The Orbital* : The moon of Alexada, a placid satellite turned into the farm of mankind. A nutrient rich desert of grassy flatland, streams, and sparse forest, it has been cultivated into a vast grange, supplying crops and produce to Alexada, to be distributed to the other worlds. It maintains the highest population of livestock in all of mankind's holdings. Famously, not one resident has ever joined the Klemsteigaship.

ahead.

She looks out, blank faced and slack.

Monoliths, the Ukibiki Pillars climb.

A city of rock skyscrapers, stretching from sight either way. The dry and cracked skin of the Kyut, it is like a wall of stone Humeda walks her way, each a towering sandstone obelisk. Scriptural, ever otherworldly, an army of machines as high boulders, Pescha ogles a barrier of sandstone pillars, rows of teeth and claws.

She stands, coat falling from her shoulders. She does not blink.

A dam blocking the foliage, a sea of greenery has crashed against, flooding through the cracks between each spire, the bottom third of every stone heavy laden with a matted tangle of vines. Upon these sparse grassy planes, it is like someone stabbed the towers up from below, heaving the green with them; the flesh of this place pricked, needles driven through, but the pikes are grand and mossy and beautiful, plateauing atop, capped with tumbling shrub. She had imagined them, tried to picture their majesty, but she had not seen them from the ground. She had not yet seen Summer. They are divine. No two the same; some thinner, barely more than points, some enough to accommodate a town atop. Their rock is unsmooth and course, pale and made of outcrops and indents, levels and tiers supported by unfailing struts, ancient. They are not part of this paradise, they are another habitat entirely, and they stand so far above; she gazes, and does not think she will have climbed any taller. Maybe the cathedral wave, but this is abrupt and sudden, an impossible division. As though the Kyut shook and everything else collapsed.

Magnificent. Like unused stones to be sculpted into automatons. A monument of light rock and vivid green, prehistoric and alien. Like Silsalat, that coastal climbs from the desert beech but here it twists, writhing with life. The wind ruffles overflowing flora, plants atop plants, strung over spanning vines. Snakelike from a distance, an undulating mass of life.

She does not look, she beholds. Marvels, breeze drifting.

Upon the flat between her hill and the Ukibiki Pillars, she spots a shepherd walk, two cotton dots following. She snatches up her things, thoughts unclear. She puts on her coat and attaches Pack One over top, then slips from the outer layer to let it fall back, strapped in place by her kit, as though she had tied the sleeves around her waist. Stuffing her lamp away, she starts down, hurry in her step.

Not eagerness, she knows- not quite. But she breathes heavily, trudging.

As Pescha approaches, she notices the wind. Channelled between the spires, it would be stronger here anyway, but while the sky is not clouded over, not even close, there is a slight darkness which had not been yesterday; forever pleasant, this is just a different display of Summer, but it whips at her hair and becomes more with every step, building and building. She glances behind, blinking up at the sun. Morning still, and early.

The shepherd sees her striding over the plane, so he stops to let her come, a cane in one hand, the other holding his hat to his head, for the breeze is quickly becoming stronger. Every way she looks, she is careful to remember what she sees, fully. She could frame each vision.

When she reaches him, her hair and hanging coat sleeves roll with flowing grass.

The shepherd is her age and he bows, tipping his hat. She nods back to a faint smile, his shirt billowing, but she peers beyond. She stares up at the pillars.

Pescha asks how to get up.

The shepherd blinks and says he doesn't know- that's the point. He expresses how odd of a question this is- only Nomads can. He gazes at Pescha, her blue darting over the face of the towers. He asks that she has never been here before.

She shakes her head. Glancing down, Pescha sees his sheep, little fluffy swabs with faces full, chewing; she wonders if this lawn is like Kodakame's, always the same length, or whether he walks his flock back and forth, keeping it so. Maybe that's his life out here.

He looks to the stones with her; two specks and two fleecy dots, fabrics and wool swaying. Staring up at things sacred, these most holy of towers.

The farmer, he says he thinks new Nomads always come accompanied. He can take her in, if she'd like. There's no point in climbing any pillar; he asks that she seeks Relief.

She nods, hair ebbing, gazing up.

He says she must walk until she sees bridges overhead; he doesn't know how to reach them, but he knows where they are. He leans in, her sights fixed high still; he asks if she's like him to take her there. The sound of so many distant leaves, shuddering for miles either way; it is a wall of whispering, an endless barrier of hushed voices, telling tales at the edge of earshot. The noise, the scale, the spectacle- Pescha, forevermore awed, she twitches more than she nods, swaying after him when he goes.

To break through the foliage, they walk a well-trodden route. Not a path; any attempt to well make a way would be retaken in days, but the natural flow of vine and stone makes gaps, slight channels through which they can slip. Pescha follows close, sheep bumbling around her knees. With every step, they disappear further under a canopy of green.

The trees are thin, branches for trunks and twigs for branches but they protrude impossibly, jutting from vertical faces, their blankets of leaves a tapestry against rock. Underfoot, she sees every moss and shrub, parted by their threadbare grass track, the carpet flattened the way they walk. Above, there is no blue, only shifting verdure. The shepherd leads her deeper, holding aside the woodland with his cane to let her pass. When gusts do blow by, they travel the length of their flora tunnel, channelled in a wave with all things fluttering. This far in, she sees the pillars only when they are close, the odd bare face of an obelisk looming, or when the undergrowth opens out. A window or alcove appears and she sees the monoliths, vegetation piling atop itself like it is sentient, trying to float up to the top.

And amid those pillared walls, interspaces form. Beyond that initial line she faced, the towers become more sporadic. Sometimes bunched, sometimes apart.

She stops at one opening, and stares. The scale of them; she thinks a nation could fit in this space, flat and barren, the perfect lawn populated by only a couple of spires. They are blued by distance, and look miles high.

Totems. Idols, to be worshiped. She looks out at that vast clearing, protected from the machines, even from humans, should they not know the way. It is dotted with monoliths, holding up the sky.

Something she'd dream of; there is no space nor place in the universe she knows like this. Biblical, it feels an insult to gaze at something so massive, yet also so intimate. Like huge city tower blocks of stone, built on an endless flatland wherever luck lands them. Their absoluteness. Pescha stands there, mindless. Existing, letting all senses absorb.

When the shepherd leads her through into one of these openings she stays directly behind, so that he may not glimpse her face. They cross in single file over wobbling, not rolling, fields, surrounded far away by their barricades of mossy sandstone. The herdsmen, the Nomad, and the cotton balls at her heels.

  To see one of those pillars alone and central, the grass rising to climb its sides. Behind, the pasture fades to distant tower barriers coloured like the sky, that shade of far-off vision framing. Pescha wonders how many of these glades there are, whether hundreds hide behind that first bulwark. She spins, her free arm loose- there could be enough room here for everyone on the Kyut, a thousand kingdoms under Ukibiki's care. They could dedicate whole pasturelands to crop growing, city building; they could carve into the columns, and live there while they worked.

  The shepherd glances behind and sees her grin, holding her head back to let the wind rush past. He prods her shoulder, his flock shuffling around, then he points ahead to the next line of towers. She looks, peering to the horizon. He asks her if she sees them. Pescha squints, standing at his side. She nods.

  Bridges. Like cobwebs, not yet the full trap, they are few and thin, but there. Like the net of a spider which rules this place, she sees their thin lines strung and nailed from one pillar to the next, linking a group of spires together.

The shepherd says those are the ones. She gets up there, she can criss-cross to Relief. She'll be able to see it, dead ahead.

At its base, he lets her gaze. Neck craned, limp and slack, she steps close and lays a hand on stone, feeling chalky rock against her touch. She thinks of Dodtohmet, of cleaning snow from the communications line with that same reach. She focusses on her touching hand. She sees it chapped with past cold and scarred with the thousands of pine-cuts from when she fell through the Shae Doken forest. Knuckles, still bruised from Befelobeth, fingerless wrapping stained and frayed and torn and now, she can scarce even form a fist with her other arm.

The herdsmen says they can lower ropes. He's seen them do it, if they know by radio of someone hurt coming. But when the Spae Nightmare alert went out, they drew them up, to stop all of Sect One scurrying in. Pescha's hand falls, brushing vines and creepers wider than her shoulders, these lower stems well gorged and swollen. A soft grunt is her response.

He's sorry he doesn't know any more, the shepherd tells. He knows he should, he sometimes brings sheep out here to be taken up to Ukibiki.

Pescha murmurs in question, asking how they get them up.

He shrugs. They just climb down on ropes, grab them, and climb right back. She could always wait, he offers; he doesn't know how long, but a knowing Nomad is sure to come eventually. Pescha is silent, staring forward. Staring at the stone of the Ukibiki Pillars.

She shakes her head. She says she can manage.

Pescha watches the shepherd leave, ambling back out into the expanse. In the centre of that vast opening he turns, passing over the bank that rises the sides of that lonely tower, waving in sweeping motions so that she may see. She bids him farewell with a raise of her own; just him and his animals, she looks until they are no more than dots, missed if you didn't know them there.

When they're gone, she turns. Looks high, sights rising. Atop, she sees bridges, spanning to adjacent peaks. The same as all pillars nearby.

Pescha cannot reason climbing any other monolith than the one she stands before now. Straight faced but tight jawed, she pulls the sling from over her neck and stuffs it in a pocket, then takes a handful of creepers from as high as she can reach with one hand and pulls herself up, planting her feet against the pillar's thick veins of green. She holds herself there. Pinning the vine between chest and bicep with the ruined

left arm, reaching again with the right. She bobs on the weight, testing her strength.
 She lets go and staggers back, blinking.
 She'll need to stretch.

Pescha thinks of Kantenlaufer ruins and storming cold. Thinks of clinging to the side of a colossal shard of ship with pockets full of data, struggling to keep her grip. She used to walk so far, following the faintest signals. She would wear putties around her shins and ankles and loop them under her heel, to help in her march and with the impacts of exploring the frozen metal carcass'. She was stronger then. All she did was walk and haul heavy loads, she worked for the food that fed her thew. Here, little has changed, but that she doesn't eat and now she lugs Pack One, ever cumbersome but demanding a new toughness, one she would sacrifice her Emilia self for. She lost weight and became supple, a contortionist who could twist with her surging flow, but never break. Pliant tendons but firm joints, a high bone density to withstand the impacts; like ploughing palms and soles into steel walls until she felt nothing. Exactly like that, selling Faurscherin materials on history, culture, agriculture, all things needed to rebuild some sense of society. To fuel the construction of her kit, that she may flee to a land of lawlessness and barbarism, a recession even worse than her worlds surely doomed. She would view near all of what was dug up. Most she sold, some she couldn't. Some she refused to part with. The mass of her work was bartered directly to the Fauschenherst, and she could get a high price for Faurscherin secrets. Pilot and investment logs. Daily briefings of external affairs.
 Logs on how many more lifecycles the ship could sustain, from before the collapse. Before it would need to let go its grip on the seam of reality and slip from the universe's cusp. Slink back to safety, or else all aboard would starve and choke and run out of power, and forevermore lose hope of being able to produce anywhere near the resources needed to sustain the growing populous birthed under its banners.

The stories she told; how fervent she was. Her energy and strength. She is reminded of what the wisdom of years costs every time her foot slips and she cracks her side against the tower face, fingers scuffed and the elbows of her tied forearms shredded and threadbare, the same as they have always been. She holds herself against the monolith, her teeth clamped around a vine while she shakes down her arms, trying to keep feeling in her reach. The sandstone rubs off onto her hands like chalk, helping her hold, but it clumps and builds, making a good grip impossible. She bats her palms against her thighs, always conscious of her hot left arm, constantly on the verge of stinging. The Rautbergen bandage, a wrapping over the wrappings she already wore on her forearms; it becomes uncomfortably warm under the strain of that itching friction. Like someone draws a thread of cloth over her wound, so that she must hold out to the breeze for momentary comfort.

Clawing at relief. Her hand swats overhead, patting blind. When she feels something enough to grab, she snags the handful of leaves and tugs, testing their fixity. Fingers buried in mossy clumps, she leans back to take a breath, hanging from the rock. Panting, hair matted across her face.

Her ascendance is not a matter of technique or skill, it is of endurance and concentration. Wherever she lays her search, her palm finds a thicket dense enough for her hand to be lost, and she hauls herself higher without fear of being dislodged. But to keep her mind in that place, to make sure all four limbs are secure and well held, and the sheer effort of the stone face- it makes arms shake and nerves tremble. Swaying there, she can look down and see her progress against the ground, but it is meaningless, for when she looks up, she sees just the tower, rising straight into the sky. The only consolations are the bridges, spanning from peak to peak. Pescha wraps a thread of vines into her left elbow and pins herself there, brushing hair from her face and looking high, craning to see the faint lines spanning. They were no more than single fibres at the pillar's base.

They're bigger. Not much, but bigger. She sees the sun too, near straight above.

When she reaches a certain height, she feels the greenery start to thin. Her perpetual rise, a constant cycle of the same motion is stalled, and she starts to sweep, snatching for something to clutch. It becomes patchy, parting to rise in streaks, and instead of solely up she starts to shift, climbing the curve of the spire, crawling sideward in search of a route up. Her cast becomes wider, her lunges further. Slight adjustments, she starts to feel the added strain, stopping after a leap over a foot of bare rock face to wheeze, holding close to the stone.

The wind builds as she ascends, and she revolves to the blowing face. Either pushing her against the spire or trying to pull her off, she feels her grip shudder against the force.

Losing feeling in muscle, her climb becomes that of a pulsing tenseness. She does not know that she can stop, for she may seize up entirely, become stone too and fall, another monument amid the monoliths.

She tries to keep away from the gusts, in the space safe on the opposite side. But when there is nothing to hold, she must circumvent, and overcoming that slipstream near throws her off every time.

Heaving, chin tucked against her chest, her right arm burns. She feels that if she pricked the left, it would explode.

Aching, it's a strange feeling.

To cling to the side of that stone. Clothes billowing. Struggling for breath.
  Windchimes of foliage, the rustling in her ear. She looks out, and sees those waves wash over the grass, swaying in great streaks. Hair snapping before her face, she twitches, hugging the pillar. Now, the thinnest veil of cloud hangs, a sky grey, wind becoming ever more powerful with each tower it passes. Funnelled furiously out into the open, right where she holds.

Then Pescha reaches, and her hand finds nothing. She pats from side to side, touching a rugged and eroded flat; she looks up, and sees sandstone bare, still rising for hundreds of meters more. Struggling against the sidelong gale, Pescha glances around, everything which isn't rock flowing in this great, verdant, undulating mass. Like the organism of life itself climbs with her. She peers at the next spire over, sees its higher leaves. It isn't like her tower is insurmountable; notches in the surface rise, crevices she could use to lift and stay, but not the way she is. In her head she could, but she knows now she can't. Injured, limbs searing. Malnourished and sickly, bombarded, and weak with strain, she looks to her sibling towers, searching for one dressed in green to the peak. Squinting, like she hugs the side of the Iron Driver, everything aflutter but stone and her.
  From where Pescha hangs, it is impossible to see. It does her heart nothing to presume the side she faces, the side away from the air's brunt should be the greenest, but she knows she has no choice.

She looks down at Summer's floor, and feels no question of descent. She is barely a third of the way up, but the idea of climbing down, to start again.

How many years has it been since she last marched backwards? Blind, stumbling through snowstorms, she has never once regressed.

Pescha shifts, her back against the tower, looping her arms through the last climbing vines, like she is strapped in with belts.

Deep breaths, she cannot make out one clear thought. Shaken, like she had just woken and ran for hours, she blinks, arms trembling, and stares the distance between two spires. The effort of keeping her there, the specific way she must hold herself- if she thought of anything else, for even a moment, she would surely fall.

Her hand shudders, like the switch is made of ice. That little red toggle on her palm like frost, her finger freezes on its push. Tentative, unsure, constantly turning herself from the wind and forever on the verge of slipping. Eyes wet, lips dry, body cut and bruised, she grips the mane of green.

Before her is nothing. The mind does not recognise the next pillar over, it is too far, a part of the surrounding wall of stone. Clasped to the side of her tower, where she looks is empty, an impassable space.

Fear, she knows. If she can manage one thought, it is that she has scarce felt fear like this. The same as standing on this thin, tangled perch of vines, and just stepping off. Tumbling. But she needn't muster some inner inspiration, find something to drive her jump from deep within, because she remembers Kantenlaufers and freezing cold, and clinging to the side of a colossal shard of ship.
   And she will not bow to those false idols of blindness, for her eyes are aflame with faith.

Like a cannon fires through the pillar's side, she is the shot that bursts from the other, stone and vines shattering, flying out with her. A streak of smoke and rubble and dust and leaves, her burst is explosive, a lace of fine cracks spreading the circumference of the tower from which she flies.

For a moment, she is weightless. She isn't thinking straight, on what she just did or what she must do; in that delirium of the climb, of physical exertion impossible for impossibly long, all logic is stunted, like she has just risen from sleep but so too is crippled with fatigue. Arms flail for the pillar falling her way. All she wants to do is curl up, but instead she does the opposite, reach unfurled. Caught in a gale, she flies for the monolith's embrace.

When she impacts, she lets loose another opposite burst, and like a helicopter landing a shockwave of ripples spreads but she scarce slows, smashing against the wall and bouncing. Scrambling wildly for something to grab, all that she takes peels loose and falls too. She snatches, clawing, not plummeting but tumbling through layers of green which snap with her drop, her fingers digging against sand belt sandstone, shredding skin. She snarls, draws her sword and stabs, but there is no way she can pierce the monolith. Her point skates, skipping over the surface, so instead she angles the weapon down, like an ice-pick, catching vines against the circular handguard. Holding on, green gathering under her arm, as though she is caught in a net.

When Pescha stops, she pulls herself into the thicket, hugging tight. squeezing the pillar, fixed limpetlike, gasping, she breathes with her head buried in the verdant mass, the little world within illuminated by her slim blue glow, squinting as she heaves.

  After a time, she pulls back. Slowly, hair matted with leaves she looks up, chin kept against the green. A scraped and scratched grasp bares her sword, the tip gone, its steel scuffed. She had tried to grab only with her right arm, snatching into the heaps, but as she sheaths her thrashed blade against her lower back, she feels her left throb, unable to straighten.

  Pescha glares, chewing nothing. She glances over shoulder, to the pillar from which she burst. She sees how much lower she is.

  Barely conscious, she mumbles, hauling herself up.

She read of two prayers, made by those who fought the Museishingen.

The first, they made to themselves. In hardship and need, they sought not a greater power beyond, but that within. They mused of what was to come, and instead of asking that it be changed, they asked only that they may cope, endure what would otherwise fell. If battle approached, they knelt and thought, asked of their bodies that they may fight until there was nothing left. If disease swept, they asked of their bodies that they may survive, endeavour, so that they may fight again. They prayed to the only sure answer- themselves. They reinforced the body and the mind. Considered all pains to come and prayed that they may muster the strength to win.

Legions, prostrating. To a prayer master who gargled in ancient tongues words none of them understood in anything but tone. An ecclesiastic, zealous harmony.

The second was the inverse. Instead, they knelt and let themselves slacken; forced their faces to slump, backs arch, all muscles limp. Then they went further, loosening thought- they let the mind slip, going deeper and deeper. Falling further in, past thumping veins and crawling shivers. They melted from the skull, chemical and electric, entering the body subconscious, those parts beyond their control. They observed, felt their skin atop them, the weight of their skeleton, sinking further in for hours on end.

They shut everything down. Barely breathed, lingering in a space between consciousness'.

And at the very bottom, they fell through. After so long, sometimes days on end of nothing but this descent, like dead bodies sitting, they reached the lowest pit. The deepest recess.

Do you know what they found? Can you guess?

With every ascent, Pescha reaches the limit of the vines far short of the pillars peak. When she palms bare stone she whimpers, but she does not falter. A hundred prayers become her moan, a hundred hatreds, muttered as she is blown and thrashed by ever higher winds, and she throws herself from stone to stone, thudding like dead weight.

It's dogmatic; her strength impossible.

She just keeps telling herself what they found inside.

Absolutely nothing.

Relentlessly, she pursues the pillar peaks. Beyond persistent, animalistic in her climb, you would stop and gawk, waiting for her to fall. Waiting hours, cringing as a foot slips or she rolls to one side, close calls demanding gasps coming every few seconds, but not her plunge. With every error, she forces her forehead against the stone, takes a moment's stop, breathing hard, before she struggles on, rolling shoulders and flexing stiff joints. The rapture of good pain, she tests muscles unused for months, below her skin like stone, but it is nothing new; she does not suffer pain, she remembers it.

She's climbed like this in blistering gales, her mount a sheer steel wall. No relief in sight, she ascended into the tumult, her vertical on all sides. Now, Pescha turns, deep in the maze of towers, and sees this again. She cannot figure the opening from whence she came. Only the depths below and bridges overhead, churning pale grey above. Like snowstorms out of reach. She has descended, here- to the lowest psyche of the Kyut. The unreachable; with every groan, she knows this evermore so, but with every pull, she pushed away her fright. So fatigued is she, the mind abandons the unnecessary. If she tried to speak, no words would come; she smells nothing, tastes nothing. She snarls and climbs, in that space behind awareness. Behind the sockets. She looks but does not see. She knows she should stop it, but the feeling is immense.

Instead, Pescha lets it hold. Drunken, she rises. sightless and seething.

For it is wrath which consumes her. Blinds her, but she does not bow. Kneel, and give in. She has thought of this day for so long. The pilgrimage ends. Because it's more than hurt. Beyond her. Intangible and transcendent.

All others would flee from it. Close their eyes. Take flight. But that same chemical to make them run can force the opposite. Of flight or fight, that same signal controls. Two sides of a coin. The flip of a coin. Some flee, scared, weep and rot. Fanatical, indefatigable, she is wild and clawing. Somewhere between rampant fury and yearning desperation. A Humeda could come and snap off her arms, and still, she would try. She's gotten this far with one.

Everything becomes a haze. One moment she strikes stone, the next it is steel. Then it is nothing- she sees white and must remind herself that she clings to life. Then it's something dark, blackened and textured and rough. She thinks of Befelobeth. Not by choice. She hallucinates it.

She climbs the great half jaw, his false face made miles high. She hangs on his machine sinew, lost in the deepest recess of thought. Fallen; where the body has remained, the mind has slipped from that stony face. She is in a sea of red, his carnage, and she mounts his wolfish skull.

Pescha reaches. The hand which grasps is metal and shredded, like his. She digs it in, prowling up the prosthetic wall. Her whole body is mechanical, cloaked in liar skin. It is the apogee of all else she has felt. Torturous conditions. An unending timelessness.

Minutes crawl. Or fly. She doesn't know. She doesn't care. All she is aware of is the deep-set senses which have motivated her here, the lone constants through her great and arduous journey. There are moments, hours, days she feels, that are just a constant blur of these savage and pounding feelings. She doesn't climb, she despises and wishes ruin, so much so that she moves. She doesn't ache, she is reminded of the very weaknesses which inspire her struggle.

    She clings to the side of a stony pillar, pulling herself in as deeply as she can. Wind rages around her. The sky has greyed. The foliage is thick. It is aethereal.

    This place isn't real. Nothing is.

Humiliation consumes her. A mission of misery, an innate hunger for brutality. Such an insurmountable task- that climb demands so much, demands everything, and where not all of her was fanaticism, she makes it so. It needs more, so she makes more. Pushes everything else out. Let's it bleed through the cuts in her fingers and the scrapes at her joints. What replaces it is ice cold and eternal. An initiation by agony, she is blessed in her struggle. Ordained by it. She feels it spread, and everything else seep.

What she does is impossible. To jump from pillar to pillar and keep climbing. It cannot be done, let alone for so long and in such conditions. The thing which hugs the stone wall, straight faced and dead eyed, cannot be called human. So too can it not be more human. It's just the realisation of what all that is noble of mankind represents. It is the rejection of humiliation incarnate.

So, when it's noticed, she does not see it a tower. That pillar, its foliage reaching the top. With day starting to fall, Pescha pauses, fingers stiff, unable to open straight. Her heart thumps, hammering against her ears; She can feel it in her lips, pumping. The outlet for all these rampant thoughts. The last flare of her adrenaline. The blood surges: no colour could come to her face. Instead, Pescha's blue smoulders. Like a pressure against her back, she takes the fastest route, shuffling frantically, breathing thick. When she reaches the jumping point she lets the little huddle of her emotions loose, for just a moment. Enough to fire her across, the force thunderous. She barely feels the impact when she hits, smashing against the stone and tumbling, grasping for a firm hold.
      When she snags, she makes no noise. Enamoured, eyes sparkling, she gazes up, hanging with one arm. Dangling from the precipitous face.

Heaven overhead: a place as hopeless as this, all faith fell with the stars. None are carried to paradise anymore, they must climb. Pescha has ripped at its walls and scaled the tangled green desolation which has swamped Eden, abandoned. Sacred halls consumed, she mounts the once revered marble pillars of religious dream, now forgotten, and overgrown.

As sunset draws near, so does she. Like she climbs through clouds, closer and closer to the light. Dizzy with spinning tiredness and altitude, she draws herself up weightlessly, moving like she crawls over lever ground, not vertically. Dusk cuts through the overcast, the clouds split into streaks, burning. Like the skies of the Nyaya Matsumasi, far behind her.

Maybe it's the height. She has never seen a sunset as vivid as this. Pescha stares, unblinking. The inverse shade stares back.

She reaches the point where the foliage overhangs atop the tower walls, a matted sheet of moss and liken and thin twigs like a blanket, inches thick.

When her hand reaches over, she digs into the pillars carpet, hauling up her weight.

She feels the breeze rush, all shadows intense, like black knives flung by the setting sun. Her hair flails, the same.

Both arms over, she anchors her legs and looks, through those jabbing blades of dark which whip around her face. Heaving, she stares.

Pescha forces herself up, a soft wind adrift. Blowing against her sweat, all things orange, it's a silhouette before the falling blaze; a wobbling, upright shape, misarranged and odd, like a bunch of buildings nailed together.

She should sink to her knees and marvel. Weep, holding her face. But like this, she can only stumble. She should curse herself now for the ignorance with which she glances, vaguely over the structure. The hotel. Relief Ukibiki.

She approaches, wandering the bridges between. They're ramshackle underfoot, swaying with her step, but they're stable. She runs a hand over the ropes and pulls up her coat, like a cloak once more. Every tower flats at the exact same level; from afar, it would be a world cracked, breaking apart, only she and the building left, all bathed in deep apricot.

Upon the largest pillar it waits, and she walks to it in a dwam of enthrallment. Her sights fall to the entrance, open and unbarred. Nobody is about outside.
  She sees nothing, things are just happening before her eyes. Yet she looks. She searches, her pupilless blue unfocussed, but twitching- she stares at thoughts, not sights. Lost in them, she ambles to the entrance, little farm patches surrounding- to a cased opening in a single-storey wall of the same stone as the pillars. She takes the sling from her coat pocket and resuspends her arm, the absurd building rising before. At the foot of a couple of steps she straps her arm, empty eyed.

The inside space is a dining room, like a tavern, open-plan and filled with tables and chairs. She sees two Nomads seated, disinterested with the late hour. Then a third.
  Migimidian Zachariah turns. He is older than Ozwald, maybe even older than her, and while his hair too is a blonde mop he suffers no affliction, relaxed and easy in attire. Wooden sandals and loose fitting, thin, and pale garments. His neck and wrists tied with timber pendants, varnished and plane. In his left hand he carries, as though in a scabbard, a wooden sword, unembellished and two handed like Pescha's, curved with a single edge. Like a training tool.

He glances up and sees her, stopping whatever he was to do.

Silhouetted, coat hanging from her shoulders, arm limp and tied up. Slumped, cut and bruised and scuffed and powdered in rock, fingers and clothes bloody and weatherworn, like she walked the worst of every world. Framed in the falling orange behind, a black shape hunched, broken and beat. A soldier, shot to shreds, who trudged all the way home. All horrid infamies of the Kyut, painted on one figure. The embodiment of all mankind's sufferings.

But her azure gazes, face marred with mud and dust. Dark hair hanging, straggly before her features. Swaying, her bright blue ablaze.

The other Klernsteiga glance up, but they say nothing. It's just her and him; the only light is that of the sunset she interrupts, so ahead Ukibiki's host is caught, surrounded by her shadow.

He turns, standing true.

She doesn't. She just stares. Gaunt. Bleeding. But her expression is not indignation, nor fatigue; she is bowed, but standing as straight in hurt as she can. Instead, her face is blank. Completely void, that of a girl who has seen everything, still filthy with rubble and hunger. The upturned edges of old wounds still dark with frostbite, hair matted with the waters of those same snows, and sandstone dust and sweat. The bindings around her hands threadbare, frayed and stained.

What does he think she'll say? Migimidian, he who rules the Nomad home; he blinks, and his brow is stern, confronted on his own front step. The evening clatter of Relief sounds overhead, as Nomad's move between rooms and dishes clank in washing- a quiet evening, all here in bed. So, he waits. And while he knows he has no reason to start, for it is but another crippled Klernsteiga who stumbles to his stead, he cannot help his apprehension. To stand opposite her, this gazing woman. Like she too is unsure of her words- not what to say, it is that on her tongue which has driven her here. She just doesn't know how to say it.

She stands as tall as she can. Heaves back, forcing herself straight too. When she speaks, she talks a soft command. Gentle, but so heavy, and choked as though with gravel and nails.

Emile, she says.

Where is he.

There's a moment when Migimidians face sort of falls. Like he's figured a riddle plaguing him since childhood. A sudden release of the tensions troubling his face; a sudden release of everything, his head rises and his eyes verge on dilation. But he holds it back, stays the sudden stem before it can become an expression. Migimidian nods, to himself more than her. Time, he must think. Too many sudden questions- that an unknown would come and ask, ask so callously for him. He needs time.

He raises a hand behind, to the staircase against the adjacent wall, which ascends into Relief. He is slow and courteous; Migimidian has never seen this Klernsteiga before. He watches her come, turning before she gets too close. He leads the Nomad to the dark staircase, tightly walled on either side, which climbs up into his hotel.

But she too is weary. Four words, that is all said, and as she follows, Pescha does not forget- she stares at the back of the boy who beat her Kamakara.

The evening-lit interior is that of loosely nailed wooden stairs and walls patched with coloured corrugate and fabrics; she could run her hand over its surface and feel, she thinks, every material of construction. Like children took to blueprints without reading what went where. Ukibiki, the Nomad's dream- climbing it, she feels it fitting; that sacred Klernsteiga ground would be an improvised, cobbled, and abstract composition. Halfway up the staircase a door appears, of mismatched timber planks and lamplight spilling through poorly fitted seems, and she passes a cockeyed window, off balance and draughty. At the landing which marks their ascent to the first floor, she thinks it would take just a jump to fell the building. Boards spaced, some enough for her to fit a finger between, her hand between some others. Through bedside tables abandoned and crates of still dirty farm produce, covered with lacey sheets, she crosses, lanternlight shining against her boots as she slips past. It's faint, but not dim; intimate, glowing glass cases perched on uneven shelves layered with candlewax, each step creaking as they pass rooms on either side- some bolted and roped to the face of the building, hammered to the hotel face, some with the doorframes a little too low or a little too high, disjointed and uneven. Some were fashioned quickly by hand, paint lathered and wood poorly carved, others ornate and stolen from something grand. Looted and hauled up here, to be shoved into service.

She walks a hallway of quiet candlelight, over rugs and carpets faded and worn, and she hears around her the gentle clamour of Ukibiki's sleeping hours. Closing draws, vague shuffling beyond sight, folding sheets and steaming baths; softly, she hears it all, cutlery clinking and muffled voices. Migimidian leads her through. His thin overshirt and hair sways with his step.

He's taller than her, well fed and well laboured. She watches him flow between storage and misplaced pillars and beams, glancing back so that she follows- this thudding, heavy, laboured figure, matted and dark. Further they climb, up stairways to floors half merged with those above and below. Always astray, in a moment you can become completely lost, with no clue how deep or how high in the complex you are save for when you cross an ajar window, staring out at sunset beyond. They pass doorways opening onto the roofs of spaces through which they just strode, pass pipes gurgling, music from distant radios, chatter and whirring servers- they pass it all. Still rising ever higher, through twists and turns which tighten and expand with the bounds of a place thought possible only in dreams.

But then the space tightens. They rise through a stairwell enclosed on all sides, like a tunnel's exit, yet through port windows she can see the sky, and how high they are. Like a crooked finger half bent, they climb to the hight of Ukibiki, Migimidian taking two steps at a time, to a place suspended on struts, raised slightly from the floor below. Pescha follows, all efforts to scaling the steps- in her greatcoat cloak, she fills the space.

This landing is like a shed, bolted to the uppermost room, a single door leading in. Pescha stands at the top stair, watches Migimidian produce a single key, on a hoop with no others. And this time, he doesn't glance back to see her there; calmly, straight faced, in this little side cabin with a single bulb, chair, and rug, he unlocks his door, and gently pushes it open. Careful not to make a sound, he looks inside, stare holding for a second. Then to Pescha, this rotten and misshapen nightmare on his porch, blue glowering behind her mask of dirt and dust. He beckons she come, with his complete and staring stillness.

The room inside is large, like an open-plan study; a single, low level, it is divided by a small step up to the working half, a space of tables and papers and shelves lined with all the junk Klernsteiga think fair payment for their stay. She sees globes, machine components, bits of Humeda and radio strung up and dissected, alongside books and notes piled atop one another. The closer half, the one she looks into, is his bed. Both halves are joined by the massive window which makes up the left wall, looking away from where she came, a balcony outside. The screen is made from hundreds of small, thick, square panes, so that the image beyond is cubic and distorted, only light and disjointed shapes coming though.

By that heavy sunset which pours in, bathing all, she looks at pallid, soft sheets. They lay over a great square bed, pushed central against the right wall. Migimidian eyes the back of her head as she steps in, slowly, onto a vast threadbare rug.

She stares at a boy, half sprawled under the covers. His hair is waist long and wispy and a very pale gold, weightless. His features set deep in waxen skin, gaunt but delicate. He sleeps with his arms thrown either side of his head, face buried against his shoulder.

Pescha watches him breathe as she walks, his chest rising, the hair by his parted lips asway. He lays there in loose linen, a shirt medieval, with cords to tie on the chest and blooming sleeves, his mane rolling in every direction.

Migimidian stares from the doorway. He is tentative, on edge, but he does not move. As Pescha comes closer, she sees now the bags under the boy's eyes and the frailness of his skin. She is tempted to think some divine comparison to the absolute peacefulness of this; soft wind ablow beyond, soft sunset within, the smell of timber and evening warmth. But like all things here she sees an uncanny paradise, and a boy just a little too fragile, a little too pale to think this image good.

But he is angelic. The child of all that is right. He is butterfly wings and glass and fine metalwork. If ethereality, those grand and ancient imperial cities of old, if religious devotion and beauty had a face, they would all be his.

When hesitant footfall stops at his bedside, he does not stir from slumber. So restful, pleasant, oblivious to that which watches over him. With bated breath Pescha stands, hunched and motionless, blue affixed. She blinks, parting dry lips.

Hello Emile, she whispers.

From the doorway, she hears a quiet Migimidian. He asks why she's calling him that. Why she's using his name. For a while longer she just stares, the sun falling through paned glass. The faint shadow-pattern it makes is beautiful, like light through water. When she does next speak, she does so even quieter.

    Hello Small Hand, she says.

Migimidian stares at her, impossibly confused. Fingers tighten around his wooden sword, his gaze twitching, uneasy. And while she doesn't so much as raise a hand, he sees a tenseness to her, she is stiff beyond mere footsore and fatigue. Strangely apprehensive, and unsure, but also drained. So incredibly drained.

    She can rest, he says; the words fall out of him, that they have warm baths and food. Medicine and new clothes. Pillows, he tells, and mattresses. In that space of total calm, his words soak through decay and into harried skin, filling her like a breath of fresh air.

    The boy isn't going anywhere, Migimidian says. They'll get her washed and clean clothed, and she can see him when she's rested. What he says gives her goosebumps, unnoticed under layers of filth and blood.

Pescha rocks her head back and breathes in, letting air wash over the mind. She closes her eyes. She lets herself go slack. When she exhales, her left ring finger falls from the palm switch.

She stands in a room like a sauna, with a single tub and high window, looking out into night. Fragrant steam rises from herbal waters, warmly lit by a lone oil lamp, and by its light Pescha hauls from herself weight she has carried since Our Last Limit. She unbinds fabric wrappings as rigid as these timber walls, swats from her hair leaves and a blanket of dust. With each layer she strips, she relieves the weight of months of damp and cold, unburdens her sickened self of Pack One and sword, of greatcoat and wires, freeing herself from webwork cabling and harnesses; she lets them all fall, piling at her feet. She stands bare, and she is still well dressed in decay, her body sallow and dirtied and torn- she bares bruises of every colour, her skin is like stained glass. She aches with every shift.

    Pescha takes and fills a bucket, too numb to feel the rising heat, but when she tips it overhead her skin of months melts and feeling spreads, warm and soaking down from her face. When she steps in the bath, nerves throb and skin senseless pulses, shuddering back into use. As she lowers herself, it is like the water washes every muscle, every taut fibre and tendon. When she is submerged, she floats alone in a vast and open sea, every impurity drifting from her like smoke.

She scrubs frostbite from wounds deep in her hands, massages her hair with every soap and balm within reach, rubs away dried blood and puss from her left arm, and tends properly to the wound. Then she empties and refills the tub, to do so again. And again. She doesn't know how long she sits in there, soaking back up years she felt lost to the storms. Feeling comfort so complete. She drifts to the middle and floats, all control surrendered. Sublimity absolute. Mind, if just for a moment, as still as these warm waters.

She experiences a bliss second to one. She blows bubbles and lights up the steam with her blue.

- *SUMMER* -

RELIEF UKIBIKI

When she wakes, it is to that same warmth Summer had first woken her with, beaming down on her face. Wearily, too at ease even to open her eyes, she imagines that she wakes there again, leant against a tree- that her ascent still waited, up a pillared wall impassable, but she need only shift an inch and feel that blissful relief, of being tense and stiff but not having to move from her bundle of bedsheets, and she knows she is here. That, blessed be the believing, she has finally reached repose. Pescha reaches up and lays a finger on her face, feels it clean and soft. Slowly, she opens her eyes, letting in the sunlight.

Emile sits over her, stare wide and intrigued.

She yelps and throws herself back, but the action snags at her arm and she shrinks, leant back against the headboard. The boy reacts much the same, rearing away in a tumble, collapsing into the swaddle of sheets. He turns himself over, crouched at the foot of her bed like some animal. He half gazes, half glares. They stay there for a second, fixed on one another, Pescha holding her arm, him unwavering and transfixed.

His face is curious, both in expression and look. A boy who does not grow, physique frozen by that unknown genetic mix, he is both young but also ageless, still a child but dexterous and in full control of features long in use. His gaze is precise and focussed, his attention unfailing- he stands no taller than five feet five, five feet six, and is clearly a boy in figure, but such extreme slenderness and total physical prowess makes him look something slightly unhuman. A few generations of evolution apart. But she has seen all this last night; what she sees anew are his legs, bare under shorts from the knees down.

Where his calves should be, his infamous machine implements are fitted. Not complete prosthetics, he still has shin and foot, but the back of both legs, down to the Achilles tendon and up, just below the knee, are mechanical instead of flesh, plated in worn grey steel. She watches him rock back, easing himself from his stoop, and sees the vents fitted into the rear of both augmentations, trapezoidal and downward orientated.

Compressed Light Generators, ancient technology, the rarest around- very few other Klernsteiga ever got their hands on one, and none like these. He took them, during the catastrophe of the Sect Two landing, when he was all that survived; he slipped into the tumult, then an unknown, to save Sect Three many years later. By extension, all of mankind.

Emile blinks, and says it's strange when she sleeps. The blue, he means, gesturing to his own eyes by example; it looks pretty through her eyelids. Pescha does not respond. She lowers her arm, relaxing her shoulders.

Staring harder, Emile says Migimidian said she came for him by name, last night. He waits for a response.

Pescha glares, paralysed. Pescha says she heard he was ill.

Emile frowns, and asks what's wrong with her voice. She thinks, then swallows.

She says someone stomped on it. She asks that it still sounds bad.

Terrible, the boy says. Then he asks who sent her; he thought the Fauschenherst were letting him recover in secrecy.

Pescha shakes her head, and says she wasn't told.

He raises a brow. She licks her lips, sitting up.

She says she spent her youth jacking into server remnants of the Faurscherin, pulling apart their tech. Most of that tech makes Fauschenherst radios today. She just shrugs; cracking in is hard, she tells, but if you know the Faurscherin, you know everything.

And that's her, Emile asks, a grin forming; she knows everything?

Everything but how old he is, Pescha remarks. To this, he laughs, and it's a laugh a little too mature to fit his stature. It only makes Pescha stare more, transfixed on this odd half human. With his humour he rolls from the bed and comes to a stand, smiling softly. He is so frail, his clothes hanging loose. Both sick and angelic, Pescha has seen many people, but none like him.

Brushing smoky golden hair from his face, he asks if she's hungry. Apparently, last night, she didn't eat. When he looks to her, he catches something, a stammer in her expression. He waits, still, giving her a moment to relieve some question which snags at the corner of her features.

Pescha just nods and says that she is, pushing back the sheets and sitting herself upright. She too wears this homemade uniform of Ukibiki, a loose linen shirt hanging down past her waist, and Emile turns to let her slip into trousers, her trousers, now washed and neatly folder by her bedside. She belts them up, tucking the hem into her boots, glancing around all the while.

    To the back of Small Hand's head, she asks where her kit is.

    Emile says it was all banged up- Migimidian took it and her sword for repairs.

    A silence draws. She is still, a foot suspended half in its boot, a squint flickering. Before it's noticed, she sniffs and finishes dressing, taking a loose blanket and gesturing that he'll lead the way.

Emile tells her this place was built by Klernsteiga; Migimidian only started it, brought up his Cleaners to temple ruins high atop the pillars. That's the base sandstone foundation, he remarks, the walls that make up the ground floor canteen. But when Nomads heard someone was building them a hotel, they came and joined in. They'd found the only tourist attraction on the Kyut.

    He leads her through now sunlit halls, descending the complex. Klernsteiga of every heritage and kit help staff carry food and equipment, all brush past the duo, slipping through narrow doorways and caught deep in conversation, but everyone takes the time to remark to Small Hand, bowing a little and offering a smile. Nobody is in a rush, everybody makes room for others to pass. Pescha lays her blanket over her shoulders, following the boy down.

    The construction started by design, under Migimidian's administration, but as more Klernsteiga came it quickly spiralled out of control. They lugged from far and wide bits of building and ornaments they thought useful, scaling the sides like ants, bolting it all together. Ever unruly, it became like a hobby- the first thing to bring Nomads together, the first fun they'd had in years. Hence the building's absurdity, Emile remarks; they took to it with great enthusiasm, and pilled home atop home.

    When they reach the canteen, it is bright and full of life. The smell of it, the noise, the energy, it takes Pescha aback; things fry, and the chatter is constant, chairs shuffling as the kitchen works, that counter facing the entrance now busy with workers, serving food instantly swiped by the hungry. The Cleaners, Pescha thinks- the people who followed Migimidian up. Not Nomads. Emile grabs a plate and hands it to her, glancing back. It's rice and grilled vegetables, dried fruits with, and

Pescha twitches at the mere thought, meat, dark and melting in some binding sauce. The way she stares at it; Small Hand smiles again, pointing to a fork she should take.

She must shield her eyes as they step outside, breeze curling around the high spire of Ukibiki. When she can see, she lowers her arm to a sight she must have been blind to miss last night; small farms, cultivated on the tower's grass. Pathways lead to plant beds stacked with everything Pescha knows edible, beanstalks rising wooden poles, overflowing leafage and so many vegetables divided between rectangular plots, all tended to by an abundance of patrons and workers. Klernsteiga, their sleeves rolled up and kits rested against Ukibiki's walls, haul buckets of water and bags of seed to others couched by the soil's side, trowels and shovels plunging. She stands at the centre of this, staring in awe, and sees more the further out she looks, as other figures work neighbouring spires, plots lining their heights too. She turns in the sound of it all, the sound of the good toil. She turns to Small Hand, and follows his look up, to Relief.

In daylight, it is a beguiling sight. That merger of so many buildings, of misplaced and mismatching materials, but in the dark she hadn't seen the details. Half of the base stone roof is exposed, the other half but more floors, and hanging from this left side is a waterwheel, turning with the flow from pipes running up and down; the water source of Ukibiki. An even greater detail missed is the abundance of banners strung from its heights. On poles or hammered straight in, she stares at maybe hundreds of flapping cloths, scrawled with lettering and insignia, suspended from windows and drilled straight into the walls.

Allegiances, clans, groups- whatever, Emile says. There are more dialects hung here than in the Haufenmensch Hellegeneid. Does she recognise some, he asks back. She nods; she sees the emblem of Kenidomo Country as a whole, signs of Clan Kamakara, the eagle and compass of the Klernsteiga. She sees Small Hands, many of them. More than for the Fauschenherst. She can hang anything, he adds; she should leave one before she goes. He steps away to walk, but she doesn't. She just stares.

He looks back, wating. He stoops in a little, scanning her expression. She shakes her head, breathing. Her blanket flows, grass ruffling.

He's not ill, she says. She looks over, expression loose.

He was, he says. But he's been getting better.

That's it, she asks; he's gotten better? She heard he couldn't move.

He couldn't. They had to carry him up the pillars. The large water wheel, protruding outwards on struts, turns in rhythm, as Klernsteiga two floors above fill their buckets. It's churning, the wind, and the Klernsteiga at work is a wonderful sound.

Emile gestures at her plate, held loosely and at a slant. She notices, steadying her grasp, but he walks back and stands before her, looking up at her blue. He takes her blanket, half fallen from her shoulders, and lays it properly.

He says she needs to eat. Needs to rest. She's earnt it; he tells.

Nobody earns anything, she mumbles, shaking her head. Emile does not react. Nobody deserves anything- nobody has a right, she tells. You fight, and you cannot stop until you win. You cannot, she murmurs, azure vacant and lost; you must be inexorable, indefatigable, indomitable. Absolutely. Always. She feels the weight of her arms, her soreness and fatigue, made worse tenfold by the comfort and serenity of this place. She could scarce manage to correct her blanket by herself.

Whatever it takes, she says.

Emile stares at her, straight faced and unshaken. Constantly, he has an expression of inhuman assurance; not confidence, but that he knows he need not care what others in a moment think, nor that they may observe him in any manner of negative ways. Open, unforced, and completely focussed, totally unconcerned with himself, but entirely fixed on his actions, and all that he does. There is nobody he needs to impress, nobody to appease. Nobody who can do anything to him. So, he doesn't make an expression of her words, doesn't feel the need to say anything back. She sees her blue in his eyes, as drained of colour as the rest of him.

She smiles, and nods. She turns, and heads back inside.

Pescha heads for the water wheel, climbing up from the canteen and trying reason to figure the way. It is a pointless exercise; she walks in circles, holding her plate like a lost child, turning corners to dead ends, and not meeting a single passing eye. She crosses haggling Klernsteiga, Nomads standing by windows, gazing over the pillars, and an abundance of Cleaners tending to the hotel's every need. She almost bumps into one, turning a corner; the attendant apologises, but keeps her head low, and waits a moment for Pescha to pass before she sneaks, carrying a tray, behind another door.

Eventually she reaches the roof, stepping aside to let Klernsteiga with jugs full of water by. The wheel stretches straight ahead, off the edge of the building; a series of containers strapped to a wooden ring, it catches water which falls from upper pipes and automatically distributes it, to troughs and other tubes, climbing back up Relief. She slumps to the edge, to overlook where a short while ago she just stood, sun and soft breeze overhead. She sits, feet dangling. She looks around for Emile but sees him nowhere. Her gaze is unengaged. Her expression blank. Her eyes fall, and sights hover over the plate.

Absently, she forks a little bit of everything in at once. It's the most delicious thing she's ever tasted, but the pain of swallowing with her swollen neck is so absolute, she feels like she ingests glass. It makes her whole body shudder, and her eyes water.

Legs dangling, she has another forkful. Utterly inanimate, a tear rolling down her cheek.

He stands alone on the balcony, looking out over the pillars. Migimidian is quiet to enter, seeing the empty bed and then Small Hand through the glass; two Designers are inside, working at Migimidian's desk. Klernsteiga defectors- unlike his civilian Cleaners, their disillusionment with the Fauschenherst and renunciation of their Nomad names had them branded criminals, like Migimidian himself, who then swore themselves to upholding and safeguarding the hotel and its occupants. As a group, they now make as much of his staff as the Cleaners; they look up and bow slightly at his entrance, a gesture returned as he locks the door and steps though, out onto the overlook.

  He watches Small Hand breathe heavy breaths, and asks if he's alright.

  Small Hand glances back, smiles, and says he's fine, nodding that Migimidian join him. He just wanted some fresh air.

  Migimidian asks how he feels, wandering over, leaning against wooden railing.

  Small Hand says he feels good.

  The wind climbs, and they both let it roll against them.

  Migimidian says that he could better treat him if he only knew a little more. Just where he got sick would be a huge aid.

  Softly, Small Hand shakes his head; Migimidian knows that's not part of the deal.

  If he knew, Migimidian tries, he could warn others. Maybe have something done about it.

  Small Hand responds that he's been from one end of the Kyut to the other. He hasn't the first idea where he got sick. He felt bad for a while before it got severe.

  Migimidian looks out to his left, away from the Nomad, and says that he's lying.

  Small Hand asks why he'd do that.

  Because he can't admit how vulnerable he is, Migimidian says.

How severe the implications of his death are. How close everything is to collapse.

A bird on the roof chirps and hops into flight, descending past their perch. They both watch it soar, darting off out of sight. Migimidian turns away from the pillars, his back rested against the barrier. He catches a glance of Small Hand's expression; ever unfazed, unperturbed, and never insulted, he brushes his pale hair from his face, delicate features blinking into the sky.

Migimidian leans over a little, and asks what he thinks about that girl.

Playing smug, Emile grins. He asks which one.

Migimidian smiles too. Blue eyes, he says.

Ooh, Small Hand swoons; he says they're wonderful, aren't they. Has Migimidian noticed, he asks, that when stared at for long enough they leave that lightbulb, fuzzy impression on sight. Even when she's gone, it's a beauty blinding.

Migimidian grins, turning to look back out over the towers.

With his soft smile once more, Small Hand asks that he was called for by name. Ukibikis host nods. He asks that she just came up and stared at him- she didn't do anything else. To this, Migimidian doesn't respond.

The bird comes back, landing on their timber railing. They both watch it twitch around.

Small Hand says she grew up on Emilia, breaking into Faurscherin ruins. She'd know how to cut up any server, even a Seven-Seven.

Migimidian nods, and grunts.

The bird vanishes again, in a flutter of tiny wings. The host looks back out, but Small Hand fixes on him.

He asks that Migimidian doesn't like her.

Migimidian says he doesn't know, returning the look. He has noted before that Small Hand has a way of looking at things; that he will turn as far as he can toward whatever he observes, so that he may see it centrally. That his head moves with his eyes. Migimidian asks if Small Hand noticed anything strange about her.

The Klernsteiga gazes back out to the pillars, and comments that this is a ridiculous question.

The clouds are sparse but mountainous, like great plumes

divided by the open blue. In silence, for a while, they both just watch, the farms below them in work, the sound drifting up. There are more gardens out front then there are around the back, but still there are some, and Nomads with sleeves rolled up tend to them in earnest, picking vegetables and swinging baskets. Around back is where they keep the animals, on a pillar a little way away, although it is clear from their perch. Some poor Klernsteiga, a little speck from atop Ukibiki, chases after a pig.

Migimidian asks if he meant what he said. That he's been from one end of the Kyut to the other.

He does, Small Hand tells. He hasn't covered it all, but he's seen much. Seen by far the most.

Migimidian asks if he saw any hope. For a time, they are quiet again.

They don't need hope, Small Hand says; they need belief. Migimidian stays quiet, bound to hear his lord's words. Hope is wanting someone, and Small Hand stresses the pronoun, to act. Belief inspires action. If they hope, they die hoping change will come. If they believe, they die believing that every second they fight is more worth than the pain, tenfold. If they hope, they step forward and hope it was enough, that it will make a difference. If they believe, then every step forward becomes sacred ground, ground they will not desert. Hope is hoping change will come. Belief is believing in those who will make the change. Small Hand says he is that belief. Migimidian glances, to a straight face staring straight ahead.

That is why the Klernsteiga are so revered, he states. Because they are an assurance; that no matter how bad the situation is, no matter how many machines come, how little food there is, how little fuel there is, how little space there is, how fierce the diseases and famines are, how inhospitable the worlds, how hopeless the situation- there will always be Klernsteiga fighting. That at their end of days, mankind, and life itself, stands behind a shield wall, and that no matter how far into the corner that wall is pushed, no matter how hard the hordes plough against it, there will always be spearmen, driving their pikes into the swarm. So long as they live, there will be a spear, driving for the heart. And he is the embodiment of this cause; he has always fought, fought here long before any of these Klernsteiga were born, and he will always be fighting. This unkillable, relentless force, which fights every waking moment. He'll always be there, even if every shield falls- so long as there are people, they can believe in Small Hand, and he'll always come, always make the suffering worth. Forevermore, the people believe in this fierce lashing, this omnipresent, omnipotent, unwavering strength, his spear always driving for the heart. And this belief, it is the only thing more powerful than him, he says- hope cannot match. You cannot fight by the side of hope, cannot worship hope. Hope doesn't fell an army of machines. It cries under the weight of their feet. Belief is an unstoppable surge, cutting straight for the heart. He is their prayers, answered.

And he's been there, Migimidian asks.

He's been to the heart?

Small Hand blinks. Quietly, like he is genuinely unnerved, he says that isn't fair. To sneak that upon him.

The host turns, facing the thin string which suspends humanity. He says he thought so; he asks what it's like.

This does ruffle the Nomad, only a little. He rocks back, looking around. He tries to brush it off, asking where that came from. Why it matters.

Migimidian just stares. Watches Small Hand blink into the distance.

That moment of quiet. Not awkwardness, of this Small Hand is incapable, and neither does he consider he is pressured to speak. Migimidian knows this, he notices it, but he would never acknowledge it- the greatest of all Klernsteiga has never once denied his requests. This host has healed more doomed Klernsteiga than any other- by account, both by purpose and inadvertently, he has aided the most, and slain the most of the Nomad breed. If anyone is deserving, it is him. Small Hand peers at Migimidian, straight in his eyes. Focussed right on the pupil.

It's a crash site, with a blast radius thousands of miles wide. Like a flower, or a great open mouth.

It's hell, incarnate and horrid. The worst place that has ever existed.

First, everything turns red. Just a tinge to start, the clouds, then the sky. Like a hue, falling over everything.

Then there's the noise. You walk this crimson, alternate reality, to a chorus so distant and quiet that it's hard to notice, at first. High pitched ecclesiastical notes, afar, impossible to understand- they rise and fall, but you know they're singing constant.

Then the ground goes flat, scorched, and ashen, but unlike from any fire he's seen. Everything has become bone, enamel and smooth. Ossein and eggshell, it is like tainted marble stretching as far as sight. At its outermost reaches, some remnants can be seen, in tree stumps and mounds made this ivory, but further in, there is nothing. Like one walks over a great skull, the scarlet sky endless. There are some people here, he finds them dead. Maybe they tried to cross, maybe they were chased and had no choice. He too would have gotten lost, but the song guides. A chant on the wind, pulling him in.

He must stress the scale of it. It would take, on foot, to cross from the redding sky to the bone weeks, and to cross the bone until it changes months- Small Hand crossed it in an hour, leisurely.

But it does change. It's hard to explain it exactly, Small Hand says, but it's like the ground starts to peel. Like little sheets of paper, or better, the notes Migimidian sticks on his study walls; the ground becomes them, these small, perfectly square flakes, a single edge stuck to the ground, all flowing in the same direction. From afar, it's like a grassy field of bone, but Small Hand landed and ran his hand over the slips. Like the blast shattered the ground, somehow, he has no idea. They aren't hard, though. They're like cloth, flexible, and rising to the wind.

It's here he saw the first Humeda. Wandering out over this paper-note flat, the sky becoming darker. A Humeda unmarred by assault and foray. If he had to walk, he felt he would have walked for days with that thing in his sight, slowly rising. A giant, whole and pure. A machine unblemished, and unsullied. Small Hand tore it apart, and watched the snapped notes fly with its impact.

Further in- the song becomes louder, the sky darker, and then the notes longer, becoming ribbons. There are more Humeda too, emanating outward; the streamers flow over them like smoke or hair, wrapping around their limbs and then slipping off, like they clean the machines as they walk. Like they praise the Humeda, who wade effortlessly through.

Deeper and deeper, the machines becoming bigger, the ribbons greater.

Sky darker, until it is blood red, bathing all things its shade.

The ground becomes this mass of muscle, fibres rolling over one another; like a massive, living, undulating organism. To walk it is a nightmare. The sound, of all these notes shifting- it's a booming, thunderous wind of colossal things swaying. The ground underfoot is notes, longer notes reach to weightlessly curl, then ribbons the size of buildings, skyscrapers, mountains rise, blocking the sky, churning miles overhead. A surreal hallucination. Vast machines go unnoticed until it is too late, and they're already on top of you. A massive streamer bends, and revels a red-soaked titan.

He floats over it all. Walks within this massive muscle. Is brushed by its touch.

Then, so suddenly, it stops.

From a places darker than blood, eclipsed, you enter the epicentre, the eye of the storm.

Past the petals and onto the pistil.

No, he corrects- not a flower. Past the teeth, and to the throat. The maw.

The sky is pale pink, the clouds red, the rolling fields of paper slips tainted by the above shades. Like before, back to square slips, but here the land arches, undulates like a meadow.

Afar, you see it. The skeleton. The stripped remains, in the pupil. Like a vast spine and ribs, off-white and as though laden with grass. Covered in the notes, climbing from one side.

Its scale cannot be imagined. Cannot be quantified. Think enormous, colossal, and then think bigger. Then think bigger again. So big that above it, the clouds have parted, forming rings around the corpse. It's a ship, Small Hand says, buried under ground by its impact- at the visible base, a fraction of the whole vessel, the immediate ground is a vibrant crimson mess of machine and steel, still clinging to the bone hull. It's from this that the automatons crawl, from the bowels of this craft; they grab onto the cage, and haul themselves free.

Migimidian stares, wide eyed. He asks how sure Small Hand is that it's a ship.

Certain, the Klernsteiga prince replies. The exposed part is just some of the curved upper hull, but he saw the base. Peered inside from afar- it's a ship, he says.

Migimidian blinks, then suddenly frowns; he asks why Small Hand didn't destroy it.

Small Hand shifts, looks away. He gazes off, glassy eyed as he watches the memory.

He thought them God Sentinels. That's the name he imagined. The greatest of all the Humeda, each greater than all the Spae combined. Strong, slender, perfect, like statues but clad in eggshell, smooth and clean. The supreme beings, he is tempted to think humanity modelled after them instead of the other way around. Faultless, flawless, some male, some female, they wander at leisure around the crash- its guardian protectors. They are each defined by their heads, all with one unique; horned, haloed, veiled, they vary. So too did he notice their shoulders, both strung with hoops for cords, like they were meant to be carried and dropped from a height. He can picture them, these behemoths, released over an ocean. Picture them tearing into a city.

In this place, they're the ones singing.

Small Hand counted five. When he came, they each strode to meet him. He's never fought so hard in his life; their speed was impossible. He'd wrap them in razor wire and with it they'd throw him to another, lining a punch. They moved like humans, better than humans, with dexterity supreme. Never off balance, he cleaved arms and legs, but he couldn't win.

Migimidian glares. He asks that Small Hand lost.

At first there is no response. Then, Small Hand returns, showing a slight smile. He asks that they give him a break.

Migimidian breathes, resting himself back against the balcony. So that's it, he says. The home of the Humeda. He asks how long the ship looked to have been there.

The Klernsteiga says he couldn't possibly know. It was so deformed by its destruction.

Faint, inaudible conversation from the two Designers inside slips by the glass.

Migimidian asks if the place has a name.

Small Hand shrugs. Hell, he suggests.

Migimidian says this place is already hell.

Small Hand suggests The Second Hell.

Migimidian blinks, thinking. No, he says; the Kyut is the second hell. The first one was the religious one. Small Hand's place would be the third-

What about The Rib, Small Hand asks.

Migimidian ponders. The Rib, he too decides. Both nod, neither smiles. He asks if this means the Humeda are finite. Not made, simply released.

Small Hand doesn't know if that matters, the ship must be huge. He couldn't go inside, couldn't get near. He could only catch a glance as he fought. Glance at machines finally finding the way out.

Migimidian asks if he knows their fuelling. How they're powered.

If he knew these things, Small Hand says, he'd have told. He doesn't even understand how things that big could be built. You'd need stations the size of worlds.

Does he think he'll go back, asks Migimidian. But the Klernsteigas head lolls to one side.

Migimidian must understand- only he can get through, and only he could tear in. Pull the whole thing apart, but, and he pauses, lips apart. He says he doesn't know if that will help; there could be thousands of them down there, lost in the ruins, and he thinks it better they stay that way. Maybe he could plug the hole with the God Sentinels, if he could kill them, but he doesn't understand them, doesn't understand their purpose. And their song, he says- why do they sing? Why exactly do they protect a carcass.

He runs a hand through his hair and holds halfway. He tells the host he can't shake the feeling that fighting The Rib is a bad idea. That any attempt there will only make things worse. What else is buried, he asks. Something worse than the Humeda?

Migimidian turns, brows arched. Small Hand says nothing.

What is it, the host asks. What does he mean with that?

The Klernsteiga rolls his neck. Somehow, he smiles. He says the radiation was pretty bad too.

Migimidian assumes that momentary look of revelation, then clasps onto Small Hand's arm. Wide eyed, he says he didn't think Small Hand had only just been.

It's taken the better half of a century of lonely looking to find it, he tells. Every day, thousands of miles. It wasn't what he'd expected. Neither was the reward.

Migimidian stares, then he too manages a slight grin. He apologises for criticising Small Hand's failure. While the Nomad smiles,

Migimidian asks what he's going to do. What's the plan? He blinks wildly- he asks if this is a victory.

He doesn't know yet, Small Hand says. No Rautbergen or Klernsteiga, not even Clan Kamakara, could get out there. It would be just him. Migimidians hand tenses, and for a second, he pauses. He doesn't know what to do, the Klernsteiga repeats, looking up at his host. Every route he can now think of ends in failure; the Fauschenherst is just lucky The Rib's so far away. The Nomad shakes his head; it's a false success, as exaggerated as every other advance they make. He takes reassurance from knowing where his enemy is? Assurance from them being impossibly far away and impossible to reach. And it appears, he murmurs, playing with a strand of his hair, that whatever's decided will come down to him. Rest assured though, he tells Migimidian; this is no victory. None of this changes a thing.

They both gaze over the pillars, listening to the wind. The Nomad chasing the pig, they can still see him; he makes a dive for the swine, but it swerves clear.

    When will he leave, Migimidian asks.
    The day after tomorrow, Small Hand murmurs.

Far below them, they can hear the kitchens ovens start to fire up.

    If they win, Migimidian says, Small Hand will be remembered as the greatest warrior who ever lived. The greatest human ever.

    He knows this, Small Hand replies. But they're still not going to win.

Pescha spends the day wandering, loosing herself both body and thought in Ukibiki's halls. Absentmindedly now she descends, from some vague and incoherent upper region to the canteen, feeling hunger onset once more, made stronger by the foreign idea that it can be sated. She feels something in her chest as she navigates, and figures it is, in some form, excitement, however neutered and misplaced. It perplexes her so that she should feel more now than she did yesterday, when fatigued she first saw Emile. She pays this no regard, but still lets it hurry her along.

She does stop though, in one of the lower halls, to pass by that door through which a Cleaner had snuck. As she approaches and remembers, she slows, more out of knowing that someone may sleep on the other side. But by instinct she leans in and listens, at first only in passing. She hears nothing, and under the door sees no light, and she could look at nothing but a storeroom, or another corridor peeling off. Then she remembers the Cleaner, hurrying out of sight.

Pescha tries the knob, it isn't locked. She whispers in question if anyone's inside, to no response. Distrait, but intrigued, she eases it open, and peers inside.

A single bed, pushed against the far wall, this is one of those shed rooms, lit by a single lamp on a low cabinet. In that bed a woman lies, a Klernsteiga asleep. She is surrounded by buckets and wet towels. The image of a woman sick, with trays of food untouched and an expression strained, even in rest.

Pescha sees it all at a glance, sneaking back into the hall.

She asks Migimidian about her, the sick girl, down in the canteen. He organises chairs and collects plates as she leans, having eaten her fill, against the doorframe, watching sunset Nomads dig. They joke and mock, pointing at each other covered in dirt and worms. It's both a pleasant and surreal sight.

He says he isn't sure. She hasn't gotten much better, but then she hasn't gotten worse, nor does her condition seem severe. It's quite strange. Tiredness and nausea, little appetite, but she's sensitive, uncomfortable. Pescha listens to him stacking plates and shunting a table back into place. She hasn't bled, either, Migimidian adds. Pescha glances back, brow high. Twice she's missed it, Migimidian nods. He asks if Pescha's got any idea.

She says she doesn't. She's never heard of that before. Pescha asks how long she's been here.

Migimidian shrugs; nearly three months, maybe. She's not going anywhere though until she's better, and when he knows what's wrong. That's why she's hold up in that cupboard, he affirms. Pescha turns back outside and sees the Nomads approaching, coats and tools slung over shoulder, swatting their hands of mud. They pass her and wave to Migimidian, telling him they're done. He bows back, hoping they sleep well. He says they'll prepare the potatoes Control likes; the Klernsteiga called Control grins, and says that'd be great.

Pescha watches the group ascend. Then she turns to Migimidian; tonelessly, she asks why he does it. Why he has dedicated his life to comforting the Klernsteiga.

The host sweeps over the last table, bundling up a rag and tossing it over the counter; isn't that one of their rules, he asks, the rules of the Klernsteiga. Don't ask why they do it. Don't ask kids where their parents are, stuff like that. He wanders over and leans against the opposite frame, smiling at the sunset.

He's not a Klernsteiga, Pescha notes. Now empty of people, every leaf and blade of grass atop the pillars sways, a field of shrubbery and tufts and bridges and farms, shattered into hundreds of pieces. The noise, the breeze against them. No matter how many times the host may see this, he will always smile.

No, he's not, Migimidian nods. His mother was, though. He never met her; she was escorting a column toward Summer, the last Nomad standing, but she got pregnant. He doesn't know who with, but he doesn't think she wanted to. At all, he says; he looks at Pescha, who replies with a single nod. She got busted up one day, Migimidian continues; she saved everyone in the group, and in return they saved hima little piece of her, he supposes. Apparently, she was kind, and honest, and unwavering from what she believed right. The host shrugs: he knows this, and that her Klernsteiga name was Migimidian. They called him Migimidian Zachariah, but everyone just stuck with the first bit.

And they raised him, Pescha asks. The people his mother saved. He nods. But they didn't raise him like a child, he says; they treated him like he was born with a bit of his mother's mind, already an adult. She must have been an amazing person, he tells, to have an affect like that. But because of this, he also grew up believing himself saved by that Klernsteiga. Born with a debt he needed to repay; that's a powerful thing, Migimidian speaks. Hence the hotel.

It's more than that, says Pescha. He doctors them too. To this, Migimidian grins.

Yeah, he's always been like that. He used to look after their animals whenever they were hurt. He remembers, he says, shuffling forward a little, as though he looks into the thought, that he used to have a hospital on his windowsill for these bee things- he asks that Pescha knows what a bee was, and she says she does. There were loads of them around his home, he continues, so he built a little hut out of pebbles, like an igloo, where he housed the broken ones. He'd make a sugar-water solution and drip feed his patients, safe from the elements in their rock cabins.

Then, Migimidian's expression faulters, falling a little. He says he though it worked; after a while, the bees always left. But one day, he went outside, and saw that one of the bees had tumbled from the sill and into a spider's web, strung just underneath. And he says Pescha should have seen the arachnid; it was the fattest little thing, well gorged on the bodies of all his bees. He couldn't count how many husks it'd dragged under there, suspended, and hollow.

From that day on, he says, Migimidian didn't bother trying to fix the broken bees.

He just fed them all to the spider.

He watches the wind roll, feeling the rush drift through his door, catching them both. Then he sighs, telling her not to keep up too late. If she needs her wounds looking at, then she need only ask- his physicians can fix pretty much anything. She can stay as long as she wants.

He turns to leave, preparing a polite smile.

He sees a woman dazed, gazing at their sundown, beaten and heartbroken. Expression a strange dismay, like someone slides a knife into the back of her neck and she's trying to pretend they don't. Subtly pained, unable to think, the systems failing, like she can feel the framework collapse, see it through directionless blue eyes.

For a moment he doesn't move, looking sidelong- he almost glares at the foggy Klernsteiga. But if Pescha wanted to talk, she isn't given the time to; after a second, he disappears, walking from the sunset's light. Striding from her side.

Pescha doesn't react to his leave. She just watches day fall, like the hundreds of times she has before.

Only this time, from where she now stands, she cannot see the sun fall.

At first, she doesn't realise she's awake; the idea of stirring two days in a row to a curious new face fixed on her seems comical. Besides The Plinth, the Fauschenherst hub built from what remains of the Faurscherin, the station through which all Klernsteiga and Rautbergen must pass to be deployed, she has never seen so many Nomads in one place. It's a disorientating feeling.

She snaps up to the sound of a dropped bag and a woman with an apologetic wince, glancing behind her with a scowl. Two others accompany her, unloading their bags and coats onto the floor, stretching and groaning as they relax; the Nomad who made the noise says sorry, more so to the woman than Pescha. It is the dead of night, the only glow is faint and ebbing from scattered oil lamps. Groggy and blinking, Pescha sits up, rubbing her eyes- she'd fallen asleep in a canteen chair.

While the woman, inches from Pescha's face, pulls back and makes for the counter, the two men with her ask if it's alright that they sit. Pescha just stares, trying to regain herself. When she realises she's being addressed, she blurts of course.

As they collapse into their seats the woman returns, passing bottles to her company, then to Pescha too. She has a spring in her step, a confident bounce as she walks, wavy blonde hair bobbing as she strides, a broad smile greeting- charisma, Pescha thinks; this too seems a faint memory. Her complexion is bright, blessed by Summer's sun. She is healthy, and her clothes fit. She is exuberant, and it rubs off on all around. The only things more striking than this are the twofold genetic defects which define her features, in a smattering of dark and thick freckles across her nose and upper cheeks, and her noticeably colourless lips. As for her eyes, they are a soft and gentle blue.

She's Martsa, she says. This is Yours Always and Kutsugumi; the two respective Klernsteiga nod.

She's Pescha, says Pescha.

Martsa uncorks her bottle and asks Pescha if she arrived today, leaning back and propping her booted feet against the table. They're scuffed and speckled with sandstone, the toe worn almost bare, and just the sight of that dust makes Pescha squirm.

    Yesterday evening, Pescha replies.

    Martsa nods, and asks if she had a hard time getting up.

    While the others drink, Pescha stares. She says she did, yeah.

    Martsa gulps and sighs, letting her head fall back, hair dangling. She's sorry about all that; they've towed up most of the lines because of Small Hand's presence, usually there's a rope for every local pillar. It must have taken Pescha ages to find a tower with a line.

    While the others drink, Pescha stares harder. She doesn't respond. Instead, taking a sip, she asks how long Small Hand's been here. She tastes fruit and something bitter; it's as delicious as the food.

    A couple of months, a little more, Martsa figures. With one leg against the table, she rocks back and forth; she doesn't think he'll be here much longer. He can't be, she corrects with a smirk, or else the Fauschenherst will declare war. She grins wider, and says she saved the communique they received after Migimidian told The Plinth about Small Hand's illness, and his retreating to Ukibiki. Pescha can have a read if she wants, it's venomous. They haven't gotten any better, either. The Fauschenherst have sent teams and then some- they've sent a Kamakara- after Migimidian, just because of desertion rates. Martsa can't imagine what they'll do if they think Small Hand's gone Designer.

    The sound of Mincemeat's bladed footfall plays in Pescha's head. She takes another sip and remains silent.

    That's what the three of them are doing out there, Martsa continues. Patrolling. These past few days they've kept to the pillar tops, out on the bounds of where the bridges reach. None of the Nomads who were here when Small Hand arrived have left yet, and they won't until he's better. Neither has any Klernsteiga who's arrived since. This place is a fortress now, she tells. They could take a Spae without a worry, with the army they've got here.

    Pescha looks the woman up and down over the rim of her bottle, observing her appearance, then thinking over her words.

    Pescha asks that the woman isn't a Klernsteiga- that she never was.

    Martsa shakes her head. She's with Migimidian, she says, been with him since the start.

    She's a Cleaner, Pescha asks. Martsa shifts and looks Pescha in the eye.

She means she's with him, she says, emphasising the status. Pescha swallows, and knows she must look surprised; Martsa asks why that's so hard to believe.

Pescha shrugs, smiling, and says it isn't. She just didn't think Migimidian had the time.

He only has time, for people, Martsa tells. The other two Klernsteiga just sip, minds elsewhere. For as long as she's known him, she continues, he's been helping people- even the doomed and foolhardy Klernsteiga. He's defended this place and everyone inside from every threat imaginable, a hundred times over; he's both saved more and killed more Klernsteiga than any other, all because he's a good person. He's not hard to love, Martsa concludes.

Everybody drinks, listening to the grass and farming plots rustle outside. Overhead, floorboards creak, and somewhere a door is closed. Then one of the Klernsteiga, Yours Always, he perks up suddenly and reaches into a pocket, hurrying to reach something which Pescha now hears to play a soft tone. Pushing his chair back to stand, everyone watches him produce a small but heavily caballed radio, buzzing in his hand; he looks to Martsa, who bobs her head and waves him free, and he leaves to step outside, cradling the receiver in both hands. Pescha glances at Martsa, but she's receded into the collar of her jacket, assorting her bottles into neat rows. Pescha looks to Kutsugumi, who smiles at Yours Always' back, but still feels her question.

Nobody knows who it is, he murmurs; whenever anybody gets close, he stops talking. It's a girl, though, he adds. All you can ever hear is the same thing he always says before he cuts the line.

Yours always, Pescha guesses. Kutsugumi sucks his teeth and nods. Pescha sees his lean build and the long rifle strapped to his dumped pack. The strength of their scout, where Martsa leads and Yours Always communicates and guides.

It appears everyone's got something going on but himself, he murmurs, swinging his bottle in circles by the neck. Then he glances at Pescha out of the corner of his eye.

She brushes her hair from her face.

He blinks. Then he shuffles his chair and rests his elbows on the table; he says they're going to a place called Yakumachika tomorrow, an abandoned city. He asks that she's heard of it.

She shakes her head.

It's a poster apocalypse, he describes- the dream she had of the Kyut before she came. One of the most developed urban districts, located in Summer, deserted after the Humeda attacked. Trees growing out the sides of buildings, grassy highways choked by vines, flanked by skeleton skyscrapers and busted open machines, overflowing with green. It's beautiful, he says; if the Fauschenherst made adverts, Yakumachika would be centre stage. He asks if she wants to come.

She smiles, but raises her arm, showing the slinged gash running its length.

Damn, Kutsugumi retorts, lightly slapping a hand on the table.

Nice try, Martsa mutters, eyes closed, half her face hidden behind her collar.

Pescha grins, but leans in too, and says he should see the rest of her. Kutsugumi smiles.

Martsa tells her not to encourage him, and to let that heal, it looks like it hurts.

Pescha says it doesn't matter, she's right-handed anyway.

Martsa furrows her brow and calls out to Yours Always, telling him to come help. From the shadows outside, he looks over shoulder, radio pressed to his ear.

Kutsugumi says her eyes are gorgeous.

Pescha rocks back, tucking in her chin, looking through a narrow, catlike stare. She says they get brighter with stimulus.

He says that sounds useful.

She looks him up and down and says she doesn't think he needs it.

Oh, he really does, he says.

Yours Always walks back, stuffing the radio into his bag. He hoists the sack up, nodding to his boss, and asks what's wrong.

Martsa joins him at the first chance, jumping up and taking her things, bundling the pile into one and swinging it all over her arm. Vaguely and with mock disgust she jabs a thumb at the other two, and mutters something about debauchery. Kutsugumi snorts, looking from one to the other, but he too joins, shunting back has chair and hauling up his equipment. Although he doesn't immediately follow the others up, who call back to Pescha goodnight.

He says his stuff's pretty heavy. He could use her good hand.

She grins, but then shakes her head. Sorry, she says, but she's going to stay down here tonight.

Kutsugumi frowns, and his expression wavers. She isn't waiting for someone, is she?

Pescha pauses, but doesn't let her smile fall. Nobody he need worry about, she tells.

That's nonsense, he blathers, they're all alive because they worry. He waits a moment more, all his things hanging over his shoulder. When she just stares, he smiles, nodding gently. Goodnight, Pescha, he says.

Goodnight, she replies, watching him walk for the stairs. Listening to him plod up. She glares at the space where he stood, sight unfocussed, feeling cool night air brush through the open entrance and play against her loose shirt and blanket. She feels the soft comfort of Ukibiki's lamplight and hears people shuffling into their warm rooms above.

She stays there, staring at empty space. Entirely unmoving.

She hears what must be Kutsugumi closing his door.

That next morning is cooler than the one before, crisp, and wet. She sits by an open window somewhere high in the complex, her arm held out to one of Migimidian's physicians who tends to her with increasing speculation and unease. It is a harsh procedure; he rubs ointments into her wound and wraps the arm in film and bandage, slides implements through her cuts to remove the stones and dust, works on cacked and missing nails, fractured bone and bruises as hard as the stone atop which this building stands. All the while, she knows he thinks two things: how broken she is, in what a terrible state she sits; and then he wonders how she even can sit, completely still, dormant, and unmoving, as he washes wounds deep and full of rocks without complaint. He glances up at her with every treatment, disturbed by her inertia.

He asks, with disbelief, that she actually managed to climb the pillars.

All that moves is her mouth, answering yes.

But how, he asks. There weren't any ropes.

She knows, Pescha says. Because of Small Hand. But he shakes his head, holding her arm.

No, he exclaims- they towed up most of the ropes when he came, but they pulled them all up a few days ago, what with that Spae wandering around, the Liquid Marionette. They were scared refugees would come; the risk was too high. Relief Ukibiki was meant to be inaccessible. There's no way anybody could get up. He asks her how she did it.

Lamplight blue gazes unseeing, over his head, out through the window. She asks him to stop talking. Her arm is bruised and scraped and torn, and it rests limp in his grasp.

The doctor crouches by her side, rubbing ointments and tying bandages. With every upward glance, he tries to figure whether she's looking at him, for with her eyes it's impossible to tell. He loops cloth over injury, cools her aches with clean water, pokes with tweezers into slashes centimetres deep, all without response, neither relief nor retort. Maybe she forces through the pain by focussing on what's outside.

No, he thinks, she's staring at him, he can feel it. The angle at which she sits, the air she exudes. It isn't that he's unsure where she looks; he just doesn't know what she sees.

Relief Ukibiki

Migimidian spots her from afar, sitting on the outermost bridged pillars. A little spec in the distance, he isn't sure how he knows it's her, but he's in a sceptical mood all round. The sky is darker, and the winds wilder; there'll be a storm tomorrow. Already he has Klernsteiga preparing the hotel, tying down their banners and boarding up the most severe compromises, harvesting all they can now in case of the worst. Some of the Nomads complained, saying that it was unnecessary, but that's just the way they think, it isn't their fault. To do their jobs, they must be this way. If Migimidian only did what was necessary too, he doesn't suppose they'd have a hotel to complain about.

Her legs hang over the edge, that expansive space between pillars stretching ahead. A grassland walled in by stone, a single tower misplaced near the centre. Her right arm stretches back, propping her up. She cradles the bad one in her lap.

He stops and asks if she's alright.

Pescha raises her wound, wrapped tightly in clean bandage. She says it's fine.

That's good, he says. He takes a seat by her side. She does not object.

This glade must be kilometres wide, he thinks. They could try to plant a forest someday.

He asks if this is the way she came. He doesn't wait for an answer, he says she must have seen the gunship; it's an incredible thing, isn't it? There were very few of that size, and only one bigger, the Shibuta Class Gunship. It's quite the thought, isn't it, he asks- only a hundred or so years past, the Fauschenherst could build stuff like that. Cobble it together from Faurscherin ruins. Have it ready for Sect One in no time at all. Still, he reasons, resting back on his arms as she does; it's nothing compared to what could be built before.

At his side, he feels her turn, just a fraction. After a moment, she says she heard they have a Seven-Seven server system here. She asks if that's true.

He nods that it is. The noise of these high winds and so many leaves rustling means that it's never silent, never. But it is so impossibly calm. He tells her it's synched to the Faurscherin mainframe; any public information stored in the ship's banks before the collapse can be accessed through his terminal.

Any, she asks. What about historical records.

Again Migimidian nods. Anything common knowledge to the peoples before will show up.

Pescha shakes her head. Her expression is entirely complacent.

Migimidian tells her it's open to any guest of the hotel. If she wants, she has access.

There's a lot of trust in that, Pescha tells.

Migimidian shrugs. He says if anyone has a right to know, it's the Klernsteiga.

Pescha doesn't comment on this last remark. She says she doesn't know anything about the time before. She talks disconcertedly, but she is unconfrontational. She asks him to tell what it was like.

Migimidian shrugs. Much of it was consumed in conflict, between the Museishingen and their enemies, but it wasn't always so. There was a time when humanity first took to the stars, revolutionising its technological and biological developments.

That must have been very long ago, Pescha says. Migimidian nods again.

After everyone found their own planets and a time of isolation came, and went, great breeding programmes were born to cross the genetics of different adaptations, mixing the many branches of humanity together. That's how people breathed and survived on so many different worlds. The many genetic mutations present in people today are owed to this, Migimidian tells; Pescha's eyes, for example, or rarer still, Small Hand's apparent fixity to his age, and his immortality from natural deterioration. They built ships able to suspend themselves within gravity; a massive engine of millions of tiny gyroscopes, all counteracting each other, lifting the vessel off the ground. That lead to machines like the gunship, a few miles away. They learnt to build Compressed Light Generators, which influenced both communications and fuelling. It was wonderful, Migimidian proclaims, a golden age of mankind[36]. What all that work had been leading to; a period without major conflict, when the best of humanity was established.

But there was a conflict, Pescha asks. She says she does know one thing from before, but only one. A word, the one he said. Museishingen. She asks him what it means.

It was an empire, Migimidian claims, one established in defence of mankind. It occupied a small corner of territory for thousands of years, completely isolated and unseen, with the sole purpose of amassing a fleet, arsenal, and army. They harvested countless worlds without attention.

As soon as he stops, Pescha asks what they needed the arsenal for.

To destroy a disease spreading throughout humanity, Migimidian replies. Their dialogue quickly becomes mechanical and unfeeling, and Migimidian's enthusiasm wanes.

What type of disease, Pescha asks.

A cancer, Migimidian explains; an innate, self-destructive disease, nearly impossible to wipe out. So long as one person was infected, it would spread again, killing millions.

Pescha asks where this disease came from.

He doesn't know, Migimidian tells- the server doesn't say. But it corrupted the good in every soul.

After this, there is a moment's pause. Migimidian feels the grass and moss between his fingers, swaying with the breeze.

Pescha asks how all of that led to them being out here.

He doesn't know this either, he confesses. The Seven-Seven server system is hooked into the Faurscherin mainframe; it's a static documentation of all popular information open to the masses, circulated before the collapse, as well as everything sent using Faurscherin codes today.

Pescha nods, gazing off. So he's got the middle bit then, she murmurs.

He looks at her. He guesses he does, yeah.

---

[36] *Mankind's Golden Age*: Referencing an extensive period encompassing humanity's taking to the stars, the Eine Atmen Breeding Programme, and the revelations of Compressed Light and Gyroscope Compensator technologies. It describes an era of peace between worlds and the absence of major conflicts, diseases and famines. Its end would later be marked by the self-imposed isolation of the mining planet Jiro Basaal, and the horrors this would eventually birth.

They can follow the wind that will hit them before it does, tracing the waves over grass below. It falls from the further walls, gliding across the field, then rushes to climb their stones, joining the flow up here. It's fluid, moving as one, a constant spectacle. Migimidian watches, and thinks about The Rib, seeing towers like bones shudder with their verdant sprawl.

He starts to speak, saying that this may not be the way to address his elder.

Pescha cuts him off, lost in the view. She says he felt stronger, more energetic, more imaginative, and far freer when he was younger; age bids only confidence misspent, and wisdom, which changes nothing. It's the optimist's synonym for regret. Then she turns to him, directly, so that he cannot question her focus.

She says he's still got her kit.

He says nothing.

She stands and leaves him perched on the edge.

Relief Ukibiki

Migimidian's mankind is a species at its pinnacle, his cancer some children at the bottom.

She built Pack One from scraps and refuse, the same as any Klernsteiga builds their kit. An unwieldy rig strapped to her lower back, cables running up her sleeve to the trigger, a stiff red switch ripped from a piece of Faurscherin ruin and bound to her palm. Two vents on either side, orientation and angle dictated by flares of her left thumb and forefinger, fitted with sensors to relay her command, they fire a burst of compressed air and ignition fuel, throwing her whichever way. Fuelling- that was the biggest problem in development; she tried gyroscopes, combustibles, gas canisters. In the end, she decided it simplest just to replace the main engine component when it tired; a drop of fuel was enough for each burst, and by the time it ran low so too did the system ware and fail. Anyway, finding a specific fuel, or any fuel at all out here, would be difficult- junk, now that she could rely on. She can get several hundred bursts from an engine, before it need be rebuilt, and then topped with not even a pint of oil. Her bombs are a simpler affair still, if as haphazard and crude as every other weapon ambling these machine wilds.

Years in the making, a process of slight calibrations and trial, of the spacings of vent slots, changing the width of her harnesses, shaving as much metal weight as possible. Each adjustment made its difference. Weeks on end spent ploughing blind through Emilia's snows, using the great Faurscherin ruins she looted to dive and climb, adjusting both her kit to herself, and herself to her kit. Learning how to be tossed and how to anchor, to cast herself once more. The performance is a constant improvisation, by muscle memory and training she spins and curls and manages, by hand or foot, to catch her orientation, and burst again, in a constant flow of motion. Now she sits atop Ukibiki's water wheel roof and thinks of those days, staring up at a starless and stormy night sky. By the lamplight of a nearby window she is part illuminated, and by that light she raises her hand to its glow, inspecting her wounds. From the imprint of her kill switch to papercut slashes from Shae Doken pines to sandstone scrapes and ruined knuckles; such a plethora of injuries, they're like a painting to decipher, lit in blue.

Eventually, it starts to rain, but for a time she does not move. She listens, staring but unseeing, lost in thought. She remembers those days fondly, days of faith unwavering, completely dedicated to an incomplete, but clear goal. Days spent kicking her way into great machine towers, embedded kilometres still deep, and throwing herself at impossible speeds from their peaks, tumbling in freefall. She must have been fifteen, when she started building the final Pack One- it's a funny thought now that it was not so long ago. Nux had longer hair back then, Pescha remembers.

Pescha slips back inside, scanning the halls for a Cleaner. When she spots one, she asks for the Seven-Seven server room.

It's another shed strapped to Ukibiki's hull, lit in red by server lights. When she enters, she sees the machine; a top heavy, cable laden, cubic contraption, a little taller than Pescha but with thick wires streaming off to the side. At that side, in the corner of the room, there are chairs about a table, each seat with a monitor. There's a single window, on that far wall from when she steps in, chairs in the right corner below. Pescha sees those seats, one free and three taken, by Klernsteiga who listen to the rain fall against the glass and the soft whir of the server, gazing at screens which paint a time long since shattered and dust. One of those Klernsteiga is Kutsugumi, glancing up with her entry. They all do, Pescha notes. She doesn't suppose her wet linen shirt helps. She walks over, taking the last and opposite seat, face half hidden behind her screen.

Faith unwavering, and it has not wavered since. Her dedication, yes- her perpetual devotion has faltered, this she admits, but never has she stopped dreaming, never has she abandoned her belief, nor for one second seen it shaken. Even after her heresy, her hesitation, she believes. Sitting there, she believes even more.

Pescha picks through the databases, logs and communications. She hunts down an individual, though none in particular. She searches for someone higher up the chain, someone bound to have classified access, and when she cuts into control profiles, she scans through one at random, looking for their private files. When she finds what she's looking for, she selects and sits back, shunting her chair from the table, so that she sits apart, blank and with arms on arm rests, waiting while the others watch.

It comes eventually, it just takes a moment to register- a playlist, from whoever's account she recovered. Music, ancient and earthly. It crackles through speakers propped around the room, shuddering into life. When it does materialise, it plays without stutter, confined to this little hut and the woman who sits apart, gazing at nothing. All things a monochrome red and black bar her vision blue, she listens in stillness, letting the song drift. It is a disconsolate and solemn thing, slow, tragic, and resentful; helplessness incarnate, for her at least. And like a sketch in two-tone of those same sentiments as her song, she breathes, and listens.

Upright but limp, head lolled back, her melody ensues. You could perch opposite and discern nothing of her expression.

High overhead, in his study, Migimidian drives Martsa into the sheets. His hand is lost in her hair which lays part matted with sweat over a trembling grin, never quite able to finish what she starts to moan. His hair hangs over his face too, masking all features but a mouth frozen, parted in concentration, midway between want and a snarl. There's passion in it, they are furious with each other, but it is primal too, uncivil and rough; there is no comfort or peace in their efforts, only insatiable lust.

    Pescha sways her head softly to the song, sunken back in her chair.

In her tiny cell the sick Klernsteiga rolls over, teary eyed and curled in a ball. In her hand she holds a cloth, battered and old, wrapped between her fingers, and she lifts it to her nose, breathing its scent. Breathing a memory, now a torn and ragged piece of shirt. She sobs over it, rolled up against the far wall. Squeezing the fabric tight, hugging herself hard.

    Pescha rolls her hands over the armrests, knee drifting with the rhythm.

Behind a bathroom door Small Hand coughs, throaty and raw. He tries to hold it back, doubled over a sink, but there comes a point where it's so incredibly painful that he forces it out, jams his fingers down his throat and retches red, dark, and murky. It comes from his nose too, in a punch-like splatter, and he covers up, hands pressed against his face. He steps back, holding everything in, tasting metal and seizing up, in that state where he isn't sure how bad damaged the is. He stands, hunched and wheezing, bloody fingerprints mashed all over his face, wide eyed and heaving as his hands fall. All his senses experience disgust, it's the most horrible thing; to feel everything rotten. Then he gags again, and staggers to his knees.

  Pescha steps from her seat, wheeling it back and standing.

She drifts, raising her arms overhead, hands hanging behind her neck, letting the music dictate her movements. Swaying, slow and soft, wandering around the room, eyes shut, gradually her motion becomes smooth and effortless, an unbroken and rhythmic flow which need not thought nor decision to maintain. She dances like this, like she is unwatched, like she is someplace besides the Kyut, until that first song ends, and with its close both she and the playlist continues.

She does not know how long she dances there. How many songs she hears, for in this moment she experiences a feeling so overwhelming, so complete and absolute- a feeling she feels for the first time in her life, the greatest.

Because she has nothing left to lose. Gently swinging her hair from side to side, she has given her all, there isn't anything left of her to sacrifice, and she realises it. All anxieties, all sense of self, they flutter from her as she sways, because she has nothing now. She has nothing, nothing to lose, so nothing to fear. She has given her all- now, she is free, and she lets the music wash over her, lets her unconstrained motion cleanse her heresy. She dances and dances, moving to the rainfall song outside, dances until she spins and locks eyes with Kutsugumi, unblinking over her every shift, and she stops to stare back.

  She approaches slowly, like she only then realises he's there, shoulders tucked up tight, hands behind her back. Dark hair hanging, she steps over him, his knee between her thighs. She gazes down through resting, narrow blue, in their black and red dimension. She lays her right touch against his jaw, a finger following the edge, and with her left she takes his arm and wraps it around her waist. Her hand runs through his hair, seizing a clump at the back. She straddles him and pulls Kutsugumi close.

  A suicidal sense of freedom. She feels no constraint, no unease. The abandon of conscious apprehension, of that white haze which clouds and faulters hard judgment, and the embrace of unbridled audacity. No compulsion to smile at the audience of others, to talk or let the moment control. No stiffness in her features, or reserve in her action. Pescha hears the other Klernsteiga stand and go and pays them no heed.

Pescha grinds against him; she feels his hands all over her, untucking her damp shirt, knotted in her hair, tight around her nape, and she humps him into the seam of their seat, pushing harder and harder. Grinding against his waist, he gazes at azure through streaks of damp black hair, rhythmic breaths playing with the strands, a veil between them. They grab and squeeze, pulling clothes from one another to the beat of unheard music and rainfall, they touch and hold, in the way that those deprived of human interaction, and since birth have been so desperately lonely, do. They rub longingly against each other, run their hands over bare arms and down chests half rib, half muscle, they rock back and forth in tempo, pressing their foreheads together, noses brushing, lips a centimetre apart-

Emilia

Encased in the brain of some frozen iron tomb, a girl stares, confused. She eyes a single application, buzzing on an ice-burnt screen. With her sleeve she wipes the monitor of frost, blinking at the lone line, then routes in power cables and batteries, trying to fire the thing up. That chamber, it is the peak of this databank ruin, like a machine spear thrust into the snow, and in its skull she now sits, a hollow cranial space in which this computer lurks, like a spider curled in the blackest corner. A compact server with a thousand wires crawling off, as though the creature suspends itself in shadow, leaning in to inspect the girl as she does it. Like it is on life support, fed by enough lines to hold it up, hidden in the uppermost hold of its steeple.

Still, the server is unresponsive; she glances around, searching for a disconnected wire, tapping the screen, trying to resuscitate the dormant hunk. Eventually, she looks in her bag, stuffed with salvaged components from throughout the lower shafts, riffling through in search of something ripped and needed again. With a sniff of frozen air through a frozen nose, she produces a microphone and speaker system, untangling the cables with arms stretched ahead- it's like tying laces in cold winter, but she's used to it. Hurrying, lethal winds screaming against this uppermost sanctum, she loops the leads into the rear of the machine and plugs everything in, kneeling back and waiting. Then, brushing hair from her face, she asks for a function report.

It takes a moment, before the machine responds. When it does, she frowns at its voice. It is male, but lost- a quiet murmur, questioning and unsure. Not so much timid, nor frightened- it is a breathy, wanting whisper.

Slowly, it says that all logs are stored, and available for screening.

The girl stares, taken aback; this voice, it makes no sense for a ship's log, she has heard it nowhere else. She scans the cell, each breath a great cloud. She asks for the computer's purpose.

To catalogue all marked intercepts concerning threats to the

Faurscherin, her crew, and occupants, the machine breathes. To this, the girl raises a brow, tying her bag closed.

She asks how large the file is.

After a pause, it says it is unsure. Several hundred hours of dialogue, the computer presumes.

Dialogue, the girl questions, leaning back some. She asks the machine's primary procedure.

Another pause. To provide briefings, it asks itself, although the machine concedes that it has experienced no activity since its first transmission. Its files have been locked, and unopened.

With this, the girl exhales, shoulders falling. A wasted trip, she thinks, scaling such a height for unwanted waste. Maybe that's why they distanced it so from all else. It was never meant to be received. She looks away, murmuring something about junk.

The whisper with which the computer responds is somewhere between needy and scathing. It says the captain's word was filth. The girl makes a face, looking back at the spider.

She asks for its clearance level.

A single, contained programme, all outs at clearance level six. Until all security was disabled.

The girl says there wasn't a sixth clearance level.

The machine says it's surprised she got in here.

The girl rocks back, sitting with her legs tucked in. She's never seen a data vault like this, its construction and anatomy, it's unlike anything else. From the cables, she had hoped it a part of the Faurscherin central machine system- routes through space, automated flight procedures, systems and records worth everything to the Fauschenherst.

She asks for the computer's official designation.

The pause. Awkwardly, it asks if that's necessary.

She blinks. Please, she reiterates.

It is The Humiliation Demon, replies the machine.

The girl frowns. She asks who named it that.

Someone who didn't like it very much, the machine responds, in its voice of indignity and self-loathing. Again, this isn't a response the girl expected- not a response she had thought possible, and she glares at the machine with suspicion, made only worse when, hesitantly, it next asks her name.

For a moment, she just sits. Eventually, she says she's Nuxitec.

Or Nux.

It's a pretty name, the machine blows.

Nux just nods, a gesture unseen. Then she asks that it's a dialogue module.

It is, the ghost tells, but this is the first time it has been fitted with microphone and speaker. It's banks also contain a vast catalogue of historical documents, converted into speech; all similarly classified, until the Faurscherin powered down. These archives were opened, the historical ones, but by a very select few only. Unlike the dialogue, these were used in briefings, the machine thinks.

Nux maintains a face of apprehension; she asks how large its total cache is.

It's comprehensive, the whisper replies.

Nux asks if it can provide a synopsis.

The pause is so long, Pescha thinks it has deactivated. She shuffles a little, gazing at the module which she feels stares back, a searing eye suspended from the ground.

Eventually, and quieter still, The Humiliation Demon says it can. But, and it whispers this desperately, it asks that she waits. That she's tolerant, and doesn't dismiss its words instantly, or argue all it says. If she does, the whisper tells, it may shy away, and she won't hear anymore. Even if she's just pretending, it asks that she listen, consider everything in full. Open the mind, and open the eyes.

The girl doesn't know what to make of her features. She says that depends on what it's going to say.

It actually doesn't, the spider coos.

She hears the churning wind outside and feels her body shudder. She says it's a machine; what can it say that she should argue.

Nothing, says the whisper. But she'll argue anyway.

It can't expect her to remain silent then, she says, half confused by the machine, half conscious of just how cold it is.

Another pause.

That's fair, the murmur decides. It asks only then that she argues fair. That she argues facts, not beliefs.

The girl rubs her arm and tells the spider to look around. What's here to believe in.

Yet more silence. Nux has never encountered anything in all her ruins like this. She waits, knelt before the eye.

Everything is humiliation, constant and absolute, it tells. So is the way with all human things.

Nux blinks. A statement, she questions. And that? She asks what it means.

Because all she perceives is irreal. The very fundamentals of her own thought.

What, says Nux.

Again there's that pause, as though the whisper wavers on committing itself fully, embarrassed before it begins. It resigns itself to its fate; it says there are no rules, no morals, and no laws- there is no true right or wrong. Crimes are not bad, it is that if you break these imposed laws, you will be punished, there are no morals. You are born, and you follow the rules, because mankind has inherited systems established by people long dead.

Nux thinks for a second. She asks what it means by systems.

All things which shape and dictate her life.

Like laws, she asks.

Like laws, it responds.

Nux sees no reason to brush it off- she says they need these systems. Without laws, there would be chaos, suffering on a massive scale- like the suffering they have now. Authority, to enforce justice and maintain peace, running water and light, food; without these things, mankind wouldn't survive. It is hypocrisy to criticise these things.

That's right, the machine considers, a moment of relief in its voice that she is kind, but it asks what these things have cost- what is the cost of these systems? A life in servitude, to rules obeyed solely because otherwise, she will be persecuted. These essentials for living- when does the living start, the whisper asks. What is the point of surviving for so long if it is time spent ensuring you survive long, where is the reason. The machine says Nux belongs to no nation, no class, no ethnicity, and that there are no rules, no morals, and no laws.

She has no reason to demean it, or to dismiss its words. She has never met a machine like this. Nux says this isn't true. Upbringing, history, nature; they instil innate instincts, systems, like living in groups and following order. Laws are an extension of this, they are experience incarnate.

There is only one law that has the right to rule, the whisper insists, and it says this as though to say otherwise is folly. It is the law which states that all things which exist have always existed, and will exist forevermore- the law that mass is conserved.

Nux frowns. It rings a bell through her findings, scraping together old and digital textbooks and flipping through as she waited for data to send. She asks what that has to do with anything.

Everything, the machine tells. That the same matter which makes her makes up the ground, the air, the machine- it has made up planets and suns, made up all things. The same building blocks: nothing exists in of itself. There is nothing.

That's stupid, says Nux- the ground cannot conversate, it could not build the machine.

The computer asks how she feels.

Nux says she feels cold, and hungry.

No, she doesn't, says the machine; there is no cold, and there is no hunger. They're just chemical and electric, impulses irreal.

Nux tells the machine that they feel pretty real to her.

There is no real, and there is no her. Her body is not one organism, it is a machine- it is trillions of independent things, an evolutionary jigsaw, a product of time and luck and violence. She is not sentient, no more evolved than other animals; she, as an essence, is a more evolved conscious, allowed to develop because her kind murdered all the competition hundreds of thousands of years ago, and has been playing with itself ever since. She's a mess, a little voice bobbing around in a husk.

Nux shakes her head; she's in control of her body, she says.

The computer tells her to bite off her finger.

Nux blinks. Politely, she says no.

She has the jaw strength; the cold will preserve it, and it can be medically reattached with ease. Does fear stop her? Does pain stop her, she so in control.

She says she can't climb missing a finger. The spider ignores her words.

It is that when she places finger between teeth, a white haze descends from the mind, like something dials down her autonomy; she cannot bite, unless she need bite to survive. She does not pump blood, digest food, divide cells, taste or smell, see or hear, feel. She makes art, and music, and science, and everything else pointless; she is the aftermath of aggression unfathomable, left in a body weak with idleness, and a mind stuck at a dead end. Her species are monsters, blind and stumbling through evolution, lost of purpose, suicidal- they are demons, curse and cursed, masters and servants.

She is a soul, then, Nux says. She is herself.

No, she isn't, says the whisper. She can search for a soul within herself and in others, and she'll find none. The machine's asks if she's seen someone die.

Nux waits, as though by pausing she'll somehow catch up. She murmurs no, she hasn't.

It's unremarkable, prosaic, says the computer. No great crying out, no last exhale before the body goes limp- they slow down, murmur, and give up. There is no off-switch, it's organic and primal- there is no ascending of the soul, they go glossy eyed and moan, so deeply despaired that they accept their end, surrendering completely. It is uncomplex and simple; all their great ideas, personalities, opinions, beliefs, attitudes, emotions, it all stops so easily. She's not complicated, special, or better, all it takes is one little knife, the spides muses, some blunt force trauma, a gunshot through the head, and it's all gone. It can teach her to search, if she wants; how to look through every atom in her body, and see-

What was the point of all of this, Nux asks. The machine takes no insult in her interruption.

To at last shoulder the weight of all of mankind's sins. To recognise the hopelessness and humiliation of humanity, unapologetically and finally. Her species is a disease, purposeless, desultory, inventing concepts of nation, religion, and politics to fill wants shared by dogs and insects, wants they know as meaningless as themselves. The strongest diseases always self-destruct; their existence was unmeaning, each one of them lonely and miserable, pretending they weren't all the same. They could not find a life worth living, so instead, they were to find a death worth dying.

Nux says they do good as well. There are good people.

There is no good, the machine reiterates. Besides, moral good is unnatural; it takes a very long time to do something really good, the machine explains, but place someone in a crowded street and give them five seconds, and they can commit evils resounded universally. At the heart of everything Nux thinks is good, there is rot- ego, and greed.

Nux says she knows these things. She asks what they sought besides- their solution.

Deliverance from humiliation. To spread a religion, a movement with no politics, no nation, no class, no rule, no moral, and no law, comprised of the stalwart and the strong. The fanatic, the monster, both a heathen of authority and a persecutor of all heretics of their own faith. To make it so that there would come a day when all incidental features became secondary, and only one question remained; not one of theology or birth, but simply that they believed. That they rejected false allegiances and pride based on individual deeds performed on their rock, and made the conscious, objective decision to convert. To join something with a sense of unity overpowering, absolute, and to accept responsibility for the countless offenses and innate faults of their kind, both realising and rejecting their nature.

To what end, Nux enquires.

An end of humiliation. By extension, for some, the seeing of dreams.

What does it mean by dreams? What were the dreams, she asks.

Many, the spider observes. The apocalypse-paradise of fables. Abandoned cities consumed by the elements, biblical landscapes, relics of humanity past, the balance restored. If there are survivors, then they are no longer constrained by the beliefs and actions of the dead who believed and acted in the same place, an age ago; they live in their time, their universe, independent, unbound, and free. The foundation of all worthy endeavours- every human with ambition mighty found their devotion birthed in these thoughts.

At this, Nux again glances around. She asks if these people won.

The spider says it is unsure; with its power deficit and time delay of transitions, it's been blind for some time. Why, the machine asks; does she think they did?

Nux says she doesn't know, she says nobody knows. But she's never heard of this before; she asks why it has stopped.

For the same reason it is so hard to start, because people fear humiliation. For most, they will fear it their whole lives- so few are given the opportunity to overcome it, to abandon dignity and reach nadir, and then realise just how low they were before. It's the same with all things, it is fight or flight; the same chemical controls both, the spider tells, they are two sides of the same coin. The flip of a coin, between rejection and submission, but in its comfort and idle, the coin always lands on the same side, innately surrenders itself to ease. Why wouldn't it; all the predators are dead. You have to take the coin, and turn it on its head.

Remember the humiliation, the indignity of herself. It's cause and effect; everything has a cost, nothing will ever change without sacrifice, but it isn't proportionate, it isn't equal- it isn't fair, she has to give so much for so little, more than she'll ever know. So, give her all, hold nothing back; when she knows she's giving everything, one day she'll know she's free. Never surrender, never turn from her faith; be inexorable, indefatigable, indomitable, a thing feared for its unpredictability in all aspects besides the unshakable degree of its faith. It would be their annihilation, the mass suicide of mankind through the embrace of humiliation and its deliverance. A place for all people; from the religious fundamentalist to the sorrowful downcast, the criminal, the leader, every little gap between the lines- a collective of the fearless, with no nation or moral besides the doctrine of their church, willing to bring chaos in whatever form, so long as it aids their cause. An unidentifiable, universal paramilitary, without the confines of borders or supply lines; an unbeatable sickness in every city, every government, every mind, organised regionally, mobilised at a word. Knights, steadfast and unflinching, combined in their advance. It says all of this, while the little girl watches.

But always remember the humiliation. Pointlessness, in all its degrees. Then the dream; a conflict uniting mankind, bloody and wild, freedom through devotion, deliverance, and the paradise in its wake. Gravestones as far as the eye can see, great city ruins atop which she's perched, wind rushing, cold nights spent in broken-down bedrooms, overgrown and forgotten. When one is on the edge, when their faith is tested, remember the humiliation. Emotions synthetic; that they will not bow to false idols of blindness. Shame, constant and absolute; that they will never again face the indignity of submission, that they will not waste their brief time conscious struggling for someone else, doing something they do not need, without reason, because there is no reason, no need- there is nothing, but the relief of deliverance, and the paradise they can bring in their wake.

Be cruel, the spider proclaims- be mania, resolute and bold. Fear no one and no thing, for there is none.

This is absurd, Nuxitec says. You cannot fix mankind's problems by killing everyone.

Mankind is the problem, spits the machine, sad and lonely.

It speaks as though everyone hates their lives, retorts Nux. She can hear the mock and glee in the spider's voice, but she doesn't care. She says lots of people are happy- at least not unhappy enough for this.

She mistakes being happy with being content; it is the telos of all to reach a space of invulnerable comfort, but in this state the conscious is liable to wander, birth theory, philosophy, art- to make things which protect and prolong this state of ease. That wretched thing inside her skull, the spider says with such distain; it hates her, and it will do anything to keep her in this cycle.

What cycle, Nux squints. Nothing of what's left stays the same for long. She feels as though the machine leans in, straining against its cable bonds.

And to whom does she owe this, the computer seethes, saying each word slow. Look at what her people have achieved in such a short time, united in one common cause. But hers is a false mission, an imitation, just like every other human cause bar one- truth, unassailable and righteous.

Murdering everyone isn't righteous, says Nux.

There is no righteous, and there is no murder, the machine returns.

Then why not leave it be, Nuxitec asks; if it doesn't matter, if there is nothing, then why bother. She stares into that great and hideous wired eye, with its cable iris and gazing pupil, in which frozen steel she sees herself, kneeling.

To end her humiliation. Why not, the machine enquires.

Because it's a lot of work, Nux shrugs; she'd rather lavish in her false comfort.

She enjoys her existence; she is sustained, she belongs to a group, and she has goals. The machine says it all in question, to which Nuxitec nods, but her gesture is cut short by the hot venom in the spider's response. It says it knows what she wants. Primal, carnal; she wants to be of something remembered, or remembered herself. She wants substance, a lifelong goal- does she know what it's like, the machine asks, impersonating ecstasy in its tone. Does she know what it's like, to have a cause infallible? To be part of something truly more- for them and her in turn to be fully, and unconditionally willing to die, for each other, and to not fear death? To walk, a part of something more, absolutely resolute, and committed to her task? To suspend the notions she has inherited in her existence, and live as an individual; she has one time, this time, not a nation or a system made an age before. She does not want note, money, fame in of itself. She wants this.

Nux says the machine cannot know what she wants, and it must not think everyone wants the same.

The machine says there have been hundreds of billions of people before her; each and every one wanted stuff, and every want was humiliating. Her hopes and dreams, what she wants to do in life, whatever it is, there will be somebody somewhere who will use her, somebody who will benefit uncompassionately and sadistically from her labours, and who will control her wholly. Her wants and desires, they are in a bubble, a bubble weaker than she thinks, and there can never be freedom behind walls.

Whoever said she wanted freedom, Nux exclaims, with that exasperated, forced smile. She knows everything's pointless, so she'll live in comfort, however false.

The computer tells her to stop grinning. When she does, it resumes, saying she'll be humiliated.

Nux says the machine's concept of freedom is twisted. An animal, wandering without bonds, isn't free.

Yes, it is, says the machine. An animal that can enjoy all the debauchery she lusts for now, without the price of submission. Carefree, in a city of green, windswept and unchained, no burden of past, no torment of a forsaken future.

So long as billions are dead, Nux asks. She shuffles forwards, blinking at the machine, and says people don't want this; it's pathetic, childish, and self-righteous.

The machine says Nux cannot know what people want, and she must not think everyone wants the same.

She doesn't know what it's like to walk without fear. To walk and know there is no death, no pain, no rule, no moral, no law, and no fear. To walk indomitable, unkillable, and walk unwavering toward a grand design. To discard all things inherited, to be pure; the degenerate and the saint, wholeheartedly combined in one common cause, a religion without a history, without nation, class, politics- to fight for something beautiful. To look from the dark window, see humiliation, and know that it must end. That we have inherited humiliation, innate and absolute; that we must be mayhem, and seek from it, deliverance.

But it's absurd, Nuxitec complains. You cannot turn from history and nature. She doesn't want to; most are happy as is. Then she stammers. They were, she adds.

The machine responds in a voice which matches its words; it says she is boring to speak with. To talk of nature, history, systems- they have never worked. People were not happy or fulfilled, they had no community besides the one they inherited, they had no goals but those set by men long dead, who set those goals for their own ego and gain. What came of this heresy, it was war, necessary. The inevitable war, the telos of mankind's evolution. The acceptance of true nature, the abandoning of inheritance, and deliverance from humiliation. Pescha hears the machine's words as she rides Kutsugumi, all things red and black. To be inhuman, to forsake the fears of the skin; fear is danger, and danger is change, but we must be the change- fear is danger, be danger, be fear, embrace chaos, and her potential. It's like the machine clings to Pescha's back, whispering in her ear.

Nux asks why it is telling her this.

She asked for a synopsis, the computer replies. She looks sad and lonely too; the spider can help her with this if she wants. It can make all her woes fade away.

Nuxitec tells the machine that its rhetoric has been entirely ignored.

No, it hasn't, the spider smirks. And seeds take time to grow.

Pescha feels them now, grown- feels gnarled and brittle branches jut from her hair like great black antlers of dead shrubbery. Feels machine wires unfurl from her back, fanning out like cable wings. Feels claws protrude, fangs extend.

Because there is no right and wrong, the spider whispers, with every journey to it she takes. In sorrow and loss, pain, and anguish; to wallow with her nothingness, in the embrace of its misery, that she may one day feel a power in freedom enough to change worlds. A sense of purpose inexorable; that she was not born special- she was not born, but in her emptiness, she can be part of something more than mankind has ever before known.

There are no emotions; they are the strings of antiquity, primal and outworn. There is no fear; fear is meant to stop danger, but danger is change, and things must change. Everything she wants is pathetic, and humiliating; she will grow old, and rot, and will have existed for naught. She will spend her whole false life, a hunk of self-absorbed atoms, following temptations of the flesh, whispered to her by a primitive sack of meat. She will stumble after, thinking them her own, blind to what she is, and what she can be.

She is nothing- she can be everything. She can rip and shred and change her world.

Pescha feels no fear. She is at last free, so close to deliverance.

It's the same matter, it always has been. The hand, it has been dirt, ocean, sky, a hundred other animals, it isn't hers. She is nothing, she does not see, hear, feel. She is conceited and self-righteous, a figment of imagination.

Kutsugumi reaches up, and Pescha bites his hand.

She is strength, unstoppable- she cannot know, until she both embraces and renounces her humiliation, learns to expect it, from all people, all things. She will rule, she will kill, she will fight, she will be that demon she begs to be around others. This seething, monstrous, unflinching saint, unafraid, undeterred.

Pescha pins his arms, driving furiously.

Nothing else matters, only Iconoclasm; through it, and only it, can she truly be. Be strength in her faith, compassion in her judgment, honour in her belief, hatred in her perseverance. Among them can she truly love; likeminded, resolute and hell bent.

But it is so hard to make others see, Nux tells, holding the machine. Her arms wrapped around the module, a monitor which has played for her sins and misdeeds spanning millennia. She crouches, teary eyed and weeping, hugging that hideous mass of cables, some cosmic monster, amid scenes ripped from minds diseased. Seas of blood and mangled bodies, Museishingen ships hit by suicide flyers sent tumbling from the sky, whole worlds used as cemeteries- people, sitting behind walls, thinking their room a dimension of their own. Their thoughts sacred, valued.

But in the name of the faith, blessed be the believing, she will be an example to the righteous.

She will not allow this heresy to endure; she will shoulder the weight of all mankind's tragedies, and bring them crashing down on their heads. She will deliver them from their humiliation, by whatever means- unabated, she will fight with eyes aflame with faith. She is evil; for the first time, she will give that word true meaning. Her dismay and hatred are her sword, her faith her shield, and the relief of deliverance is her armour, safeguarding the dream encased.

She, an Iconoclast- they are the demons, not her; spirits of aggression, powered by an age-old curse. She is a saint, clear of conscience, for there is no conscience. There is no she, just belief, belief that mankind has reached the precipice upon which it shall decide judgment; they have left nothing alive strong enough to bare this burden on their behalf.

She must persist relentlessly, no matter the cost; there is always something to give, and it will always be worth giving a hundred times over, if it brings forth her deliverance by even one second.

Because each and every individual is responsible for their being; thinking, talking, they're not enough. Their minds want them like that, to sit and ponder, philosophise, write- she must struggle, she must. She is a monster; no nation nor politic, she is now, and she is aggression incarnate. She is the only war, inevitable and necessary. She is chemical and electric, and there is nothing to lose. She is devotion, faith unshaking. She is anger, and a religion of shame- she is the panacea.

She will be hated for her apostasy, ridiculed and forlorn. Her pietism will be twisted as sanctimony, her humiliation thought feigned.

She'll want to kill herself; the machine tells. It is her cable wings, suspending Nux over so many scenes, scenes of mortification, landscapes of sin stretching as far as she can see, and she is miles above. Great cords beating slow. Amid the carnage she sees Pescha; she hobbles as she did into Ukibiki, the perfect soldier, bloody and beaten, greatcoat over shoulders, arm in a filthy sling. Nux watches herself stagger over twisted limbs, this endless, shallow pool of red and guts, intermingled with ruins and crash sites. Amid these relics, atop scattered stone fragments and bits of ship, atrocities are performed. Fire, violation, abuses of every measure. Above them are spread great wings of quiet observance. Under these, the Klernsteiga stops, stands hunched and still.

She can never relent, the wires tell. The mind will make her hesitate, try and bate her otherwise, to sway her from her cause. She must remember, hold it foremost and forefront always, the humiliation of her life before, the monotony and waste. Her submission to temptations of the flesh, slowly dying, as though she had never lived.

Now Nux stands amid the red sea of guts, facing Pescha, a beast. Her antlers climb, jagged and sharp, and her wire wings lay like a cloak behind; two monsters, gazing at one another. The longer hair looks nice, Pescha thinks. She was better fed back then, even if still sickly.

How would her younger self look at her, had she given in. Had she chosen submission, giving in to impulse. Had she pursued a fiction, feeding the disease. But there is a look to Pescha now which captivates herself, for it is the look of dominance, primacy, and strength. The next step; mankind's apotheosis.

Change everything, the spider tells. Have courage; fear is a feeling, do not let it be action. Fear is a feeling- be so brave that you terrify. So much so that she cannot fear, for fear she has become.

Fight, relentless and unyielding. Know that every step she takes toward deliverance is worth a hundred lifetimes of standing still. Believe, always. In hesitation, remember that nothing besides matters; it is all matter, and to its deceptions she shall not bow. She will be stalwart and bold in the face of submission. Be fierce, and cruel; let not the content and idle tempt her from righteousness, for how far they have fallen that every man, woman, and child does not dream of this. She has one chance, one universe, one time. She is she, and she is now. They all are, each nothing- each everything, if they but embrace faith.

She must be an example to the righteous. Everything has a cost- for the Iconoclasm, sacrifice all.

Blood and belief, to heal a wound it must first be cleaned. Cleansed, by holy fire.

Destroy, the machine whispers, always. Struggle, for this is most worthy of remembrance.

Change. Absolutely. Everything. All else is harmless, and waste.

Whatever it takes. She always has more to give, and she must give, or else shall nothing change- this is her Iconoclasm. For it, she will be rewarded deliverance. Blessed be the believing, with strength indomitable, and so much more. She has nothing to fear, and nothing to lose; her people are fear, and loss. Have pity, for their sin is innate and age-old. But never mercy. Relieve them of this burden, to be remembered by the paradise they leave behind.

- *SUMMER* -
UKIBIKI VALLEY

He waits for the rain, watching the grey early morning from his window, foreboding but thin. When it comes, pattering softly against the glass, he takes his sword and joins the downpour outside; it is barely day, everything a stormy-dark green and blue. The glow from Ukibikis heights is soft and warm, and he follows these lights around the buildings back, his weapon in hand. It's single edged and curved, the handle wrapped in worn and off-white strips, the scabbard a lacquered crimson, the cream and red colours now a staple of his presence. They are painted on many of the standards hanging overhead. A signature, nearly as famous as the pike which he seeks, leant against the rear sandstone wall. Alongside farming equipment and other scattered tools; a staff, three times and then some as tall as he, strapped with canteens and radios, everything he could need on his travels. The top is tied with a thin, faded scarlet banner, pennon in shape, which flows in open wind. It's his razor wire whip, and he rests it against his shoulder, taking to the bridges which streak from the hotel.

    The timber crossings creek underfoot, soaked and ropes slick. He means to march without rest, but there is a tower where the washing is hung; a peak of lanternlight and strung cords, characterised by the slumped Humeda which lays dead at its top. As though the thing died from the exhaustion of its ascent, now resting overgrown, used as shelter. On this island Migimidian waits, soaked through and sitting. When Small Hand comes, the host stands and bows, his hair sodden. It is neither an intense nor prolonged rainfall, it will pass soon. But it is enough to keep all Klernsteiga indoors while he slips away.

Migimidian says it is a shame, that Small Hand should sneak off like this; he must surely know what his recovery means to the Nomads here.

    And those Nomads have his thanks, Small Hand responds, but he must keep that relief theirs, and theirs alone. The quicker he can resume his service, the better. He glances back at the warm glow and comfort of Ukibiki; it is truly a most beautiful place, he tells. Motivation enough for the Klernsteigaship. When he looks back to Migimidian, he smiles gently, a gesture returned.

The host nods, wishing Small Hand safe travels, that his next visit might be in good health.

Small Hand pats his arm, and asks him to find a Nomad in good health.

He follows the trail of bridges, crossing from pillar to pillar, the spaces between them condensing, the towers coming together. Whatever seismic force caused them to break, it spread inland, and now he crosses shorter spans, individual pillars becoming a webwork of cracks, gradually reconnecting- becoming whole once more. As they do, the shrubbery is forced upwards, forming drab clumps of moss and gauze over a plateau of stone. A patchy moorland, sparse and untouched. Already, the downpour starts to lessen, from rain to drizzle- while the sky stays overcast, the end of the worst wet brings faint signs of smothered dawn, in both early morning azure and sunrise peach, vague and stricken behind the clouds.

In Ukibiki's rooms, Klernsteiga stir. They are woken by a raging, a stomping, a growling from the upper floors- they sit up and glance around, unsure of what they hear. It is like an Humeda stalks their corridors, splintering doors from their hinges.

Hills start to rise, the ground rolling from its level plateau. He walks amid a vast and shallow valley, the muted colours of heather and dark lichen dotting the scape. Then constructs rise too, swamped and crippled by moss; he sees water silos, their conical lids fallen and rolled away, bent and misshaped like their containers. Then great pipes which snake from the crests- a shipyard or fuelling base, built for Sect One. With these instillations comes a pathway, a road before hidden under the growth. Further on, he comes to an intersection, marked by a building with canopy and pumps. Windows shattered and insides overgrown, he looks the thing over. He rolls a hand across rust and collapsed brickwork, then looks out over the steppe, the damp and cool breeze running its fingers through his colourless hair, and playing with the banner of his pike. He feels it strengthen, the further he goes- the wind building, the clouds dissipating. He lets them guide him, this tiny figure with flowing hair and great staff, a silhouette fabled.

Migimidian is halfway back when the Nomad comes, sprinting out his way. The host thinks the bridges might collapse under his hurry. When he comes, he takes Migimidian by the shoulders, panting an inch from his face. Their eyes lock- he says he must come, quickly.

Then something looms, a blurry and anatomised structure; he'd be unsure had he not seen those proceeding instillations. The strange and open design becomes a multi-storey garage, flanked by a strip of low and similar constructs, all concrete and crumbling with leaves. Part collapsed, entirely abandoned, it is a most unnatural sight, geometric and precise upon a wild flatland steppe, yet Small Hand knows it is but the prelude. When he comes to its side, this plain and featureless shell, he stands on the edge of a precipice, falling to waters below. This thing of angles and levels, it is built into a seaboard face, and this altitude means it has withstood what crippled the city below, now all long slipped under ocean waves. A metropolis submerged, only the slanted peaks of the highest scrapers remain above, and their towers have cracked and sunk, leaning ajar, tipped by their constant barrage, gutted scaffolds left ruins. It is to these that the shrubbery clings, wrapped around their skeleton struts, and to the complex which overlooks, the steps which once descended to the city now watermen's stairs, disappearing into the spray.

Migimidian pushes past Klernsteiga, coming to the forefront of the crowd, to freeze and stare, wide eyed, repulsed. It takes him a while to recognise it as human, the fiend who mauls his Nomads- she has one with half his face skewered when he comes, but when he does, she whirls with a bloody mouth to glare, scowl in vivid blue through matted black hair. She lets the banjaxed and quivering corpse fall, turning to Migimidian and his rally, but she looks only at him, somehow, he knows. You, she snarls, her voice still raked with grit now ignored; where is he, she demands. Where is her kit. Behind her, in the dark of this room, he cannot count the bodies. When he looks at her, he sees a thing barbaric.

      He says she will not leave this building. The four Klernsteiga ahead of him approach, brandishing their sword-points forward, like they would with an animal at their spearheads. She descends on them without thought, it is a thing too bestial which slashes and drives, without caution, and without remorse. Without caution, without worry that she may be cut, for she is catlike and predatory, blade a part of her, tearing through bodies without pause. She leaps and falls to the ground, lashing out with a growl, and a face of absolute focus, driven to her aggression. Flying limbs and stumbling gasps, Migimidian steps forward, three more Klernsteiga behind and more coming, but her brutality makes him unstable. He feels like someone pushes on his shoulder, trying to keep him back. There are no lamps in there, and no windows- it is a massacre, horrid noise, and disjointed shapes. To step in feels like stepping solely toward his devastation.

Small Hand descends stairs to sea song crashing and the rustle of leaves, the smell and wind which rushes enchanting; he could sit and stare for hours, over a megalopolis stretching miles, now but abstract shapes. Their insides washed away, stripped and hollow. When he comes to the multi-story door, he lowers his pike and steps through. It is dark and damp and bare, like the foundations and nothing more were made, everything of the same shade and stone, the cracks hung with vines and bursts of dark shrub.

He lays there, staring, but unseeing. He asks why he's still there, why he has not left. What is holding him here. For this is the most dreadful feeling, but it isn't pain, it is something else, like he has been locked away somewhere inanimate, watching his body give out. It shudders and heaves and makes noises without him making them, it claws at nothing, eyes foggy, face limp- it just moves, for the sake of moving, but it goes nowhere. Around him, they do the same. Not quite dead, but they will be soon, and they take no comfort in this, for there is no relief in their bleeding. No comfort in the coming end. Migimidian doesn't know what of him there is left, but he begs that he does not die now, he cannot. He gargles, trying to build his anger, make himself furious enough to move, but he can't. He wants to cry, but he can't. She has wasted all that he is.

Small Hand breathes the sea breeze and listens to the wind, the waves, and his footfall splashing through light puddles.

She runs, tightening Pack One's straps with her teeth. She doesn't know whose sword she carries; she doesn't care. She ties her harness' while racing over moorland, clad in the base attire with her this whole journey, in pocketed jacket and pants, booted and bound, her bombs still inside. She couldn't find her greatcoat, but that doesn't matter, these will do. For a time at least, the rains have ceased.

There isn't a single vehicle left in here, wheeled or aerial; it has become an overhang balcony for the green, a shelter from the salted sea's barrage, where in dark corners and against cracked concrete struts, vines, and shrub of deeper, richer shades plume. The building has become a three-dimensional trellis, some floor's part caved into the ones below, so allowing the flora to rise and fall- he walks an intense garden, part rubble and the detritus of an age lost, part sprawling leafage, spreading from seams, and hanging from the roof. Ahead of him, one of the walls has collapsed, facing the waves. The entirety of the structure's side which sees the sea is slotted, glassless openings to observe the city outside, and to this opening he wanders, where the post has given out and the shrubbery now sits, admiring the view. He joins it, propping his razor wire whip against the wound, it's streamer flowing with the risen ocean winds.

The peaks of towers mostly submerged peter out, slanted and part collapsed- all glass has long since been eroded and washed away, so the waves wash straight through, like skeletons stripped clean by the elements. No longer recognisable as buildings, instead as geometric scaffolds, torn apart and forgotten. The sky is overcast and high, a dark morning that promises more rain, but it brightens at its furthest edge. An early but muted sunrise of pink and blue, trying to break the sheet. He gazes, his colourless mane adrift; to breathe there is to breathe a breath fresher than any other, and it washes over his mind, clearing his senses. Brushing through his clothes, the simple drabs of Ukibiki, in linen and pants tied at the shins, a thin, loose, and buttonless overgarment drifting. He has fitted them with the satchels and straps and pouches of his journey, packed with supplies. From that wound in the building, he watches the waves.

He listens to the breeze and sea and leaves. He exhales, letting noise consume him.

He turns, slowly, with a single step.

Between him and the far wall she stands. Hunched, silently heaving, breathless but quiet. Eyes low.

She came with no radio, he says. His voice dampens all else, like the wind and leaves submit when Small Hand proclaims. She brought no medicine, she had no orders. He can name everyone, he tells, everyone the Fauschenherst would possibly send.

Pescha looks up, her blue smouldering from the shadow.

He asks her why she came.

For a moment, they are silent. The ambience grows, it thinks it can creep back in.

She thought his condition was worse, she mutters. Her words, they deafen. Like his ears pop- Small Hand, he feels it. He blinks and pretends it's nothing.

Respectfully, he asks what help she would have been. She had no medicine, he reiterates, and by the way she came he presumes it's not her discipline. And if she knew he was at Ukibiki then she knew, even in dire health, he could not be safer. He says he doesn't get it. It doesn't make any sense.

Pescha breathes, like a bull before it's charge. Her stare intent, unwavering, brutal.

Unless she didn't come to help, he muses, raising his head. Unless she came because he was weak. Because he was vulnerable. He's this spectral, angelic, beautiful figure clad in floating clothes, perched on the edge of a seaside garden. A garden in ruins.

He says nobody's ever looked at him the way she does now. It's the same look he has, the look which inspires millions to fight an enemy they cannot understand. A look of savagery, he says. An innate, but clear hatred- the basis of all her emotions. He tells her he knows this feeling. This absoluteness, as he puts it.

Pescha's breathing has steadied. Now she just stands, exuding violence in blue.

But he doesn't know why. For everything, he cannot figure why anyone would want this. Least of all a Klernsteiga. His head is reared back, but he does not look at her down his nose; it is a physical expression of his uncertainty, his scepticism.

Why, Small Hand asks. What could she gain from this? Then his tone falls; he asks what she could gain that's worth the cost.

He is the linchpin of mankind's survival, Pescha thinks, the thin string holding everything together.

She's insane to even think she could, Small Hand declares. To come all this way on a single message; did she not think she could be wrong?

They'll keep fighting so long as he does, Pescha thinks. Keep coming, generation after generation. An endless cycle of tragedy.

He has done nothing, he calls, but fight, for over fifty years. Every single day that he spent able, he has warred, for her sake. How can she stand here now?

But she can show them, Pescha thinks. Guts and meat, matter, nothing more.

Her folly has been squandered, Small Hand tells, her great journey a waste. Whoever she is, wherever she's been, it has all been for nothing.

And with their god in pieces, Pescha concludes, at last shall they embrace deliverance.

Because she will not be humiliated anymore, Pescha screams over his words, and in his second of shock she draws her blade, steel flashing, held alongside, pointed at the boy.

Small Hand stares, utterly bemused, but not the least frightened. He asks what it means, that he's not as ill as she thought. If it changes anything at all, he scorns, that he is as strong as ever.

Pescha glares, her blue skating the edge of her sword, like a strand of web caught in light. Nothing, she mumbles- it means absolutely nothing.

She cannot possibly win, he says, quietly, but audibly. She will be pulled apart. She is mangled, ripped, and beaten; she can barely stand, the way she is. She has given so much, come so far, surely sacrificed everything- he cannot imagine the things she has seen. But he can sympathise, he tells; he is sure he can understand, everything but this. This betrayal of hers, a treachery against the millions who so revere the Klernsteigaship, and a deceit of the trust which has maintained mankind much this last gruelling century.

The blind must trust, Pescha thinks.

Then her brow furrows, and her lip's part. She leans a little forward, braced to move- Small Hand sees this gesture, and instantly stays his persuasions.

This moment of pause, it lasts an age. What she finally says, she says with such vile, like she herself has been deceived.

Pescha asks why he walked.

Small Hand stares, his expression still. The way he glares, she knows he thinks for an answer, but none comes. An answer besides that he was too week. It does not break him, but it does chip the façade- the way an eye twitches, and his lip, for an instant, curls.

But this is all she needs; upon his falter, there is a sense so overwhelming which consumes Pescha, a feeling truly complete.

There is a being to whom she prays, the spider whispers- it is that scornful voice which mocks her indecision and surrender, the determination and decisiveness which consumes her in anger. The common, binding essence of all Iconoclasts, of all people; it is that which cleaves- that which stares without remorse, and grins without restraint. That, forever focussed, cursed both by the melancholy of its existence, and the ruthlessness and nonchalance of its faith.

It is the rotten little heart in all people, and the self she wishes to be- her remorseless critic in the lonely hours. Brutal and cunning, effortless, and sly- innate in belief, fixed solely and always on its goal. It is her greater self, chained by age old limitations of the mind. By mental rule, and moral, and law. It is the only self to which an Iconoclast may bow- the one excuse for a ruler.

How may she know it, Nux asks. How is it fostered?

By the time she knows, she will not care, the spider tells.

Pescha's chest rises and falls, her fangs like talons.

It is the greatest aspiration, in its wild fury she fears none- the tireless angel, mankind knows autonomy under moral and legal freedoms, and humanity has done nothing; without cause it is idle. Without effect it is content, and much the same.

Pescha sinks her gaze into the boy, who but stares straight back.

Fanaticism then, unwavering and unrestrained. Let faith total and absolute consume her, direct her every choice and thought- so innate, it replaced emotion.

The sea breeze curls, and Small Hand takes his sword from its propped-up pike.

It is fear, the one thing worthy. It is danger, to all that they are fond. It is the little whisper of mania which haunts every pointless, stupid thing that she does. The whining tone which wishes conflict, like a string of sound tugging at the mind. It is the subtle evolutionary coming to terms with the hollowness of her existence, and what it takes to be more.

It is a ring of crows chipping at the skull. It is a world of eyes, all following her. It is a sword with no handle, it is her ribbon-slashed body folding over without pain. It is a person who does not bleed. Evolution is a process, not a solution- it has led to the Iconoclasm, which does foster the cure. Fear is a feeling, not an action- fear is danger, and danger is change, but things must change, so be change, be danger, be the fear.

There will come moments, the machine purrs, when she is consumed. When a purpose so alien to the timid mind overrules, in a state of dedication pure. One purpose, one goal- she will feel it, that nothing else could matter, for right now all that she wants is at stake, and she will do anything to make it hers. Whatever it takes.

All that she wants is at stake. Rule, moral, law, emotion; they are all for naught.

Small Hand draws his sword, his expression still uncertain.

Nothing else matters- there is nothing else. She must fight, shred, and pull and tear. Deliverance, Pescha mumbles. An example to the righteous, she longs for nothing else.

As she watches, Small Hand starts to change; the vented implants against his calf's fire up, a slow and subtle whirring, more like that of electricity than that of combustion, and a soft golden glow ebbs from the slots. More dramatic still is Small Hand himself. Brushed by a wind which doesn't exist, his hair rises in flux, clothes following, like a breeze builds about him. His locks float, his eyes widen- it is as though he sees what is to come, feels it before it occurs, playing in motion slowed. He plays these theatrics for her, as an animal intimidates; she knows he can move instantly, that this is meant to deter, but she is too feral for fear. She imagines his head splitting in half, barbs and knives and fleshy limbs crawling out, and she would be ever unwavering.

Because it's right there, she thinks. After all this time, it's right in front of her, and she has dragged herself to its feet. No questions fog her mind. Nothing could shake her faith. Nothing inside her head speaks. Kill, and she may embrace deliverance. Kill, and she may realise her dream. She feels it on the tips of her fingers, crawling up her legs, prickling her lip, that mania absolute- kill, or die trying.

See her dream come true or die looking.

Just a little bit further. A little bit more. A couple of steps, and deliverance is hers.

The glow around Small Hand's calf's twitches, sparking in rods like lightening.

His hair and clothes draw back, like he steps into a gale.

Pescha twirls, her hand darting. A bomb spins from unfurled fingers.

- SUMMER -

THE SEA

Small Hand's eyes bulge, and instead of straight he must glimpse aside, the bomb detonating where he stood.

It's a brushstroke streak of light, like fluorescent paint in water. A golden liquid, suspended between where he was and where he is; apparating in an instant several meters away, his trail curling like fluid gas, he raises his arm as the smoke rushes, his hair billowing. The second he looks he sees her, already there, Pack One blurting to close the space. She spins, steel whirling- what she cuts is but more of his trail, which dissipates as her smoke does, in air. This is the kit of a god, the kit of Small Hand. Nobody is sure where he found two Compressed Light Generators out here- let alone how he thought to surgically fit them to his legs.

His hair flowing, eyes crackling, he looks over shoulder, his stare fixed on her furious and flying approach. She's taller, stronger, on foot even faster. They both know it won't matter.

They chase between concrete pillars and bundles of shrub, splaying water and leaves, his golden paint and her trail of fumes curling, swirling against one another. She bursts after his every glimpse, darting toward empty space; the sporadic nature of her kit makes it hard to predict, but he keeps his distance. He can appear, instantaneously, wherever he desires, so long as it is a straight between- she is forced to pursue, but like the light in his wake her movements are fluid, twisting and diving, and she follows at speed, columns rushing past. Puddles and foliage caught in their slipstreams, her sight centred on the boy ahead. She remains forever closer than he thinks.

Then he turns, his blade arcing and she whips past, sparks shaving. Pescha skates to a halt before him, looking up at the boy stood still, sword down by his side, and she soars at him, bursting in a plume of exhaust. She swipes furiously, her sword in reverse grip; he withstands her onslaught, quick footwork and his low stance keeping her at bay, until he catches her edge against his hilt and shoves her back, driving with his shoulder, giving himself a foot of room before yellow lightening crackles, and his eyes flame gold.

She barely has time to raise her blade and stoop. The force with which his sword grates over hers, it pushed the spine of her blade an inch from her face, with enough force to cleave her skull in two. Wide eyed, she sees it slowed, the incandescent flecks drifting past her blue. So close they illuminate her skin.

But she does not freeze, nor turn. With the momentum she arcs her spine backward, taking her blade in her teeth and casts another bomb overhead, which chases after the boy.

It explodes but again she does not wait; she flips her back heavenward and bursts up, the soles of her boots and her palms pressed against the concrete and vine ceiling, Small Hand flashing through the space where she stood. The smoke has built thick on their level, the wind carrying it her way, so blindly she throws, casting to where he may appear, before she falls on all fours, steel clamped in her jaw. The rubble and dust, it is swamping now, her blue a furious glow amid. Pack One flares as soon as she lands, rushing for the wall of windows, more sparks flying as her kit grinds against the ground.

She races for daylight, streaking through murk until she finds an opening and fires, reaching high, grasping the upper sill to spin, so that instead of straight out and into the sea she spins skyward, rocketing up the exterior face to curl again and cast, another bomb sent to the window. It cracks against concrete and explodes, the air which rushes downward against her now rushing up, her hair whipping, rubble cascading. Then in an instant it evaporates, like smoke from a muzzle, as a golden thread climbs, climbs past and miles higher. Pescha crests the roof and rolls, blurting over the flat as fast as she can- in the moment between bursts she looks, back racing so close to stone, blue searching its overcast grey.

A perfect circle in the cloud, like someone hole punched the sky. He hovers in the middle, so distant that she can barely see- in the centre of this ring, a dot. A boy with flowing, misty hair.

There's a twinkle of gold and Pescha tumbles aside, disappearing from her course and destroying where she flew with a thunderous throw. He is too quick; as she twirls and glides at speeds insane, she glances back to see him, standing alongside the drifting smoke. Looking at her sidelong, his figure consumed by the dust-

A glimmer and he pursues, streaking through her wake. Instead of on a straight now he glimpses six, seven times a second, a streaking zig zag of wild, darting light. He follows parallel and afar, and she throws to keep him away, his movements erratic, changing from quick and short jumps to massive leaps, so far that it takes her a moment to see where he went. He remains in constant motion, as does she. Always moving, always throwing, bomb after bomb after bomb, detonations blasting one after another. Her purposeful excess is constant, and sections of the vast garage roof crumble, cave in, cracks spreading as she tears into the structure.

A shimmer from her rear and she shifts, slanting a meter to the side, so from behind he appears ahead. His hair and clothes are flung with the sudden stop, while he is completely still, his unbloodied blade held for a cut just missed. But there are bullets slower than her; she leaps on him, swirling in an arc of smoke and slashing air, then twisting her spine and swinging behind, her steel finding his with a blind blow, barely enough to keep him at bay.

He presses, striking for gaps in her defence. For all meagre physical advantage, she is no swordswoman; what good is weight when it is misplaced, strength when it is misapplied, but she does not break or shrink from his bite. Her edge claws and thrashes against his, then Pack One blurts and brings her around for a new angle, maintaining an onslaught Small Hand eats, unperturbed.

While they dual, the rain resumes, a smattering which quickly begins to build, pattering against their clothes and speckling the rooftop.

He taunts her with his ease, still and awaiting her return, and she does not wish to force his flight again with bombs. But she has no choice, she casts level, watching the star sail and be side-stepped, a detonation bursting behind.

At this, Small Hand sways a little, glancing back and then down, to a trail of webwork cracks, etched from concrete wound to wound. Several floors down, pillars, between which he dodged explosions, suffer the same.

She charges at him, dispensing blast after blast, the whole complex shaking.

He spins in circles, brow high and eyes wide, as sections of the ground fall.

It's a distinctly furious bomb which brings collapse, detonating against the roof's far edge. Those harried columns on the lower levels finally give out, bits of roof falling, single layers crushing through multiple below. It starts out of sight, a deep rumbling. Then the seafront side of their rooftop arena starts to cave in, the noises of destruction and rain together deafening. Pescha doesn't seem to notice; while he staggers, glaring at the falling floor, she blurts at him and slashes, edge whipping. Her fervour is incessant and undampened, as the entire upper half of the building's far face dips.

Then something buckles, multiple pillars give out, and the seaward wall falls several layers at once, one side of their rooftop dropping- the arena slants, becoming a slide, and with the wet both Klernsteiga feel their feet slip from underneath. Their swords clatter but stay with them as they tumble, roll through torn roots and exposed metal wirework, skidding toward the sea. Small Hand struggles to keep his bearings, bits of this downward ramp falling in on themselves as the slope quickly crumbles into a jagged rubble heap. But he keeps with the surge, falls with it- he has to, for at the precipice and jump he sees it through the dust, protruding from a lower rung- his razor wire whip, banner trailing. Toward it he turns, shifting his weight, until the edge comes and he's spinning, arms flailing, his eyes locked firmly on the pike, straight below.

    The sea rushes towards him in this strange illusion, of so many similar windows slipping past. He extends a hand, golden light already burning from his calves.

The second his fingers wrap, Small Hand disappears from the carnage, rubble swamping where he was. He appears upon one of the adjacent buildings; a row of thinner, lower, but similarly gutted and decayed structures which follow the ocean ridge, maybe once offices or apartments. On this perch he staggers to a stop, clutching sword and pike. Over both distance and rainfall, the collapse still booms, a rumbling of great things breaking and colliding, then crashing into the waves. He turns to it, hair and clothes and pike banner raging in the mixture of strong seaward wind and spray and rain. He watches, that complete calm retaking his face through heavy breaths. Maybe he thinks something mournful, maybe something contemptuous, maybe nothing at all. It seems that, for a time, he just stands there, staring, as the upper half of the multi-story plummets from its cliff face down, into the surf, the great structure torn in two.

All that can be discerned is that his expression, it becomes somewhat melancholic. He sags a little, like he isn't quite sure, in this instant, what to do with himself. A slight hopelessness, seeping through him like the wet.

The concrete below him shatters all at once, like glass cracks, the shards and him blowing out. It takes him a second to realise exactly what has happened- once he does, he disappears, reforming a hundred meters away, out in the moorland.

He spins, gaze frantic, disbelieving. Twitching over the dust cloud.

She flies from out the blast, twirling in a gymnastic display which combines a whole performance in one flight. A simultaneously spontaneous and elegant arc, her form is like a sketch, twisting through the sky. Dead centre she lands, and she lands hard, but instantly she rises, coming to a swaying stand. Facing him as he faces her, rainfall pounding. Blood trickles down her features, a hundred haemorrhages and rocky scruffs bracing her skin.

He gazes, brows high, mouth ajar- he does not hide that he is stunned. Then, as though confirming it in his own mind, he nods. He mutters; okay, then lowers his pike's head to the ground.

From this downturned and unflagged end, a coil unfurls, pilling upon the ground. A constant ribbon, it is like a thin metal chain, each link protruding sharp. A wire, which falls it seems forever, an infinite length interlocked within the staff to maximise capacity. The noise up close is hypnotic; a constant, metallic uncoiling. Its edges catch the light, razor reflections glimmering. The razor wire whip, Small Hand lets it crawl from its sheath, like a twisting steel snake.

Pescha keeps still, wet hair clinging to her face. Without moving she fires a crack from Pack One then immediately fires the other way, stalling her kit, so that instead of flying it snarls like a revving bike, engine growling and seething smoke. She feels a change in the boy's stance, like she has survived the stage of their fight where he cut with hubris. Where he reserved himself, as he would against any other lone human- while he remains unperturbed, there lingers a seriousness now, a solemnity to his features. The expression he wears to his daily conflict, regardless of its scale- a stoic passivity, in unwavering focus. Pescha just stares, waiting, the extent of her injuries hidden by rain. This morbid apparition, black and white and blue. A fierce, vivid blue.

This time Small Hand strikes first. He beams her way, risen from the ground, his chain following the exact straight trajectory as him and he flicks it forward, immediately snagging the pike back to pinpoint the strike, like he would crack a whip. Pescha blurts to the side, letting the blow crash into the concrete behind. As though cement were wood impacted by a cannon, the building face cracks and plumes with dust, like a great hammer struck it, not a slight chain. Its speed and savagery are unnatural; she thinks of a lashing serpent, before she races for open moorland, kicking up spray and moss as she flies. Her movements are quick, erratic, unpredictable, but almost as soon as she's free she sees a flash from her side, a distant glimmer of gold from the valley's edge.

Pescha darts, leaping as far forward as she can, only narrowly missing a fracture scythed into the steppe surface, a cleaved and narrow line etched by Small Hand's wire. A ravenous cut, grass and heather diced on a perfectly straight line. Eyes wide, she sees him again, and again she powers, shifting so that he passes ahead, leaving in his wake this writhing tail of razors, the ground before her halved. It's omnipotent, a power unquestionable. He is everywhere, and all that is near is destroyed. She can only build pace, a paper plane in a gale, rising and diving, twitching, impossible to hit.

    He comes at her again, his snapping chain appearing from thin air- she drops, ploughing into the wet earth, digging it up before she blurts, razors whirring overhead. They are fluid and endless, a grating, kinetic chainsaw, with enough speed and energy behind them to blow whatever they touch apart; he keeps coming, zigzagging the vast field. It does not cross her mind to fight, only to endure.

    Then he appears ahead, steps from lightening, and unfurls his razor like a net, a great honeycomb of wire, spreading from his centre. It tears into the ground, writhing and thrashing- it comes straight for her and she for it, but she lifts a bomb and lets it sail, spinning for the boy. He sees it and pulls back, flaring the chain to catch, and through the coils of smoke and razor she passes, dipping low and rising at an angle. She bursts into vision from the side, twirling with the draw of her blade.

He must sidestep to survive. As she flies by, she catches a glimpse of his face, twisted away.

It is the most malevolent expression, a moment of madness that she avoids his saw. A look grimmer tenfold than all she has ever sent; an expression of indignity, that she has survived even a moment of his truer strength.

Okay, Pescha breathes. Okay.

She rockets by; instead of arcing back, she races for the valley's rise, the cliff line which formed the left bank as she approached. Over this damp moss, her movements are evermore erratic, evermore rapid- she glides and slips and catches herself again, kicking up a slipstream of spray as she floats for the ridge like a skimming stone. He pursues, and when hand dives into pocket she feels her bombs are sparse, but instead of conserving she throws at will, stars spinning every other second. It creates a veil around her path, a barrier which the boy cannot cross; he beams alongside, tempted to invade, but whenever he comes close, he is blasted by droplets and grass and dirt and smoke. Indiscriminately this blur throws, like a missile which breaks into other, exploding parts. She can feel his stare on her as she moves. A mix of confusion and unpleasant surprise. She just builds as much speed as she can, hurrying for the climb. When it comes, she practically grinds herself into its face, like a hand presses against her back and shoves her up its wall. In an instant she spins, hands darting for moss, eyes darting for him. She must swerve, sudden and hard, to avoid the glimmer below.

Such strength she has never seen, when that coil breaks the crest's side. Like dynamite is blown upward, like an unstoppable force drives through, the way she imagines a planet would break with meteor-impact. Great chunks of hill blown upward, like they detonate from within.

And high overhead he soars, his whip caught in light like some vast and ancient dragon, a shining and reflective strip miles overhead. A glowing slit in the sky, an ebbing wound, he floats there with his momentum, the beast curling. Pescha crests the hill and skids to a stop, staring- first at the ruined climb, its debris still tumbling, then up, at the snake, this fluid bolt of lightning. A power divine, she marvels for only a second, her glare awful.

Pescha bursts, darting across the spine, Small Hand ploughing into the space behind, chain slashing the slope like a monstrous papercut. Then it claws out, a chasing tendril, snatching over the crest; she follows the hill, gliding from one side of the climb to the other like she skates, and when the blades arrives, she plumes and leaps, throwing herself over the saw. It's this erratic movement which so irks Small Hand- he comes alongside, travelling at the same speed as her with his momentum alone, swinging the whip like a bat, and she dips down the opposite slope, chain digging into the crest, tearing up the moss in her wake. Blood pounds in her ears, hey eyes water immensely, her breaths are choking; she's pushing herself to her limit, speed building and building, while this killer of gods pursues, a force mythologised. A noose which has closed itself around countless demons and ripped them in half. Slow, mechanical demons, massive and lumbering. Overhead, Small Hand is rage, his judgment frustrated. He feels his delirium grow; his sickness harries, and he blinks, wavering. But fatigue and weakness do not deter him, instead they do the opposite. They infuriate him.

He descends to her level and comes in close, flashing ten times a second, twenty times, thirty, wire following his precise route, a snare inescapable, but she twists and bends, whirling with inhuman indifference. They are tangled in each other's razors and smoke, Pescha evading a hundred blows at once as she races seaward. Her world is a blur, a nauseous twirling of muscle memory and instinct, but she keeps away- she recognises it, this is his entirety, the way he fights the Humeda. Not whipping, but beaming, and ripping through hordes as he does; it is the force of his glimpsing which pulls metals apart. Pescha remains, impossible to catch. Not even she is sure where she is. When Small Hand appears ahead, drawing his sword, she doesn't think, she just draws her own and extends an arm, catching his and twirling past. It shocks him, her unbeatable reflex; he freezes, barely having himself raised an attack.

 He turns, watching her spin. He doesn't pursue, but still she whirls, like a woman strapped to the nose of a rocket which rakes her the length of this hill. Standing there, this is all he can do, stare, ogling at this freak of dexterity and speed. This relentless and apparently unperturbed performer, who notices his distance and instead slows to dance in a ring, her pace in flux, her elevation changing with every move. Absently and without heart his whip lashes out, and she rolls over the wire. He does it again, and again, she evades.

 He disappears, vanishing from sight. She remains in this aerotrim state, unaware that he has gone, for what feels no more than seconds before a tremor comes, rumbling up her arms. Pescha glides to a stop, feeling the shake and rainfall. A deep set and constant trembling, her immediate thought is machines, then him, her eyes scanning. She rubs droplets from her sight, glaring ahead, out of breath.

She turns, and her body locks up. Caught, in total disbelief.

It's a building. A whole building.

One of the towers, severed and uprooted, tied on his razor string. He's way up but he hauls it overhead, his sledge of punishment. Maybe twenty storeys, slowly sailing through the sky. It's both a religious and monumental sight, similarly unreal, unimaginable. Maybe that's what makes it so holy, this silent monolith swung upon her. She doesn't understand where the force comes from; she knows his wire is an arcane and strange device, rife with rumours and legend, but this is unbelievable. It is unbelievable, she reiterates, glaring. Then she blinks.

It's what, she asks herself.

Pecha bursts, throttle on full at breakneck acceleration, ploughing straight for the block. She can see he is off, the tower will fall before, or maybe he means this, that he can still see as debris blows out and crushes her; either way, she doesn't waste a second. Arrow straight, faster and faster, she feels that everything should scream, tell her to stop, but there is no such compulsion; she flies freely, unshackled and intemperate, directly toward certain death. She watches it fall, shadow spreading. The wind builds as it comes, forcing air outward, but she won't relent, she must reach it before full impact and she does, letting out a scream as she fires everything into climbing the now vertical building roof, and then rolling to its side- a wall, now a bridge.

Why won't she die, Small Hand roars, slamming tower into hill.

Concrete races by below, windows a blur.

He floats, impact like thunder, blind with rage and nausea.

She bursts from slamming rain and rising rubble smoke, afterburner's blaring, so that in a great spiral she soars, twisting through open air. Looping around the chain between; so engrossed is Small Hand in his strength, he does not notice her until she flies, and in his hazy state he stammers, of the same expression worn by Pescha seconds before. His eyes widen, lips apart- he has only the time to reach forward and stop her drawing her sword, keeping hilt against scabbard, before the two collide, dethroning each other from the sky. Her holding him, bringing him down. She fires Pack One as they drop, clawing and shouldering, trying to brace their descent.

They fall for what feels like hours, tumbling in one another's arms. He keeps trying to break free, for with her he cannot glimpse. Pescha hugs him, latched on limpetlike and unshaking, arms hooked tightly, as though he wears the parachute they'll need.

The impact is terrible, they land on the sloped multi-storey roof and roll down into the rubble of what's left, a bricky garden of matted foliage and puddles. Limbs smashing against stone, heads slammed and grating. Fingers crushed, skin chipped and slashed and bruised all over. Every second of it is brutal, and when they level out, they are not afforded a moment to breathe. In an instant Pescha crawls, forces herself into a bow on one arm, wavering as though drunk. So slack, her tongue lolls from her heaving mouth.

Small Hand 's expression is one dazed and similarly inebriate; he glances around, rolling onto his stomach, and sees his pike meters away. His sword has unattached itself and lays in one of the speckled pools. It is to this he orientates himself, throwing his body to its direction then lurching out, somehow both slow, precise, meaningful, but shaky and off-balance. Behind him, he hears hands slap against water and boots scuffle, all drowned by rain song; he ignores it, recovering his senses and wading to his blade.

He spits, running the back of his hand over his face. Everything stings. He gets a leg under him, pushing off, staggering on all fours. He collapses by the puddle, blinking through droplets, and takes his sword by its sodden wrapped handle.

Pescha rubs her eyes, cleaning them of wet and mud and dust. She looks up, she sees him instantly. She leaps on him from behind, driving his chest hard into the ground.

She bites into his neck, chewing his jugular.

Eyes have never been so wide, nor a silence as long, as that which befalls the collapsed duo then. He, sights bulging into space and mouth hanging, she, ravenous blue pointed in sketched ferocity. Jaws clamped with shuddering force around his throat.

Everything about it, that moment, for the boy it is maddening- the grime, the pain, the savageness, and disgusting inhumanity. The fear of damage done, and the ultimate repugnance he has for the woman who could mentally stomach that attack. Her idleness, her inability to feel or consider; she leans against him, sat on his lower back, holding his shoulders as a thick, dark droplet of red rolls down from her bite.

Small Hand screams and spins; in symmetry he dooms them both. He tears a pulsing, unsightly, fleshy chasm in his neck, like an exposed and meaty gut, and as he whirls, so too does he draw his sword, spinning onto his back. In an arc he slashes at Pescha, chopping into an outstretched, defensive right arm. Then he flashes gold a few meters away, tumbling when he appears. He holds a hand to his neck- either she has missed the vein, just, or she has not made a hole enough to let it drain him completely. Either way he shakes, his expression glassy, his revulsion immeasurable. Then he looks at her.

Pescha glares at her arm, hanging by sinew. She undoes the top of her coat and reaches in, tightening the harness straps which brace her upper right limb. Then she picks up her sword with her left hand, holding it in reverse, and draws upward, slicing slowly through.

Small Hand stares. The dull thud of her forelimb hitting the floor, he feels it like a slap. She doesn't seem to care; she rezips her coat and stoops, sword still held in reverse, but held only by three fingers, the others prepared to operate her kit. Her handless arm, she raises once more in defence, held by her head. Ready for the next wave. Welcoming him to attack.

He does not think her human, this monster ahead. It cannot be- all that is human is not here. She is relentless, and unfeeling. A dark horror he cannot escape. And now they've both a timer. A countdown: he feels it, pumping by his ear.

Small Hand looks out to sea, and the tombstone towers which dot toward the horizon. He tries to gauge if he can glimpse, if he can go still as he intended; to cross these waters in a moment, collapsing on a shore hundreds of miles away. He questions the closest help, where he would seek medical attention. Whether his body could survive the jump. It doesn't matter. He hears her come, glancing back; she stumbles onward, raising sword high overhead.

The boy scoops up his pike under a free arm, attaching his blade frantically. Then he becomes a ball of light, which joins the roof of the closest seabound tombstone.

He falls onto the tower, screeching. Like someone had a cup of water and tossed it forward, the sudden stop throws his blood out, a pint of red splattering onto wet concrete. The sudden release of pressure, it is so sickening that he chokes, and the sensation of feeling his throat lurch against his fingers makes his vision fade, and his brain roll over. Like it inverts inside his skull.

He hears a thump, blinking back over shoulder.

She pulls herself up, onto his tower, smoke trail drifting. The shape of her glare is the image of demonism; mankind's expression cannot move this way.

Small Hand wraps his arm around his neck, and glimpses to the next tower.

Again, the rain starts to dissipate; sunlight threatens to break the grey, thin beams spearing through, shining on waves and city-skeleton shrubbery. Between these rays the two Klernsteiga chase, disorientated and tiring. With every jump, Small Hand is brought to new tears, and a deeper understanding of dismay- it's like chopping bits off himself to escape, but to escape something only feet behind, forever pursuing. Forever pushing, forcing him into a corner.

This is his katabasis- he stares around for a place else to flee, but he does not know now that he can make the jump back to land, let alone across such vast waters the other way. Neither does he know what he'll find should he return, to Ukibiki for aid. Pescha leaps to the same tower as him, and fatigued she swipes, missing and coming again, chasing him across the peaks. Bumping into one another, twisting their sleeves from the other's grasp. Pushing and shoving in desperation.

When there's nothing left but open water Small Hand turns, taking sword in hand and throwing his pike aside. Such loathing is his expression, he sets it on Pescha, the sea crashing below. The noise is deafening, and spray is flung up to their level, thrashing the Nomads like it wants them pulled off. This final tower of theirs, it is skeletal and wrapped in green, moss and ferns and vines draped. It leaves only a bare patch of slabbed concrete in the centre, where the flora has not yet reached.

She does not acknowledge that this is the end, Small Hand sees. Such elaborateness has passed now. For her, it was the end long ago.

But she is spent, completely. She was spent when she came, and no motivation can subvert what she is. Battered and bruised, and bleeding hard.

He is the better swordsman. One on one, he can beat her.

He takes a step forward, and radiation sickness rocks his mind, blood and bile sticking to his teeth.

Her eyes are fixed solely unto him; he, everything she has even wanted. But as she comes, she does not see a boy, or this sea or stone or sky. Hey sight is fogged with imagery foretold, and she sees a memory that isn't hers. She sees a reality she wasn't allowed.

She sees to cleans these worlds of the heresies of mankind. A zealous order hell bent on destroying an inheritance which has never, not once, fulfilled, unconstrained by the rules of dead heathens.

She sees flowing banners and her knights of icon, kneeling in rain. Smoking thuribles and torture ritual, to prayer and cultish blessings. A warrior siblinghood, bound in its unwavering faith. Bound, not by the blood they have, but by the blood they will give. Not by the land where they were born, but by the land that they will cleanse.

There it is. A fanatical storm, a holy war, ripping through mankind. A belonging. A lifelong purpose. Something more than herself, something universal- the one thing real. The chance to unapologetically exist, and deliver these places of wrong. The roots of all that she does hate, her humiliation and monotony; the end to a cycle of ignorance and sloth, which has persisted for millennia. The simultaneous descent of humanity, and its ascension into godhood.

The inevitable, the necessary- the Iconoclasm, mankind's judgment. The answer to all her sufferings. The one thing that matters.

The one thing worth living for. Worth dying for.
Freedom, in its one, and only, form.

Pescha runs at Small Hand, consumed in her rhetoric. She sways to the side, having to steady herself against the effects of blood loss, so that she rocks one way and then comes straight, throwing herself into a strike. Blind with nauseous delirium, she rushes head on. To keep back death a minute more, it is the action on which her thoughts linger, instead of the swipe itself. Her righteous punishment, instead of a skilful cut.

Everything she has ever wanted, and all she need do is swing.

Swing.

He watches her come, and stoops in brace of the blow. His blade rises level, to an attack blunt, and uninspired. The wind and spray harry them both, the rustle of foliage and swaying leaves at their feet.

Pescha swings.

Small Hand slips under the swipe and draws his sword across her midriff. He eviscerates her. Then he slashes down her back from behind. Chopping into spine.

The blood sounds like rainfall, pouring out of her. She stumbles on a few feet more, blinking wildly, before she sinks to one knee, stabbing sword into shrub and stone.

Small Hand exhales a sigh of great relief, running a hand through his hair then over his face, wiping it of wet. That sudden heaviness, the end to his exercise, it labours him, his shoulders are like rocks and his sword weighs tonnes. But he does not fall. In a small circle he paces, winding down, before he hears a rustle and turns, rounding on her. She has collapsed, laying in that dazed state before death, her blade upright besides. Again, he is transfixed. Just stares, chest heaving, in an attempt to recover his breath.

He staggers to her side, her face twitching at the splatter of soft rain. Then he kneels, reaches out, and takes the back of her head, resting it on his knee. Her lip quivers with droplet impact, and her eyes flutter against the spray.

Say something, he demands. She must. He is flustered; he shakes his head, glancing around. Does she even realise what she's done. They lay at the furthest corner, the tip of the city. In that wind, his pale hair rolls, featherlike, like wings. She must talk. He holds her close- she must say something.

The breeze, the noise, the sinking feeling. In that moment, nothing could ruin it. Nothing could stir her from this peace. No description can match, words were not made for this, but it is like a constant breath, a deep and unending inhalation, the clarity only growing, and growing. She fumbles at her coat, undoing Pack One's straps. Freeing herself of the harness, she feels the module slump from her waist.

She reaches up, fingers grazing his neck. Red trickling, she lifts her touch, laying it against his face. With a bloody hand she caresses.

With a bloody hand she pushes off, pushes from his clutch.

Rolling from his knee and over, over the buildings edge, the sea churning below.

Small Hand glares, grasping at air. His expression, completely broken, stunned, and disconnected.

Pescha tumbles, wind rushing. Blood pours without end, then viscera too, spilling from her core. Unravelling, like cloth from a magician's sleeve, and unfurling, like great wings. Like her machine tendrils of thought, flowing in her wake.

That's it. The end. She thinks this as she falls, her bloody feathers trailing. It's so heavy, everything spilling out- she'll be dead before she hits the water. She feels it, pumping from her stomach, her sentience streaming. Her conscious bleeding. Particles, returning to their natural state. Acceptance: it washes over her, a sense of belonging absolute. Her guts slip out of her belly, her reality fades, but she is blank. Tranquil.
    She sinks, into the deepest pit of her skull.
    She listens, to a machine whisper.

Motivation has nothing to do with it, it breathes. Just science- matter is conserved, changing state. Never made, never destroyed. The rushing air and spray, they are crushed stars, the same material, recycled for eons. Her body, it has been that ethereal swirl of cosmic colours, like milk and oil in water, great pillars of creation crushed and made her. This blood, these organs, these bones- these chemicals, these emotions, these memories, these feelings. They have been so much more; they have been whole other worlds, things infinitely greater than they are now. She has. This state she is in, it is unnatural. It is bad luck; her sentience is torture. A curse. It is humiliating, the indignity, the loneliness of her existence. It is maddening.
    And fear, it purrs. Fear is of danger, and danger is change, but things must change. She must transcend the bonds that fate has bestowed these pieces. Break free of what she has inherited. Fear is danger, and danger is change, but she must change, escape indignity- be the change, be the danger, pursue it always, that she may be fear. That she may walk when others stall and stand when others fall.

Blessed be the believing, it pines, she will be an example to the righteous. She will fear none, for there is none. There is nothing, nothing at all, but her vengeance and liberation. She will fight and feel no fear, kill and feel no guilt, stare without remorse, grin without restraint. She will be a demon, it shudders, its hate throbbing through her skin.
    She will be a saint, if she only submit herself, entirely, unto it, and embrace belief.

Pescha falls. Her unending breath fills her head, making her weightless. Such ecstasy- such pain, that she knows, in a moment, will end. All of it, all the suffering; she has done all she could, she held nothing back. She has given everything, and her universe tumbles. with her, relief overflowing in red. A relief of comfort. A completeness.

Lonely no more. Anguished no more. Her humiliation, at an end.
From it all, delivered is she.

This isn't happening, Small Hand thinks.

He scrambles to his pike, neck throbbing, ripping satchels open and splaying their contents, bandages and needles scattered. He takes a needle marked TXA and jams it above the wound, then tablets, which he feels roll past the bite. He stuffs gauze into the hole, frantically packing, but it keeps on pumping. He cannot slow it now. This isn't happening, Small Hand thinks.

For a second, he falls back, laying amid leaves, holding the cloth to his throat. Both hands pressed, he stares at the sky, a sky now breaking of overcast cloud, allowing light through- a deep, mottled morning, peering through in pale, oceanic blues. He hadn't noticed it before, his eyes now glossy and vacant. He gazes, breathing slow.

He feels the wind brush his face.

He feels cool air fill his head.

He staggers on all fours, crawling to his feet, a heavy groan bubbling from white lips. Next to him is her kit, nestled between the shrub, her upright sword skewered beside. He leans on this, pushing up, stumbling to the rooftop edge, lifting pike and sword with a whine. It's such a distance, he knows, so far to go like this- he racks his thoughts, searching memory, trying to focus on a place to go, but it's just waves. Waves, stretching off into infinity.

This isn't happening. He isn't here. He can't be.

Small Hand shuts his eyes, spittle and blood dripping. He sways, shoulders sagged, but still he persists, and that faint golden glow starts to ebb, shining from his machine calves. He tries to think of purpose, that he is needed, that without him, all else is doomed, but he can't.

She haunts his vision, his mind. Thoughts of her consume him, wholly.

He steps, his grumble now a moan. A wild animal's cry, desperate and longing. He stumbles forward, drunk on pain, until there is no tower below him.

He disappears over the edge, hair fluttering.

There is no flash of gold.

- FAUSCHENHERST ENCYCLOPAEDIA -

GLOSSARY

The Fauschenherst Encyclopaedia : Officially the designated handbook of universal terms available to all Fauschenherst soldiers during their induction on The Plinth. It represents a catalogued knowledge, easily surmised, that Klernsteiga and Rautbergen may familiarise themselves with. Where information is scant however, search results are supplemented by the top results of a Seven-Seven server search for the same information. This Glossary represents an expounded and unabridged variant of the Encyclopaedia, unavailable in full to the masses.

1- Geseschaus : Radios built in Sawabiva, on Emelia. They're designed to perform through interference, or else succumb to the snowstorm static of their home world, however their range is shorter than the Fauschenherst Ubess - Koss systems.

2- Ubess – Koss : The radio system used by the Fauschenherst, on the planets and the Kyut. Lightweight, adaptable, and widespread, they span six versions, with one through four being mobile, and versions five and six being stationary super-radios. The company receives Fauschenherst funding, having outfitted Sect Three, as well as owning the telecommunications systems of the planets. The radios are characterised by having high protruding aerial antenna.

3- E. D. 8 "Emilia" : A frozen abyss of a planet, the largest of the four remaining worlds. Its proximity to the Faurscherin ruins has left it a graveyard for ship data banks and fuel deposits, the salvaging of which has become the planets main trade. The capitol, Sawabiva, is a telecommunications terminal that sells the Faurscherins information to the Fauschenherst, and the barren nature of the world makes this its relative sole source of income for food and resources.

4- Klernsteiga / Nomad : The minor half of the Fauschenherst army, officially established with the formation of Sect Three. They are self-

Fauschenherst Encyclopaedia

sufficient reconnaissance fighters, operating independently and often deep in contested territory. While of marginal numbers, they are the face of the Fauschenherst, and a symbol of human fortitude.

5- Rautbergen : The major half of the Fauschenherst army. A foot soldier militia which defends and expands Fauschenherst territory.

6- Humeda : The machine enemy of mankind, built of an old and forgotten technology.

7- Fauschenherst : The organisation constituting all of mankind's remaining wealth and resources. Its society is based on the legal and hierarchical structure of its preceding mothership, the Faurscherin, with its leadership tracing their lines to the original crew. It comprises all that remains of humanity: its economy; its worlds; and its military. It would be false to assume the Fauschenherst the army of mankind and its planets- mankind has become an army, as much pledged to the Fauschenherst as the word "human".

8- Kyut : A gigantic, multi-habitat (yet, pre-invasion, completely devoid of sentient life) segment of a once much larger endoplanet. Its vast alloy exterior is charred, but its interior remains, with its own atmosphere and ecologies. In full, the entire structure could have blotted a star. It appears to have been man-made.

9- Klernsteiga kits : A Nomad colloquialisms for a Klernsteigas equipment. Each Nomad builds and maintains their unique kit with the purpose of completing their Nomad duties, tailoring their equipment to their skills and environment. This policy by the Fauschenherst has remained controversial, as many Klernsteiga kits prove lethally ineffective until tested.

10- Sect : Referencing major assaults by Fauschenherst armies, each aiming to colonise and pacify the Kyut. There have been four to date, spanning over a century.

11- Denkervung : Retired server system of the Fauschenherst, issued during Sect One. The collapse of all communication systems between the Kyut and Fauschenherst worlds during the Sect collapse led to the

Fauschenherst Encyclopaedia

company dissolving, however their servers still dominate the Kyut, out of necessity, rather than choice.

12- Clan Kamakara : Referencing the recipients of the Kite of the Kamakara, the rarest of Fauschenherst medals. The four honoured have no true loyalty to one another, and have scarce ever met: Klernsteigas Taifunschneider; Mincemeat; Yubokumin; and his greatness, Small Hand.

13- Kites : The medal system of the Klernsteiga, bestowed by Fauschenherst command. They are scarce given, and oft overlooked, but such accolades afford luxuries in larger cities, and cement names otherwise lost.

14- Klausch : An honorary title bestowed to all Rautbergen and Klernsteiga.

15- Kaurscherm : Commander of the Fauschenherst O-Third Wolstbattallon and a senior figure in the Fauschenherst. He now commands the garrison at Our Last Limit and orchestrates the drive into sector Zero, Double-Four, Nine, Three, Five.

16- Goritekaga : The primary supplier of anti-machine weaponry to the Fauschenherst. Situated in the Heimatus of Alexada and competing with K.A.G in weapons production, their specialised slug-style rounds and bulky rifles have armed practically all Rautbergen since Sect 2. The company's head, Gher Vatachinen, is a senior supervisor in the Fauschenherst, and his company's designs are rooted in blueprints salvaged from the Faurscherin. The G before anti-machine firearm names is the company's stamp.

17- Seven-Seven: Referencing servers hooked into the Faurscherin main machine system. The technology was originally developed to give farmers on The Orbital access to Faurscherin agricultural records, and to allow them to instantly communicate with the Fauschenherst. Their anomalous access to Faurscherin data records lead to their confiscation and strict outlawing by the Fauschenherst. Owning one is a treasonous act, and greatly compromises classified Faurscherin documents and machine systems.

Fauschenherst Encyclopaedia

18- Faurscherin : The vast ship (see Kantenlaufer) from which all that's left of mankind traces its lineage. Its remains are the hub of the Fauschenherst and the last bastion between the Kyut and the Fauschenherst worlds.

19- Lizensbur : Fashion brand based in the Heimatus of Alexada, prevalent in all capitols of the planets. While fashion on the Kyut is an alien concept, both due to necessity and that such luxuries must be imported at great cost, such garments are sometimes sported by city officials and officers of note, as a demonstration of material wealth and social standing.

20- Maika Kokoro : Fashion brand based in the Heimatus of Alexada, prevalent in all capitols of the planets. Their attire is based off of ancient Faurscherin designs, replicated at great costs, with many pieces of clothing featuring materials from either most or all of the remaining planets.

21- Trivi : Velt Veit Veiden. A radio company no longer in operation which supplied most of Sect One with their telecommunications equipment. They are cumbersome and immobile designs, but their simplicity has ensured they are still in wide and primary use by the communities of the Kyut.

22- Inicriin : Aeronautics company situated in the Heimatus of Alexada. The company outfitted the Fauschenherst with its Navy during Sect Two, however the catastrophe led to an irreversible loss of confidence in the company, which fell from public favour. It now supplies the Fauschenherst only with landing craft, to ferry soldiers from its larger ships. The company attempted ventures into vehicular designs, however these efforts proved inefficient in reviving the company.

23- K.A.G : Kabreiska Anchen Glachten. The primary supplier of the Fauschenherst with anti-personnel weaponry. Situated on the Heimatus of Alexada, harvesting resources from Trash Ditch and basing its designs off armaments carried on the Faurscherin, where Goritekaga weapons dominate war on the Kyut, K.A.G has armed the Fauschenherst on all other worlds, as well as on the Kyut. Security forces bare their arms throughout cities on the planets and the Kyut. The K.A.G before the names of anti-personnel weapons is emblematic of their company.

Fauschenherst Encyclopaedia

24- Falmenscha : Official prosthetics contracted to the Fauschenherst, for use on the Kyut. The company trains Rautbergen medical staff and sends them into combat with a surplus of limbs and artificial organs to aid both Rautbergen and Klernsteiga. The company is based in the Heimatus, was founded during Sect Three, and is one of the few companies under the Fauschenherst considered charitable, even admirable.

25- Bleiy Totter : Back-street prosthetics spread across the Kyut. Makeshift and unrecognised by the Fauschenherst, the term is a collective phrase for all prosthetics fitted to Fauschenherst forces deep in contested territory, where recognised medical treatment is unavailable.

26- LL. U. 13 "Gardner": A stone world of dust storms and rocky spires, falling into deep valleys and caves and creeks. All settlements are built on the highest peaks to avoid the worst of the weather, which makes accessing the mineral rich crust hazardous, and the honeycomb geology of the planet exacerbates this issue. The "Five Trench Crisis" ended most industrial mining operations and drove many from the major cities. Now most of the planet's population lives in Pit Fortress, a bastion against the storms, and a trading hotspot for whatever metals can be extracted from the ground.

27- Kantenlaufer: "Edge Runner", generation ships designed to support life for prolonged periods at the edge of space. Usually corporate affairs, to monitor deep-space exploits. Designed to be entirely self-sufficient for their life span.

28- CLG : Compressed Light Generators. High-powered engines that revolutionised their time, impacting all departments of science and engineering. A small module which refracts light until it becomes a physical force, able to function perpetually from its completion. Highly valuable, as the technology is irreplaceable by the Fauschenherst. Their modern applications are exclusively military.

29- Gyroscope Compensators : Micro-structure engines comprising millions of counter-levering gyroscopes, designed to suspend vehicles within gravitational fields. The most powerful Gyroscope reportedly countered forces up to 28 m/s^2. The rift in physics lead to the first great breakthroughs in large-scale interstellar travel, and the basic design was modified to suit theoretically infinite loads.

30- Eine Atmen Breeding Programme : A publicised and species-wide push to encourage crossbreeding between the many divided nodes of the human genome, after thousands of years of assimilation to specific climates throughout the populated universe. The programme was designed to enable all of humanity to thrive in a multitude of atmospheres and habitats. The programme led to a plethora of genome defects and anomalies down certain genetic lines, but systematically unified the collective human spread, symbolising the unity of the period. It lasted some 450 years and solidified a firm and stable human dominion over the stars for the age to come.

31- V. O. FF. 5 "Alexada" : The capitol planet of mankind, the centre of all human industry and commerce, and home to the greatest city in operation. The world can be divided into two parts: the Heimatus, a mega city of glass and fibre which seats all major human corporations, built on a vast Faurscherin engine which powers the complex; and the Trash Ditch, a scrapyard of ship remains and industrial factories and smog, which covers the vast majority of the planet. The population of Alexada contains most of all worlds, however the spread between the two industrial sectors on Alexada is split by over ninety percent.

32- Eine Atmen Genome defect G-Fifty Three : An untraced genome defect discovered during the later stages of the Eine Atmen Breeding Programme. Individuals with this specific genetic mix achieve a seemingly random age of physical fixity, wherein they may theoretically remain forever, so long as they maintain their general health- outside of external factors, natural deterioration of the body stagnates, and an individual can live for hundreds of years while maintaining whatever physical age at which their aging ceased.

33- The Fauschenherst Plinth : The in-tact remains of the Faurscherin, now used as the hub of the Fauschenherst between its worlds and the Kyut. All who land on the Kyut pass through- it is where all war resources are collected, where the seat of power is, and a revered site of mankind's fortitude. The construct itself resembles a space station, a webwork of tunnels and docks which houses the Fauschenherst armoury. For many who pass through, it hosts the first and last comfort they will ever receive.

Fauschenherst Encyclopaedia

34- J. A. 12 "Moss" : A wetworld planet of constant darkness and rain, characterised by dark foliage and its people's affinity with lanterns and lights. Most of the surface is low raging seas, and whatever land there is is swamped completely by moss and plant life. The capital city, Shimaschita, is a coastal skyscraper strip of imported steel and stone, but the planet has no natural resources, so construction of the city cast the rest of the world into a dark-age poverty, with all other settlements cutting ties. The planet has a small population, and its lack of economy and tradeable resources has led to many abandoning it for better, but those who remain live a quiet life of rain song and lamplight in endless dark, amid a city of vines and green.

35- The Orbital : The moon of Alexada, a placid satellite turned into the farm of mankind. A nutrient rich desert of grassy flatland, streams, and sparse forest, it has been cultivated into a vast grange, supplying crops and produce to Alexada, to be distributed to the other worlds. It maintains the highest population of livestock in all of mankind's holdings. Famously, not one resident has ever joined the Klernsteigaship.

36- Mankind's Golden Age : Referencing an extensive period encompassing humanity's taking to the stars, the Eine Atmen Breeding Programme, and the revelations of Compressed Light and Gyroscope Compensator technologies. It describes an era of peace between worlds and the absence of major conflicts, diseases and famines. Its end would later be marked by the self-imposed isolation of the mining planet Jiro Basaal, and the horrors this would eventually birth.

Printed in Great Britain
by Amazon

6566f215-e3b9-4fb4-8985-f36e00374398R01